STEALING THE LIGHT

LISA HOFMANN

Stealing the Light

- a fantasy novel -

Text copyright © 2016 by Lisa Hofmann
Coverdesign: Magicalcover.de/Giusy Ame,
images: Depositphoto

Published by Elisabeth Hofmann Verlag, Netphen

This book is dedicated to my husband and children.
Thank you for your infinite patience with my dream.
It's also dedicated to my friend, Dana Winslett, who
encouraged me to get this project underway.

Many thanks to Patti Geesey (editing) for walking
down this road with me. It's been, and still is, a great
pleasure knowing you and working with you.

Lisa Hofmann, June 2016

‹ช Prologue ฿๖

A wispy, insubstantial thing was she, rawboned and filthy. Here one minute and gone the next, Catherine was a clever little weasel dodging the owl in that one mere moment of silence when darkest night surrendered to the first hope of dawn. Off she went, raggedy and on her bare feet, toward the forest and the hillside upon which the old castle ruins stood.

There was nothing like a good downpour to wash the grime off a child, the girl's mother thought.

Maebh slouched in the doorway, wrapping a tattered shawl around her shoulders against the cool morning air. She watched her daughter disappear in the thicket between ropes of rain and the lower branches of old beech trees and elderberry bushes. Pretty was different, to Maebh's mind, but that might change if Catherine ever got enough to eat when she was older and able to contribute to their household.

It was a shame the rain wouldn't rinse away what was beneath the dirt. Catherine would never be good or even easy to handle. No amount of water could cleanse the polluted blood in her veins. She was a burden to them and always would be, and she was smart enough to know it.

"Damn that brat," her father muttered. "Close the bloody door."

Caleb had given Maebh several other children besides, but none of them had survived infancy, and now, there was only Catherine.

Turning over on the lumpy straw mattress in the corner by the hearth, he yawned and languidly scratched his backside. Then, he pulled their coarse blanket about him more snugly and went back to sleep. Getting up would have been pointless. He had nowhere to be. No one had died in their nameless little village over the last days, so there were no graves to be dug today.

Maebh was sure he'd deal with Catherine later and give her a good whacking when she came home if he was still sober then, and *if* Catherine actually *did* come home. One of these days she wouldn't, the still-young woman was certain. Times were tough, and evil bred danger in these woods.

She shuddered and closed the door, and Catherine ran.

Chapter One

---

෪ Vidimus ๛

The golden woods dripped and creaked with rain-heavy foliage. A cold breeze murmured through leaves barely hanging on to the remaining strands of a short summer life. Shafts of early morning sunlight were determined to breach the leaden clouds but didn't quite manage it.

Catherine ached from lying on the packed dirt floor of her parents' hovel. She ran nonetheless. It felt good to be outside and finally breathing again. Running sorted her bones, and it sorted her thoughts, and she soon found a steady pace.

She'd had the strangest dream again that night, and she'd awoken with a start. Wonderful images ghosted around in her head even still, and the urgent need to get to the castle added speed to her stride. She had to see if something fundamental had changed up there. It was her firm belief that, sometimes, things *did* change when you weren't looking.

To Catherine, the basic assumption that people could appear from out of nowhere only to disappear again, that things could change form, and that places were swimming islands in time didn't seem odd. She'd never given it any thought because she assumed it was a common knowledge mankind shared. To her, there was no such thing as a reliable constant in reality, and she neither looked nor longed for any kind of fixed star in the evening sky. Her world was full of the unexpected.

Only recently had she begun to guess that she was different from the other village children, but she couldn't quite grasp why. They felt it, and they let her know. She felt it, too, but she couldn't put a name with it. Up until now, she'd been convinced they avoided her because her father was a gravedigger.

It didn't help that the boundaries between the physical world as others perceived it and the world that was woven into its fabrics were often so indistinct. The blending color and texture of past and present made it hard for the ten-year-old to decide which was which. Sometimes, she just didn't know what was really there for everyone to see in the here and now, and what wasn't.

That morning, two huntsmen in pursuit of a large deer were having as much trouble with this as Catherine. They'd finally had a perfect angle on the animal when she unwittingly spooked it in passing. The frightened creature bolted and vanished into the undergrowth.

Swearing under his breath, one of the huntsmen released an arrow after it in frustration, and Catherine felt it miss her head by a hair's breadth. She ducked and ran even faster, blending in with the scrub. He was about to send another one flying when his companion stopped him, a gut feeling guiding his hand as she fled.

Neither man could say they'd actually *seen* her there in the brush, but at least one of them thought he'd spotted a movement that could have been a child in the bushes. This wasn't their day; they'd almost killed someone, *and* they'd be going home empty-handed.

Catherine didn't think about it too intently as she pushed onward. Near misses were a reoccurring thing with her. It wasn't that she believed she was invincible – she knew a thing or two about pain – but she was fearless in a way only a child with plenty of experience in dealing with fear could be. Never having been taught the concept of valuing her life, she wasn't sure it *had* value, and that made her brave. What did have real value was the other side of her reality where things seemed so much more logical.

She'd been dreaming vividly, intensely and unusually often of late, always of the castle on the hill, and always the same dream.

At the old ruin, Catherine's dreams tended to melt into living images that revolved around the stronghold's past and the dark-haired woman she assumed would be the Lady of the House. She couldn't say why, but she kept running across that woman, and she was fascinated.

The castle on the hill was an abandoned, decaying relic of an era that lay decades behind the Northern Forest. It had been almost completely destroyed by a siege and the fire that had ended the blockade during a war around the time of her grandmother's birth.

Catherine knew that.

She was a smart girl who knew a lot of things because she listened when others talked, but that didn't mean she had to accept everything she heard without question or doubt.

What she saw when she'd eventually cleared the forest and was nearing the neglected winding cobble road that led up the hillside wasn't a testament to disaster or defeated hopes with broken parapets and sunken towers. It was a functional fortress in its prime that dominated the hummocky landscape. Its walls were high and thick, and there were many buildings around its whitewashed keep, which was the heart of the complex.

Passing through the tunnel-like entrance of the grand gatehouse, she was met with the sight of a bustling market-day crowd in the baily and the sweet smell of honey biscuits and fresh bread. Traveling vendors were barking songs of praise for their livestock or peddling odds and ends from handcarts in various parts of the courtyard. Guildsmen were giving demonstrations of their crafts by the side of the walkway near the stables. A red-faced herald was proclaiming new edicts on the chapel square opposite them. Unbeknown to the man, a jester stood behind him, pantomiming his earnest demeanor. The herald had no idea why people were giggling at him. Ignoring them, his cheeks glowed as he plowed on.

For the first time in days, Catherine laughed. The sound of her own clear, silvery voice ringing out almost startled her, but since it would probably remain unheard, she allowed herself to enjoy it and relaxed. It felt good.

Suddenly, there was an abrupt surge of energy, and a burst of light exploded behind her eyelids, blinding her. For a second or two, she thought she couldn't breathe and started to panic, but then she realized she was all right again, if slightly dazed.

One of the armed guards who'd been on patrol by the gatehouse when she'd arrived had passed right through her from behind as though she wasn't there, as if *she* was the ghostly intruder upon veracity, and not he. Reappearing immediately in front of her and facing in the other direction, he walked on unaware, chatting with his comrade as they shared a flask of water.

Disorientated, Catherine stumbled forward and nearly fell as the guard walked on, but then she caught a glimpse of the Lady she'd come to see, moving along with the tides of good-spirited buyers going from one stand to the next. She was alone and she looked lost, Catherine thought, asking herself how that could be. Then, she looked at the Lady more closely.

The pale-skinned woman wasn't dressed as elegantly as she had been when Catherine had last seen her. She wore peasants' clothes and colors, and there was nothing remotely noble about her appearance, though that didn't take away from the air of dignity she exuded. She was purchasing something. Catherine wove her way around the people surrounding her to see what that might be, trying to avoid touching anyone.

She wanted to make herself known to the woman. It was now or never, she told herself. No one else here could see her, but something linked her to this woman, she felt, so perhaps this time it would be different, and she would see, or at least feel her presence in some way.

"Hello?" she said timidly, standing beside the woman who didn't even raise her head to look around. "Hello?" Catherine repeated more persistently, her eyes brimming and lip quivering as she drew a breath and placed a hand on the Lady's arm, ready for the painful sensation this would cause. Pins and needles assaulted her skin and the flesh beneath it until her hand passed through the apparition.

In her dream, the woman had looked right at her. She'd smiled and beckoned her, and Catherine was convinced that this had to mean something. Things happened for a reason.

Still, she could have guessed this was how it would be. She'd wanted to put off acknowledging that she'd hoped it wouldn't, but now she had to face it.

"Can't you hear me at all?" she whimpered, wiping her runny nose on her sleeve before rubbing her hurting hand.

Obviously, the woman couldn't. And why should she? Catherine scolded herself for crying. She was such a baby, at times.

Young as she was in years, she realized that everything here was only a reflection time had cast on the mirror of eternity's glass. No one heard or saw her because she was standing on the wrong side of that glass. She was alive in the present, and everything and everyone she saw on the other side was in the past. No one could change the past, no matter how much they wanted to. That was one rule of nature Catherine would have liked to change, if she could.

She had many questions, and knowing they'd remain unanswered today was beyond discouraging – but there was always tomorrow.

And yet, she felt like howling even still as the Lady continued ignoring her, digging around in her purse for some coins to pay for the trinket she meant to acquire. Trying to refocus her attention, Catherine's gaze fell upon the little object the Lady was holding in her hand, and she discovered that it oddly resembled the thin, worn-down old locket her mother possessed. That in itself didn't seem very important; she supposed there could be any number of those in the satchel the merchant had on him, and her mother wouldn't be the only one with an heirloom like it. Her chest heaved despite herself.

Maebh's locket had a tiny dent on the side, and she wore it around her neck on a delicate chain with a clasp at the back. It did have the look of something valuable to someone who'd never seen more precious jewelry, but if it had been costly her father would have sold it by now. Her parents didn't own anything of real worth, and they never would. She had a hunch the woman in front of her was no better off than they were, and she couldn't help but wonder where she'd gotten the coppers she was counting.

Just as the Lady handed the locket to the vendor along with her coins, Catherine felt the world spinning out of focus, and she started to lose her footing. Looking down, she could see the cobbles underfoot crack and disappear, and the people all around her started to fade away.

Concentrating on the vendor, Catherine saw him take the locket and fasten it to an elegant chain he produced from the satchel before giving it back. Her gaze came to rest on the miniscule flaw on its side.

Then, the imagery vanished like the rising vapor of the rainwater heated up on the shattered sandstones scattered about her, and she found herself alone on the overgrown, deserted street. She didn't know what to make of what she'd just witnessed, but suddenly she was fairly certain that she'd been meant to be here to see what she had. There was a connection here – *she* had a connection here – and she was determined to find out about it.

Her feet squished over soggy patches of grass that had taken root in the interstices between the chipped, uneven cobblestones. She tried to calm herself as she wandered through the silent, weathered maze of desolation, but her thoughts tumbled around inside of her head like autumn leaves in a storm.

Some of the more sturdy load-bearing walls had endured and towered above her, stained with scorch marks even after more than half a century of snow and rain had washed away the soot and destruction. Here and there, the splintered, charred remains of beams jutted out like a great fanged maw above her head to mark where upper stories had existed when the castle had been intact.

There was no roof anywhere above the structure, yet the sun refused to reach into the darkened clefts of the dusty and forgotten place. Sickly shafts of light resembling broken spirits floated in and out of the empty halls and rooms, and an eerie wind coursed through the hollows, sounding like the moans of ghosts long past.

Moving through the gaping entrance of the gutted chapel where the herald had stood just minutes before, she noted that only elements of the western partition and the back of the sanctuary remained. Vegetation had taken over as it had everywhere, forcing its way through every crack and crevice in the floor. Tangles of weeds and wild flowers grew in proliferation on the eastern side, ending where the western wall blocked the afternoon sun.

Shadows lived here, hiding in dark corners, trapped by the violence that had shattered the foundations of the once stronghold of her people, but Catherine wasn't afraid. She could sense the excruciatingly narrow divide between this world and the next, and the in-between space was occupied by tormented souls that knew she was here, their soundless screams assigned to the stillness all around. Yet, she was sure they weren't there to haunt her; they appeared to welcome her as if they could feel her presence among them, too, her voice adding to the canon, her confusion supplementing their bizarre composition's theme.

A beech tree grew next to the wall, its limbs reaching up to and out of a huge pointed arch that must have been an impressive artwork when it had been fitted with its tracings, the twin lancets, and the oculus near the top. Catherine could picture it easily as she gazed up at the yawning hole that it was now with a branch protruding audaciously from it, and she held her breath as colors began to swirl above her in the air, coalescing into the opening and settling into the resplendent patterns and symbolic motifs the chapel had worn in years past. The leaden framings that held the small panes of stained glass were shaped like scrolls, and they formed intricate patterns within the lancets, like the scales of a fish, all bursting in an array of crisp, rich colors she'd never seen like this before.

On impulse, she climbed up the smooth trunk of the beech to the first forking boughs which her father would have called the heart of the tree. Fearlessly rising to her feet, she stretched out her arms and balanced along the branch that would lead her to the wide window seat, putting one foot in front of the other until she'd reached it.

It was in surprisingly good repair, she discovered as she stepped out onto the ledge, testing if it would hold her weight, slight as it was. Affirming that it did, she reached out her hands and placed her palms on the cool, shining panes. They seemed to vibrate under her touch as if the tiny particles of matter they were made from were abuzz with a life of their own. The sun illuminated them from the opposite side, blending light and pigments, and brilliant violets and greens, noble purples and warm yellows spilled over onto the awed child until Catherine was completely enveloped in a radiant haze.

Careful not to lean into it too much, she gently pushed against the glass, and the panes wavered for a moment before exploding outward. Millions of miniscule shards hung suspended in the air like sparkling fairy dust for the span of two breaths before shimmering outward in a firework that dissolved on the breeze, making her skin tingle long after the last vestiges of them had vanished.

One more reason to love this place, she decided, and sat down with her legs dangling over the edge of the ancient window seat. She pulled a plum from her pocket and took a bite. The sweet, sticky juice trickled down her chin as she surveyed the ruins from above, and she found that – with the walls on the east side gone – she was able to see quite a few of the overgrown paths and avenues.

Her mind kept wandering back to the woman she'd assumed to be the Lady of the great stone fortress slowly disintegrating below her, and there were many scenarios playing in her head. The person she'd seen buying her mother's locket today had surely been a peasant. But, she'd also been beautiful; as beautiful as though she'd been of noble birth, and the Lord had treated her so on the occasions she'd seen them together. That was why Catherine has mistaken her for his wife.

There was beauty all around, she surmised, because beautiful people had lived here and created it over the centuries before the wind and the years had stripped away its effects. It was the absence of that beauty that had left the ugliness most everyone else who came here now perceived, and that was both sad and unfair, Catherine thought.

Neither of her parents were beautiful, unfortunately, and all they'd created was ugliness, herself included as Maebh never grew weary of telling her. Imagining what life might have been like if she'd been born to a nobleman's wife, she pictured a lot of beauty in it. Her standing would have commanded respect from the other children, or at least some form of appreciation, and no one would have dared push her aside or overlook her.

She would have been beautiful.

She might have become a duchess or even a queen, one day, and she'd have turned the fates with a wave of her hand. She knew she was strong, stronger than most, and perhaps that was enough to make up for a lack of nobility.

Chapter Two

⟡ Honey ⟡

"Where do you think you're going?" Maebh yelled as Catherine ran for the door.

Catherine had developed ways of protecting herself against the fallout of her parents' life very early on. It was probably haughty to think she was any better than the other children her mother had born, but she suspected she was made of *more* than they'd been, at least, or she wouldn't have lived. She was perhaps *blessed* in a way.

Blessed wasn't quite the word that would have come to her mother's mind while revisiting the hard birth of the only child of seven she'd brought to full term in the dank hovel littering the edge of a nameless cluster of dwellings in the Northern Forest. This was where the poorest of the poor lived and died, and no one felt *blessed* here. They felt hunger, and the cold, and they were grateful for mild winters, at best.

Catherine tried to tune out Maebh's voice whenever the woman got started on how Catherine had nearly killed her the day she'd been born. Conveying grisly details with all the drama and resentfulness of someone turned bitter by too much contemplation and little else to occupy her mind was a craft the sour-faced woman honed with a vengeance.

Occasionally, the girl caught herself wishing her mother really *had* bled to death.

This unusually sunny morning was one of those occasions, and she was determined to escape the one-sided discussion about to ensue.

It was still early, and this alone was enough to explain Maebh's terrible mood just before Catherine attempted to flee the hovel. Maebh would be glad to see the back of her, Catherine was sure, but the chase and the argument were a part of their game.

Rebecca, her mother's older sister, didn't play games. She was already there on the makeshift porch when Catherine opened the door.

The honey-blonde woman seized the moment of surprise and caught hold of the started girl to keep her from bolting. Securely wrapping her free arm around the child's middle, she hauled her back inside the ramshackle cabin on her way in. Rebecca didn't bother with a greeting as she pushed past Maebh, who'd been about to shout something nasty after Catherine by way of a goodbye.

Catherine kicked and writhed, growling like a wild cat, but Rebecca was stronger than she looked and had practice in restraining felons. She was the midwife in these parts, and she visited the home of every mother in the area on a regular basis.

Rebecca firmly believed in taming and civilizing the local *wildlife*, lecturing parents on feeding their children properly and hosing them down every so often. She was convinced the high mortality rate among infants had something to do with a general lack of cleanliness, but everyone knew it was just the hunger.

Rebecca was also convinced Catherine's grandmother would be turning in her grave if she could see the state of Maebh's household. She'd raised Maebh and Rebecca on nothing herself, but the one thing they'd always had was their dignity, and she never grew tired of preaching that to Catherine.

"Quiet, now, or I'll tell your father to put you in the dugout," Rebecca said.

Catherine stopped struggling instantly even though her father wasn't at home.

The dugout at the far end of the room was no more than a small cavity in the ground, meant to hold stores before Caleb had discovered that it was too wet. He'd simply covered it up rather than go to the trouble of refilling it, and its sole purpose now was to confine Catherine whenever her mother or aunt decided she was in need of some discipline.

That had nothing whatsoever to do with dignity, as far as Catherine was concerned. Secretly, she knew Caleb shared that opinion. Being a hands-on man himself, he preferred the more immediate approach to settling things. He was generally inclined to give her what he called "a well-deserved smacking" for some forms of misbehavior while ignoring others that would have evoked a fit from Rebecca. But, he wasn't one to object to his wife or his sister-in-law when it came to bothersome little things he saw no sense in arguing, or when he was too tired or too drunk to object.

The pit he'd shoveled was too shallow to sit up in properly, much less stand. Even for a girl of Catherine's size, it was cramped, with a good inch of fouling moisture pooled at the bottom. Lying on her side with trembling knees drawn to her chest, she'd spent a lot of time there, huddled in the mud, trying not to cry, trying not to move.

It wasn't the water, the darkness or the restrictiveness of the hole that scared her; it was the maggots and insects crawling beneath the heavy wooden boards that covered it. Maggots were the one thing Catherine couldn't stomach because she'd seen them on the corpses her father buried, burrowing into every opening, eating their way through tissue and flesh. She felt them squirming against her own skin at the mere mention of the scraped-out hollow in the dirt floor, and imagined them creeping into her eyes and ears.

"Sit," Rebecca said.

Catherine did as she was told, plopping down on the rickety stool by the empty hearth as Rebecca put the basket she'd been carrying on the table.

Looking around disdainfully, Rebecca took note that Caleb wasn't there, and her eyes questioningly found Maebh's.

The younger woman closed the door. "Gone to town for a job, digging a new well for the steward."

"Finally decided to get out of bed, has he?" Rebecca smirked. "Bit of a walk there and back, but maybe he'll bring home his pay this time, seeing as they don't have to see someone off if it's just a well he's digging."

Maebh's mien betrayed her thinning patience as she crossed her arms beneath her breasts. "What do you want?"

"Just paying you a friendly visit, dear."

Rebecca was a mystery to Catherine. She didn't like her aunt any more than she did most people, but although she knew her mother felt much the same, Rebecca kept coming back week after week. She'd been doing so ever since Charlie had died.

The widowed midwife brought them supplies whenever she could, and Catherine was aware that she had her to thank for the thick barley soup they got every few days, as well as most of the clothes she was wearing. She had no idea how Rebecca did what she did, but it wasn't something she'd ask her about. She supposed Rebecca was simply a little cleverer than Maebh and Caleb were. The clay jar of honey she'd placed on the table for Catherine to see was proof of that.

"A little something for Sunday," Rebecca declared merrily, smiling that thin-lipped smile of hers. It irritated Catherine beyond measure because it wasn't really a smile at all. It didn't reach her eyes, and it could mean anything. "I got it from the miller's wife today as payment for... well, a little help with her troubles."

Catherine had learned that in Rebecca's line of work, there were *joys* and there were *troubles*. *Troubles* usually involved unwanted children or women's ailments, and both were brought on by *troubled* men, she'd told Catherine. Rebecca was an expert when it came to troubled men and the damage they caused. She was sought out for medicinal herbs and ointments, and she was called upon to either help with deliveries or prevent them.

Catherine often wondered why her aunt hadn't prevented her delivery. It was evident Caleb was troubled, and even more so that she wasn't wanted; not by Maebh, in any case. Rebecca had told her how the clergyman had come calling the day after her birth to see if she'd survived it, and he'd christened her Catherine after Maebh's and her mother – the one who'd turn in her grave if she knew how they lived.

Many children born during the cruel, hard winters in the Northern Forest were weak and feeble. When their mothers had no milk for them or dried up too early, they were set outside at night so the cold could have mercy on them and end their suffering more swiftly than pneumonia or starvation would.

The clergyman stoically did his rounds when he'd been told a woman was close to birthing, and he tried to help where he could with donations of food, but his means were restricted, his parish too big, his mule too lame, and he often came too late. The only thing he'd had for Catherine was a name.

Catherine had no idea why she hadn't been among those children who'd been set outside in the winter of her birth, and she didn't know why she was still alive today. She did know for certain that neither maggots nor the cold were ever going to get the better of her. And, she was going to enjoy that jar of honey someplace more amiable, come hell or high water.

Looking up, she could see Rebecca rummaging around in Maebh's broken chest next to the bed. She was searching for a comb to use on Catherine's mop of black hair. Rebecca habitually did this whenever she was there. Maebh watched her crossly, seething in silence as she did every time.

Ruling out that anyone was paying attention, Catherine carefully edged toward the table. Quick as a weasel and unnoticed, she swiped the jar and made a break for it before either woman could stop her.

Out the door she went, up the mucky lane and into the woods, the pot of golden goodness pressed against the flat of her rumbling tummy. Sometimes, life was just plain precious despite everything.

Early autumn had begun to paint all of nature, and the woods smelled gloriously of damp moss and puffballs. Slippery Jacks were in season, and she positively loved those. She knew how to find and cook them because her Uncle Charlie had taught her how.

But, *a whole jar of honey* to herself was a treat she'd never live down, she thought, well pleased with herself. She'd eat half and hide the rest for the next day.

Maybe.

Or she'd eat it all, if she could, and hide the jar that in itself seemed useful.

She'd never have gotten so much as the empty jar if she'd stuck around and waited for Rebecca to leave. Maebh would have squirreled it away, and it would have been used in trade for Caleb's ale, in the end.

Uncle Charlie and Caleb had been close, though they'd hardly had anything in common, least of all the drinking. Charlie's absence saddened her whenever she neared the river, half expecting to see him there on the bank, fishing pole in hand and waving to her.

She stopped running when she'd reached the spot where he'd liked to stand, pulling one trout after the other from the still, barely streaming water. Cross-legged, she sat down beneath the tree he'd called his *whispering birch* for the way its tear-shaped leaves stirred, gently murmuring on the breeze. She noted that it was already next to bare.

Untying the string that held the white waxed cloth closing off the jar in place of a lid, she carefully peeled back the thick piece of linen, licking her lips in anticipation of the sweet delicacy.

It melted on her tongue and coated the inside of her throat, every bit as creamy and wonderful as she'd hoped it would be. She couldn't stop dipping her sticky fingers in for more until the little pot was almost empty and she felt nauseated. The final dollop she put in her mouth before she vowed to stop tasted gritty, and she spat it out. Wiping her chin on her sleeve, she bent over to look at just what had spoiled her last taste of heaven, and her eyes widened in disgust.

Heaving and retching within seconds at the thought of having swallowed any number of the vile, dreadful creatures that twisted and wound beside her ankle, she discovered more of the tiny grain-like bodies inside the jar, preserved in the sugary mass. Scrambling to her feet, she dropped it, and it fell into the piling green and yellow spotted leaves, bouncing several times before it cracked on the rock where it came to rest. The last of its contents slowly trickled out along with an impossible amount of more dead maggots.

There were hundreds of them spilling all over the place suddenly, and Catherine retreated in panic, way past repulsed. She stumbled as she frantically rubbed her hands on the bodice of her dress. Some part of her clever, near-grown mind knew this couldn't be real, but the very young heart beating inside of her told her differently.

Charlie had taught her to keep away from the boletuses as long as she couldn't tell them apart from their poisonous doppelgangers. He'd accumulated a vast knowledge in his years of experience, but somehow, this hadn't kept him from erring. She remembered how his life had ended, wretched, and warped with agony. From that day on, she'd meticulously heeded his warning and concentrated on the things she could classify as edible without a doubt. She was *always* careful, and not just with mushrooms.

Of course she'd looked into the jar when she'd opened it, sniffing the intense sweetness before she'd begun to gorge herself. She was certain she would have seen the larvae in the honey if they'd really been there. Telling herself this over and over again, she stopped backing away and took deep breaths, closing her eyes for a second before she forced herself to have another look.

The maggots were gone, and all that was left was a chipped clay jar holding the remains of something she'd probably never again bring herself to eat.

Rebecca was calling for her somewhere in the woods. Catherine heard her voice in the distance, but there was no way she was going back to the house today. Or tomorrow, for that matter.

Her aunt wasn't looking for her because she cared. No. Rebecca was a boletus, and if you couldn't be completely sure, you kept away from those.

Minutes later, Rebecca passed the spot where Catherine stood, but she didn't see the girl. She found the jar on the ground and prodded it with the tip of her shoe, sighed, looked around, and headed off one direction while Catherine scurried away in the other.

Chapter Three

❦ Sisters ❦

"Sit still, girl, you're stirring the water."

Catherine squirmed uncomfortably in the wooden tub Rebecca had deposited her in after dragging her home. Tossing the child's filthy clothes into a corner for wash day, she set about scrubbing her hair with a hard lump of lye soap.

It hurt when her aunt picked the bits of leaves and twigs from her dark tresses, but she sat stoically as the woman worked, grateful that the water was at least warm this time. Rebecca and her mother were cross at each other again, and any protest she had for the scrubbing would go unheeded anyway.

"You have to do something with this daughter of yours," Rebecca told Maebh. "She's becoming a wildling."

The girl's mother shrugged. "She likes keeping to herself."

Rebecca had brought a length of thick homespun fabric over to cut a new skirt for Catherine. She'd laid it out on the rough plank table. She'd also brought along a red square left over from her wedding cloths to use as an apron. Catherine watched Maebh idly draping it over her own drab skirt, admiring the color contrast.

Rebecca poured a cupful of water over Catherine's head to rinse off the soap and grime. "She's half-grown and runs the woods like an animal. Four or five more summers and she'll be ready to be married, and she knows nothing of keeping a house."

Four or five more summers and then marriage… That sounded almost like a threat. Catherine had no intention of keeping house or marrying. Both were filthy jobs.

"Who would have her in this village?" Maebh grumbled, and Catherine pictured some of the candidates, shuddering.

Maebh threw the cloth back on the table and stood cross-armed in the open doorway to look down the path leading away from the hovel. Catherine knew what she was thinking. Her mother wanted out. She would leave if she had somewhere to go, and she'd never look back. She didn't want any of this. Catherine didn't either. She hadn't asked to be born.

"All she'll get from this place is brats and boredom," Maebh said. "Better she amuse herself while she can."

Catherine hated it when they talked about her as though she wasn't there.

Shaking her head, Rebecca helped Catherine from the tub. She wrapped a coarse towel around her and went to fetch a comb while Catherine stood by the fire, running her fingers through her hair to draw the worst of the tangles from the long wet strands. That way, the comb wouldn't be quite as much of a punishment.

"She's had plenty of amusement, dear," Rebecca said. "She needs to learn a few things from her *mother*. She's fair to look at, so she's bound to be with child not long after she starts bleeding, if you don't watch her. She needs to know what's expected of her."

Catherine startled. A child? Never! She didn't want to be anyone's mother.

"If you're so keen on her learning, then you teach her," Maebh responded irritably.

Rebecca laughed, shaking her head. "She's *your* daughter."

"Yes, she is," Maebh hissed, glaring first at Rebecca and then briefly at Catherine, as if that was something she'd had the power to change. "She is, so leave her to me. If you have a daughter of your own you can do as you think best. Until then, keep your opinions to yourself."

Catherine knew that was meant to hurt, but observing Rebecca, her aunt looked more bored than upset. She'd asked Rebecca why she'd never had children, and her aunt had told her it was because she'd never wanted any. Children were nothing but a bother. Rebecca held her sister's stare without flinching, her lips tight, as always.

Realizing she hadn't achieved the result she'd hoped for, Maebh turned her back on Rebecca and Catherine and fled the house, seething.

Rebecca sighed. "You know, she's actually the child I never wanted and got stuck with."

Catherine grinned, and they both laughed.

From the tiny window, Catherine watched Maebh striding away. She knew she'd be back before long, but her mother was always determined to put on a good show. Maebh was the undisputed queen of drama.

Pulling a chair up to the hearth, Rebecca called her back and directed her to kneel on the small reed rug while she worked the comb through her messy hair.

There was something about the interactions between the two women that made it nearly worthwhile to stick around, sometimes. It wasn't as entertaining as this every time Rebecca came by, but Catherine knew Rebecca enjoyed lecturing Maebh every bit as much as Maebh hated her constant nagging.

Neither her aunt nor her mother ever spoke badly of the other to anyone else, but watching them go at each other Catherine often wondered just why two people who were so much alike beneath the surface never found a common denominator somewhere along the line.

Catherine didn't know much of how people's hearts connected yet, but she often thought Rebecca and Maebh would have overcome their differences in some parallel world where she didn't exist if they'd only found a single thing they could agree on or laugh about. A world where her Uncle Charlie hadn't died so

young, and where her mother hadn't married her
father. Much later in life, she came to understand that
it was the mirroring effect the two of them had on each
other that put them so thoroughly at odds.

Weakness recognized weakness in others, and it
consumed amity.

Catherine knew Rebecca didn't have much love for
her in her heart, either. She was young, but she wasn't
entirely blind, so she could see things for what they
were: Rebecca was afraid of the talk in the village, for
one thing. She simply didn't have it in her to turn her
back on the child her husband had taken such a liking
to, for another.

People would talk anyway – they always did – but
Catherine had heard Rebecca telling Maebh repeatedly
to think of their poor mother and what she would say
if she knew how Maebh and Caleb were neglecting
their duties, and the shame of it all. Catherine didn't
believe Maebh held the memory of their mother very
dear, so that wasn't an argument that carried much
weight with the woman. Nothing much did, and
Rebecca's chances of taking influence were minimal,
although she'd never admit defeat.

Charlie, on the other hand, had always loved
children, and things had been different when he'd still
been around. She thought he'd have been a great father,
and she'd wished he'd been hers, but things were what
they were. His passing had been Catherine's first

glimpse at the pain of loss, and she'd grieved, though that seemed to have struck Rebecca as odd.

Catherine remembered how her uncle had told her she was a clever girl. No one else thought she was clever. Rebecca insisted Catherine was practically a lost cause, and she'd been saying it more often after Charlie had gone. Catherine didn't think she was completely useless because she knew for a fact by now that everything in creation had its place, and she was more inclined to believe what Charlie had told her than what Rebecca was trying to get across. She didn't doubt that there would be a place for her in this world, even if she'd have to put an effort into finding it for herself. There were very vivid images in her mind of where she was going, and they didn't include a ramshackle hovel in the muck with a gaggle of children around her.

When Rebecca had finished combing the almost dry locks of Catherine's hair, she plaited it. Catherine didn't like it plaited, but she didn't object. She'd open it the moment her aunt had left the house.

"Here," Rebecca said, tossing a clean chemise and skirt at her. "Get that on you, and we'll see about cutting you a new dress. You've outgrown yours."

Catherine complied, and Rebecca held the fabric to her form, roughly judging where she'd need to cut its length.

Catherine's father didn't have money for cloth, and her mother didn't have patience to cut and sew it. If it wasn't for Rebecca, Catherine would never have had a decent stitch of clothing on her, but she was still too young to appreciate that.

All she knew was that the coming winter would be far more bearable in warm garbs and drawstring shoes than in the thin dress she'd worn to a rag. If she played her cards right, Rebecca might even throw in some cork and a piece of wire or a length of yarn. Cork would make her shoes much more comfortable in the snow, and trapping squirrels and rabbits would be easier if she had some wire. The best thing she'd gotten from Rebecca over the summer was a new knife. The old blade Charlie had given her to dig for roots with and cut branches was dull and nicked, and its only value was sentimental. The new one did what it was supposed to.

She had no idea of the strain Rebecca's consistent trickle of odds and ends put on the widow's household. She didn't know the cost of a piece of tanned leather, and she was clueless as to the asking price for cork; all she knew was that it was freely given, and the rants and tirades she had to endure in exchange for these things were only a small and quite acceptable part of the package.

Catherine took what she was freely given. This part of her life was only time that had to be measured off by the hour, day and week until she was old enough to think of a means of survival by herself. It didn't even occur to her that she wouldn't, so she patiently waited for her aunt to mark and fold the cloth, and she nodded when Rebecca told her to come to her next week for the dress and a new shawl.

Chapter Four

❧ The Other Catherine ☙

The dark-haired Lady's daughter appeared near the gatehouse. Catherine knew it was her because she bore a great resemblance to the woman; her steel-blue eyes and the shiny black curls cascading over her shoulders and down her back gave her away. The girl was about her own age and height and she was just as thin, but prettier than she by far, Catherine thought, though she didn't hold that against her.

She was curious about the other child. She walked right up to her, not expecting to be seen. The dark-haired Lady couldn't see Catherine, after all. That was why she was surprised to find the girl's eyes following her now. Looking around, she discovered nothing else had changed, and she realized this was neither a dream nor a vision. The ruins stood unaltered, a dark reminder of past times with sink-holes in the walkways and in between the crumbling buildings, tumbling towers and derelict walls.

She decided to walk by, just to see what the other girl would do, and sauntered past the chapel toward the inner defenses of the stronghold. She was glad she was wearing her new dress and shawl. Rebecca had embroidered a crisscross pattern on a portion of the front of the dress and on the collar and sleeves, and she'd dyed the shawl a pretty green. The homespun fabrics still stood in stark contrast to the other child's fine, soft velvet garments and proper leather shoes, but Catherine didn't feel quite as inadequate as she might have in the company of her new posh acquaintance.

The girl followed her for a while, but she wasn't very talkative, so Catherine finally resolved to take her under her wing. She slowed and cast a glance over her shoulder, motioning her. When the other girl saw she was being invited to join Catherine, she made haste to catch up with her and smiled.

"Not much going on here this morning," Catherine remarked casually, and the other girl nodded her head in agreement.

She wondered if the child had ever seen the castle's market or the people who came and went. She wanted to touch the girl's arm, but dared not. It was nice having her here, and she didn't want to do anything to spoil that.

The castle was empty except for the crows perched on the parapets and pointed rooftops of the four slender towers beside the keep. Catherine had become such a regular here, the silly birds didn't bother complaining about her presence and tended to ignore her, save for when she threw stones at them for stealing her food.

"Do you eat?" she asked the other Catherine.

She didn't, she let Catherine know, which was quite a relief. That meant she wouldn't have to share.

A few weeks earlier, she could have provided for both of them, but winter was coming in leaps and bounds. This year's meager harvest had already been brought in from the fields, and the fruit gardens were almost bare.

The only literate man in the village owned several orchards she knew like the back of her hand. Sweet cherry trees, plums and pears grew there, as well as big bushes with blackcurrants and thick-skinned gooseberries. She loved them all, and she'd had her fill, but the season was over. The last of the waning year's spoils were the sour apples that grew on the rocky slopes farthest from the farmer's house, but they gave her tummy aches if she ate more than two of them in one meal. Catherine had picked as many as she could carry before dawn on a daily routine over the last weeks nonetheless so she wouldn't have to go without too soon.

She showed the other Catherine where she was storing them. The alcove of the chapel's sanctuary where the tabernacle had once been made for a good, dry hiding place. They kept quite nicely there in the cool dark niche unless they were bruised, and she thought if she rationed them, they might take her well into the next month.

She wasn't hungry right now, and neither was her friend, of course, so she decided they'd take a peek in on the tiger tabby who was rearing her kittens under the stairwell in the keep.

The other Catherine loved kittens and clapped her hands in delight at the prospect. Catherine herself had spent many happy hours just sitting there holding them, silently stroking their downy-delicate fur and watching them drift in and out of sleep on her lap.

"The litter's becoming really lively," she said. "They've been getting out and about to do some exploring while their mama's hunting for mice in the kitchens or near the breadhouse. They could be anywhere, so don't be disappointed if we don't find them there today."

She remembered the frantic search she'd conducted when the tabby had moved her kittens a week after they'd been born, but the other girl just smiled and shrugged. If they weren't under the stairwell, they'd just have to look for them together.

They weren't half way to the keep when the earth suddenly started shaking. It wasn't much of a tremor, but it was enough to topple parts of the upper walls still standing.

The other Catherine looked at her in dismay, and again Catherine wanted to reach out and touch her. She tried to grab her hand, but the other Catherine retreated from her, seemingly torn between running and staying.

Earthquakes were rare in these parts, and she didn't know what to make of this, or how to react. She fixed a questioning gaze to her friend's, but the girl was fading away as the structure around them continued crumbling. Close to panic and unsure of what to do,

Catherine ran toward the keep, avoiding the rubble and the scattered sandstone blocks on the bumpy cobble street and barely dodging the new stones that crashed down around her.

Entering the Great Hall through the opening that had once held massive iron-studded double winged doors, she caught a flash of brightly colored wall tapestries. For a few seconds, there was a grand vaulted ceiling above her, but the biggest part of it faded away as quickly as it had appeared, giving a clear view of cloudy skies.

Catherine knew she was alone in the ruins once again, save for the crows circling excitedly overhead, and everything became still. Looking about, she could see there had been a great amount of damage. Large sections of the rear end of the building had collapsed, and the dust particles hadn't settled yet. Also, the floor beneath the stairwell had partially caved in.

The kittens, she thought, and hurried to the gaping hole under the stairs. Her heart beat like a drum in her throat. She'd promised the other Catherine she could hold those kittens, and she was sure the girl would be devastated if anything had happened to them.

Kneeling to inspect the opening in the floor, she couldn't see any jagged edges or crumbling fringes. It was perfectly rectangular, and it didn't seem as though anything had really *caved in* – it was rather as if a sealed door of sorts had been shaken loose from its bracings. The stone slab that had covered this section of the floor had fallen onto stone treads leading into a dark cavern of sorts below, shattering as it had tumbled downwards. The kittens were nowhere to be seen.

"Kitties?" she called, trying to decide if it was wise to climb down. There was no telling if it was safe yet, and she couldn't see to the bottom of the stairs or imagine what would be down there. The dungeons were on the other side of the inner wards near the stables, partially underground, and the kitchen storage wouldn't be beneath the keep, she assumed, but farther to the east of where she was standing, so what *was* this?

"Kitties!" she called again, and this time, she heard a faint mewing in reply.

The first of the black and gray quadruplets appeared out of the darkness of the chamber and scuttled over the rubble and treads to the top of the stairs with some difficulty, throwing itself at her legs. It was followed by one of its siblings, but the tiny creature was dragging its hind leg. She carefully picked them both up, awkwardly cradling them in her arms.

"Where are your sisters?" she whispered, pushing her nose into their dusty fur. "Where's your mama?"

Since they couldn't answer her, she decided she was going to have to go and look for them. They'd probably been hurt, if not killed, she realized, but she'd have to see if she could find out for sure.

Whatever was she going to tell Catherine? Her friend was bound to be much more sensitive in these things, being of noble birth. Noble people had nice things, but they were really squeamish.

Cathy the Brave of Unknown Village was the one of them who knew how to light a fire, trap squirrels and rabbits, dig for roots and steal fruit. The dark-haired Lady probably hadn't taught her daughter much besides a curtsey, the letters that made up her name, and how to behave like a Lady; all straight backs and posture, the kind of things Rebecca was always on and on about, though Catherine knew her aunt was most definitely *not* a Lady. No more than she was.

Her hands trembled as she set down the tiny kittens. She got to her feet and stood at the top of the stairs for a moment, staring down, before she took the first step. Once she'd accomplished that, the following were much easier, she found, despite the darkness and the tightness in her stomach. She had to clamber across the pieces of the broken slab about half way down and hesitated to go any farther, but her eyes quickly adjusted to the dark. All she had to do now was to keep her footing.

She'd almost made it to the bottom, when her toes touched something soft, and she bent to have a closer look. It was one of the kittens. Its skull had been crushed by the fall, or by a falling stone, Catherine couldn't say. She gasped.

The tabby lay not far from it, half trapped beneath a large rock. She, too, was dead; her spine most likely broken by the falling debris. Moving the rock over the side of the staircase, she found the fourth kitten. It was in a terrible way, but still breathing. Not bothering to look around any longer, she carefully lifted it and brought it back up to the daylight.

It died on her lap a few minutes later.

After that, things became clearer.

None of them stood a chance. One had broken its leg, their mother was dead, and they were hungry. They didn't eat meat yet, and they couldn't survive on sour apples. She couldn't bring them back to the village because most people were afraid of cats. Some folks claimed they were the Devil's underlings, but although neither Caleb nor Maebh believed in things like that, they did share the general common dislike of the felines with a passion. If she brought them to the hovel, they'd make short work of them.

What*ever* was she going to tell the other Catherine, she thought again, but nothing would come to mind, and so she sat with the kittens until the setting sun had reached the horizon. Then, she wrapped a small but strong-fingered hand around the neck of the healthy kitten and twisted it until it snapped, and the tiny creature stopped struggling. The second kitten was already too weak to fight, and it went faster.

Lying down on the damp ground, she curled up, pulled the three little furballs to her and listened to the sounds of night descending. She didn't feel the rain, and she didn't feel the cold, but when the clouds broke, revealing a silvery crescent moon that bathed the old ruin in an eerie gray light, she resolved never to look for or speak to the other Catherine again.

She couldn't.

And she didn't.

Chapter Five

❦ The Rat ❧

Her mother was sitting at the plank table when Catherine returned to the hovel. Caleb was nowhere to be seen. Perhaps he was still digging the steward's well, or had a six-foot hole to dig for someone else, or lay drunk at the bottom of some other hole. Catherine hadn't been home in a few days, so she could only guess.

Maebh was so engrossed in what she was doing, she didn't hear her come in. She looked like she was concentrating on something at the far end of the room. Catherine strained to see, and caught a glimpse of a big fat rat. It writhed in agony for a few moments, and then it lay still on the dirt floor.

The wind freshened up and sent a gust at the open door behind Catherine, banging it.

Maebh spun around, a mixture of fear and anger on her face. She rose and swiftly closed the distance between them, grabbing Catherine by the arms.

"How long have you been standing there?"

When Catherine didn't answer straight away, Maebh shook her. "Answer me!"

Catherine's heart thumped wildly. She knew she'd walked in on something she wasn't meant to see.

"I… I just got here." She tried to keep her eyes on Maebh and not look at the dead rat by the hearth.

"What did you see?"

"Nothing… what were you doing?"

Maebh loosened her grip on her arms, releasing the tense breath she'd been holding. "Nothing."

But Catherine knew she'd been doing something forbidden. She thought it might have something to do with why Maebh didn't leave the house anymore, but she wasn't sure. There were a lot of things about her mother she didn't understand. Things didn't get broken around other people when they got mad, and other people certainly didn't kill rats just by looking at them.

Caleb sometimes called her mother a *bloody Cine* when he was in a rage. *Cine* was a word you didn't use in public because it was evil. Evil words drew evil deeds and evil people, Rebecca didn't tire of telling her, but she'd never told her what it meant.

The clergyman had spoken of the Cine once at Mass – the one time Rebecca had made her attend. He'd praised the Good Lord for delivering them from the evil that had resided amongst them in the Northern Forest, the Middlelands and the Sudlands. He said God had armed the king with a blade of steel, wisdom and foresight to free them from the *Unnaturals*, from *the Tainted*.

Catherine imagined the Fairypeople he'd spoken of as having bats' wings to fly off on when they'd stolen a child from its cradle. She'd pictured man-eating

Shapeshifters in the form of wolves or bears tearing into the hapless humans they encountered in the woods. The Cine had been the vaguest of the priests' monsters, so, in her mind, she'd painted them sharp, pointy teeth and claws.

She'd spent a few weeks thinking on all of this, but finally decided for herself the clergyman was only trying to scare them into staying home at night. There was nothing whatsoever to be afraid of in the forest, while the dugout at home contained creatures truly capable of eating your insides.

Catherine didn't think her mother was a Cine, or even really evil. Killing rats wasn't such a bad deed. They ate your food if you didn't do away with them.

The way Maebh had dealt with the rodent was fascinating, of course, and somewhere deep inside, Catherine knew it was something Maebh wouldn't want getting around, least of all to the priest. Normal humans trapped or impaled rats, and then they skinned and ate them. She wondered if the rat her mother had somehow willed to die would still be edible.

"I'm hungry," she said.

"There's no food in the house."

"There's a rat."

Maebh looked around. "Diseased. Stay away from it."

Catherine twisted away from her and scuttled to the fireplace. She picked the rat up by the tail. "Doesn't look sick."

Maebh slapped it out of her hand. It flew across the room. "You never listen to a word I say, do you?" she yelled at Catherine and smacked her across the face.

Catherine retreated backward from her toward the door, but ran into Caleb.

He already smelled of ale, and it wasn't midday yet. He grabbed her far too tight. "What's going on?"

"Nothing," Maebh hissed at him, searching the floor for the rat she'd just sent flying.

Catherine struggled to free herself, kicking at him.

"She being a bother?" he asked her mother.

Maebh didn't answer right away, but picked up the rat, pushed past him and threw it out the open door.

Catherine thought he was going to choke her. She wasn't strong enough to get away from him. "She just killed that rat by looking at it," she labored to tell him between two attempts to breathe.

Abruptly, he let go of her and redirected all of his attention at Maebh.

"You stupid wench... what the hell are you doing?"

Catherine needed a moment to steady herself, and she would have made a break for it, but her father was still blocking her from the door.

"That's not true," Maebh said, and Catherine could see the fear in her eyes again.

"It is, I saw."

Caleb was shaking with rage. "It's in you. You're

47

cursed, and you're going to burn for it. You're going to get us all burned for it."

"No, you're wrong, I told you–"

"You lied," he cut her off, clenching his fists. "You ruined my life, you're ruining *everything!*"

The look on Maebh's face changed: fear turned into spiteful outrage. "What on earth could I have ruined for *you?* Look at yourself!"

When Caleb stormed at Maebh, Catherine knew she was off the hook and made a break for it. No one gave chase. She supposed they'd be busy for a while.

Chapter Six

⊗ Straw ⊗

Catherine sat on a fallen tree trunk by the muddy river bank, throwing pebbles and sticks into the black rapids. She still hurt from where Caleb had snagged her around the neck and shoulders a few days earlier.

She hadn't been home or to the castle since she'd left her arguing parents. Neither place seemed like a good idea at present, but she wasn't starving.

The Plum-Man had two cows, and she knew how to get inside his stable. Cow milk was warm and good, she'd discovered, much tastier than the goats' milk Rebecca had brought her sometimes when she'd been younger.

The miller a few miles downstream kept pigs, and his wife fed them on flour-mush, some manner of root vegetables and old bread. She left that out on a bench in her yard to soak in a bucket of warm water before she gave it to them. This wasn't quite as good as the milk, but a few handfuls filled Catherine's stomach for the entire day, and the burley red-faced woman never seemed to notice there was any missing.

The Plum-Man always seemed to vanish indoors at the same time every night with some girl or other, so he wasn't a problem to get around. The miller and his wife were less predictable, and they had recently acquired a new dog, so she knew she had to be careful around them.

Getting caught stealing wasn't an option. The bread wouldn't be worth it because Catherine knew what they did to thieves when they were caught. Children stealing bread were thieves every inch as much as adults in the eyes of the law and in the eyes of the Lord.

God, however, was probably more lenient than the law, she imagined, because hell couldn't be as hot as the angry red lashes she'd seen on the back of one of the crofters' misbehaving boys some weeks ago when they'd dragged him from the church square. He'd died of a nasty infection a week or two after his whipping, and she wondered if Saint Peter had found it in him to overlook his sins, in this special case, and wave him through for the suffering he'd already endured. God wasn't cruel, and thievery wasn't heresy or devilry, after all. It couldn't be as high up on His list of unforgivable sins as those things were. She wasn't sure she'd have been forgiven if she'd been caught stealing and died in the crofters' boy's place. She suspected not.

The icy, swirling currents swallowed the stones she tossed into the water, and one after the other, they vanished without a trace, just as disobedient boys and girls did.

She wished it was warmer so she'd have a chance at catching some fish without catching her death. She'd lost her hook and yarn and couldn't find a decent replacement, and these were high up on her list of wishes too, but wishing didn't make things happen or feed you when you were hungry. A new hook would. She'd simply have to find a way to get ahold of one, and wondered if the shed beside the Plum-Man's stable would be as easy to access as the stable was without breaking anything.

Lost in thought, she didn't hear her aunt coming at her from behind. She nearly jumped out of her skin because that didn't happen very often. Rebecca must have been looking for her for a while, judging by the state of her hair and clothes.

"You're coming home," the woman said, standing in front of her.

She was breathing heavily as she pushed her hands into her sides. Catherine could tell she'd been making haste the last stretch of the way. Perhaps she'd been afraid of losing sight of her. That tended to happen when Catherine knew she was approaching.

She made a mental note to go back to paying more attention to her surroundings, but it was harder by the riverside at this time of the year. The gush of the water made it difficult to hear, and between that and the memories she attached to this place, there was hardly room for anything else in her perception.

"No."

She wasn't going home.

"That wasn't a request. Your mother's leaving. She's packing, and she wants to say goodbye to you."

That was news, though not entirely unexpected. This was her fault.

"Is *she* leaving, or did *he* throw her out?"

"A bit of both, maybe."

Giving a small sigh, Catherine rose. She brushed off her behind, and let Rebecca lead the way.

"Where is she going?"

Rebecca didn't answer. Two *I-don't-knows* in a row were a bit much to admit, Catherine supposed. At least for Rebecca.

When they got back to the hovel, they found Catherine's father clearing the old filling out of his dirty mattress. He was surprisingly sober. He'd gotten half a small cartful of new straw to stuff the coarse woven sack with from somewhere. Catherine wasn't sure it was better than what he'd just dumped outside, but this was the first time she'd ever seen him do anything toward cleanliness in his little house.

Maebh's locket lay on the board table. She was already gone.

Catherine didn't know how to feel about that.

She'd never perceived either of her parents as people who'd function on their own. Neither of them was very clever, and winter was coming, so where was Maebh going to go if she wasn't staying with Rebecca? Her father had no kind of measure, virtue or talent, and she wondered how he was going to manage to stay alive without Maebh there to drag him in out of the cold when he was too drunk to make it home or hide his ale when he could take no more.

Rebecca frowned, picking up the locket. "Where is she? I told her to wait."

"You did," he returned. "And then she left." His eyes wandered to Catherine. "I can't have *her* here, Rebecca."

Several heartbeats passed in silence.

"What?" she finally bit out, fighting for composure before spinning around with a hint of uncharacteristic emotion peeking through her otherwise stony, guarded mien. "What do you mean, *'you can't have her here?'"*

"What I said," he returned evenly, not looking up at either of them. He proceeded to stuff armfuls of straw into the coarse cover. "I can't raise her on my own, and–" He paused there, avoiding her stare.

Catherine could see he was going over his excuses while pretending to concentrate on what he was doing. He always did that when he couldn't think of how to say what he needed to.

She was frozen in space, it seemed, fighting the urge to turn and run back into the forest, and as the silence spread, she asked herself why she was still here. The answer was simple. She wanted up front clarity on what came now. She didn't *need* Maebh or Caleb; she didn't need anybody. She was convinced she could survive on her own. And yet, she was hurting. The lump in her throat felt as though it was suffocating her. This was worse than when Caleb had restrained her too harshly the other day because it came from the inside. Injury or illness were only on the surface, and they went away, but this ache came from another place much deeper, like when the kittens had died.

"Let me get this straight… *you can't raise her on your own?*" Rebecca reiterated, waving a hand in Catherine's direction without casting a glance back. "Look at her! She's ten years old, and you've never done a *thing* for her. She's been raising *herself. Out there.*"

She violently jabbed a hand toward the woods.

"You don't understand," Caleb went on then, his voice as cold as Rebecca's was heated. "Catherine is like Maebh."

The open statement grew out of the earth and loomed over them all solidly like a dark, bat-winged, wolf-headed monster with pointy teeth, ready to dig its claws into them.

Rebecca quietly closed the door and crossed the dirt floor to where he was standing. Leaning in to him, she placed a hand on his shoulder.

"Well, guess what?" she said, her voice low and carefully controlled. "That's too bad, because Catherine is still a child, and you don't have a choice in the matter of dealing with this. No one here will take the burden from you."

When he didn't answer, she turned to Catherine.

Catherine's feet were rooted to the ground. She fought against her tears and the urge to bolt for the door was overwhelming.

"I have something to take care of now, but I'll be back tomorrow, and I expect you to be here when I am."

Chapter Seven

⊙ Promises ⊙

The Master Sorcerer stood at his son's bed, watching the boy sleep, as he'd often done when Dean had been younger. It was only now that he realized he didn't quite know where those years had gone; between the lad's first coherently spoken words and the pile of books at his bedside, it seemed like they'd slipped through his fingers like sand.

The boy with the head of haphazard copper hair was fourteen now, and Greenleaf regretted every moment he hadn't spent with his family, but he didn't know whether he'd really change anything if he could have all of those moments back. He'd always been torn.

He hadn't expected to become a father at fifty after he'd married a woman not much younger than himself, but he wasn't inclined to question this particular wisdom of Fate. He'd loved the woman deeply and they'd shared wonderful years. Dean was a blessing. Whatever else he'd done with his life, Dean had to be the best part of it.

On nights like these, when the house was quiet and he got to thinking, he imagined that he probably wouldn't be around anymore if it hadn't been for his son and the hopes he inspired. Not with Gwyneth dead and things as they were.

Generally, the Sorcerer's inert optimism and stoic determination to find pinpoints of light even in the most hopeless situations encouraged positive thinking in others. Lately, however, he didn't think he was much good at reaching out to people anymore. Much of his inborn happiness had quietly slipped away, and he'd been dwelling on the past rather than stretching his fingers to touch upon a future worth fighting for. His own inner demons kept misleading him, and he tended to get lost in the abysmal chasms of the two hard realities he found himself facing outside of his son's room and the house they lived in.

One was a reality he couldn't change, no matter how hard he tried or thought about it. Gwyneth had fallen ill and died, and there was nothing he could have done to help her because healing wasn't a Talent of his. He hadn't heard of such a thing as a *real* Healer. The Cine had no real Healers, and neither did the humans. Perhaps there had been Fairypeople with that Ability once, but there weren't too many Fairypeople left to verify that. Humans and Cine could mix potions and elixirs that worked on some ailments to an extent, but there were illnesses no one could cure because they weren't *meant* to be cured. Gwyneth had known that, and she'd made her peace with it. He hadn't.

The second reality he'd had to confront was the ongoing persecution and slaughtering of his people. If the killing didn't stop, the Cine were soon going to be as extinct as the Fairypeople practically were, and he felt a deep-seated obligation to help his kind survive the storm that was sweeping the lands.

Both struggles he'd been dealing with were equally personal, and they'd shown him his limitations over the last months in ways he hadn't imagined possible, but Dean was his anchor when he thought he couldn't fight anymore. Dean was his inner haven. At moments like these, the mere presence of his son, the mere fact that he existed in the world gave him strength.

He'd told Gwyneth the truth about himself only days before she'd passed away. She may have suspected what he really was and speculated on how he spent his time away from his family, but she'd never asked or accused him of keeping secrets. She could have, and he wouldn't have denied it, but she simply never had.

He recalled holding her hand when she'd finally admitted to worrying about him, sometimes – she, who was so sick, she hadn't been able to leave the bed anymore – and he'd smiled and told her of his father. He'd described the great magician to her as he remembered him; tall, dark but rather unspectacular to look at. Sober. Practical. Brother and advisor to the last Lord of the Northern Forest before the war. Cine.

He'd told her of the small community of outlaws and refugees he'd been trying to keep alive and fed just a few hours' ride away from their home. He'd shown her his father's work, the incomplete book he'd left to him on protective wards, creating pocket dimensions, and even crossing dimensions to give what was left of his race a fighting chance.

She'd accepted all that without criticism. The only thing she'd asked of him was his promise that he'd find a way to complete his father's work and make his people and the children born to their kind safe. The children of the Cine were important to her, because their child was Cine, too. That hadn't been clear to him up until then. Saving everyone else had taken up so much of his time and energy, he hadn't been aware of what was going on right under his own roof until Gwyneth had told him. He'd hoped Dean's Talent wouldn't surface. Things would have been so much easier for the boy if it hadn't.

Greenleaf blew out the candle that had burned down to a stump by the side of the bed. Tucking the covers more snugly about Dean's shoulders, he planted a kiss on his son's cheek before he left the room. He didn't have to grasp the iron handle; the heavy oak door opened and closed quietly for him, his mind over the wooden matter.

The chill of descending night crept into his bones as he stepped out into the hall, and he shuddered. His footsteps resounded in the corridor that changed as he walked its increasing length. The planks on the floor beneath his leather soles turned to stone tiles, and he became aware that someone was coming. The cloaking spell he'd cast to protect his family's home had started taking effect.

A flick of his hand lit a blaze in the fireplace of the living area, and a mere thought levitated some logs from the inglenook to feed the flames. Sitting in a chair that was the same in his home as it was in the make-believe place where he received visitors who weren't human, he waited for the knock on the door.

The flames grew, and heat began to radiate out from the iron panel behind the grate, but it didn't warm away the cold stillness that seemed to breathe holes into the heavy fabric of this night.

His visitor was having trouble deciding. The Sorcerer knew the feeling well. In the early days, he would have jumped up, opened that door and invited whoever it was to enter, but he was past that stage now. The Cine had to choose their own destiny. All he could do was offer help, and those who really wanted it knocked.

He was going to take Dean to The Fair tomorrow so he could begin to understand the choices he'd be facing one day soon. This was the first time the boy would see the Sorcerer's *other life* and meet people who were – more or less – like him. Perhaps this would be the definitive end of Dean's childhood.

Greenleaf wasn't sure what reaction to expect. Deep down, he didn't want Dean to like it there too much. The Fair was a safer place for the refugees who'd made it their home than the places they'd been forced to flee, but it was more dangerous there for Dean than anywhere else his boy had been before.

Knowledge was always both a power and a burden. To date, he'd kept his family out of his *other life* and out of harm's way. That was going to change now. He trusted most people at The Fair with his life, but he'd have to learn to trust them with Dean's life also, and that was another thing entirely.

Cine people came and went. Sometimes, he took in Shapeshifters when he was convinced they weren't a danger, but they were generally bad company and inclined to make trouble. A number of Dwarven fugitives had made The Fair their home for a while, but they'd left to go back to the Winter Mountains after a year or so. He didn't know whether they'd made it or not.

He'd always been afraid that those who left The Fair would reveal its secret and betray their little working community. It didn't matter whether it was a Cine, a Shapeshifter or a Dwarve; when the Inquisitor's henchman applied the hot irons or decided to cut off fingers and toes, who would blame them for telling the man what he wanted to know? Well-paid executioners knew how to kill swiftly and mercifully, but they also knew how to prolong death, and, contrary to popular belief, the Tainted felt pain like any other creature under the sun.

Involving Dean in this *other life* of his hadn't been his intention when he'd been younger and more naïve, but he now knew that both Dean and he would have to accept that life wouldn't be the same again for either of them. Dean wouldn't be fourteen forever. He'd need to learn how to be judicious about using the Gifts that had just emerged, if he was going to use them, or how to hide them away from the rest of the world cleverly enough so no one would find out. In order to make choices, you had to know what those choices were.

Finally, the knock came, and he answered.

A haggard, raggedy woman stood at his door. Despite the gloom, he saw how tarnished the thin silver aura around her irises was. Weariness didn't discolor Cine eyes as completely as this, and he wondered what story she'd have to tell.

When she didn't say anything, he came to her rescue.

"I'm Ortus Greenleaf. How can I help you?"

She didn't even look at his eyes. "Are you… are you…"

She didn't look because she obviously couldn't tell him apart from a Troll. There was too much human in her blood, and she couldn't ask what she'd come to ask because the words were so alien to her.

"I'm the Master Sorcerer, if that's what you want to know. The title was my father's, but I carry it since his death. And you are?"

Again, no answer. Many of the people who came to see him were afraid to reveal too much about themselves until they'd made sure they were on the same side. Titles didn't mean anything to a Cine nowadays.

"Your name, dear," he insisted nonetheless.

"Maebh Salt."

"From?"

She finally lifted her eyes to his. "The village where I grew up doesn't have a name."

"Well, then it's a good thing *you* do." He stepped aside, inviting her in.

She seemed genuinely grateful to get in out of the cold.

"I wasn't expecting this," she said, rubbing her arms as he led her to the fireplace and offered her the seat nearest to it.

"Expecting what?"

"The house... it looks much smaller from the outside."

He smiled. He'd modelled the cloaking spell to disguise the house so no one could describe it to the Inquisitor or his henchmen. It was never the same twice. Sometimes, it was a mansion with the finest furnishings and sometimes a hovel with flaking, rotting window frames, depending on what his visitor was hoping or presuming to find. This woman had hoped to find wealth and a hand up from where she was. She might not have expected it, but she'd hoped for it.

He would have liked to know where she'd seen the heavy sandstone blocks she'd imagined into being for the house's walls, but he didn't want to ask. Not yet, at least.

"How did you find me?"

"I've been traveling," she said.

"Far and on foot," he thought out loud, and she nodded.

"I was looking for work at the alehouse, but there was none. The alewife said I should go and find you because you... you..." She didn't seem to dare say it.

The alewife was a good woman. She saw the silver, but had no Talent herself beyond brewing the bitter concoction her locals loved. She knew the risks she was taking by helping the Cine, but she'd lost her husband to the fever, two daughters to a marauding horde of robbers in the woods, and her youngest son to the promise of the Western Tribelands. She'd let Ortus know she wasn't about to be intimidated by the people who took her taxes and gave her nothing in return.

"I provide Cine with a safe place to be and work to earn their keep."

She looked relieved.

He didn't think she'd been raised by anyone knowledgeable of magic. "Can you control it?"

Maebh hesitated. "If I don't use it."

At least she had some humor.

She shifted about uncomfortably. "The alewife said you teach the local children to read Scripture and do sums."

He did. He also wrote up contracts for the governing nobleman, and he taught the Duke's children old languages no one but the clergy spoke so they'd be smarter than their father, one day. He didn't know what she was getting at, though. What had old Maude been telling this woman?

"I taught her son to sign his name and count his coins, too."

"Maybe you could teach me to handle my magic better than I can right now."

"Or handle it at all," he returned, and vanished, reappearing at the other end of the room. He could feel her heart missing a beat as he picked up a decanter to pour mead into two earthenware cups. In an instant, he was back with her and handed her one while already drinking from the other.

He watched her tensely nipping at the thick, sweet drink, and reclaimed his seat, settling back for what might or might not be a long conversation.

"I can do *some* magic," she told him haltingly after a silence, "but nothing like *that*, of course."

He smiled. He'd hoped the drink would melt away the knot in her stomach and loosen her tongue. Her natural curiosity outweighed her fear of the unknown, and that was good. That was Cine.

"Well, you wouldn't have found me if you didn't have a Talent, but not every Cine has the same amount or kind of Talent."

"I think I'm a fast learner."

"The place where I'd take you would require it."

Her eyes widened in shock and she nearly spilled what was left of her mead.

He bit his lip. "Nothing to be afraid of. It's only a fair."

"So I'd have work selling things?"

"Probably not the kind of Fair you're thinking of, although there are cloth weavers who might need a hand, maybe, and there's a toymaker who's got more than enough to do. No, we have performers there, who do daily shows on three days a week for the pleasure of audiences all over the kingdom."

Her face told him she had no idea what he was talking about. "Performers?"

"Yes. Let me show you." He set down his cup on the floor next to his chair, stood and offered his hand. "Don't be afraid. You have my word nothing will happen to you, and if you don't like what you see, you can leave anytime."

He realized she might not be inclined to believe what he was telling her, but it was her choice to take a chance or go back to sleeping in the woods. He could go on talking for an hour, but if she didn't see for herself, she wouldn't understand that the only thing left to them was to hide in plain sight.

"You're joking, right?"

He chortled a laugh and shook his head. "Come and see."

Reluctantly, she placed her hand in his. It felt cold, but she was at the end of her rope, and if she made a smart decision tonight, that could change. He concentrated, thinking of where he wanted to be, and the world became unhinged.

A flurry of glistening particles engulfed them. Lights in white and silver whirled and came alive in the air. The space they were in was torn apart for the fraction of a moment, and another layer opened up beneath the first. Ortus barely heard the static anymore, but he realized Maebh Salt did. He felt a little guilty at not having warned her, though there was just no way to prepare anyone for a Helper's Passageway. He was no Fairyman, so he couldn't make the trip any easier on her senses than this.

When the blinding haze had faded, he could see by the expression on her face she was somewhere between confused and horrified.

"Are you alright?" He had to help her steady herself.

She nodded, blinking around breathlessly. "What was that, and where are we?"

"Welcome to *The Fair*."

They were standing in the drizzle on a big, mucky field with makeshift shelters and tents nestled around a large, round blue and golden Big Top. He had to admit this wasn't the best of nights to bring someone here, but she hadn't chosen the best of nights to come to him.

The shelters they passed in heading for the Big Top were small and shabby, but the people scurrying about in the cold light of the smoking putty torches and Swedish Fires were dressed in the brightest of forbidden colors, and they didn't seem to mind the damp. They laughed and joked as they went about their chores, and they saluted him in passing like an old friend, nodding to Maebh pleasantly. She was a guest who'd stay only for the night or for the rest of her life. Every last one of the people they encountered had come here the way she did now, and they all knew how difficult and strange it was to walk this unfamiliar road.

The Big Top's tarp looked as though it had seen better days, but it kept the weather out. Two poles set on either side of a flap large enough to allow for three or four people to walk through side by side marked the main entrance. It stood wide open and they entered. Their feet crunched on dry wood shavings, and the smell of wax and oil, horses, fresh cut pine and acrid paint filled the air around them.

Glowing torches of the same make as those outside lit the arena. Scores of artists scattered about the tent. It looked so much larger from the inside than it had upon their approach, large enough to absorb the noise they made as they occupied themselves with various strange and wonderful endeavors that seemed to captivate their newcomer's imagination.

On the south side of the circus ring, a group of about a dozen men were erecting risers for spectators, twelve rows high and sturdily built. Next to them, several youths were painting a set that had already been completed. Huge nets occupied the center of the arena. Above them was a network of aerial trapeze apparatuses. His stomach still clenched when he watched the small group of performers flying out toward one another on swings with absolutely perfect timing and complete confidence, swapping grips in mid-flight.

Jugglers and Acrobats practiced their acts a little way from the net on one side, while a bear-tamer led two of his animals past them toward the back exit on the other. Maebh flinched at the sight of the beasts. They had no chains to hold them, and he couldn't blame her.

A man and woman entered the tent through the main entrance behind them with five fine black Iberian horses. They directing them around the outer ring. The animals trotted in unison, and the woman uttered her commands quietly and without raising her voice. The horses obeyed her to the word even from the other side of the tent.

A group of musicians, seemingly oblivious to those about them, rehearsed on a stand raised above the back exit. There were horns and drums, zithers, lyres and a host of other instruments.

"Everyone with a Talent has another talent they can employ it for," the Sorcerer told Maebh. "We don't sit around here and wait for Fate's biddings. We decide it for ourselves."

"But how can this work?"

He smiled. She wouldn't comprehend. "Suffice it to say this Fair is protected, and we move quickly from place to place. The people who come here bear no ill will. They'll see all the wonders they could ever dream of and live a day in awe. When they go home, they'll take all their memories of that day along with them, except for where they spent it."

"Stand back," shouted a voice nearby.

Maebh startled and turned toward a family – father, mother, three nearly grown boys and a daughter – standing in a rough circle some ten feet from her, each of their hands upon the shoulders of those flanking them. They were dark haired, their oriental faces flushed, and their eyes locked on some unseen point fixed in the middle of their sphere. After a few seconds, a light began glowing in the middle, growing brighter and larger until it erupted into a soft ball of flame hovering about four feet above the floor. Slowly, as one person, they moved their hands away, their left arms dropping to their sides as they extended their right hands in beckoning toward the luminescence in the midst of them.

Tendrils of flames stretched from the center, seeking a channel through those who called them, and the Firestarters received them in the palms of their hands.

"One, two, three, four," the mother counted softly as the group moved about in rehearsed dance steps. "Two, two, three, four," she continued as they whirled and vaulted in a flawless routine, the flames dancing about them in patterns and shapes at the command of each holder. The daughter, maybe ten or eleven years old, pirouetted into the center of the group while her family circled her in an easy step-lock pattern. As they danced, the flames rose above their outstretched palms and swirled, creating rings that slowly floated upward, spinning elegantly some twenty feet above them before exploding into a shower of sparks that rained down on them like the stars.

Picking up the pace, the woman counted faster as the two older boys faced each other and tossed rings of fire back and forth between them. Ortus watched Maebh holding her breath as the flames traced patterns about the Firestarters like the symbols of ancient runes.

"Maebh, this isn't a fair where people bargain for goods or watch a jester ridicule his king. This is a Fair of Souls," he told her. "It's where souls like ours can come to heal and be returned to themselves. This is where we can be who we really are without fear of discovery because we don't have to hide who we are. The people who come to see what we have to offer *expect* to find magic here, in whatever form their imagination will allow them to accept. They'd never guess they're getting anything but trickery, but they'll get their fill of what they choose to make of this, and perhaps lead a happier life for a night or a little while longer."

Leading her back to the entrance, he could see she wasn't convinced.

"But *why* do they live like this?" she asked, gesturing to the shelters and small tents outside. "They have magic, and they could do so much better…"

"How do you mean?"

She stared first at her feet, then into the light of one of the Swedish Fires a few yards from the Big Top. "They live in *tents*."

"We're still working on that…" he said, but she cut him off, revealing a side of her he wouldn't have presumed.

"Magic can make you rich and powerful, and I just don't understand… *You* live better than they do."

"That's right," he said. "I do. But I don't live here because I'm still working on something that demands my attention elsewhere. I run the risk of going back to a place where any village wench can turn up on my doorstep knowing I'm a Cine. But this is where you're wrong: most of us don't have the kind of power you're thinking of. You haven't seen much of the world, have you?"

"But *you* have that kind of power. Why don't you use it to create… *more* here?"

"You can't just create *something* from *nothing*." He laughed. "There's a balance to keep, and you have to give something for everything you take. You'd do well to remember that. It's the first lesson we all must learn if we hope to control the Talent inside of us."

He turned around to the young man in the ring who was juggling hoops of fire. Focusing on one of the burning hoops, he willed it to appear in his own hand.

"Hey!" the young Firestarter called out, losing his rhythm and dropping the rest.

The hoop continued burning in Ortus' hand as he elegantly waved it from side to side several times in a figure-eight pattern. The flames traced patterns in the night, but the heat didn't affect the Sorcerer.

"Everything you take for yourself in this world will be missed by someone else," he told her, "and get you attention you certainly don't want."

Chapter Eight

❧ Legacy Children ❧

Rebecca didn't bother going back to the house the following day. It had been raining since the early hours of the morning, and the ground was soggy, but she knew better than to assume her niece would have listened to her. Why should a girl who'd just been abandoned by her mother and openly rejected by her father listen to *anyone?* Rebecca thought Catherine probably didn't feel like she'd ever been given much incentive to.

She was a mess by the time she reached the castle ruins, but she found Catherine there in the chapel without really looking for her.

It was where she would have gone when she'd been Catherine's age if everything around her had been falling apart. This old place had an air of peacefulness, and she'd often imagined that if you listened closely, you could still hear the people who'd attended Mass here singing on Sunday mornings. Aside from the river, this had been her favorite place.

She was clear on the fact that she could see Catherine only because the girl allowed her to. If that was all her Talent encompassed, then maybe she'd be spared a life of hardship and persecution, Rebecca thought. This was something you could keep to yourself if you were smart. She wondered if Catherine would grow up to be that kind of smart, because smart people survived.

The girl was sitting on the broad window seat in the arched opening of the only remaining thick bearing wall. Rebecca remembered how Maebh and she had sifted the rubble below to find tiny shards of the colored glass that had made up that window before it had been shattered. They'd given away the pieces of it as tokens and gifts to friends. She still had one or two of them.

A red beech grew right next to the wall. It seemed to shelter the girl beneath its boughs and canopy of waxy new leaves as though it had no other purpose, and Rebecca felt somehow touched by the sight of her niece there. If things had been different, Catherine might have grown up here, and life would have been good; a good life for a beautiful child.

The irony made Rebecca smile. Life wasn't kind, or permissive, and although Catherine must have realized that already, she was just a child, and children sometimes needed guidance. This little wildling certainly did today. She didn't feel comfortable handling these kinds of things because she didn't want to be; personal closeness always ended in personal suffering one way or the other. Nonetheless, she somehow felt a sense of duty toward Catherine now that Maebh was gone. Whether or not her sister's daughter would accept this was up to her.

Catherine was sharpening one of an impressive number of sticks with her knife in a very unladylike fashion – for one of her traps, no doubt – and she didn't look up even when Rebecca appeared beside her, huffing and panting from the break-neck ascent.

She was getting too old for this.

"I'll say that I do admire your patience," she began chirpily after watching her niece for a moment. "I think you have enough to last you the year."

"I'm not *like* my mother at all," the girl remarked so quietly, the older woman barely heard.

Rebecca didn't know what to reply, at first, and sighed. She pushed aside the pile of stakes to sit down. "You know, I don't think Caleb meant that to sound the way it did."

Oh, he'd meant it all right.

"He was hurt," she plowed on nonetheless, "and he will be hurting for a while. He was lashing out, and you happened to be in the way."

"But what *did* he mean, then?" Catherine was attacking the stick so ferociously, Rebecca briefly considered taking it away from her. "I'm *nothing* like my mother."

"Did you know your grandmother was a very special person?"

Of course Catherine couldn't possibly know that. Maebh had never had a good word for the woman.

Maybe that was why she'd never bonded with the child. Catherine was the mirror image of her.

Catherine's smooth brow creased, but she didn't stop assaulting the stake. "Whatever. So?"

"Well, your grandmother was the child of the nobleman who once lived here and ruled over the land."

The girl stopped what she was doing and looked at Rebecca, eyes wide, as though something she'd given a lot of thought to without being able to figure it out had just sunk in.

"Seriously?"

"Seriously." Rebecca quirked an eyebrow. "It didn't do her much good, though." It had done no one in her family any good, least of all her mother. She'd been the bastard daughter of a *defeated* nobleman, and they were lucky the story had blown over. "Lord Tierney never wanted to know her."

"Why not?"

"Because your grandmother wasn't lucky enough to be born to a *Lady*. She wasn't born to the nobleman's wife."

There was a silence as Catherine tried to process this, but then the coherencies seemed to become clear to her.

"Things don't always work out as we'd like them to," Rebecca went on absently. "That's the way of the world, dear. She was just a few days old when the castle was burned to the ground, and the Tierneys had to flee through one of the secret tunnels underneath the earth here somewhere."

"Was there a war? Why did they have to flee?"

Rebecca thought about it for a moment. "Do you know what they call people like your mother?"

Catherine nodded, not looking at her. "She's *tainted*."

Rebecca chuckled. "Well, they have many names for the *Tainted*, dear. *Unnaturals* or *Witches*, but the correct term is *Cine,* and *they* like to refer to themselves as the *Talented*." She paused briefly and pulled a face. "Although… I wouldn't quite call your mother *talented*."

Catherine rarely smiled, but Rebecca saw that she did now.

"She *can* fry rats."

Rebecca's nose scrunched. "Indeed she can."

She wondered if the child understood what she was getting at.

"Well, the Cine built this castle at a time when magic wasn't forbidden because no one thought it was godless."

Catherine stopped hacking away at her stick and put the knife down.

"I didn't know that."

"Lord Tierney was the last Cine nobleman in the Northern Forest before the Pope in Remulum decided magic was evil, and anyone with an Ability for it was to stop using it. Needless to say, people tend to use what they have if it's to their benefit."

"What kind of Abilities do Unnaturals have?"

Rebecca had to think about this. "Nothing really harmful, I'd say. If you don't count frying rats as harmful."

Again, Catherine smiled.

"Nonetheless, after a while, the use of magic became punishable by death. That stirred a lot of protest, of course, but neither the Fairypeople nor the Cine were ever very strong, or numerous. The Pope sent his bishops to the Sudlands first before the Inquisition moved north and got here. Lord Tierney served a king who was very weak and impressionable, and he was sitting on dry farmland, while Tierney had copper mines in this part of the Forest. The people around here actually made a decent living. You could say Tierney was a wealthy man compared to his king, no matter how hard that king taxed him."

Catherine sniffed. Rebecca thought she might not even know what taxes were, but it didn't matter.

"So the king wanted what Lord Tierney had," Catherine said, and Rebecca thought that hit the mark accurately enough.

She nodded. "He had the Church behind him. When someone is charged and found guilty of being an Unnatural, they execute them and take away their property and their lands. Some of it goes to the church, and the rest goes to the nobleman in charge. The king really looked forward to owning the Tierneys' mines, and he even bought the church's share back before the siege was over and he'd even had his advisors look at those mines."

Rebecca had always found this part of the story would have been very satisfying, if it hadn't meant the complete ruin of the people who lived here as well.

"Did the Tierneys get away, and did they take your mother with them?"

"No, child, no." Rebecca laughed so hard, she almost lost her balance. "She didn't belong with them. The Cine who got away scattered, and no one really knows what became of the nobleman or his wife. Rumor had it Lady Tierney made a pact of some sort with the king before the siege. He'd promised to spare her and her daughter and grant them both amnesty if she'd reveal the secret of the copper mines to him. But she couldn't. Something went wrong. They say Lady Tierney was killed before she got to wherever they were going. Lord Tierney was said to have died of some illness a while later. In any case, those mines didn't yield an ounce of ore to the king's laborers, and the king was left with nothing but more worthless land, a burned-out castle and impoverished peasants who couldn't feed themselves, never mind pay him taxes and repairs."

"He must have been pretty mad."

Rebecca nodded.

"Your grandmother, was she *tainted*, too?"

"By birth, yes. She was half *Cine*." Her lips closed to a thin line again in disdain when she said the word. "The blood is in our family through her, and there's nothing to be done about that. But, you have to understand this: we don't talk about it to *anyone*. When Caleb said you were like Maebh, he meant he thinks you've inherited her Ability."

Again, the girl's eyes widened as it dawned on her that he knew she also had a Talent. How had he guessed? Or was a guess all it was? She was sure what she had wasn't anything dark. How could making yourself unseen be anything dark when it did nothing but protect you? She didn't even fry rats or anything, unlike Maebh.

"Do you –" she began, but halted, hardly daring to ask. "Do you have a Talent?"

"No!" Rebecca hastened to establish, raising a hand in her defense. "Heavens, no."

She wouldn't call what she had a *Talent* any more than Maebh's ridiculous attempts at getting attention. She just had a good feel for what herbs could do by sight and smell, and she knew a little about the human body. "I was spared. Not every child born to a Cine descendent has the affliction."

"You really make it sound like a curse," Catherine mumbled.

Rebecca was convinced this was what magic was: a curse. It was a burden to bear, and it needed to be concealed, or it would get you killed. Life was hard enough as it was. One envious neighbor, one unlucky birth too many, or one misjudgment in measurement of some elixir or other to relieve urinary problems in the pregnancy, and she could be in for trouble, whether she had a Gift or not.

She doubted Catherine had ever been consciously aware she manipulated other people's perception when she blended in with her background. She assumed it was the others who weren't paying attention.

"A lot of people can't control it," she said. "*It* controls *them*, and they always end up hurting someone and getting caught. Using magic can make you reliant on it, and the more you use it, the more you want to use it," Rebecca explained. "That's why it's forbidden, and that's why they put any person they suspect of using magic or being a Cine to death. They think it can't be controlled, no matter how hard you try."

"Did Catherine control it?" the girl inquired cautiously.

The truth was, Rebecca thought her mother hadn't had much of a Talent. Not that she knew of anyway. "She did. That's why I think you could also learn."

Her gut feeling told her something different, but she didn't want to admit defeat quite yet. Caleb would simply have to toughen up, and she would too, or this Catherine was going to do a lot more than rid the world of some louse-ridden vermin.

Reaching around her neck, she unfastened the delicate clasps of the necklace Maebh had left at her house before she'd gone, and placed it around Catherine's, pulling the empty locket gently to the front. She'd cleaned and polished it the previous night after she'd tried to find out if anyone had at least seen the general direction Maebh had taken.

"This might help you," she said. "It was your grandmother's."

Catherine's eyes widened in delight as her thin fingers undid the two halves that opened like a butterfly's wings or a cockle shell.

"Why did she never put anything in it?" she asked. "Why is it empty?"

Rebecca turned this over in her head but found herself groping in the dark. Maebh wasn't the sentimental kind. The locket had initially been her mother's gift to Rebecca, a hand-me-down and keepsake to her oldest child. It had been empty when she'd first gotten it. She'd never thought it very pretty, and she'd easily parted with it on the day Catherine had been born. Rebecca had always known she herself would never have a child to pass it down to, and that was why Maebh had worn it these past ten years. She supposed her sister had left it behind as a small thing of small monetary value rather than because she wanted Catherine to have something of hers to remember her by.

She hummed as she considered her answer. Then,

she said, "It's possible your mother never thought she had anything worthwhile to fill it with. But, since it's yours now, you can start filling it with any memory you see fit."

Chapter Nine

♋ The Fair ♌

"How far is this going to put us behind schedule with the wagons?" Ortus wanted to know of Thaddeus, entering the fairground through the narrow glowing Portal on the edge of the field near the tree line. The brawny man's wife, Mary, had opened it for them. She closed it when they'd come through, and left them to their conversation.

"Not too far," Thaddeus said. "The lumber we've already cut isn't lost, but we weren't finished, and it's just not in the right place for when we'll need it. We have friends both there and here who'll help us with that, though, so I suppose we'll just have to rethink our route and plan a little more loosely."

Plan and *loosely* weren't two words the carpenter would have used in the same sentence when they'd met ten years ago, and Ortus smiled. They'd both learned a lot. Things didn't always go smoothly, and you had no choice but to *plan loosely*.

Glancing around, the Sorcerer thought Mary had chosen the new location well. She always did, even when they were in a hurry. Their site nested in a wide valley enclosed by ancient woodland. A clear stream dissected the gorge. There would be good fishing and hunting.

"How far to the nearest town?"

"Nuremthal is a little over three hours' march south, and there are smaller villages in every valley along the way as well as to the west of here."

Ortus was sure they'd easily have their income over the summer.

They'd had to move The Fair ahead of time from its last location because some of the king's cavalrymen on leave had gotten inside the Haven. The soldiers had displayed no signs of bad intent, but they'd asked too many questions. Thaddeus had dispatched someone to follow them when they'd left, and the young man had sent back a dovelen, reporting the men had gone to inform their captain. There was no sense in taking risks. Ortus didn't think anyone could breach the Haven, but the locals would have paid the price. Endangering the humans who helped and supported them wasn't an option.

The new fairground was bustling; everyone was busy setting themselves up again, rebuilding their hastily dismantled shelters and tents, and sorting their possessions. Fences for the horses and goats were already up. Some of the older women were gathering wood in the forest, and twenty men were toiling with the framework for the Big Top.

"I'll need a few hours to reinstall the wards," he informed Thaddeus.

"That's not a problem. I've already posted sentries."

Ortus had to recreate the Haven to protect every new site they settled on. They rarely stayed in one place longer than three or four weeks with the exception of the winter months when life seemed to stand still. Casting wards to cloak The Fair's presence had become as much a routine for him as ushering people with their possessions through her Portals had become for Mary, but it took him some hours even still, and the grounds were wide open during that time.

His glance fell upon a woman crossing their path just then. He knew her face, and he remembered having brought her into The Fair himself, but couldn't recall her name. There was something about her eyes that bothered him. She nodded curtly by way of a greeting when she noticed his unintentional stare, and he returned the gesture. There had been so many newcomers lately, and it annoyed him to discover he wasn't keeping up anymore.

"Who's she, again?"

Thaddeus sighed and halted in mid-stride so as to wait until she was out of earshot. He looked as though he needed to gather his thoughts before speaking, but that seemed like an unsavory task, and Ortus didn't take that as a good sign.

"Maebh Salt. She's not… uncomplicated."

Ortus grinned. "*Not uncomplicated* or *difficult*?"

Thaddeus frowned. "To be honest, difficult."

"Where's the problem?"

"She isn't adapting. She doesn't pull her weight." He motioned to the woman who'd seated herself by the cooking fire while everyone around her was in motion.

She unhurriedly poured herself some tea as though she had nothing else to do.

"What jobs has Mary given her? Is she unhappy about them?"

Thaddeus' wife usually had a good eye for people and their Abilities. She was a Fairywoman by descent, and liked by all. Despite the challenging situations they sometimes faced when new refugees brought their broken souls' baggage to The Fair, she'd proven to be a very good mediator.

"*Any* job seems to make our Maebh unhappy." Thaddeus smirked. "Mary's had her with the washing women, but people started complaining. She's had her mending costumes, but she's no talent. She's had her helping the cooks, but she's slower than the children and grousing about the others to Mary. I'm letting her muck the goats at the moment, but they're in a terrible state most of the time, so someone always has to double for her."

So Maebh Salt didn't have an affinity for chores. "Is she taking an interest in any performance acts?"

Thaddeus scoffed. "She likes watching them, and she's tried and failed at a few things over the months she's been with us. But, she does seem to be quite good with animals – as long as she doesn't have to clean them and they don't smell."

Both men laughed.

"Has she made any friends yet?"

Thaddeus hesitated, watching a slender man with short brown hair crouch down beside her to fill his own cup from the heavy kettle over the fire.

"If so, then it's the wrong ones, I'd say. If there's trouble on the grounds, Aurum is never far."

The man exchanged a word or two with Maebh, but each of them pointedly looked past the other while sipping their tea.

"Well, I wonder where this is going…" the Sorcerer thought out loud.

Jaden Aurum had come to The Fair with his son and a small group of survivors from the massacres in the Sudlands three or four years ago. Ortus knew him as a talented Illusionist who could captivate an audience, but in private, he was as unpleasant a character as they came.

The only thing that prevented him from throwing the man out on his ear was the fact that Aurum would be taking his boy out there with him if he left, and neither Ortus nor Thaddeus wanted to have that on them. Mostly, Aurum was all bark and no bite toward anyone bigger or stronger than he was in any case, so they'd simply been keeping him in check by monitoring him.

"Maybe Mary should talk to her again – and point her toward more pleasant company. Let's give her another while, shall we?"

Thaddeus shrugged. Ortus knew his best man was always good for second or even third and fourth chances, and most people did end up finding their niche and staying. Sometimes they just needed time. Perhaps he should be giving Maebh some of his own – she'd asked him to when she'd come to him – but his time had become so scarce and so precious, he was always afraid he'd run out one of these days before he'd found a more permanent solution for protecting the growing community he'd dedicated most of his life to.

"You're late," Dean told him from behind, coming from where he'd been helping the Snake Sisters with their tents. Dean had been spending a lot of his time at The Fair recently because he wanted to and because of the new project they'd set their sights on. Ortus was relieved at how easily he seemed to deal with his new life situation.

"And you're being smart with me," he replied, turning to him and smiling.

Chapter Ten

ଓ Names ଏ

Catherine believed in dreams.

She wasn't sure whether the one she'd had that night meant anything or not because Caleb's words, Maebh's absence, and the subsequent silence in the hovel had kept her somewhere in between asleep and awake for most of the hours she'd lain on the hard dirt floor beside the newly stuffed mattress, but she was inclined to follow her instincts, and they told her to go. So, she did.

Her father wasn't awake yet. He wouldn't be for another hour at least, and he wouldn't miss her when he was, she thought, quietly closing the door behind her. She was up the lane before she realized it was raining again, but she didn't care. Rain increased the chances of not having Rebecca out looking for her.

On one hand, she knew Rebecca was the one person who might yet straighten out a few things, but on the other, she wasn't the *thing* that needed straightening out. Her father was. She doubted he'd *want* to be straightened out, though, so he was on his own, just like she was, and just like Maebh was. They all were. Perhaps everyone in this entire world was, when it came to the crunch.

In her dream, she'd seen *the other Catherine*. They'd been down in that secret room she hadn't dared return to, and it had been all clean and new, as though the master builder and his brick masons had just completed it. There were no furnishings, only echoes and the coolness of a place the sun couldn't reach.

The other Catherine was lying down in the middle of the most extraordinary floor as though she was a part of the imagery depicted thereupon, arms and legs spread wide and staring at the ceiling into nothingness. At first, Catherine thought the girl might be dead, her life-force somehow linked to the kittens the tremors had killed – *she* had killed – but then she realized that the child was merely dreaming, perhaps of her.

She'd never seen anything so beautiful as the rich, warm glow of the golden ivy border that ran the perimeter of the six hexagonal shapes around the centerpiece the other Catherine was lying on in stillness. The leaves seemed to move, like an unheard breeze was stirring them, and the colors of the illustrations inside the hexagons were lucid like the panes of the stained-glass window in the chapel. When she'd awoken, she couldn't remember exactly what they'd shown, but she wanted to find out. The faraway, unearthly look on her friend's face made her believe she had to. She owed her that. And, she owed that to herself.

The hillside seemed to have become steeper over the winter, but that was impossible, she observed disgruntledly. Or was it? Was anything *really* impossible?

She was puffing and panting by the time she'd reached the overgrown cobble road cutting through the landscape like an old scar, so it had to be her. She hadn't done a lot of hill-climbing over the last months, and to add to the thorn in her side, all she saw was an old pile of rubble in the drizzle when she looked at the vestiges of the walls and gatehouse of the stronghold.

Nothing shifted, nothing changed for her the way it usually did, and she was momentarily disheartened. Walking across the crumpled courtyard, she half expected and very much dreaded to see the other Catherine and have to look her in the eyes. She didn't know what she'd say to her. Having buried the kittens and their mother in the soft earth of what had once been the kitchen's herb garden, she knew she'd had no other choice than to do what she had. Life was tough, and death lurked everywhere, but maybe the other Catherine had already had an idea of that. Still, she doubted she'd find it in her to justify herself.

Mercifully, the girl failed to appear, just like the last time she'd been here, and just as the castle refused to.

The Great Hall was silent and empty, stripped bare of all dignity. A crow sat on the chimney top, laughing down at her. It was a hoarse cackling sound that made her want to throw a few stones, but she knew she'd never hit, and that infuriated her. Red hot anger welled within, and she bit down on her teeth so hard it hurt.

Suddenly, the creature plunged, seemingly lunging itself at her in a downward arc, but Catherine wasn't certain it was actually targeting her. Its flight was uncontrolled, uncoordinated, and she wasn't alarmed by its descent, oddly enough, so she didn't even step aside when its wing brushed one of the remaining bearing walls close to her, throwing it off course before its dilapidated body smacked into a partial column opposite her – hard. Then, the broken creature fell to the ground at Catherine's feet, dead.

Looking up incredulously, Catherine watched the other huge crows fleeing the ruins in an outraged medley of screams that coalesced into a single voice testifying to their dire indignation. They had never been in the least bit afraid of her sticks and stones, but something had made them change their minds about her all at once. Smiling to herself, she found some satisfaction in that, a morbid kind of amusement. She hated the wretched birds.

The stairwell was as she remembered it. Nothing more had moved or collapsed since she'd last been here, and she carefully began her descent. It was quite dark in the hidden chamber and she'd need a lot of light if she wanted to be able to look around properly. She'd known that, and about half way down, she pulled the tallow candles she'd taken along from her pocket. There were three of them, already burned to stumps, but that was all she'd been able to find. Maebh would have been furious that she'd dared to sneak off with them, but Maebh wasn't there anymore.

Lighting the kindling she'd brought with a flint and a firestone, she got a little flame going and quickly held the first candle's wick to it. It caught immediately, and Catherine lit the other two stumps on the first. The effect wasn't overwhelming, but it was better than nothing, and it gave her the visibility she needed to make her way safely down the remaining steps and into the low underground room of about three hundred square feet.

She distributed her precious candles as well as she could, but the blackness in the room swallowed up most of their luminosity. Allowing her eyes a moment to adjust to the gloom, she stood in the profound silence, thinking as time raced on and tallow melted.

There had to be a way to see this place properly, and as it *had* been, like she'd seen the rest of the castle in its prime. There was something down here she very much *needed* to see, and the strange floorcovering she felt beneath her bare feet was perhaps only a part of that.

Dropping on all fours, she discovered that the cold stone surface wasn't like anything she'd encountered before, and she wondered just what she was feeling as she swept her hands over it, noting the grouted clefts. At first, she'd thought she was standing on aged and fragmented stone tiles that had cracked in the heat of the fire that had consumed the fortress, but that hadn't made much sense; the Great Hall had tiles on the floor cut from stone, and so did the chapel, but the cracks and fissures there were less regular and less frequent, more gaping and jagged.

The portion she was looking at here within the restricted radial glow of the solitary candle in her hand consisted of small, differently shaped fragments of painted stones almost reminding of the window in the chapel and of what she'd seen in her dream. They were masterfully cemented to make for an almost perfectly even overlay. Scuttling around and trying to determine whether this was consistent for the whole of the flooring in this room, she crawled from one end to the other, her hands roaming where her eyes strained to but hardly could. It seemed to her the colored pieces were arranged to show something bigger, some significant entirety you couldn't grasp if you only had plate-sized portions to look at.

The increasing irritation that was gnawing at her with sharp teeth, pinching at her patience wasn't going to help her, she realized. Rocking back on her calves, she tried to focus, groping around inside of herself for something, *anything* to anchor her mind to.

She generally found it extremely hard to concentrate on inanimate things, but she couldn't bring herself to envision the Lady or the other Catherine. She didn't need people, much less dead ones who hadn't turned out to be helpful for all the hope she'd placed in them. All they'd ended up doing was stirring dull aches and confusing her when she hadn't been before. The only person she could rely on was herself.

She'd come here for a reason, and she wasn't going to leave without having something to show for it. Whoever had built this chamber below the earth would have had to install a source of light.

She remembered having seen torches fastened to the decorative iron holders that were mounted on the walls of the Great Hall, and she thought that was a good place to start. Imagining how they would have looked here, she focused all her energy on the light they would have given off.

It took a while for things to begin reforming, but time was the one thing Catherine had plenty of. The first tentative glow barely half a lumen above what the candles were putting out was like the dawning of day when you were waiting for morning, unaware of the first rays of sun already touching the horizon. But, that glow soon spread, and most of the chamber was presently bathed in the buttery, if flickering light provided by tangible pitch and tow torches fading in and out of sight. The heavy smell of burning tar was less than bearable, but even if it hadn't been, Catherine wouldn't have left the underground room for gold and silver now that she could see what the darkness had concealed.

Part of the floor was still drowning in shadows, but getting to her feet to have a better view of the imagery revealing itself to her, she didn't know where to begin. She found herself open-mouthed and surrounded by the astonishing and wonderful realities of her dream's waning impressions.

A full, silvery moon gained a third dimension and rose up from its allocated place on the floor mosaic, describing a partial arc before coming to a halt in the now star-filled sky above her. The illusion of a huge gray wolf bounded through the forest that grew from the dust about her, and she stood there on the center piece inside of an artwork she had no name for. Everything was translucent, everything was made of blue energy, but it was there nonetheless, and Catherine felt like her mind's own rendering of the dreamscape she perceived on the floor beneath her bare feet was a world in itself, and she was one of its defining characteristics.

Suddenly, the torches flared up, and they made the chamber day-bright. The shadows were gone, and the pictures on the mosaic went back to being what they were and always had been: colored images on the floor of a collapsing relic. They were breathtaking even still, or maybe solely because of this – Catherine couldn't decide.

One of the works in particular caught her eye, the rest weren't as interesting to her. It was of a woman seated on a throne, a child on her lap. That woman was a queen for sure. She was wearing a crown adorned with sparkling gems, and she was dressed in a gown so opulent she couldn't be anything else, but she looked remarkably lonely despite the baby she was holding. Somehow, Catherine understood completely.

Leaning closer, she discovered that someone had carved letters across the bottom section of the hexagon depicting the noblewoman. They'd been scratched deep into the color pigments and spelled the only written word Catherine could recognize because Rebecca had taught her to. It spelled her own name: C-A-T-H-E-R-I-N-E.

Chapter Eleven

ೞ Illusions ೞ

"Need a hand with that?" Jaden Aurum inquired, startling Maebh as she left the tent she'd been sharing with two other women for the past six months.

She turned to see who would be up to watch her sneak off at this hour. The man smiled, gesticulating toward the bag she was lugging out into the cool of early morning.

She'd been tossing and turning all night before she'd finally decided she wasn't going to wash pots and pans and help other people with their props for the rest of her life. She'd had enough of that at home. It was still dark and she'd hoped to get away without causing a scene – no questions asked, no explanations. She owed no one here anything.

Aurum wasn't a handsome man; a crooked nose protruded starkly from his face, and his teeth were bad. She'd seen him around more than she'd been happy to because *around* her was where he always seemed to be. The wicked gleam in his dark eyes told her he was trouble, though he wasn't a thug. He wasn't very tall or built for it, and he didn't have the kind of close buddies he would have needed to pull off passing for one, but there was something mean about him, and she knew it.

Not wanting to encourage him, she huffed a "No," clear and simple, and tried to shuffle past him.

Putting himself in her path, he appeared reluctant to take this dismissal for her final word.

"I wouldn't do that, now," he told her, a light, dancing melody over the thick Sudlands accent in his voice, almost as though he was speaking to a naughty child in need of boundaries.

Again, she tried to push past him, but he blocked her way. She wondered if the Master Sorcerer had been having her watched by Aurum, but then discarded the thought; Ortus had no interest in her whatsoever, and it was all the same to him whether she stayed or left his little illusion of a sanctuary.

She had no idea why Aurum was here, but it was infuriating.

"Look," she told him agitatedly, "I don't see how what I'm doing would be any of your concern."

"You're right." Folding his arms across his chest, he stepped aside, giving her space. He seemed amused. A knowing smile tugged at his lips, and it irritated her beyond measure.

"Then what are you *grinning* at?"

She wanted to give him a good kick, but didn't dare to. He didn't strike her as a man who might take a humiliation and back off. He wasn't like Caleb. Aurum seemed the erratic type, and she couldn't tell how he'd react.

Just then, he burst out laughing, and she couldn't help herself and did kick him before hastening to get some distance between them.

A few seconds later, he caught up with her, limping slightly, but able to keep pace. He was still chuckling and seemed disinclined to retaliate.

"I'm sorry, I really am," he offered, but she ignored him. Finally, he appeared to grow tired of her game and grabbed her arm, stopping her in her tracks. "Just hold on a minute, will you?"

"What do you want from me?" she screeched, unable to keep her voice down as she pulled free of him. She no longer cared who she'd wake as long as he let go of her.

Raising his hands in surrender, he understood and motioned her to calm down and stop yelling. "I just want you to reconsider leaving."

She tossed down her bag. "Why should I?"

Chewing his lower lip, he studied her face intently for a moment. "Because I've been watching you, and I think we could be very useful to one another."

"Useful?" she returned dryly, picking up her bag to be on her way. "Why should I want to be *useful* to the likes of you?" Why on earth had she let him keep her?

"Because there are things *the likes of me* can do for *you*, if you just stop being so determined to make a dramatic exit." The timbre of his voice had changed, nearing a growl, but not quite, though he still didn't *look* angry, and she started walking toward the perimeter again. The sun was rising, and people were starting to stir on the grounds. It was now or never.

"I'm not making a dramatic exit – I was trying to leave quietly," she mumbled as she went, taking note that he still wasn't giving up. She found that odd, and, keeping her eyes on the muddy ground ahead, she heard herself telling him why, though it was really none of his business.

"I don't belong here," she admitted softly, and he didn't object. "This wasn't what I was hoping for. I came to the Master Sorcerer thinking he could help me, maybe teach me how to use my Talent so it would pay off and get me out of the mud, at least. I've been here for over six months now and nothing's happened. I don't want to spend the rest of my life camping out here, hiding, washing dishes and mucking the goats."

An awkward silence ensued, and she bit her tongue, conscious of how she must sound.

He drew a deep breath, not hiding his scorn. "Well, are you good at anything else but mucking? Because you're not very good at that, says the girl half your age who's been trying to teach you. If you can't even learn a simple thing like how to muck, why should the Master Sorcerer waste his time trying to teach you to control your magic?"

He put himself between her and the place where she knew The Fair's protections ended. The perimeter was marked so the children would know how far they could safely venture. Ten-foot poles set at regular intervals propped up lines which had been hung with brightly colored scraps of cloth like pennants on a Church holiday. "You're not making an effort," he continued, "and that's why nobody is bothering much with you."

He was right, as far as the goats were concerned; she hated the smelly creatures, and she hated the smelly creature in charge of them. However, she failed to see the correlation. The Master Sorcerer had brought her here and left, and he'd barely talked to her again. So, unless he had an enchanted mirror or made a habit of breezing in at night to have in-depth conversations with the goat-girl about her work ethics, he wouldn't know if she was carting off the manure with a song on her lips or a swear-word for every shovelful of crap she scooped up.

No, she was certain Ortus wouldn't even remember her name at this stage. All of this had been a mistake, and the fact that she didn't have a better plan didn't deter her. Aurum was really starting to annoy her. There had to be a reason for his interest in her.

Raising her chin defiantly, she circled around him. "Then tell me why *you* would bother with me?"

He didn't reply right away, confirming her suspicion that he'd probably just been ordered to keep tabs on her. The small and quite ridiculous flicker of hope that his interest might have been more personal died.

She marched off, traversing the narrow space that separated The Fair from the world around it.

A tingling sensation on her skin made her shiver, and a brief rush of static hummed in her ears from the transition. She knew if she looked back now, she might no longer see the slightest trace of the little community of fools she was leaving behind because she didn't *want* to see it anymore, but she was making the right decision.

The Fair had nothing to offer to anyone with an ounce of self-respect, really, because if the Cine herding together there, hiding, hadn't been aging away with the wind and the weather, you might have thought they were suspended in time. The bubble-like blind spot the Sorcerer had designed to conceal them may keep out the Inquisitor's henchmen – for however long – but it also made them prisoners. The pitiful bit of trade they had going with some of the locals they trusted, the merchandise they peddled, and the pittance they charged for the shows they put on in the Big Top three nights a week couldn't possibly feed them. If she'd wanted to live out her days in poverty, cowering in a damp shelter with nothing to show for her Abilities, she could have stayed home and waited for death there more effortlessly.

"You know, if you weren't so busy snubbing your nose at everyone else, you'd have found what you were looking for."

She couldn't believe the nerve of him. He'd

followed her. She hadn't expected him to, but he obviously had. All at once he was right in front of her, much closer than he should have been. She could feel his breath on her cheek and neck as he lithely moved around her.

"Leave now, and something will find *you* before the year is out, love."

Not having an alternative plan did have its quirks, but she'd think of something. She wasn't stupid.

"Come back with me, and I'll show you a few things," he suggested in a low voice, and she wasn't sure what *exactly* he was getting at. "You'd be surprised at what you've been missing out on."

For a minute, she thought she was seeing things, and then she realized he was *making* her see things: he stood to the right of her one second, and to her left the other. Then, he was gone, only to reappear behind her. It was impossible, he couldn't be that fast. No man was *that* fast. It had to have something to do with his particular Talent, she guessed. He was an Illusionist, but there was more to him than she'd been aware of.

Watching him closely – or thinking she was – she discovered it wasn't him who was moving fast at all, though. It took a while, but it soon dawned on her he was merely *slowing her down*, making her think he was speeding up. Observing a blackbird in the brush a few yards off affirmed what she derived by contrast. It was perched on a branch near the ground when it first caught her attention. Although she tried to keep her eyes trained on it, it suddenly vanished, and when she next saw it, it was in a bush some distance off. In the meantime, Jaden had leisurely strolled away from her and into the forest, and he waved to her, looking extremely pleased with himself.

This was intriguing. His Talent wasn't so far from the Sorcerer's. She wondered if anyone else knew the true nature of Jaden Aurum's Gift, but she thought not, and she believed he'd shown her for a reason. He did have *some* personal interest, after all.

She was still pondering this when he popped up next to her, a long-stemmed rose in his hand. Handing her the flower, he gave a little bow. Genuinely delighted at the gesture, she accepted it, not minding at all as his fingers brushed her hand ever so lightly. Something about his smile made her reconsider leaving – for now. It couldn't hurt to stick around for another few weeks, she thought, and the perfect red blossom turned into a marguerite, like the ones that grew near the tree line on the south end of the clearing. She raised an eyebrow at him, but he merely shrugged.

"One thing goes, and another comes in its place," he mused.

Taking her hand and waving his own over it, he conjured a white dove that sat on her finger, digging its tiny talons into the flesh, but before she'd even gotten a good look at the bird, it had already returned to what it had previously really been: one of the ordinary pigeons he kept in a cage by his tent.

"Things aren't always what they seem," he said, "but we make of our Talents what we can. I know yours is special – it's not meant to entertain the farmers for a few eggs, a measure of flour or some coins while we wait for deliverance. That's not going to happen. But your Talent is meant for *much* more. *You're* meant for much more. Come back with me and let's talk. Give me the chance to help you find out."

He held out his hand for her bag. She had no idea why she was letting him talk her into this, but she handed it to him and followed him back to his tent.

Chapter Twelve

ಜ The Siege ಖಾ

When Catherine came back to the castle, she was down to her last candle and decided to save it for emergencies. Concentrating on the torches, she managed to light up the room once again, but something was different this time. Something was off. Only every other torch was lit, and she thought she smelled smoke that wasn't from the burning tar.

Voices filled with fear and urgency reverberated in the Hall above. Booming, cracking, crashing noises thundered through the castle as though walls were being toppled. She was afraid.

A woman she hadn't noticed before knelt in the middle of the room, clutching a baby to her chest in one arm. With her free hand, she was scratching something into one of the mosaic's hexagonal segments with an old nail.

"Hello?" Catherine said, but the raging, roaring storm above ground – if that was indeed what she was hearing – drowned out the word.

Moving a little closer, she recognized the woman as the dark-haired Lady she'd been seeing at the castle so often, and hunkered down beside her.

She instinctively reached up to touch the locket

Rebecca had given her. She wore it all the time now. Her mind reeled at the thought that she could be clutching it while at the same time seeing it on a chain around someone else's neck.

It was strangely relieving to discover for sure it was this woman who'd carved the letters of her name into the floor beneath the picture of the lonely queen. She'd nearly finished the last of the letters, and Catherine's heart was beating like a drum.

She tried to get a glimpse of the sleeping child. The infant was no older than a few days, and she wondered if this was the child Rebecca had told her about. If it was, then this was her grandmother – perhaps this was *the other Catherine*.

All at once, hurried footsteps slapped the stone stairs behind her. Catherine was about to start looking for a place to hide, but then she remembered she wouldn't be seen. Turning, she observed a woman dressed in fine clothes leading a group of peasants down to them.

"What are you still doing here?" the red-faced woman snapped at the young mother.

The baby began crying, and its mother shifted the child from one arm onto the other.

"Waiting, Milady Tierney," she said simply. "I won't leave until he's seen her."

"Do as you please," Lady Tierney told her indifferently as the room filled with people, "but this is neither the time nor the place, and don't think for a moment he'll be in the least bit interested in your bastard."

Lady Tierney opened the heavy oak door that closed off the tunnel and ushered the peasants toward the dark passageway. "Go," she urged them. There was genuine concern in her voice. "Don't come back, no matter what happens."

"What about you, Milady?" one of the maids asked.

"I'll be alright. I'm going to wait for my husband and his brother. They shouldn't be very long."

The maid seemed torn, but she finally followed the others, casting the young mother a disdainful glance.

With the servants gone, Lady Tierney pushed her hands into her sides and returned her attention to the younger woman.

"Why do you insist on doing this? If you valued your daughter's life you'd just go – *now*," she said.

"No."

Lady Tierney shook her head, smirking. "You're even more stupid than you look, Angela."

Angela. At last Catherine had a name to put with the face.

"I want you to take her with you," Angela said, a pained look in her eyes.

Shock was written all over Lady Tierney's mien. "You can't be serious. No."

"Why not? She isn't to blame for any of this, and I know she'd have a better life with you than I could ever give her – we don't know what's coming after the siege. Even if the king's troops spare the farms, there's nothing left for us here."

"You selfish little witch! Have you not been listening to me?"

Catherine thought the noblewoman was going to strike Angela.

"*He is not interested,*" she continued from between clenched teeth, and another explosion shook the walls as though to emphasize the statement. "He *might* have been if you'd given him the son I couldn't, but let me assure you, he doesn't give a damn about you or that little girl. Now, it's going to get very ugly here shortly, so you decide whether you're going to leave or stay, but don't expect anything from him, or from any of us."

"I'm not asking for myself," Angela cut in, but the noblewoman grabbed her arms and all but shook her.

"If the king's troops catch up with us, they're going to lead us back to Trondenburgh in chains, torture us, and dismember us on the public market place. What do you think they're going to do with that child? You'll be lucky if they kill her before they burn her."

Lady Tierney ran a hand through her hair, pausing to calm herself. Catherine could see the tears welling in Angela's defiant eyes, but she didn't budge.

"Look, this has to end here. Take your child and get the hell away from me and my family. Stop wasting my time and yours."

With that, the noblewoman turned and hurried back up the stairs.

Catherine didn't know what to think. Feet rooted to the floor, she stood staring at Angela and her wailing child. The young woman was at a complete loss as she pressed her cheek to the baby's, considering her options, and Catherine felt her emptiness and frustration as though they were her own.

Eventually, Angela crouched down and finished scratching the last letters of the name she'd been working on into the mosaic. When she was done, she flung the nail carelessly away, tucked the coarse blanket more snugly about little Catherine and left without looking back.

Catherine thought about following her, but then the booming noise abruptly stopped, and she heard yelling, scuffling and fighting above. She made herself small in one corner of the room, more afraid than ever, but she wanted to see who was coming now and what was going to happen next.

A bloodied, exhausted man carrying a boy of about four or five hastened downward, Lady Tierney in his wake. Behind them, another man who resembled the first lugged a broken sword. He stopped about half down the stairs for a few seconds and turned to face back, raising his hands with his palms outward in front of him. Catherine strained to see what he was up to. She couldn't understand what he was saying, but his mumbled words sounded like a chant in some foreign language she didn't know.

A stone slab appeared above him where there had been nothing before, closing off the top of the stairway completely. It looked solid, as though it had always been there, and Catherine thought she wasn't seeing right.

"Papa!" the boy cried, struggling on the first man's arm.

The Sorcerer looked at his child and his brother, wiping his filthy face on his sleeve.

"I'm coming, Ortus," he said, and made his way down into the chamber. "Stay with your uncle."

Lord Tierney motioned him to hurry, but he waved, telling them to go ahead. He still seemed to have something to attend to and remained behind in the room. When the others were out of sight, he dropped his sword, or what remained of it, and knelt down close to where Catherine was standing. It looked as though he was searching for something along the stone surface, and all at once, a small portion in the wall opened, revealing a vault. From that vault, he pulled a wooden chest. Rummaging around in it, he quickly found what he was looking for and tossed the object on the floor to have his hands free so he could replace the chest in the vault.

Catherine moved around the man so she could get a better look at the object he was risking his life to retrieve. It was a book or a journal of sorts, bound in brown leather. A golden border of ivy boughs ran around the edges of the front cover, encompassing an ornate centerpiece she couldn't quite distinguish.

With the wall closed, the Sorcerer grabbed his battered blade and the book, got to his feet and ran after the others. Catherine was about to follow him, but once he was inside the tunnel, he began to seal this entrance also. She stood right in front of him as he did this, and she could have reached out to touch him. He was a handsome man and radiated strength, and she was tempted to, but she knew what would come of it.

When he was done, a new wall separated them, and Catherine could stand it no more. She tried to press her palms to the cool stone surface, but they passed right through the solid matter. The tingling sensation on her skin was painful, but it stopped the moment the vision ended.

The noise above her in the castle faded out, and the light of the torches died.

Frantically, she turned to check the stairway. It was open, as it had been before, and she scurried up to the Great Hall and out into the courtyard. She needed air.

Chapter Thirteen

☙ Two Books ❧

A night's troubled sleep brought on new determination. Catherine made her way back to the concealed room beneath the Great Hall well before midday. She knelt down on the dusty floor by the wall to the left of the tunnel entrance and ran her fingertips around the edges of the only protruding stone she could find. She took her time about it, scratching away at the crumbling mortar first with her fingernails and then with the tip of her knife. When nothing happened despite her patient efforts, she began wondering if this was the right stone or even the right place.

Rocking back on her thighs to sort out her legs, she nimbly rose and turned about. Impatiently, she scanned the walls around her and tried to remember what she'd seen in her vision. She needed more light, but she was down to her last pitiful candle stump, barely a finger high, and she mightn't even get ahold of another one for a week when this one was spent.

Chewing on her lip, she closed her eyes and tried to bring the images back, if only for the sake of the light. She just had to concentrate, she told herself, and took a few deep breaths to calm her blood. She was aware she couldn't do this if she wanted it too much.

Nothing ever worked out the way you meant for it to if you went about doing it too hastily. She really wanted to know what else was in that vault, and finding out might just take a while longer than she'd hoped, but it would be worth it. The Magician wouldn't have gone to the trouble of locking that chest away if it didn't have any value, and she wouldn't have seen him do it if she hadn't been meant to.

Eventually, things came together again, and her perception of the castle's grand past faded back in, but she wasn't back in the time she'd witnessed the previous day; this had to be some earlier time, a while before the siege, because all was quiet, and the entrance to the stairway wasn't blocked yet.

The pitch torches flared up and cast a warm artificial glow in the room. It enhanced the contrasts of green and autumn red on the winding leaf patterns of the mosaic floor. Every unevenness and crevice in the sandstone became visible in the new interaction of light and shadow.

She inspected the stone she'd been working on and decided this wasn't it. Exhaling, she accidently triggered the mechanisms of the one next to it. The whisper of air from her lungs caressed the smooth, sandy surface, disturbing what was hardly more than a memory now, but it was the memory of an enchantment cast by a desperate man many years ago. A dull, scraping noise alerted Catherine to the change before the stone that had been giving her so much bother slid back and out of sight, revealing the cubic compartment that held the chest. She smiled. Triumph was sweet, even if it was begotten by chance.

The wooden chest sat in the middle of the three-by-three square feet repository. It was almost untouched by the hands of time, and she struggled to haul it out of its hiding place by one of the ornate copper handles fixed to its front.

It wasn't quite as heavy as it looked, and she slowly managed to drag it forth enough to open it. She half expected to find it locked, but it wasn't, and the lid tilted back easily and completely.

Her breath hitched when she saw what was inside: dresses of finest satin in reds and royal blues, a baby's christening blanket, a dagger, some rings with pretty stones and several more books that looked very much like the one the Magician had taken with him.

The garments and jewelry were exquisite, but the books were fascinating. They were by far more beautiful and valuable, she decided, taking them out one after the other. Running her fingers over their leather bindings, she relished their warm velvety texture beneath her chapped hands.

They were almost identical; both had the same golden border of small-petaled, delicate spring ivy twining around its rims on both sides, and both had the central motif of something that, to Catherine, resembled a floral design. It was, in fact, a repetitive infinity sign. The only outward difference between the volumes was that one was bound in a cowhide dyed dark crimson with symbols depicting the element *earth* in a rectangle around the infinity sign, and the other was bound in cowhide dyed a rich, chunky green with symbols for the element *air* arranged in a circle around the middle motif.

The covers were firmly held shut by two locks that divided the length of them into thirds – no, not locks, but clasps, she realized. She knew that locks were complicated devices that needed keys to open them, but these fastenings were much simpler by design. They were small, sturdy catches, hinged to the copper plates on the back with a gib, and latched into the front plates with an ornate, but functional hook.

She couldn't open either of the two on the first book she tried. One of the clasps on the second was broken, but when she couldn't undo its twin, she eventually tried to force it, hoping something would give. Tugging with all her strength, she tried to insert her fingers between binding and parchment, but when it wouldn't budge, she suspected there had to be a trick to this, just as there had been with the wall.

Gently, she tried blowing on it. Nothing. Then, she spat on it. Again, nothing. Wiping the spittle off of the book with the raggedy sleeve of her dress, she turned this over in her mind. It was as though the author of those books was mocking her, and it just didn't seem fair, but she was absolutely determined to find out how to disengage what she'd decided was a lock, after all.

She was convinced that she had the key – somewhere.

Time passed, and the torches died. When Catherine's candle did, too, she felt hot tears of frustration leaking down her cheeks in runnels, dripping from her chin. She hated herself for crying and told herself not to be such a baby, but she couldn't stop and finally surrendered to the feeling of defeat.

Eventually, she'd wept as much as she'd needed to and decided to bring both books upstairs to the Great Hall. Swiping at her wet face with her hands before she picked them up, she touched the catches on one of them with her wet, sticky fingers, and the locks came undone as though they'd never been blocked. She felt the volume open in her hands before she could see it properly and ran, tripping and falling up the stairs toward the daylight.

Sitting down in the hole where the main entrance of the keep had once been, she opened the tome in the middle. At first, she didn't know which way was up. There didn't seem to be any text passages on its pages; maps dominated the parchments instead. The names of the places they showed were a mystery to her because she couldn't read them, but she recognized the depictions around them as mountains, rivers, woods and settlements. Like her parents, she was illiterate, and she didn't know what she'd been hoping for, but it was only now that the irony of this dawned on her. She continued leafing through the volume nonetheless.

Strange symbols and little drawings she couldn't place kept cropping up. Some of the renderings depicted rudimentary likenesses of wolves' heads or swarms of creatures that could have been bees, maybe. Others were more like bizarre shapes and stars, and she could make even less of those, but they seemed so exciting, she desperately wanted to know what they meant and what they had to do with her.

She tried the other book.

One tear shed on the metal for her Uncle Charlie was enough to open the lock, and she thumbed her way through the pages. This time, there was only text; page upon page of tiny letters that wouldn't disclose themselves to her.

At the very back, she recognized a whole block of the same symbols she'd found on the maps in the other book, and she was sure the words behind them explained what they stood for – but she couldn't read them.

The other Catherine would easily have deciphered what they stood for, but Catherine couldn't, and felt so ignorant. She hated herself, she hated her father, and she hated the humans who'd driven her Cine ancestors from this place. She hated the Cine who'd rejected his daughter, her grandmother, and she hated her aunt for telling her all of this. She hated everything. The only thing she loved fiercely was this castle, and she mourned its ruin.

The words written on the pages of the books in front of her were secret and sacred, and they very likely held the key to the magic that might restore the fortress to its former beauty. She'd found a way to open them, and now she had to find a way to discover what was inside and how she could use it to become as powerful, no *more powerful,* than the Magician she'd seen work his magic down in the hidden chamber. If she had that kind of power one day, she'd rebuild this place. She'd be rich and people would respect her, and she'd show them all she was so much more than just the gravedigger's daughter.

Chapter Fourteen

❧ Cooper ☙

Morning had melted into afternoon by the time Catherine replaced the books in their hiding place.

She resisted the temptation to take anything else out of the chest because there wasn't a single item in there that could be of any use to her. Poor girls did not have treasures, and if they did, they'd surely be forced to tell where they'd gotten them. She felt her way to the stairs in the gloom and felt both elated and anxiously relieved to be heading back above ground.

There was no breeze to stir the hot air as she fled from the chill of the ruins, charging through the abandoned, overgrown streets with dirty streaks on her face. Like a moving shadow, she plunged headlong into the woods. It wasn't any cooler in the ancient forest, but the shade of the green oak- and beech leaf canopy above offered some relief to her eyes. Running to get some air in her lungs felt good, despite the heat.

The books had been protected by a spell, but that spell had recognized her. She was sure no human could have gotten past it, and maybe no other Cine, either. Her tears had opened it, and she realized that perhaps it was the desperation, or the emotion as such that had solved this particular riddle. A loss, a sacrifice. Next time, if they didn't recognize her as someone who had a right to open them, she'd try her blood to see if that would work as well.

And still – she couldn't read what was in them. She was nothing but the gravedigger's daughter, nothing but dirt-poor, filthy Catherine Salt until she found a way to change that. She had the power to break a protective enchantment, but she didn't have the Ability to find out what knowledge it protected. The irony of that was staggering.

It took the better part of an hour before the land leveled out, and another one before she'd reached the wide valley where the river Leigne meandered through the forest. She stopped to kneel down for a long drink and a wash of her face and neck. The dust and sweat had become uncomfortable, and she briefly considered going for a swim, but it was still early in the day; she hated the thought of anyone chancing by and catching her alone, so she dried her hands on her ragged skirt and decided to return to the nameless village. Another hour would easily take her there.

Few good things thrived on the edge of the forest aside from a handful of scraggly sheep bleating behind a wattle fence, half a dozen mite-eaten hens, and some goats.

A small hovel not dissimilar to that of her parents' marked the eastern boundary of the village. Its doors had been flung wide open to let in a little air. Barefoot children scampered about under the watchful eyes of mothers whose work was making them old before their time, but no one paid attention to the ragged girl walking past them, lost in thoughts as foreign to them as their occupations were to her.

It was as though they couldn't see her, and Catherine felt every bit as much a ghost here as she did at the castle.

Her own home was on the other side of the glade, away from the main cluster of buildings, and she wondered if there would be any food in the house. Perhaps Rebecca had been around – but she doubted it, since Caleb had been so hostile toward her on her last visit, and that always meant she'd keep her distance for a while.

So she wouldn't go hungry, she opted to make a small detour and slowed down when she came upon the familiar grove of plum trees.

The cloying fragrance of the ripe fruit hung in the air, and her mouth watered for the honey-sweet taste of the juicy plums she'd grown adept at stealing. Usually, she'd sneak by in the late evening hours after the fat man who owned the plantation had gone home, but he didn't seem to be here now, so she decided to take the risk.

Untended brown grass lay down and crunched beneath her slight weight where her feet unwittingly traced a path toward the tree line. She looked up into the awning of thick, green leaves and saw the plums hanging tantalizing above her, begging to be picked so they could still her hunger.

Loosening her long shawl from her waist, she looped it around her neck as she searched for the easiest candidate to climb. When she'd made her choice, she grabbed one of the lower branches and hauled herself up onto the slender tree, lighting into it with practiced ease. She anchored herself onto the trunk, quickly unwound the shawl and looped it in one hand. Then, she filled it with ripe fruit. It wasn't long before she felt the cloth sag with the weight of her dinner.

Not many people in this godforsaken place managed to scrape more than a few coins together in the course of a week, but the farmer whom she was stealing from, Cooper, grew about the only fruit that consistently made it to market, and he'd done well for himself. He earned enough to pay a couple of youths so they'd come by and water the trees every day when it was hot, and during harvesting time, he'd hire some of the village men, Caleb included, to help him with the picking and take it to the nearest town.

Catherine knew from Rebecca's stories that he'd had a wife and two pretty daughters many years back, but they'd left him. Rumors floated about the village, and Catherine had a good idea of what it was the women were saying he'd done to warrant his family's departure.

Still, a man of means came and went as he pleased, and although parents warned their girls away from

Cooper, he always seemed to find plenty of people willing to take the wages he paid for their work.

A twig snapped somewhere beneath her, and the noise made her freeze.

"Well, well," a voice drawled up to her lazily, "what have we got here?"

Glancing down, she saw the old man himself looking up at her through the leaves. An amused smile twisted his jowly face, and her heart missed a beat.

"You might as well come down, girl," he coaxed. "Hand me that shawl and let's see what you've got."

She could have kicked herself for not being more careful.

Reaching up his hand, he waited patiently until Catherine complied. When she'd lowered her shawl to him about half way, she suddenly let go of it so that the ripe plums pelted his face and skull, and she leapt from the branch as he tried to free himself from the shawl.

Once her feet had touched the ground, she turned to run, but the man was quicker than she'd thought. He snagged her thin arm in a grip she couldn't break no matter how much she struggled.

"Let go of me!" She pulled away with all she had, but he was too strong.

"Hold on, girl, no need to get all upset," he told her calmly and reeled her in, taking her kicks in his stride. "There's no harm done. You saved me the trouble of climbing up myself to check the fruit."

He held her until she was spent and smiled when

she finally stopped struggling and looked up at him distrustfully, panting with anger. She was aware of his watery eyes roving over her for a moment, assessing the ragged clothing covering her thin frame and the dark tangled hair falling about her shoulders.

Fixing her defiant gaze to his, she was determined to take her beating without making a sound, but he was still smiling by the time he noticed her glare, and he didn't look as though he was going to hit her. On the contrary.

"You're Salt's daughter, aren't you?" he asked. "The gravedigger's wench!"

She was aware he already knew the answer.

"I know your papa very well. I'd hate to tell him his daughter's a thief."

When she merely snorted and rolled her eyes, he laughed outright.

"Well, likely as not, he knows that for himself, eh? And probably profits from it too, I'd wager. Did he send you to steal some nice fat plums from me?"

Catherine didn't reply to that. Whatever she said, it was bound to be wrong. He wouldn't believe her no matter what she told him. She could have said Caleb didn't feed her, or care where she got the food she brought home for the both of them, but what difference would it make? She didn't want anyone's pity, and if Cooper didn't give her a good thrashing now, Caleb would if Cooper brought her home and told him what he'd caught her doing. The fact that she was stealing wouldn't bother her father as much as the fact that she got caught.

Cooper was some ten years older than Caleb and a great deal heavier. Being one of the wealthier men in their village, he enjoyed a better quality and quantity of food than the rest of them. The work clothes he wore were newer and more valuable than anything Caleb could afford, and he was hairy. The rolled up sleeves of his shirt showed a wealth of light brown fur growing on a meaty arm, the same color as the thinning thatch of hair crowning his head. He looked at her strangely, like a famished man looked at a pot of stew. A knot of apprehension grew in her stomach.

"Not much for talking, are you," he stated rather than asked. "You know what they do with thieves?"

Despite herself, she shook her head. She didn't want to be afraid, but she was.

"They tie their hands up high to a post in the village center." He raised her arm up for emphasis by the wrist. "Then, they lay bare the back of your dress and give you twenty lashes for your trouble." He looked down at the small girl speculatively. "A little snip like you would hardly last through the first ten, I'd bet."

She shivered, and the farmer winked at her, obviously pleased at the fact that he was frightening her without even having raised his voice.

"Well, I don't think a few plums are worth all that,

do you, girl?" Leaning down, he pulled her closer to him until his mouth was so close to hers, she could feel his breath on her lips. "Well? Do you?"

"No," she said through clenched teeth.

"We're agreed, then. I won't have you whipped for stealing, but I can't let you walk away with my goods, either. I work hard for a living, you see, and I don't like anyone just coming here and taking things from me. I won't have that."

Catherine stood very still for a moment, staring into eyes that seemed more amused than angry, but there was a glint of something else in them, too, and it gave her the creeps. She tried to shake the feeling and puffed her chest. Fear wouldn't help her now. Fear only crippled people. It wouldn't save her from Caleb, and it wouldn't feed her tonight. Her glance fell on the harvesting baskets that he'd already stacked for the pickers who would be coming over the next days, and a thought came to mind.

"I'll make you a deal," she offered. "I'll gather up what I dropped here, and I'll pick two more baskets full. I'll carry all of that home for you, but I'll take a dozen plums in payment for that."

Cooper laughed, but the croaking sounds he made turned into a crippling cough almost instantly. Red-faced and tearing at the excursion, he let go of her.

"You're a cheeky little bugger, I'll say that for you!"

She held her ground, and she could see the cog wheels in his head turning as she waited for his answer.

"You seem like a smart girl, but you won't lift half a basket, never mind a full one. Here's what I'll give you: you come to work for me in my house a couple of times a week, and I'll let you have all the plums you can carry, and maybe a few coins in the off season. What do you say?"

Catherine stared at him a moment. "What kind of work?"

Cooper scratched his head while he considered. She watched him warily, ready to bolt if he reached for her again. "Just a little housework, seeing as I don't have a wife to do it for me. Sweep, wash and cook, the like of that. I had another girl in to help up until recently, but her mama has a new baby, so she can't come right now."

Catherine didn't trust him. He'd caught her stealing, and he could change his mind about having her punished any time if he wanted to. Still, he was offering her something different to do from what she always did, and he was letting her decide what she wanted for herself. Working for him meant being more than just a thief, a nothing, a filthy little ghost, and she imagined she'd have a certain degree of respectability. She liked the idea of that.

True, he was big and he'd been quick to catch her, but she wouldn't let that happen again. Besides, she could get away from him if he tried to hurt her, and she could hurt him back.

"All I'd have to do is sweep your house and cook a little?"

The farmer nodded and gave her a genuine smile. "That's right. You can start today for all of the plums you've already picked. My house is just through the trees." He pointed to a trail that led back into the forest. She knew roughly where.

He waited until she'd picked up her plums, and then walked ahead of her to his cabin. Hazel and ash lined the well-worn trail for a few hundred yards, and elderberry bushes strained toward the sun beyond that on the clearing where the house stood.

Catherine had been here before today, but she'd never come by daylight. He owned a whole gaggle of snowy geese that patrolled his property, and they made all kinds of a commotion when people they didn't know came too close.

Catherine also counted a dozen red hens take off in all directions around the perimeter as she walked behind Cooper. Four rows of rough plank tables occupied his trim yard. He'd already set heaps of baskets atop them, ready for the sorters to start with their work early the next day when the first of the pickers started coming in.

The cabin was built of long, smooth oak timbers stacked one upon the other, and its roof was covered with shag shingles. Painted shutters stood open against windows from which fluttered dark blue curtains. To the right of the main building stood a small barn framed from oak logs like the house. Two brown and white cows were hobbled and grazing nearby, and a dog guarded a small herd of sheep further afield.

It was as opulent a display of wealth as Catherine had ever seen.

Catherine wasn't entirely aware of Cooper's hungry eyes on her as he watched her assess his holdings. She barely heard him invite her inside, holding the door for her. He left it open when she didn't follow him right away, and that made her feel a little safer about entering.

Inside, she took note of the wooden floor beneath her feet. It was beautiful, she thought, worn smooth by years of walking beneath the dust that coated it. She wondered how long the other girl he'd spoken of hadn't been here.

A door leading out back stood slightly ajar to one side of the big fireplace, and a third door, perhaps that of a pantry or separate bedroom, was on the other side, but it was shut.

There was a chunky table with a chair and two benches in the center of the large living and working room. Dirty pots and dishes, stinking and crusted with food were stacked on it, as well as in the tin basin on the worktable that was set against the wall between the fireplace and the back door. A large bedstead with blankets askew occupied the far corner near the closed door, and wrinkled clothes were scattered about.

He crossed the floor to an open shelf that may have been installed to hold the clean dishes when there had still been clean ones to hold, and he picked up a wooden pail covered on the outside with pitch.

"Well's out back, and it'll take three hauls to fill the kettle," he said, handing it to her. "I'll start a fire so you can heat the water, but I'll expect you to do it yourself next time."

She found the new stone well easily enough, and returned a few minutes later with the first pail. Cooper looked up at her. His grin told her that he'd half expected her to bolt as soon as she was out of the door. She said nothing and merely poured the water into the kettle before going out for more. By the time she'd filled that kettle, the fire was going nicely, and she set about straightening the room while the water heated.

The farmer sat at the central table working on a set of leather straps for his plow.

"You can do my clothes down by the stream some morning in the next few days. There isn't enough sunlight left to dry them properly today."

"What's in there?" she asked, pointing to the closed door.

"Nothing for you to concern yourself with. It's locked, and that's how it's going to stay." That sounded final, and Catherine decided she'd have to find out by herself first chance she got. She nodded at him despite herself, and when he offered no further explanation, she continued tidying in silence, keeping an eye on both the open and the closed doors.

The disarray in Cooper's cottage was similar to what she was used to seeing in her own home when her mother had still been with them, but she'd been to Rebecca's house often enough to know how to organize and clean so she and her father wouldn't die of the plague if they touched anything.

Her aunt had taught her to work top to bottom, so she made the bed as best she could, found a broom and pushed the discarded, smelly clothing into the corner for wash day before sweeping the rest of the room. Afterward, she took the kettle from the hearth and scrubbed the pots and dishes fouling the cabin. By the time she was done, it was nearly dark outside, and Catherine was at the end of her patience for both the farmer's pig sty and his company.

"I'll be going, then," she told him, hoping for her plums.

Cooper rose and took a quick survey of the room. She could tell he was pleased with what she'd been able to do, and more or less trusting that she hadn't robbed him blind while he hadn't been looking.

He picked up her shawl, tied the ends together and walked over to the door, holding it out to her. She pulled it from his hands and ran off without another word, his laughter following her out into the hazel thicket.

Making halt in the orchard, she swiped some more

plums from the lower branches of the younger trees to fill up her shawl until she could hardly carry it.

The walk up the path to her father's hovel was a laborious one, but she couldn't get the smile off of her face. For the first time in her life, she'd earned something by the sweat of her brow, and the sense of accomplishment was divine.

Chapter Fifteen

ເຊ The Third of Three ຂວ

Thaddeus had found a grove with tall, straight trees just a few hours' march from the fairgrounds, and he'd spent the previous afternoon marking the ones they needed to fell. Walking the perimeter of the area they'd be working in to shield it off, Ortus thought they'd get even better building lumber from these trees than they would have from the last lot they'd had to abandon; the wood was slow-grown and stronger here. Every down had its upside.

Their work troop comprised of fifteen good-spirited Cine men and older boys as well as a host of human helpers. Ortus had decided to keep watch; Dean was with them. The Master Sorcerer's son wasn't anywhere near as hardy as most of the other Cine boys. He was unaccustomed to manual labor but determined to make his dent in the workload, so he was putting his back into everything he was doing here.

By midday, they'd felled a dozen good oaks, and they'd already stripped and cut half of those to size. The Sorcerer sat on a log not far from where the others were resting. Some of the boys, including Dean, had gone for a swim in the brook nearby. He had a book open on his lap and was chewing on a piece of pan bread while revising a text his father had written but never completed before he'd died.

"You always carry that with you," a dark-haired lad observed, pointing at the book as he sat down next to him.

Wiping the sweat from his brow with his sleeve, Lorcan Aurum looked like he hadn't had his time out yet.

His shirt stuck to his back in the heat. It was too big for him, and its patches had patches – an adult's ruined cast-off. His threadbare pants were torn at the knees, and calloused hands told of both skill and toil, but he didn't even have shoes on his feet to show for it.

Ortus watched him take a long drink from the ladle in the water bucket Dean had left there before he'd gone swimming.

"I do," he replied. "That's because I've been trying to figure out its secrets for most of my life, and I'm almost there." He paused. "Some bread, my friend?" He held out a chunk of his own.

Lorcan briefly considered, but then shook his head, and the Sorcerer wondered if he would have taken it from anyone else.

Young Aurum looked like a boy whose mother would need to remind him to eat, but Ortus knew he didn't have a mother. Still, he was stronger than he looked, and the Sorcerer had the feeling this wasn't just physical. The silver was clear and bright in his eyes, almost as though there was more in his blood than just his father's lineage.

"Secrets?"

Ortus nodded. "It's the third of three. The other two were lost a long time ago, and that's a secret in and of itself. The other secret is that magic is never what you think it is, and it's hard to understand sometimes, just as the words that describe it."

Lorcan considered this. "Magic is different for everyone. Every Cine, I mean. We all have different Talents, even though we're all Cine at The Fair, so it would be difficult for someone to explain their magic to someone else who has a different kind of magic."

It never ceased to baffle Ortus how the young generation of this community had gotten so wise, whether they were the sons and daughters of merchants or scoundrels. It was a curse and a blessing, but perhaps this was where their true assets lay.

Thaddeus had been considering taking on another apprentice to manage the workload coming at him with the construction of the new wagons that would replace their old tents and shelters, and Ortus made a mental note to speak to him about Lorcan. The carpenter might not be thrilled at the prospect of hiring Aurum's offspring, but Lorcan wasn't anything like his twisted father, and Ortus was sure this would be a worthwhile investment if the lad was willing. The silver in his eyes was truly astounding, at least to the Sorcerer's perception, and he speculated if Lorcan was one of The

Few whose inherited Talents were *all* active. A thing like this was rare, and it needed to be cultivated.

"Can you read, son?"

Lorcan shook his head and looked at his feet, shame burning on his cheeks. "No, sir."

Studying him intently, he concentrated on the aura around the lad's dark pupils. It was purer than anything he'd seen recently. Perhaps he was more Fairyman than Cine; a Gift from his mother, whatever had become of the unfortunate woman. Jaden's aura was dull and weak – tainted like the bowl of a spoon that hadn't been polished.

Most of The Fair's Cine could read and write at least a little. Their community prided itself on that. He could see how it troubled the fourteen-year-old to admit that he couldn't, and he handed him the book, nudging him when he hesitated to accept it.

Reluctantly Lorcan wiped his hands on his pants and took the volume. He handled it with great reverence, running his fingers over the golden ivy border on the soft leather binding as he deliberated the centerpiece of interlaced infinity signs and drank in every detail of the rendering.

Then, he opened it.

The Master Sorcerer watched the boy's face light up at the neatly written passages of text as though they made sense to him, somehow. Lorcan turned page upon page until he'd reached the portion of the volume where his father had stopped making entries and Ortus had picked up where the old Magician had left off.

"This is different," Lorcan remarked, muttering more to himself than speaking to the Master Sorcerer. "But it is the same language – the letters are the same…"

Leafing through the next pages, something caught his attention, and Ortus leant in to him to get a better look at what that might be. His gaze fell upon one of the drawings he'd done more recently, the sketch of an idea that had been ghosting around in his head while contemplating the problem of The Fair's safety.

The boy laid the book down on his lap, open side up, and placed the back of his left hand on it, palm upward, laying the other hand across it so both palms were touching. Then, very slowly, he lifted his right hand, and a faint blue glow emitted from the space in between. Inch by inch, he drew out the space until a restless globe of light about the size of a large goose egg sat on his left palm. The blue luminescence faded, and a crystalline orb filled with images of castles and landscapes appeared, perched on a wooden base bearing the same ivy border the book did.

"That's beautiful," the Master Sorcerer told the boy, staring at the globe. An idea he'd thought impossible had just quite literally taken shape and gained a third – and maybe fourth – dimension. "And whoever told you that you couldn't read?"

Bewildered by that statement, Lorcan directed his attention toward Ortus for a second, away from his projection, and it dissolved into thin air instantly.

Ortus took back the book from him and briefly pondered the picture, his eyebrows knitting.

"I'm sorry, I shouldn't have done that, sir," Lorcan said, rising, but the Sorcerer held him back and called out to Thaddeus, who'd resumed sawing a log into manageable segments a little way off.

The carpenter stopped what he was doing and came over to where Ortus and Lorcan sat, unraveling the rags he'd bound around his blistering hands.

"Thaddeus, tell me, can you spare this lad for a few days?" the Sorcerer inquired.

The burly man eyed Lorcan suspiciously. "His father wouldn't come. Said he had a pain in his back and an infection in his foot. At least leave me the lad."

Ortus rose, straightening his aging bones with some difficulty. He could have sympathized with Aurum, had he believed a word of it.

"Half days, then," he persisted. "Lorcan here needs to learn how to read. Trust me, you and your wife in particular would benefit from that as well."

Thaddeus thought about it. Finally, he grunted and turned away to go back to work.

Ortus took that as a yes and bent down to retrieve another book he'd brought. It wasn't as pretty, but it would do better to teach how the letters were sounded and formed into words, he thought. That, and he could see Lorcan recognized it, so it wouldn't be all new and the content wouldn't be too challenging for a boy from the Sudlands who would have knowledge of the language it was written in. Opening it at the first page, he began to read, copying the Latin words he was speaking into the dry, sandy ground at his feet with a stick.

"In principio," he wrote slowly, making sure Lorcan was following, "creavit Deus caelum et terram."

"In the beginning," Lorcan translated, "God made heaven and earth." He didn't seem quite satisfied though, and his eyes wandered between the words and the Sorcerer.

Ortus put down the stick. "What's wrong?"

Lorcan hesitated before speaking, but when he did, the Master Sorcerer realized he was in for a lot of long and interesting discussions over the next months – discussions that would never have been possible anywhere but here.

"Shouldn't that be *ex nihilo?*" Lorcan wanted to know. "*Out of nothing,* God made heaven and earth?"

Chapter Sixteen

❦ The Gravedigger's Daughter ❧

"Well, think of the Devil, and you find her shinnied up a tree and barefoot to boot."

Catherine looked down from her perch in the ancient oak just inside the wood line of Cooper's property. His rather abrupt appearance didn't surprise her. She'd heard him tromping through the underbrush, alerting every bit of game between here and the river to his presence for a while now.

She'd been concentrating on a hare munching on dandelions nearby, willing it to stretch out on the grass and sleep. She'd yet to determine if she'd wielded any influence over it, but it had begun to settle down in a soft spot just inside a brushy area when the farmer's clumsy footfalls had startled both her and the hare, and the animal had bolted to safety deeper into the forest.

The big man grinned up at her expectantly. She heaved a sigh and rolled her eyes before climbing down from the thick bough she'd been balanced on.

"What are you doing out here?" she asked, straightening her skirt.

The Plum-Man laughed as though she'd said something funny she wasn't aware of. He'd been seeking her out more often lately, as if her weekly visits to his trees merited more of her time than just an afternoon or two of washing and cleaning.

He never asked much about her but preferred to talk himself senseless over things she had little interest in. She'd managed to learn a little about his bees' hives anyway, and what his profits would be in the fall, but most of his other topics of conversation revolved around people she didn't give a hoot about and places she didn't know. Not that she really minded his endless prattling, even if a lot of it was just his need to fill up the silence. Most of the people she knew either ignored her or talked to her as though she was soft in the head, and over the past two years, she'd discovered he could actually be quite entertaining, sometimes.

For some reason, he always seemed to know when she was in the grove taking plums now, and he would just happen to come down to check the crops and engage her in a conversation she didn't want but felt obligated to have. Lately, he'd even taken to walking about in the woods, looking for her in the places she'd usually forage from. She hated it when he did that.

"You have leaves in your hair," he said, reaching out to brush them aside.

Vexed, she swatted his hand away before he could make contact and raked her fingers through her tangled tresses herself. Over the last weeks, he'd been finding excuses to touch her more often than she was comfortable with, and it made her shudder.

"You were telling me why you were stomping through the forest, scaring the game away?"

Cooper smirked. "I was just setting some traps. A fox has been raiding my hens and the poor biddies are too nervous to lay."

Catherine shrugged and started up the trail. The farmer lumbered alongside of her, sweating and wiping his brow with the heel of his hand. She held no sympathy for his dead birds, or his lack of eggs. Foxes did what they did, and if the hens were too stupid to get out of the way, then what did she care?

"Maybe I'll take one of your scrawny hens home myself one of these days. You've warned everything off around here – I won't be getting my dinner tonight because of you."

"Now, don't be like that," he said. "If I ever catch that fox, I'll make you a nice hat from its pelt."

"I don't need a hat."

"Well, then come home with me and I'll make you a nice meal for the one I seem to have spoiled."

"You mean *I'll* make us a nice dinner after I've washed your moldy pots and dishes?"

He laughed again, and the noise made her think of a hoarse mule, but she agreed to go with him because she was beyond hungry. Caleb would have to take care of himself. Very likely he was too drunk to notice the absence of food in his stomach anyway.

They continued up the trail together, and yet again Cooper delivered a consistent stream of chatter that eventually dissolved in her own lines of thought until she managed to ignore most of the words spilling from his mouth.

The woods soon ended and opened to his orchard. A couple of weeks ago, the trees had been bedecked with soft pink flowers, bees swarming, sunlight reflecting off of their quick wings like twinkling jewels among the budding foliage. She remembered breathing in the warm air, heady with the perfume of blossoms. She'd spent hours and days among the boughs, her hair and ragged dress coated in the dancing petals as they snowed down from the branches. Now, there was nothing left of the delicate blooms save for the small nodules that promised a good harvest in the months to come. She smiled as she reached up and her fingers brushed the cool green leaves.

It took a moment for her to realize Cooper's droning voice had stilled, and that he was watching her. His mouth hung slightly and his eyes were wide as a child's. Noticing he'd been caught staring, he grinned wryly.

"Come on," he said, "let's eat."

Oddly enough, the house wasn't its usual state of chaos when she entered it behind him. He'd been doing some tidying, it seemed.

The door that had always been locked when she'd come to do the cleaning was standing ajar, and through the crack she spied a bedstead almost as large as Cooper's centered on the far wall of the room. An old quilt was lying atop it all haphazard, as if someone had wallowed on it through the night and then just left it askew when he'd gotten up in the morning.

She turned to him with a questioning glance. "And here I was, wondering what was in there."

At his nod, she crossed the floor, opened the door completely and peered inside.

The small room was cool. It smelled of must and mildew. Her footfalls thudded with a faint echo as she stepped inside, edging around the bed. She coughed at the dust she stirred with her bare feet. It was gloomy, and she decided to let in some light by opening the window shutters. They groaned in protest as she pushed against them, but they surrendered to her will in the end, and she turned around to find Cooper standing in the doorway. For a second, he looked as though he'd seen a ghost.

"This is beautiful," she told him. "I don't know why you keep it locked."

He forced a smile and shrugged. "Everything has its time."

Then, he left her to explore on her own, and she understood that the real question was why he'd left this room open today. He'd meant for her to come in here. All at once she recalled having been told he'd had two daughters, once upon a time, hard as it was to imagine, and she wondered if she'd venture to ask what had become of them.

She let her gaze wander and startled when it fell upon a mirror half as big as she was tall. The looking-glass was secured to the wall above a porcelain bowl in an ornate washstand opposite the bed, and she thought she'd caught a glimpse of *the other Catherine* reflected inside. The image drew her, but common sense told her it had to be her own, and she was mesmerized by the solemn likeness staring back at her.

Maebh had owned a mirror a bit larger than her hand. She'd used it to take stock of herself every morning, but it had been too precious an item to risk letting her clumsy daughter touch it. Catherine had gotten a few nights in the hole under the house just for trying, and she hadn't dared to ask again after that.

The only place where Catherine saw her own likeness was in the rippling reflection of the water in the river when it was still enough on a warm summer's day. The image cast back at her there wavered in pale grays and other fleeting tones. It was forever in motion, like Catherine, and so very different from what she was seeing now. The face looking at her from the mirror in this room seemed entirely unreal by comparison, and she raised her hand to touch her cheek as though she needed to test which of them was the flesh, and which the image.

She half expected the girl in the mirror to vanish, as the other Catherine at the castle had, but she didn't. Her twin in the looking-glass copied everything Catherine did in perfect synch, and it dawned on her why Maebh hadn't let her look in the hand mirror; she wasn't as ugly as her mother had led her to believe.

She'd never really thought about her appearance, but what she saw now gave her cause to.

She studied her oval face, sun-kissed and framed by a wild tangle of coal black hair that tumbled in waves down to her waist. Wide, steel-gray eyes blinked at her through long dark lashes the color of her hair. Some early childhood accident she didn't remember had left a small vertical scar over her upper lip. The flaw wasn't disfiguring, but it called attention to the pouty quality of her plump red lips and her perfect white teeth. Her nose was pert with just a hint of an upturn and delicately peppered with freckles.

Stepping back a little from the looking-glass, her eyes moved from face to figure, and she discovered that she was tall and thin, perhaps skinnier than the other girls in the village, but not boney anymore. At the age of twelve, she was on the cusp of womanhood. She'd known that since she'd started bleeding a few months ago. It had irritated her at first, especially when Rebecca had lectured her on things she already knew from observing her parents and the animals in the woods, but a deeper understanding was beginning to sink in.

She was the very image of the noble Lady she'd seen in her visions at the castle.

"You're a pretty girl, Catherine."

She hadn't heard him return, and the quality of Cooper's deep, velvety tone unsettled her. She stood in silence for a few heartbeats, processing what he'd said, and how he'd said it.

Was she more than just *not unsightly*? Was she really *pretty*? Did that even mean anything to her, coming from Cooper? She'd think on it later, she decided, when he wasn't blocking her from the outside world and gaping at her like a hungry dog.

Looking to distract both him and herself, she pointed to the trunk near the door. It was half the length of the bed, and almost as high. "What's in there?"

The farmer pasted a knowing smile to his lips and knelt to open it for her.

Looking over his shoulder as he raised the top on creaky hinges, she gasped at the contents he revealed. Fabrics she'd only seen in her visions of the castle swirled about in a tangle of shifts and dresses, leggings and corsets. She knelt beside him and gingerly lifted out a shift of white linen, soft and fine as the petals of a rose. Painfully aware of how dirty her hands were, she tried not to hold it too tightly for fear of smudging the silky fabric of the garment.

"Where did you get these?" she asked.

"From the markets in Ironstone and Saint Aeden. They were my daughters'. This was their room."

He sat back on his thighs thoughtfully, his mind on the past as Catherine rummaged through the clothes a little more bravely, raising them high so the sunlight filtering in through the window could enliven the colors; dark greens, wool whites, every shade of brown, and even a garment in a rich, royal blue that commoners would never be permitted to wear. She breathed in the sweet fragrance of soap that still lingered in the fabric.

"Where are they?" she asked. "Your daughters, I mean."

"Gone," he said simply, reaching for the blue overdress. His eyes misted as he looked back in time, and she wondered what he'd see there.

"Just like that?"

He showed her another of his forced smiles. "They were very ungrateful for what I worked so hard to give them, and their mother never set boundaries. They didn't know their place, didn't honor and obey me, and my wife thought I was being too strict with them. One day, a week or two after planting time, she up and left with them while I was out."

She couldn't imagine that. *What really happened?* she thought, hard, probing, testing, burrowing, training her eyes on him, and his expression changed.

"How could she do that to me?" he whined. "All I wanted was for them to love me like I loved them. I *loved* them, and I know they wanted it. She had no right to do that!"

Catherine didn't understand what he meant, and again, his expression abruptly changed; this time to shock, and he shuddered. He'd heard himself speak, but she knew he hadn't intended to say what he had. His mind seemed to wander for a moment.

"Wanted what?" she persisted, but he shook his head, avoiding her eyes.

"Boundaries, dear," he said more softly. "Children need to know their place, and their place was with their daddy. I guess I'm still hurting that they left me even though I was always good to them, and being here with you is bringing all that back to me. You remind me very much of my oldest daughter, only I know *you're* a good girl. *She* wasn't, but *you* are."

She had no idea what he was talking about.

He held the dress up to her shoulders, letting it drape down her slender body. "You may as well have this. It's a bit big on you yet, but you'll grow into it."

She gaped at him, her eyes wide. No one but Rebecca ever gave her gifts, and certainly nothing that matched the beauty or value of the velvety dress lying over the filthy, threadbare rags she wore. A voice in the back of her head screamed a warning, but she shut it out as quickly as it had risen.

She'd always wondered what it would be like to wear something truly beautiful. The garments in the chest at the castle would never have fit her, and she'd never have dared wear them, but this was different. These weren't a noblewoman's ball gowns or wedding dresses, but they were wonderful all the same, and they were meant to be worn. Rising from the floor, she snatched the dress out of Cooper's big paws and made her way back to the mirror. Holding the garment against her, she turned in various angles to see how she'd look in it.

Cooper watched with unabashed amusement, but she was too busy admiring herself to perceive the amusement in his eyes turn to starving desire.

He was giving her a gift because he thought she was good, she told herself, and she *felt* good. Cooper talked a lot of rubbish, but he'd probably been a good father to his daughters, and now he was being good to her. They'd left him, but she was here, and even though it felt all wrong to accept the dress, especially since she'd never get to wear it for fear of the flogging it would get her if the steward or the clergyman saw her in it, she wanted it. She'd been denied so many things, she wasn't about to deny herself this.

"I'm going to see to the stew now," he finally said, pushing off of the floor. She barely noticed him doing so. Turning to face her at the door, he added, "You know that this is an overdress, right?"

Snapping back, she smiled at him. "Yes."

"Well, there's bound to be a shift and maybe some boots in the trunk. You might as well be trussed up properly. I'll have supper ready when you're done."

He closed the door pointedly behind him, and Catherine wasted no time in sorting through the dozens of articles in the trunk. She found undergarments, stockings and a pair of soft leather boots somewhat too big, but manageable.

Casting off her own grubby garbs to exchange them for the finery at her disposal, she was unaware of

Cooper behind the door. He'd pushed a small, round piece of wood out of one corner of the panel when he'd left her alone in the room and peeped through it, relishing every moment of her enjoyment.

The snug quality of the textiles caressed her skin, and she felt glorious. She couldn't say she'd ever had anything as wonderful on her body. When she'd finished trying everything on, she folded the shifts and dresses to fit them back in the trunk, but something more caught her eye as she bent over it. Digging down a bit further, she felt her heart flutter when her hand connected with several books stored at the bottom.

More books. She hesitated, not knowing what to do, but then curiosity got the better of her, and she drew them out of the trunk one after the other. There were five volumes in all, and there was nothing magical about them, but she stacked them on the floor in front of her anyway, and an idea took shape in her mind.

Snatching one up, she lifted the skirt of the too-big dress to keep from tripping and practically flew into the next room, nearly bowling over the old farmer, who'd only just managed to retreat from the door.

"You have books!" she exclaimed, shaking the tome in his face excitedly. "Can you read?"

He took it from her hands and leafed through it. "Of course I can. They were mine when I was a boy. They were my lesson books, and I taught my daughters from them."

Her breath caught a moment. He could read, and if

he'd taught his daughters to read, then he could teach her.

Pushing the book back into her hands, he casually went back to the pot resting on the grate in the hearth and stirred the stew. "It's warm. Let's eat."

He took a rag from the hook beside the mantelpiece and used it to carry the pot to the table.

"Would you teach me?" she asked.

He chuckled. Setting two plates and spoons out for them, he motioned her to sit down. "What would you want to learn how to read for?"

"Why did *you* want to learn how to read?" she gave back boldly. Did he assume she wasn't smart enough?

He sat down opposite her and started ladling the hot food onto her plate. Peas were her favorite.

"You know, I was the fourth son of a landed knight. Titles and properties fell to my brothers. My father thought I'd make a good barrister, so he had me taught by a scholar. I would have been a great disappointment to him, had he lived to see me run off and marry the penniless daughter of a nobleman because I'd gotten her with child – for *love*." He said that with a bitter twist of regret, and Catherine realized how much he'd given up – *for love*.

"But maybe it wasn't such a great loss. I like farming and I've always made a good living at it, even in *this* place and in *these* times." He wrinkled his nose almost comically, and she laughed.

All of the hours she'd wasted listening to him

drone on and on about so many unimportant things, and she hadn't known the least bit about who he really was. She'd never once thought he might actually serve any good purpose for her, but he was likely the only person around who could help her discover the mysteries that surrounded her heritage. If Cooper was willing to teach her, she'd discover the magic they held, and her world would become everything she could imagine it to be.

"Well, I don't *like* farming…" she began, and he barked a laugh, cutting her off.

"No, you just like to harvest, darling, but there's nothing wrong with that."

He was back to being annoying, but she was glad to see this less broody, less saddened side of him again. It made for much safer ground, because she'd learned to navigate it. She ignored the remark; she couldn't very well tell him about the hidden chamber and the magic books. No one could ever know about all that, ever.

"I just want to learn. If you *really* can teach me, that is." She casually spooned some stew into her mouth.

The farmer's brows arched. *"If I really can?* Of course I can. If *you* can really learn. It's not easy."

"I can learn *anything.*"

He drew a deep breath, scratching the stubble on his chin as though he needed to think about it.

"A young woman who can read… that's

something even some noble ladies can't do. But it would take time."

"I've got time."

"You'd have to come here a few days a week, and that would take me away from the things I need to do. What would it be worth to you to have reading lessons?"

She held his gaze as well as her breath. He hadn't said no, and this was where they got to bargaining. What could she give the wealthiest man in the village? She had nothing he could possibly want. Neither she nor her father possessed anything of value to trade him, and she had no doubt Caleb would think the entire notion absurd if she spoke to him about it.

All she really had were her own two hands and her determination. "I can work for you; clean the house and wash, gather eggs, feed the livestock."

The farmer shrugged apologetically. "You already clean and wash."

Feeling her chance falter, she clamped her jaw shut in frustration.

Cooper kept his face blank as he appeared to ponder the predicament.

His plate was empty, and he pushed it aside. She felt his eyes roam slowly over her.

"I'm a lonely man," he finally told her. "And I know you're a smart girl, and a good girl. A *really* good girl. If I was to teach you to read, I'd ask just one thing in return."

She felt her chest close up. He reached for her hand, and she almost pulled away. The stiff, intense way he was scrutinizing her made her squirm inwardly, but she told herself not to be stupid. This was Cooper. He was like this, and he was harmless. She wasn't a baby anymore. What he'd told her about his daughters... he'd said he'd loved them, and she knew it was true. She knew it was true because he'd given them all these things, including the dress she was now wearing. She had to mean something to him, or he wouldn't have given it to her. He'd been nothing but kind to her, and he'd never expected anything of her in return. Whatever he was asking for, it couldn't be so bad, and it was almost like he was entitled to it.

"Catherine, you're beautiful and you're smart, and I *know* you can learn *anything*. If I teach you to read, then I want you to let me teach you something else besides."

His fingers wandered around her hand in a warm, sweaty caress.

Grimacing, she drew back from him despite herself, rubbing her palm on her leg. "I can clean for you and feed the animals. That ought to be enough to pay for your time."

He gave her another moment, and when she found nothing to add to that, he picked up the book she'd set on the table. "Alright," he said brightly, his tone a notch above his usual.

He rose and carried it back into the small bedroom,

put it in the chest and closed the lid as though nothing was amiss.

Panic welled inside of Catherine, and she knew she had to do something, or she'd lose the only chance she'd ever have at finding out what was in those books the Magician had left for her in that hidden chamber. She'd never be able to live with herself if she threw away the only means of learning who she really was and what she could do if she applied herself, because she was most certainly more than just the gravedigger's daughter. She had a right to her heritage, and Cooper was the key to unlocking the secrets of the magic she'd stumbled upon in her forefathers' castle. She was destined for more than just thieving and stealing and foraging in the woods to get by, and Cooper wasn't so bad. He cared for her, and she was convinced she could give him what he wanted most from her in return for what she wanted most from him. She wasn't stupid, and she wasn't a child anymore.

Putting herself in his way as he was just about to leave his daughters' room, she looked at her feet before fixing her gaze to his.

"I can learn anything," she repeated, placing her hand gently on his belly like she'd seen her mother do with Caleb sometimes. "I'll do whatever you ask."

He smiled, and she shivered as he took her hand and led her to his daughters' bed.

Chapter Seventeen

ભ Temptation ૭

Waking up on Jaden's straw mattress, Maebh discovered she hadn't felt this much at ease in years. Stretching out beside him, she thought her luck had finally turned. Life was *nearly* good this way. She mattered to him.

"Are you off to feed the goats, now?" he murmured, smiling sleepily with his eyes still closed, and she thumped him playfully for it.

"I thought you'd taken care of that problem for me."

"Oh, I have, love, I have."

Unexpectedly, he grabbed her arm and pulled her to him, and in an instant, she found herself beneath him, held down by his weight as he kissed her ravenously, invading her mouth, caressing her skin, stroking her most sensitive spots. He knew what he was doing, she had to leave him that. He wasn't anything like Caleb, whose clumsy, fumbling, short-lived efforts had never been half as pleasurable as any of Jaden's attentions.

Smiling to herself, she decided she was going to enjoy every second of being with him, just as she had all these past days, and she put Caleb out of her mind.

She wanted to put him out of her mind for good, and Catherine along with him. They were the past, and Jaden was her future – a *good* future once they'd gotten out of here.

Spooning with him in a sated huddle an hour later when most people were already going about their chores outside, she became aware of a movement at the entrance of the tent. The flap was pushed back, and she sat up, squinting into the glaring light as someone ducked into the shelter and began rummaging through the chest where Jaden kept his clothes.

She pulled his blanket about her and shook him.

"Jaden?" she hissed, and he briefly looked up, sighed and lay down again.

"It's just me," a boy mumbled, determinedly keeping his eyes on his hands as they worked their way through spare shirts and breeches to find whatever it was he was looking for. Jaden didn't seem in the least alarmed, and Maebh was puzzled because she had no idea who *just me* might be.

"I told you not to come here for a while," Jaden said impatiently.

The boy stopped what he was doing, turned to face them and came a few steps closer. He pushed his hands into his sides, and Maebh could see that his face was a mess. His nose looked like it had been broken, one eye was nearly swollen shut, and there was blood all over his shirt and pants.

"You did, aye," he said, "but I do need a change of clothes so I can wash mine. Got in a fight down by the goat cote."

Jaden snorted a laugh. Finally, he got up and pulled on some breeches. "I hope you didn't embarrass yourself, laddie."

The boy's gaze wandered from his muddy bare feet to Jaden and then came to rest on Maebh. Getting a better look at him, it dawned on her who he was and that made her feel very uncomfortable.

She was certain she'd never seen her lover's son by the goat cote. Lorcan usually worked with the carpenters on the new wagons Thaddeus was having them build. Was this how Jaden had dealt with her problem? Had he sent the boy as her replacement?

"You should see the other guy," he muttered.

"Good man. Good man indeed." Jaden forced a wide smile, thumping him on the back as he edged around him to hold back the flap of the tent so Lorcan would know he'd overstayed his welcome. Lorcan randomly snatched a shirt from the chest, cast one last contemptuous glance back at Maebh, and left.

"Children!" Jaden scoffed, and sat back down next to her. "But let's talk about more important things. Breakfast, for instance."

Chapter Eighteen

---

୪ The Boy ๛

Ortus couldn't help but smile as he approached Lorcan from behind. The lad was completely engrossed in his book and didn't hear him coming.

This particular book wasn't something Lorcan should be looking at yet, but there was an odd connection between the boy and that leather volume. It was Ortus' most valued possession because it had belonged to his father. His father had died when he was eleven. He would never have let anyone else borrow it – but Lorcan was different. The Master Sorcerer couldn't explain why, but he felt obliged to allow Lorcan access to it. While Dean still labored with the words on the rare occasions he let him try to read it, Lorcan's mind would conjure images from the texts and the sketches he found.

Sometimes Ortus thought his father had cast an enchantment on the vellum, or on the words so they'd disclose themselves to the people who were meant to understand what was written there. He didn't know if he was really one of those. Dean probably wasn't, he had to admit, but it was his hope that Lorcan would help Dean with this when the time came.

Ortus had only left Lorcan alone with the volume briefly to talk to Thaddeus, and already there was a blue-glowing three dimensional model of a Portal growing in the dirt at the boy's feet. The image of the Gate was made from light and thought spilling liquidly through Lorcan's fingers into reality as he slowly raised his hands to create what his mind's eye could see. Stretching the construction upwards to the height of a grown man and holding it there with one hand, the boy worked a pattern into the space where the Passageway opened with the tips of his other hand's fingers.

Although rudimentary, the logic behind Lorcan's interpretation of the workings of a transitional aid such as this was astounding. The Sorcerer didn't think he'd have any difficulty creating it from memory soon. He wondered if the boy could fully grasp what lay on its other side or how to complete the enchantment that would take him there.

Lorcan might have watched Mary creating Portals when The Fair moved, but Ortus was sure she hadn't tried to teach him. He wasn't certain she even knew he had the Ability. Lorcan could do a lot of things no one had ever demonstrated to him, but Ortus had come to realize his student's mind was made to create beauty and magic from nothing. Supplementing any information still missing from the Magician's writings about Portals didn't seem to pose a problem to him; the descriptions in the book were never complete, but

Lorcan's results were. He always played things through in his head until they made sense.

The Portal faded when Ortus seated himself next to the lad.

"You're doing well," he remarked, and Lorcan looked at his feet.

The boy had no idea of his own steadily increasing potential, and Ortus was glad he wasn't putting any of it on display. There was no telling what Jaden – or that woman he was currently shacking up with – would do if either of them caught on.

There were great things in Lorcan Aurum's future, if he didn't stray from the path. Ortus was optimistic his father's influence wouldn't change that. Lorcan had a good heart, though he guarded it well.

"How are the writing exercises coming along?"

"Alright, I suppose." Lorcan handed him back his book and then picked up the journal he'd brought to the lesson.

Opening it near the middle, he showed the Master Sorcerer the text he'd been copying. It was a passage from the Bible Ortus had given him. Another precious possession he didn't normally lend to anyone. Ortus thought he'd possibly need to acquire a new one for himself soon. He could see how fond Lorcan was of it, and he was getting used to the idea of giving it to him to keep. Maybe he'd ask for the journal in return.

Looking at the neat script, he could hardly find any misspellings or omissions. Lorcan worked with great accuracy and patience, no matter what the task. Thaddeus had often remarked on how he treated the hatchets and saws he used for boards and planks with the same respect he gave the quill and the vellum, keeping everything he did just as orderly and clean as his handwriting was. He'd be a good craftsman with an eye for detail in both disciplines, one day.

"So, when's the scholar going to come milk the goats?" Jaden asked, coming around the tent that stood between them and the encampment. There was nothing humorous about the way he said it, even though he was smiling.

Ortus smiled back, rising. "As I recall, he wasn't assigned that duty."

Jaden shuffled about. His expression changed briefly to malice and back.

"No, sir, but he has freely taken it upon himself to do this while the person who *was* assigned to it is working hard on practicing the use of her magic under my instruction, since she's not getting the benefit of lessons from the Master Sorcerer, as she's repeatedly asked." He shifted his gaze to Lorcan. "The cooks have already complained, asking why they're not getting their milk. We have children going hungry."

Lorcan was about to gather his things, but Ortus stopped him.

"Your son isn't milking the goats today, Jaden. We've all got our duties here, and he's Thaddeus' apprentice now. That means he's spending his days here, doing hard manual labor. He's got as much as a boy his age can handle. If he chooses to muck, feed and milk those goats after Thaddeus tells him he's done or during his breaks, then that's his decision. However, right now, he's studying instead of eating while Maebh is probably still asleep in your tent, and he's going back to his own work as soon as we're finished here."

Jaden's glance darted back and forth between Ortus and Lorcan, and he snorted. That was all. Then, he left.

Realizing what he'd probably just set in motion, Ortus turned to Lorcan. "I'm sorry. I guess I shouldn't have done that. He's going to give you a hard time, isn't he?"

Lorcan was unreadable. "I can handle myself."

He believed the boy could. Lorcan was growing up to handle himself without depending on help from anyone. Jaden Aurum didn't have a whole lot of real friends at The Fair aside from his gambling buddies, the shady artefacts-and-talisman dealers and sham-potion makers he kept company with, and Ortus assumed this was one of the reasons Lorcan was so cagey. The boy didn't fit in there.

"Do you have any memories of your mother?" he asked out of interest. The thought had only just entered his mind, but he regretted it the moment the words left his mouth.

Lorcan's expression clouded over, and the Sorcerer recognized the kind of pain that nestled in his eyes all too well. Again, he felt the need to apologize. That was twice in as many minutes, and he wondered how he could have gotten so attached.

"I think I should be getting back to work," the boy said too brightly, swiping at his eyes as he rose and turned away.

Ortus let him go. "Alright. I'll see you here tomorrow, then," he said to his back.

Lorcan nodded, but he didn't return the next day.

Chapter Nineteen

---

෪ Lessons Learned ෧

"The bell pe… a… pell-ed mou… mou-ern-fully…"

"The bell pealed mournfully," Cooper corrected her patiently. "There's no double *l*, and the *a* makes the *e*-sound long here."

He dragged his finger under the written text Catherine had laid out before her. "It's *pealed*. Try it again, altogether."

Catherine took a deep breath and started over. "The bell pealed mournfully for the noble knight; seven times it peal-ed… pealed… in honor of his years of service to his Lady Queen."

Pealed? What kind of word was that? she thought.

She only knew you *peeled* apples when the skin was very brown and blotchy. It didn't seem like that was what was meant here, but she'd be damned if she couldn't keep her ignorance to herself.

"A somber dirge rose from the gal… gal… er… gallery as his com… rads in arms marched four abreast under the colors of the house of Orin." She plowed on, sounding at least four more words she didn't know, and the farmer-turned-teacher smiled because he didn't have the slightest clue.

"Much better," he acknowledged proudly, and Catherine took some satisfaction in that. She'd made a lot of progress through the winter and spring months, and his encouragement made her feel good about herself. He seemed to enjoy teaching her.

She'd worked her way through several chapters of a *History of the Northern Forest* and had quickly grasped a working knowledge of mathematics, and he'd told her how impressed he was with her ability to master the challenge. It wasn't hard, and the more she practiced, the better she got.

Golden maple leaves in the woods heralded late summer now, and they'd fallen into a routine. She came for her lessons twice a week, usually in the mid-morning when he was still in the orchards, so she'd have the house to herself for a while. She loved the peaceful warmth it offered and the good furnishings, the pretty little odds and ends on the mantelpiece above the hearth, and even the tin basin where she washed the dishes that tended to pile up on the days she wasn't there.

She never came in from the village road where she'd be seen by the laborers, but by the path through the woods because she didn't want everyone to know where she was going. It was bad enough she'd had to inform Caleb, who worked for Cooper on and off, though he'd thankfully displayed the same indifference at this that he did at everything she got up to.

Unfortunately, however, he'd told Rebecca, and

171

she'd had plenty to say on the subject before predictably reverting to her typical narrow-lipped mien and teaching her how to bake bread and mend clothes so she'd be more useful all round. Rebecca knew she'd have done it anyway.

By the time Cooper came home on lesson days, she'd have his clothes washed and hanging on a rope stretched between two trees, the house by and large tidied and swept, and the dishes put away. A pleasant, yeasty aroma would spread through the cabin from a towel-covered bowl of rising bread dough, and she'd have warmed whatever he'd cooked the previous day. After a brief repast, she'd clear the table and roll the dough into pans to bake on the hearth while he brought in the dried clothes from the line and laid them out on the bed.

Catherine's lessons lasted for several hours, depending on Cooper's mood and her patience, but those hours seemed to fly. She really didn't care what they read – letters became syllables, syllables formed words, words made sentences, and sentences became knowledge. It was quite simple, to her mind. Not everything in Cooper's books was interesting, but it was a means to an end, and it seemed too important to abandon even the most boring exercise because it offered the opportunity to get practice.

When they'd first started, Cooper had dipped into his precious store of parchment to sketch the letters for her, sounding each one out and making her repeat the sounds back to him. She'd committed the letters to memory almost from that day, and she'd begun scratching them in the sandy ground on the river bank where she'd sit in the evenings after she'd left the cabin.

He'd written some of the more common words down for her – *and, the, he, she, they* and so forth – and given her the vellum to keep so she could look at it whenever she pleased. He'd had her point those words out to him page after page in one of the volumes he'd dug out of the trunk, and it hadn't been long before she'd gotten the hang of it.

She'd tried to apply this method to the books she'd found in the chest at the castle, but it hadn't worked out for her too well, somehow. It appeared these words weren't as common in her books as they were in his, and she'd been wondering why until she'd come to understand that her books were very different from the ones in Cooper's old trunk. Hers didn't have stories in them.

Pealing – peeling – bells, she thought again, pausing in the text and smiling to herself. *Imagine that.* She'd never found anything about skinning bells in either of her own tomes. To be entirely truthful with herself, she had to admit she still didn't have the foggiest idea what they were about.

The History of the Northern Forest hadn't offered much of a transfer for them yet, but maybe it would by the time she'd finished it. She needed to get more of a feel for meaning and broaden her command of words. If she could manage that by coming here twice a week, then she'd do so until kingdom come. It would improve her chances of understanding the words in her books, and she was positive it would be worth it.

Realizing Cooper was staring at her with a look in his eyes that meant lessons were over for the day, her smile froze before it dissolved, and she looked down at her hands for a moment before closing the history book. She knew what he expected of her now.

A knot formed in her chest as she quietly rose to wrap the cooled bread in towels and place them in the pantry while Cooper put the leather volumes and writing supplies away. Briefly glancing out the window in passing, she noted how the shadows were already beginning to lengthen as the sun tilted westward. The old man didn't have any workers in the orchards today, so no one would be coming to the house. There would be no interruptions.

It got dark earlier every day now, but that was just as well, she thought, taking off her dress with her back to him as he settled into a chair to watch her *peel* off her undergarments and step out of the puddle they formed at her feet where they fell. She could feel his eyes burning into her pale flesh, scrutinizing her form, making her writhe inwardly though she'd always believed she'd get used to it, get over it, and get on with it better than she was.

Leaning over the bed, she started to fold the clothes she'd washed during the morning, the heat of shame blotching her cheeks red when she imagined him there behind her, his sparkling, beady eyes on her rear. She tried not to think of anything, conscious that there wasn't much to see, though he seemed to think very differently.

Her breasts were starting to take shape, and she'd been bleeding once in every moon cycle for almost a year now. That meant she could bear and nourish children, but she felt far from being a woman yet, even if he treated her as one whenever he lay with her.

Cooper never spoke while he watched her work to clear the bed for them because it heightened his lust for her. He'd sit there with one hand down the front of his pants, rubbing himself so he'd harden, his gaze roaming incessantly over her bareness until she was done and he was ready for her.

The silence around the little sounds he was making was deafening. She couldn't bring herself to look at him over her shoulder, but she could hear his breathing growing ever heavier as she finished her task. Turning the covers down after she'd put his garments into his trunk, she felt the bile rising in her throat, but she knew there was no sense in drawing this out any longer when he called to her, so she faced him, shivering slightly, rehearsed indifference masking her repulsion.

"You know what I like," she heard him say, her gaze not quite meeting his when she started walking toward him, hesitating on the last steps. "Come here, darling – don't look at the floor, look at me."

He sounded as though he was speaking to a kitten or a lost puppy. His voice was soft and gentle, maybe a notch higher than it normally would be. She obeyed, promising herself it would hardly hurt anymore, and that he'd be done quickly after he'd had such a good time with himself already.

She wasn't really there with him, she kept telling herself, closing her eyes and compliantly parting her legs for him the way he'd taught her, first on the chair, straddling him, and then on the bed beneath him. The stench of his breath and unwashed body turned her stomach as he pawed and tugged at her to accommodate himself while he violated her.

In her mind, she was reviewing the letters and numbers she'd learned, repeating interesting lines, the pealing of bells, and the names of people and places she'd read about to herself. She went over the maps in the crimson book, and the strange and mysterious creatures that supposedly lived there. She conjured images of the symbols and their meanings, wondering how the names of the magical beings in the Westerwoods or the Black Sea should be correctly pronounced.

Finally, Cooper collapsed heavily on top of her with a growl and a sigh, and it was over.

She could hardly breathe under his weight, and when she was unable to take any more, she wriggled out from under him. Scampering off of the bed, his seed trickling from her folds, she grabbed her clothes.

He tried to pull her back into his embrace when he realized she was leaving, but she managed to twist free of him and hurriedly started to get dressed. Disgusted by the sticky, angrily throbbing mess he'd reduced her lower half to, all she wanted to do was get away from him – fast.

"Oh, come on," he whined, lying back, a wounded look about him. "For Heaven's sake! You really could stay for another while, you know. Who'd miss you?"

He was right about that, but the last thing she wanted to do was stay for another round when he'd recovered, and he knew it. Sometimes she thought he said the things he did to make it seem as though she was always wronging him in some way. She couldn't tell what it was he really wanted from her. All she knew was that he had needs, and she had the means to satisfy them so he'd be good to her and give her what *she* wanted. That was the deal.

She couldn't stand the sight of him for a minute longer right now though. She had to get away from him and his stench, so she ignored the remark. Crossing the floor, she unlatched the door and bolted, fleeing into the waning light without looking back.

The fact that he let her go and never came after her was one small mercy she was infinitely grateful for. He was smart enough not to stop her because it was the only way to ensure she'd always come back.

He stoically kept reminding her she was free to choose whether she wanted him to bed her or not. He wasn't forcing himself on her or hurting her; a woman's body was made for a man's use, he'd once said, and she was here of her own free will, but she didn't believe this was what her body was made for, and she didn't see any kind of choice in the matter anymore, either. She took his food, his clothes, his money, and the lessons he offered her in reading, writing, and simple arithmetic, and in return, he took her.

If she just kept on running and didn't come back to him one day, he wouldn't come after her. But, she wouldn't learn to read well enough to understand who she really was or still could be, and she'd go hungry over the winter.

Telling herself she was going to be all right, this time as every time, she sprinted off into the forest.

Broken and debased, she melted into the undergrowth, her fists clenched tightly and her jaw set as she ran. Twigs snapped beneath her calloused feet, and her dress kept catching on brush and brambles, but she didn't care. It felt good to be outside and breathing again.

Running sorted her bones and it sorted her thoughts, so she ran as fast as she could.

Any manner of creature nearby could have heard her, she realized, but she couldn't bring herself to slow down or stop.

Making her way deep into the heart of the wildwood to the river where her uncle had fished when he'd been alive, she tried to calm her hammering heart and quiet her screaming mind, but she didn't quite succeed until she'd reached its bank.

Being in the spot where she could still imagine Charlie standing in the fading daylight consoled her, and it was safe because no one came here at this time of the evening. No one would see her, *look* at her, or ask questions, and no one would touch her here.

Cooper often asked her where she went when she wasn't with him or at her father's house, but she pretended not to understand what he meant. She refused to tell him about the castle or the riverbank. Letting him use her to get his relief was one thing, but she wasn't about to share where she went to mend after he was done with her. He'd contaminate this place with his presence if he ever decided to come and take a look, and she didn't want a memory of him here or by the old ruins, whatever else happened.

Without hesitating, she stripped off the clothes she'd so hastily donned not half an hour before. Dropping everything in the grass, she waded into the clear, chilly water right down to her chest. The iciness of it was overwhelming, but it was also numbing, and that was good.

She rubbed frantically at her face and arms without feeling anything. Ferociously assaulting her breasts and thighs, she tried to wash off the grime the old man's hands and drooling mouth had left on her skin before lastly and tentatively cleaning her stinging privates of his fluids and the vicious dull ache he'd inflicted there. She'd be hurting for a day or two, and there was nothing to be done about it, but she needed to get Cooper's stench off of herself. Washing and scrubbing until she was raw and shaking from cold, she vehemently willed the reek of his breath and the feel of his sweat and stickiness away, but it never seemed to come off of her completely no matter how hard she worked to rid herself of it.

Later, sore and red, she slipped back into her dress and stiffly climbed onto the bough of the ancient oak near the shoreline where she'd be hard to see from below on the off chance that anyone did happen by. She didn't allow herself to think of anything but the letters and words she was learning – *pealing, mournfully, somber* and *dirge* – it was ironic how well they seemed to fit her, but the knight had had his honor, and she'd yet to recover hers, some day.

It never occurred to her to cry about her circumstances like a child might have, like *the other Catherine* might have. She wasn't a child anymore, and she had no one to cry to. She'd made her arrangement with old Cooper knowing full well what she was trading and what she'd be getting in return, and this was the price she had to pay, plain and simple. She'd have to get over it.

Of course, she had no illusions as to what that made her. She'd heard the names the villagers called women who bargained for things with their bodies: *harlot, strumpet, whore…*

It was inconsequential why some women did what she did when they saw no other option. They were scorned and shunned, whether they sold themselves for money or drink, or for food and another week's shelter. They were pitied by no one, but pity was something that had never been directed at her anyway, so she had little need for it. She detested the prospect of what pity might make of her. Pity was a fate worse than having to acknowledge she was a whore. She had nothing in this world, really, but she could still pretend she had at least some dignity as long as no one dared pity her. She'd deal with this and move on, and then she'd reclaim her honor. She wasn't doing this for *today*, she was doing it for *tomorrow* and for her *future*. She could worry about honor when she'd learned the secrets her ancestors had bequeathed her through the books she'd be able to read and understand by then.

She didn't hate the old farmer all of the time, but she loathed him a little bit more every time he took her. She knew she had to cope with his attentions twice a week for another while to come, no matter what.

They had names for men like him, too, and when this was over, she'd make sure he knew what they were. She'd find a way to teach him a lesson or two of her own, somehow, though she didn't know how she was going to do that just at the moment.

Something would come to mind, she was sure.
Exhausted, she began drifting in and out of sleep.

Chapter Twenty

∾ Hopes and Dreams ∾

Ortus found Jaden Aurum in the Big Top. The Illusionist was practicing for the evening show.

"You!" Ortus barked, marching into the ring. "Where's the boy?"

The other artists present in the tent stared for a moment but decided to keep out of it when they caught whiff of his fury. The Firestarters left, and the six Acrobats got busy sweeping off seats farther back in favor of continuing to work on their act. Maebh stayed. She actually managed to look bored, and he wondered why he'd ever brought her here.

When he'd gotten close enough to see, Ortus noticed an impressive bruise on Aurum's cheek. The Illusionist's eyes flared, and he casually threw all three of the small apples he'd been holding in his right hand at the Master Sorcerer, one after the other. Ortus automatically raised his hands to catch them, but the apples appeared to fall apart in mid-air, turning into a good dozen bats that flew over his shoulders and head, startling him. Then, they faded away. They rematerialized in Aurum's hand, and Ortus realized they'd never left it in the first place.

"What boy?" Aurum inquired, his tone a mockery. "Do you mean that good-for-nothing son of mine?"

Maebh huffed a laugh. "Hasn't mucked the goats yet, even though he promised he would so I can help his father."

Aurum wrapped his arm around her middle. "Show's on tonight, as you know. How do you like my new piece?"

Ortus couldn't believe the nerve of the man. "You're not throwing *bats* at anyone tonight. We're a fair, not a horror show. We want people to be happy here. We want them to come back, not go running to the steward or the Duke with a story to tell."

The smile on Aurum's face froze.

"Aside from that, your son didn't come to work today," Thaddeus said as he entered the Big Top behind Ortus, "and I'd also be interested to know where he is."

Ortus could see Aurum was seething beneath the surface.

"I really couldn't tell you," he replied, "but I'll make sure to tell *him* you're looking for him when I see him." He faced back to Ortus. "As for the show…"

"You're not doing it," the Master Sorcerer cut him short, "and that's that. Get the hell out of here."

Aurum looked as though he'd bitten into a lemon, but Ortus didn't care if he'd been out of line. All he cared about was finding the boy. Aurum turned and walked away from him without another word, Maebh trailing behind him.

"He's going to love you for that," Thaddeus remarked when they were out of earshot.

"He doesn't have to love me – he needs to understand what we're trying to do here."

"I'm not saying you're wrong. If that boy's dead, I want to know so we can bury him – Jaden, I mean. Piece of crap, he is, but Lorcan is *his* son, so what are you going to do about it? There is nothing you can do short of throwing him out, in which case we might have to accept that he'll take the lad with him. It's his right. Think about that."

Ortus hummed. "Can't have that, my friend," Ortus returned. "That boy is staying right here. You and I, we both know he's special, and The Fair is going to need him when neither of us is around anymore. He could be one of The Few."

Thaddeus nodded. "Aye. I know what you mean."

As they were talking, one of the Acrobats left his group and came toward them. The Sorcerer recognized him as Freya's son. He was older than Lorcan by several years and more muscular. Beyond that, Ortus knew he'd inherited his mother's Ability to influence reptiles. Freya was no Shapeshifter, but she could work miracles with anything that had scales. Dorian hated snakes. Ortus could identify with that.

"I heard you talking just now. Lorcan's at my mother's. He wasn't... He wasn't in good shape last night, but he should be alright to work again in a few days. Nothing's broken. She's fixed him up. Jaden himself brought him last night. Said he'd had a run-in with some boys."

Ortus exchanged a glance with Thaddeus, and they made their way to the Snake Sisters' dwelling.

The sisters shared a yurt that was cram-packed with old crockery and knickknack, and the Sorcerer had always wondered how they moved about without breaking anything, and how they got all of their belongings from one place to the other every few weeks. It had to take them days to box all of their possessions, and days to unpack them again. That, and they shared their accommodations with living beings no one could possibly want to sleep around. Ortus knew this was their idea of comfort, and he respected it, but he wouldn't have wanted to trade with any of the men they'd scared for all the king's treasures.

Stooping to enter the yurt after Thaddeus, his gaze fell upon Lorcan sitting by the brazier. The boy's lower lip was swollen to the size of a ripe plum, and he had a nasty gash above his left eyebrow that had obviously bled into his eye. He rose stiffly when he saw the carpenter and the Master Sorcerer, more like an old man than a fellow of his age.

Ortus tried not to let on he'd been worried. "Got in a fight, did you?" he asked casually.

"Yes, sir. I'm sorry I missed our lesson…" He looked at Thaddeus. "… and work."

"Did you win, at least?" Thaddeus probed, grinning.

To Ortus' surprise, Lorcan grinned right back as much as his lip would allow. "Oh, you should see the other guy," he said. "Took a few punches he never would have expected."

Ortus laughed, folding his arms across his chest. "I'll bet he did."

Lorcan's eyes wandered back and forth between the two men. "I'll be back to work tomorrow," he told them, but Ortus waved him off, already turning to leave. The lad needed his rest.

"Nonsense," he said, "you just take care of yourself for a few days. After that, I've got a special order job for you. I need you to carve something for me – a music box that will have to have exact measurements. You'll need to be all there and concentrated for that."

He could see Lorcan was both curious and delighted. That was a good sign. Healing had a lot to do with goals and hopes, and both were easy to give to a boy with humor who was capable of dreaming as vividly as Lorcan was.

Chapter Twenty-One

⚘ Blight ⚘

The orchards weren't doing well. They hadn't been doing well over the whole of the past year or more. It was as though they'd been cursed. Trees infected with fungi and blight brought forth the second consecutive crippled harvest in a row, and half of that was spotty and worm-riddled. Ailing barren plums and pears stood fouling in the grove, and there was nothing Cooper could do about it but watch… with Catherine watching him.

A morbid sense of satisfaction settled snugly into her bowels as she did so.

Although she didn't think for a moment this would benefit her in any way, she loved his bewildered, helpless mien. Observing him from a distance just inside the tree line, she could sense the ever-patient farmer's endurance wearing thin. His trees were dying, and his comfortable income evaporating.

He hadn't bothered employing anyone to do the picking for him this year – it hardly seemed worthwhile. Some of the women from the village talked behind the farmer's back, Caleb had told Catherine, wondering for the very first time what he was paying her, and *if* he was still paying her, because their arrangement was valid nonetheless. She'd assured him she was getting exactly what she was asking of him, and he didn't inquire any further.

The men who usually helped Cooper would not be getting their wages from him this season because he simply couldn't remunerate them, and they blamed him for that. Caleb did, too. Although the old smallholder's misfortune probably wasn't due to a lack of care or foresight on his behalf, Fate had turned against him. He'd have to think of something or he'd be eating barley soup like the rest of them before winter, Catherine thought, but she wasn't about to pity him for it. No one else would, either.

Her contempt for him ran close to the surface of late, like lava just beneath the earth's crust, building and building and bubbling until it was nearly ready to tear the mountain apart, but she needed one last thing from him all the same. She could read fairly well now, but reading wasn't the same as understanding, and she felt brave today.

A wind stirred in the bushes around her and, without warning, Cooper abruptly spun around, his eyes scanning the brush. She smiled and walked toward him. It took him a few seconds to realize she was there, and the puzzled look about him changed to apprehension for the merest fraction of a moment before he pasted his own smile – the one he reserved just for her – back on his face.

"Hello, darling," he sang.

He obviously hadn't been expecting her. It wasn't one of *their* days. Reaching for her, he cupped her cheeks in his hands, and his greedy mouth found her lips. When he released her, he took note of the package she was carrying and raised an eyebrow, silently asking for an explanation she did not give. She never brought along anything when she came to him.

"To what do I owe the pleasure of your company?"

"I'd like you to take a look at something," she said, patting the book she'd tucked under her arm as she headed off in direction of the house. He hastened to keep pace with her.

"That's not a present for me, is it?" A boyish hope gleamed in his eyes.

"No."

He was a clever man, and the question was a tease, so she marched on without meeting his gaze. He didn't seriously assume she'd be able to afford a book for a present for him. He just wanted to make a point of the fact.

When they'd arrived at the house, he almost threw himself in front of the door to stop her from entering.

"The place is a mess, dear," he explained. "Give me a minute."

She rolled her eyes. "Your house is always a mess. That's why you have me clean it."

Ducking under his arm, she opened the door and noticed nothing out of the ordinary. He'd left his dirty dishes on the table, and his clothes were strewn about.

Muddy boots had left tracks all over the floor.

Hurrying past her, he yanked the door that led to the small bedroom at the back of the house shut. She wondered why. What didn't he want her to see? She couldn't make sense of the drama, and she guessed he was hiding something. It was very likely nothing she wanted to concern herself with, though, so she let it go. She'd spent weeks debating on whether or not to show him the crimson book she carried with her today. Having to admit defeat, having to ask for his help was difficult. She hated it, and she just wanted this over with.

Ushering her to the table, he pulled out a chair for her to sit on, mimicking the perfect gentleman he most definitely wasn't.

She cleared several used plates to one side far enough so she could set down the book and began ridding it of the linen she'd swathed it in. He sat next to her, moving uncomfortably close, and immediately reached for the leather volume, his eyes wide as he ran his fingers across the intertwining infinity signs in the center of the front covering.

"Where did you get this, love?"

"It's mine." She tried to keep her voice even, watching him intently. Perhaps this had been a mistake. He looked like he recognized the symbol, if not the book as such, and she had to fight for restraint to keep from snatching it back from him.

"I never doubted it was," he lied sweetly. "I just want to know where you found it."

He had lying down to an art, but Catherine knew him so well, she could practically hear the questions that were forming in his head, and she briefly and very surprisingly saw herself through his eyes. He was wondering whom she'd stolen her prize from, or what on earth she might have traded for it.

With whom did she sleep to get it?

Catherine could feel something akin to jealousy crawling beneath his skin as though it was her own, digging into his flesh and hers. He was getting angry. In an instant, she was back to her own perception and slightly shocked at what she'd just experienced, but informed nonetheless.

"It's a family heirloom."

"Is it, now?"

He still didn't believe her, but she held his gaze, and he smiled permissively when she refused to elaborate. She was sure he was going to try to get to the bottom of this, but she was determined to keep what was hers to herself.

Eventually turning his attention back to the book, he opened it to the first page and skimmed the words thereupon. Looking back and forth between the densely packed passage of neatly penned script and the illustrations on the next page, a grin he could barely disguise slowly twisted his features into a superior kind of amusement.

He eyed her with new interest. "Well… if this is a family heirloom, then that would make you a descendent of the Cine, my dear. What a dangerous legacy in this day and age!"

She knew what a Cine was, and she'd guessed as much, going by what Rebecca had told her, and what she'd seen Maebh do. She'd also known he'd react to this in some manner, but she hadn't expected him to be enjoying himself this immensely. It was unsettling. He was by nature keenly interested in the unusual and curious about everything and everyone because knowledge was power, as he never grew tired of telling her. He collected it like the village children collected pretty pebbles or flowers to dry and look at in winter. She'd never seen him put it to use, though. It was like he was storing it away for the sake of having it.

She had the gnawing feeling she'd been right in her reluctance to show him her treasure, but she knew he wouldn't use the book's content against her.

He wasn't a religious man, and he was no friend of the local clergy or the Inquisitor's quest in matters of ethnical purity for humankind. The fact that she was letting him in on something prohibited per se made this attractive to him.

Cooper was a fool for the lure of danger, as long as he thought he was calling all the shots. He was far too arrogant to believe he wasn't in complete control over what others perceived of him, but she'd learned more about him than he'd ever believe. He had a few secret passions no one knew about. Sex with children was one, and the History of the Tainted and Unnaturals was another.

She'd seen him mixing potions to treat the sickly fruit trees, and she'd seen him agonize over the problem he'd been having lately with bedding her, though he'd never get to the bottom of that. She smiled to herself. She'd been employing a little of Rebecca's magic in form of a powder she'd learned about when the miller's wife had come to her complaining about her husband's frequent unwelcome attentions. A pinch of it in the miller's dinner was enough to ensure his wife's peace for the night, and a spoonful of it in the farmer's tea at lunch was enough to ensure Catherine's for several days.

No, what Cooper *would* undoubtedly use to his own advantage over her at some point was the personal value it represented to her. He was always looking for leverage over the people he had dealings with, especially in the last year since everything had seemed to be going wrong.

The latter was a necessary evil she might have to deal with on some level sooner or later when he'd try to cash in, but the former was what she was banking on.

She waited patiently while he turned several more pages, studying them as if she wasn't even there until he finally sat back in his chair, crossing his arms over his chest.

"Love, do you know what this is?"

"Well, you *did* teach me to read."

Shifting toward him slightly, she began leafing through the tome. Roughly in the middle, she stopped and showed him a map of the Northern Forest. This was a part of the book she'd been looking at very intently because it depicted the place where they lived.

The woods around the castle were marked with specs of gold, and there was a golden ring in one place where the glistening specs were most prominent.

"Every map in this is marked with symbols, but I haven't been able to figure most of them out yet." Catherine tapped a finger on the markings in the woods, *their* woods. "This says there are *Fairyflies* in the forest near here – but what are Fairyflies? What can they do, what do they have to do with me, and how do I find them?"

Barking a hearty laugh, he slapped his hand on the table, stirring the crockery so that the earthenware clinked. "Well, this is a very old book," he snorted, "and I hate to disappoint you, but there's no such thing as Fairyflies. Not anymore. They've been extinct for decades."

She frowned. The year was now 1497, and the first page of the book had the date 1437 on it. Her mathematical abilities were sufficiently developed to tell her that the sum difference was sixty years.

Studying the partial key at the back of this book and then localizing the symbols it held and all the others as she had been doing over the last months, she was sure Fairyflies had been widespread throughout the kingdom and beyond. As a matter of fact, the golden flecks representing them were to be found in almost every forest inked in the entire work, which would have made them quite a common species.

She'd never heard anyone speak of Fairyflies. How could they have been stamped out of existence so completely and without a trace in that time?

Goblins and Shapeshifters had existed in these parts centuries ago, as the Cine had, but they were monsters, and dangerous to humans and Cine alike, she'd been told, just as Fairypeople had been dangerous to everyone but their own kind. The Church had set up guidelines for dealing with them, and they'd been eradicated from the civilized world.

She'd even seen an actual Dwarve on the back of a hangman's cart one day, heading for his execution for being an Unnatural. They'd claimed he'd brought illness and misfortune upon the places he'd traversed on his journey by his mere presence, and they'd put him to death in the same manner in which they dealt with Cine or human witches and blasphemers.

No one had ever mentioned Fairyflies to her before, though, and she began to wonder if the author of this book had managed to confuse reality and superstition. Or, perhaps she'd misinterpreted, and this was a book of tales, rather than of the history of her ancestors' people.

She wasn't familiar with the names of the other creatures the author had troubled himself to pen beside their symbols on the key either. Grottlins, for instance, were marked as endemic to parts of the mountainous fiefdom *Sunderland*, and there were beings known as Nightsoarers in the lowlands of a place mapped as *The Valleys*. The writer hadn't gotten round to identifying the other species he'd marked on the maps with various pictograms at all, and try as she might, she couldn't put meaning to them.

There were no pictures of Grottlins or Nightsoarers or Fairyflies in either this book or the other one, so she had no way of finding out about them except to ask the only person she thought might know. She'd started with the Fairyflies since they seemed most common.

"Extinct...?" she pondered. "Real, but extinct?"

"Yes, they were real. Very frightening, very deadly, and very real. *Extinct* means they no longer exist, darling. Probably like every other creature named in this book. Some of these places don't even exist anymore."

"So, they once *did* exist in *this* place?" She tapped her finger on the map of the Northern Forest. "All of the symbols on this page stand for beings that existed – *here*?"

"Maybe." He looked slightly bemused, and she found that irritating.

"What manner of magical creature were Fairyflies, and *who* eradicated them?"

He sighed, his fingers toying with a piece of lint on the table before him.

"They were said to be tiny demons in the guise of the most beautiful, winged elves. Eyes the color of emeralds, ears like those of a cat, teeth sharp as those of a rat."

He got up and walked over to the window to look out. He seemed sad for a moment. "Their true nature was hidden beneath the very appearance of innocence, but they were thoroughly evil. If you encountered them in the woods, they'd mislead you, and you'd never find your way back home." He paused, and then his voice became hard and cruel as he turned to face her. "They were hunted and exterminated in most every kingdom like the vermin they were by *us*. Well, by *humans*." He let that sink in for a moment, but she didn't know whether she should take offense or not.

"Did you ever come across one?" she cautiously ventured.

"Me? No… but my father was lost to their kind." Another image passed before Catherine's inner eye because the old farmer was so caught up in the memory.

His recollection of a king's knight came rushing at her without warning.

She saw a man on horseback in leather armor and heavily armed. He had the look of a mercenary. His wife and sons were seeing him off from their family home.

"Do as your mother says," the man told his smallest son sternly, and Catherine recognized the boy as young Cooper.

He wiped the snot from his nose with his sleeve, and the man tossed a penny at him. He wasn't quick enough, and the copper fell into the mud. Crouching down to retrieve it, he watched his father ride off.

Catherine wondered what had become of Cooper's father, because this was where the vision ended, and she was expelled from his mind as abruptly as she'd found herself drawn into it. Possible he'd just left them. People were generally inclined to do that kind of thing, and those who remained behind needed somewhere to lay the blame.

Catherine didn't think any manner of *unnatural creature* was born to this world *evil*, not the way Cooper meant it.

Fairyflies probably weren't any more *evil* than the wolves or the vipers hiding beneath the bushes during the day – but they weren't *good* either. She didn't quite know what they were. *Fair*, perhaps, though she didn't know what moral standards they assumed for themselves, or who made their rules, any more than she could say what drove wolves to hunt or vipers to bite instead of flee if you stepped on them.

Perhaps Fairyflies were only dangerous to those who were afraid of the dark, deep down inside, because knowing they were there would mean risking a bite if you didn't know how to tread carefully enough.

"Was there proof that Fairyflies actually killed your father?"

"Look, how is this important to you?" Cooper snapped. He was getting agitated as he turned to her, his eyes flashing dangerously. She wondered if he was very afraid of the dark. She was almost certain of it.

"It's not, really," she said, "but there are a lot of things in this book that are new to me, and I want to find out about them."

He appeared to understand that and regained his natural quiescence, somewhat. Oddly, his mien never betrayed what lay within for long. In that, he was unlike most people she knew.

Standing beside her, he began leafing through the tome again, stopping at a page with a map of the river delta around a stronghold called *Rathsbridge*. The meandering watercourse that was carved deep into the surrounding countryside and parts of the narrow delta were marked with blue triangles and a wavy line beneath them in places.

"Legend has it there used to be Streampeople here," he mused, studying the ink rendering. "They were said to have the Ability to command the tides of the river and the direction of the water flow. The millers blamed them for their losses when arms of the river went dry and their livelihood along with it."

Thumbing on through the pages, he found another map of the woods around a large fortress and town named *Trondenburgh*. The topographical overview of the woods were speckled with black circular symbols containing what resembled a side view of a set of pointy-toothed jowls.

"Shapeshifters," the old farmer informed her pointedly without having to look at the key. "Whole clans of vicious, murdering Unnaturals that were hunted to the last individual. They were said to take on human shape during the day and walk among men as though they *were* men, mating with humans and bringing forth half-breeds that were bound to the full moon and couldn't change at will like their forefathers."

He paused, waiting for a reaction, but she didn't speak.

Browsing onward, he randomly stopped when he'd found a kingdom labeled *Vaygard,* and pointed at what looked like an omega turned topside over the castle.

"Travelers. They look like humans and act like humans, but they're one kind of the Cine said to have the Ability to travel miles in split seconds. The royal family of Vaygard was charged and found guilty of conspiring with the Devil, and the entire family was wiped out – that was just before the Cine were declared Unnaturals."

On another map, he showed her a symbol he knew to stand for *Trolls*, and a few pages on, he directed her attention toward the magical properties of trees said to grow in that area. Then, he snapped the book shut.

"Intriguing stuff, isn't it?" he smirked, straightening up and slowly moving to stand behind her. "But… about your Fairyflies, and all the other *fascinating* beings in your *fascinating* book…"

She felt him putting his hands on her shoulders, kneading them almost affectionately as he put his lips to her ear.

"You'd do well to remember that those are things you shouldn't mention to anyone else, love. Be advised to keep your heirloom and your lineage to yourself, unless you want to die young."

She hated him touching her, but she stood her ground nonetheless. "I think I can keep a secret."

Cooper sighed. "I do believe you can," he murmured, his hot breath making her skin crawl. A shiver ran down her spine as he slid one of his hands in under the neckline of her dress, moving downward.

Her involuntary squirming seemed to arouse him, and she could feel his excitement building as his fingers touched her breast, cupping and caressing her tenderly at first before grasping her more firmly. Her jaw clenched, and she went rigid.

"I also know you're always good for a surprise," he continued, encouraging her to stand and bend over the table as he pulled up her skirts, his hands all over her, "and who knows where this will end? I *do* love surprises."

Fleeing the cabin an hour later, she already regretted that she'd left him the book to see if he could find other things that looked familiar. He'd insisted, and she'd had enough of him. She'd have had to grab it from his hands if she'd wanted to take it with her, and she hadn't felt like giving him that kind of power over her.

She'd been right, in any case: he did know a lot about the Unnaturals, but she'd be paying extra tuition if she wanted him to share his knowledge.

Rebecca's brand of magic hadn't helped her with that today, and that was another thing she regretted. She was certain it was worth it, but she was also certain things needed to change when this was over very radically before the blight spread much farther than it already had.

Chapter Twenty-Two

∽ The Snow Globe ∾

Bending over his workbench and the transparent three-quarters sphere of blown glass from the Winter Mountains, the Master Sorcerer took a deep breath and held it briefly. He had to admit to himself that he was afraid for what he was giving up, but he'd come too far to turn back now.

Lorcan's vision was coming true in his hands, and his father's dream was, too. The Snow Globe was almost completed, and it would protect his people more effectively than he could ever hope to do with the cloaking enchantments he cast every time The Fair moved. This was so much more than a cloaking spell.

He was aware he might lose his Abilities if he poured too much of himself into this. His father's book was quite clear about the consequences, but he wasn't afraid. He didn't fear the personal repercussions that would go with the sacrifice; what he did fear was the loss of control over a magic others could so easily abuse if it fell into the wrong hands.

Still, he saw no other way, and he had an idea of the *right* hands he would like to place the Globe in for safe-keeping when it was finished. Aoife of Ironstone would take good care of his life's work until the insanity of this new world his grandparents wouldn't have recognized had ceased, and humaneness and common sense were in place again. He still held hopes for mankind.

Slowly releasing the breath he'd been holding into the clear orb, the words he'd memorized from the open text next to him called upon the first of the elements this world was made of, and the Globe filled with the essence of its magic – his *Cine* magic.

It took more out of him than he'd thought it would, and he felt the waning of his powers like the pains of sudden exertion. Realizing there was no time to lose, he quickly added in echoes of the other three elements: fine soil from the fields of Ironstone, black volcanic ashes from an active crater in the Middlelands, and water from the deep blue seas of the Taigean Ocean.

Flurries of color churned dynamically in a kaleidoscope of luminescence, and the Sorcerer smiled wearily.

This was what he'd hoped for.

It felt right.

It was done.

The drifting particles settled into tones of silver and white, glittering sparkles and swirls that reminded him of snow. He was more than pleased with the result as he fitted the carefully crafted ceramic base into the Globe, watching the enchanted flakes coast about until he was sure the special seal of plaster he'd applied would hold. He discovered there wasn't an ounce of regret anywhere within, and eventually, he turned his creation the right way over to observe a carpet of white descending upon the silent hillside where the miniature model of his ancestors' castle stood.

He'd sculpted the small-scale landscape on the ceramic from a mere childhood memory, detailing it with the images his father's stories had imprinted in his mind and the hopes he had for the future. Doing this had been like a long journey back in time that he'd both loved and dreaded for the intensity of the recollections it had evoked as he'd worked in tiny scraps of the copper ore his father had extracted from the mines, and mineral sands from the Winter Mountains. He'd loved his father's dream, and he'd been dreaming it every bit as determinedly as the Magician had, almost as though it had been his own from the very beginning.

He had made it his own over time.

Something stirred, and he looked up. His son stood in the doorway of the cluttered attic room, a blanket wrapped around himself. Summer was over, and the nights were getting chilly.

"Can I help?" Dean inquired, his copper locks askew.

The Master Sorcerer's lips curved upward, but he shook his head as he reached out a welcoming hand to his son. "No, thank you, I'm almost finished. Come and see."

Dragging a stool up next to his father's, Dean plopped down, drawing his legs up and hugging his knees as he studied the Snow Globe in silence.

"This is going to protect The Fair, isn't it?"

"It is, even when I'm not around." Ortus was confident about that.

He hadn't managed to finalize all of the protective mechanisms because he didn't have all of his father's books, but most of the spells he'd used would suffice. They weren't as strong or as active as they might have been if he'd had more of an idea of what was in the books he was missing, but he believed what he was doing would take The Fair's wards eons beyond anything they'd had before, even if something happened to him. Most every enchantment ended when the Cine who'd cast it left this earth, but this one wouldn't, because it was made of everything the earth was made of.

Shaking the glass lightly as he turned it, Ortus held it up for Dean to see the effects of the shimmering fragments' synergy. There had never been a thing like this in all the realm, and the longing look of fascination reflecting upon his open-mouthed child's face alone was worth the years he'd put into this project. Dean was mesmerized by the magical snowstorm inside the Globe, and the Sorcerer knew it wouldn't stop for as long as he stared into the churning blizzard. Dean's unadulterated wonder fed the dynamics. Ortus thought he might lose himself in the imagery of the glass just as easily if he allowed himself to, and his gaze wandered between his son and the Globe.

Finally giving himself a jolt, he set the orb on the worktop.

"It's so beautiful," the boy breathed, and Ortus picked up the round ornate box he'd carved from maplewood to form a sturdy foot for the Snow Globe.

Lorcan had spent the last weeks scraping and shaping miniscule ivy leaves and rose buds from the well-dried piece of lumber, fashioning tendrils and shoots that wound upward to where the glass would go. The lad had done a fine job.

When Ortus placed the sphere between the tendrils of leaves and blossoms, he was relieved to find that it fit perfectly. You could never be sure how or in what way magic would affect the properties of a solid object, but nothing seemed amiss.

Slowly waving his hand over the Globe and the box, he softly intoned a string of words from an ancient language his father had taught him. He repeated them over and over until a faint light emanated from his palm, reflecting onto the smooth surface of the Globe. Gradually, as the flakes absorbed the additional energy, they gently began to counter-spin as Ortus directed them, each particle dancing with silver refraction until the whole swirling flurry within the perfect sphere had absorbed the magic from the Sorcerer's nimble fingers and created a light of its own.

Heat radiated from the glass sphere, softening the maple base it rested in, and the delicate carvings began to quiver and draw inward to cradle the glowing ball into the tiny vines, adhering to the outer glass, fixing themselves as tightly as moss burrowing into to the miniscule pores and crevices of the mortar in a stone wall. Here and there, some of the diminutive wooden rosebuds burst open into perfect blooms, releasing the sweet fragrance of maple sap and summer. Winding up the glass surface about half way in three places, the stems and shoots looked as though they were stretching their flowers toward the sun.

As the magic settled and the Globe cooled, its brightness faded into a weaker glow. Taking hold of it once more, Ortus turned it over to reveal the music box fixed to the bottom inside. He brought forth an unusually formed key from his pocket and set it in the rose-shaped lock at the front of the wooden base and turned it, winding the music box. A melody started playing. It was the one he'd spent his childhood listening to, and Dean also knew it from the crib.

The boy startled when he recognized it. Ortus couldn't quite tell whether the surprised look on his son's face was hurt or happiness, but the moment of uncertainty passed as the music played, and what could have been a flicker of pain yielded to the familiar kind of comforting warmth he felt himself imbibed in whenever he heard the tune.

His own father had obtained the filigree mechanism it came from through bargaining with a gifted Dwarven silversmith in the Winter Mountains. Skilled in the art of crafting the most delicate moving parts for inventions beyond imagining, the craftsman hoarded his secrets for almost a century now, as Ortus knew, and he'd leave many breathtaking things to the afterworld.

This particular music box was unique and irreplaceable, and it had always been one of the Sorcerer's most prized personal possessions. He'd been much younger than Dean when his father had brought it home in a small polished pentagonal box. It had played its tune by his bedside each night before he'd gone to sleep, just as it had played for Dean, decades later. They'd both listened to the gently rising and falling notes night after night and year after year, and it reminded father and son of the same things. Ortus recalled how his mother had hummed along every now and then, just as Gwyneth had loved to do when Dean had come along. There were times when he'd swear he could still hear her voice.

Ortus wished Gwyneth had been here to see this. He'd been wrong to keep his other world from her, he could see that now, but he'd been so worried about his human family. He'd failed to see how the challenge might have strengthened them all.

Dean had grown with the task over the past year, although he was as much a dreamer as he'd ever been. His ability to dream was one of the very things he loved so much about him, but Ortus understood that this was probably also what would make his heart so vulnerable to the hard, cruel realities he'd be met with before long.

He'd need a good friend to help him through all that, and he hoped Lorcan might fill the role, if they ever managed to become friends.

When the music stopped, he smiled at his son.

Dean was resting his head on his arms. "Tell me again how exactly this will work, father."

Ortus was tired, but there was nothing more important than answering Dean's questions. He'd ignored them far too long.

"See this?" he said, running two fingers lightly over the glass. "It's glass from the Winter Mountains, one of the most secret places in this world, and only the craftsmen there can blow an orb like this."

Ortus gave the Globe a gentle shake, and the flurries of magic started whirling through the miniature landscape of the Inner Haven and the sky above it again.

"It looks so fragile, but it's not, really, when you consider what it would take to crush it."

He placed a palm on either side of it, fingers splayed, and pushed. Dean looked on in horror, but nothing happened, and Ortus handed him the Globe to try for himself. The boy was fearful at first, but he soon realized he couldn't possibly crush it with his hands, no matter how he strained. Finally, he handed it back.

The Sorcerer set it aside and rummaged through the shelf above the workbench for the candle glass he'd been using for his experiments before he'd had the orb. He lit one of the slender white candles from the drawer underneath the tabletop, placed it in the metal holder he'd made for the purpose and turned the glass over on it. The room instantly grew brighter.

"The people of the Winter Mountains discovered that their glass can amplify spells like ordinary glass will enhance the light of a candle," he explained, gazing into the buttery glow. "The enchantment is intensified by the breaking of light magic on the particles and its reflection. It becomes much more radiant than it was before; its volume is increased *hundredfold*. And, if the enchantment is done correctly, it can project the conditions of the model onto a real place, connecting one with the other. So, the protective spell I've cast on the Snow Globe tonight is a hundred times stronger when it's applied to The Fair."

He didn't know if he was breaking down the correlations sufficiently so Dean would understand, but when the boy nodded, encouraging him to go on, he felt his attempts validated.

"There really isn't much more to it, but this is so much better than casting temporary cloaking spells or building walls that can break; a spell of this kind is much stronger, and it's by far more durable than stone or iron could ever be."

The Sorcerer was sure that even a king with ten armies could never have taken his ancestors' castle if his father had had the time to complete this.

Then Dean surprised him. "But that means it's *just* meant to keep harm out, like the cloaking spells you're using now, doesn't it?"

"*Just* to keep harm out?" he asked back, and Dean grinned. "It's far more than that. It's more than just a cloaking spell – it creates a new dimension where The Fair is completely detached from the space it should be occupying in this world."

"I know that's already a whole lot," he returned, "but it doesn't make the bad intentions on the outside go away. It's like a hedgehog rolling up when the fox comes round, or am I wrong?"

The Sorcerer smiled. "If that were all, it would be like that, yes," he admitted, "but there's more. What you see inside the Snow Globe isn't bound to *one* dimension or *one* particular place."

He motioned his son to take another look, and to Dean's amazement, the Globe's imagery changed.

The scene depicted within now showed a narrow valley nestling between rolling green hills. A bandy-legged man in rough garb herded a flock of highland sheep toward a cold, blue loch. The sun had barely risen and hung low in a waking sky of orange hues, and as young and inexperienced in matters of magic as he was, the boy comprehended the scope of a magic that could transport an entire group of people to the far reaches of the world in the blink of an eye.

Before this, they'd had to use a Portal that could only accommodate one or two travelers at a time, carrying what they could from one side of the gateway to the other. This new enchantment could be triggered by someone capable of creating a Portal, someone like Mary, and it would take the entire Fair to a new location in one instant.

"It's still hedgehogging, though," Dean persisted after a moment. "Taking the hedgehog out of harm's reach won't make the fox go away. There are foxes in every forest."

The Sorcerer chortled a laugh. Dean had really put some thought into this over the last months. He wouldn't be fobbed off with less than a feasible solution to the problem at hand, but the trouble was that Ortus didn't have the fitting answer to everything just yet. There was so much that needed dealing with, he wasn't fighting yet at this stage – he was merely trying to survive and ensure that as many of their kind as possible did, too.

"You've got a point." He paused, leaning back in his chair and folding his arms across his chest. "But, being out of harm's way will give our people a place to be without fear, a place to heal and recover, and learn to harness their powers. Having a home, having a community that's as strong as all that will make them brave enough to start fighting for their rights when… when the time comes."

When and *if* the time ever came when they stood a chance, he meant to say, but bit back the words. There weren't enough of them left, and they might never recover from the slaughters of the past decades. They didn't fit in with the majority's ideas, and they were feared and hated for their disparity. Tolerance wasn't a thing you could impose or gain by force, and it took so little to uproot it.

He hoped things would settle down again, one day. If his vision came true the Cine would be living in plain sight of the humans at The Fair, but out of reach of anyone set on destroying them. That put them in the position of having choices and controlling their fate. If people started believing in the good of magic again and stopped making them responsible for everything that went wrong, if they saw things they liked, then they'd come round sooner or later, and their kind wouldn't be contingent on the whims of a ruler. They wouldn't have to hide anymore, or *hedgehog*, as Dean put it. When this madness was over, they'd live alongside the humans again, as they had a thousand years before.

Ortus was fairly certain he wouldn't live to see that day, but he thought Dean might.

Chapter Twenty-Three

⟡ Blood ⟡

Going back and forth between The Fair and his house by magic was growing arduous and Ortus was tired, especially since he'd had two to cater for on this trip and he'd never been good with the rudimentary Portals he could cast.

Dean had no idea how using his powers drew on him now, and that was how he wanted it. It was the price he'd known he'd have to pay at some stage, but the Sorcerer didn't regret a single thing as he quietly walked the perimeter of The Fair's Outer Haven in the descending night.

The circumference he'd traced with his steps glowed golden on the ground. When he'd made sure it was perfect and complete, he continued uphill until he reached a place that overlooked the entire little valley he'd chosen with Mary and Thaddeus for their first trials.

Gazing down on the peaceful encampment by the light of the full moon, he was happy with what he'd achieved over the last years. He didn't think there was any great discontent among the people he'd brought together here, shady artefact-and-talisman folk aside.

People were what they were everywhere, and there would always be some who'd go against the grain or claim they'd rather be elsewhere. Between himself and Thaddeus, they'd done a lot of weeding over time – thieves and the like – but the truth was that most of the Cine didn't have anywhere else to go. Whatever baggage they'd brought with them when they'd come looking for or stumbled upon this community, they'd be carrying a part of it for the rest of their lives. Ortus always tried to bear this in mind before he resorted to the last measure of asking someone to leave, or throwing them out.

Despite his dreaminess, Dean had developed well and was quite comfortable with his people. Ortus was confident he'd handle himself and The Fair's Cine and human relations when the time came. He was accepted and liked already, and it was clear Dean would follow in his footsteps one day.

What Dean sorely lacked was Cine Talent. He had the basic Ability to slow other people's perception of time, but this wasn't enough to earn him the lasting recognition of his kind because there was nothing else besides. Late in emerging, even this Gift hadn't notably increased in its qualities for Dean.

Not that this mattered, not one little bit; Dean could have been human, for all Ortus cared. Ortus had married a human for love, and he loved Dean for himself, and not for what he might have been. However, that meant his son would need stability and continuity in matters of security for The Fair, and a friend who had what he lacked to have his back. The most promising of the Talented here was Lorcan Aurum, and one day soon, Lorcan would be the kind of man Dean would need to have on his side, and not against him.

It also meant the Sorcerer would have to hurry along the last lengths of the journey he'd begun while the moon was full and before winter was upon them again. He'd need to seal the connection between the Inner and the Outer Havens tonight, and when that was done, he had to get the Globe to Ironstone. The longer he waited, the more difficult the roads would become, and Ironstone was a long ride away.

Inhaling the cool night air, he was sure he was alone on the hillside until he suddenly realized he wasn't. Purring around his legs was a kitten too small to be out all on its own, and he instinctively bent to pick her up.

"Look at you," he said, and the beige feline with the chunky paws and huge ears struggled upward for a more comfortable position.

He thought he saw the merest suggestion of silver in her eyes, and was fascinated for a moment because he'd never seen a kitten with it before, but then he decided it was just his own reflecting back at him. Tensing and writhing, she unintentionally scratched his hand with her tiny, needle-sharp claws as he attempted to aid her in climbing up to rest on his shoulder. A drop of blood formed on his wrist, but he hardly noticed.

"Where did you come from, darling?"

As if in answer, she mewed at him accusingly, eying him with an almost comical, challenging earnestness. Eventually, she seemed satisfied with what she assumed to have conveyed and settled down, nestling into the crock of the Sorcerer's neck.

He supposed she might have lost her mother and found herself in need of some warmth and food. The warmth he could provide for a while right now, but the food would have to wait.

"I've got some work to do, but I wouldn't mind company," he told the kitten, and she commenced purring, rubbing her head against his jaw in approval.

He smiled, but he didn't think she'd stick around when he carefully detached her tiny claws from the fabric of his coat and set her down so he could retrieve the Snow Globe from his satchel. The little creature surprised him by staying exactly where he put her, watching him patiently as he took the Globe from the cloth he'd wrapped around the glass for protection. She cautiously sniffed the satchel and burrowed inside of it, disappearing from sight for a second before her head reemerged. Briefly studying him, she curled up near the opening, still purring.

Turning his attention back to the Globe with a smile on his lips, Ortus held the sphere up and shook it slightly, observing the glistening magical snowflakes within as they began churning, reflecting the light of the moon that was now high in the sky. When the liquid inside the glass cleared, he could see a perfect mirror of the fairground as it lay before him tonight down in the valley: this was the Inner Haven.

The dozens of tents in the Inner Haven were detailed models of those that housed the little Cine community; each of them different, each of them telling of the individual characters they sheltered. The Big Top rose on the south end with booths sprinkled all around it and the animal pens behind it. Swedish Fires marked an aisle to the main entrance. The Snake Sisters' yurt was dimly lit on the west side of the compound, and his own square marquee on the east side where the first rays of sun woke him whenever he and Dean spent the night there.

Taking a small knife from his pocket, his unsheathed it with his teeth and let the leather scabbard fall to the ground. Tucking the Globe between his arm and his belly, he swiftly nicked his left hand with the blade.

Scarlet runnels of blood formed on the palm, seeping from a wound he knew he'd have to sew. He might no longer have the power to close it any other way after tonight. Holding it out in front of him, fingers to the fore, he gently blew on it.

Millions of tiny crimson droplets dispersed out toward The Fair like a ghostly mist. It was hardly visible once it had found its way into the floating particles of oxygen, water, and dust, mingling with the air.

A sudden lack of light made Ortus look up at the sky, and he saw that although nothing else seemed to have changed, the haze had tainted the silver of the moon's face. Its glow had taken on a deep shade of red. He hadn't expected this, and stood staring at it for a time before he noticed that the blood from his hand was dripping all over the kitten. He clenched his fingers to a fist around the cloth he'd used to wrap the Globe. His mouth had gone dry, but there was no time to be lost by searching for his flask for a drink of water, so he licked his lips, cleared his throat, and held the Globe up in his good hand, concentrating on it. The snowflakes inside had turned the same color as the moon.

"Blood of my ancestors," he softly recited from the book without taking his eyes off the glass, "and blood of my blood, I call upon thee to salvage and deliver, to shelter and to protect the spirit of these outcasts for as long as it will exist within the community of the Cine. A space within the space will be home to the homeless, hope to the hopeless, and a haven to the persecuted. No human with ill intent and nothing made by humans with ill intent to harm one of our own will enter the Haven's boundaries or penetrate the layered folds of the place within the place."

He felt faint all at once, and he almost dropped the Globe. The kitten protested woefully when he barely avoided stepping on her, and her cry startled him enough to secure the Globe, but he stumbled and fell backward, landing on his rear. The kitten was upon him immediately, pressing herself against his hands and whatever else of him she could rub her head on. He smiled wearily at the dilapidated thing.

"Silly Sorcerer nearly shatters the Globe he's spent all of his energies creating," he mumbled. Then, something else occurred to him.

What if the glass ever did break? He'd told Dean it couldn't, but even this special glass had its weaknesses.

"Shatters the Globe…" he repeated, and then a little more loudly, smearing his blood on the glass. "Shatters the Globe, then bring back the magic to itself and to its people. Gather the shards and gather the people. Seek the seekers so the seekers can seek. Find the key so the key can be found."

The blood soaked through the surface as though solid matter didn't represent a barrier at all and vanished within the reality inside of the orb. The moon returned to its normal color, and the kitten fell asleep.

Chortling a laugh, Ortus allowed himself to lie back for a few moments. He realized he was just as much in need of a rest as the little creature he'd picked up.

The sun had already touched the horizon by the time he was able to rise, and he nearly forgot about his new little friend. The tiny furball tumbled off of him stiffly but soon regained her feet. Yawning, and stretching out her limbs beside him, she watched as he stuffed the Globe back into his satchel, mindful to keep his injured hand covered.

The wound was throbbing, and he thought he'd have to do something about that, but not before he'd woken Dean and spoken to Jaden about Lorcan accompanying them to Ironstone. It was time the boys got to know each other a little better.

Chapter Twenty-Four

❦ The Shelter ❧

Silvery-glistening hoar frost crusted the grass on the field where Lorcan was busy in the goat pen. In passing, Ortus observed him shoveling the last of the night's muck from the new shelter he'd helped Thaddeus build some days earlier. The lad nodded at the Sorcerer in a friendly good morning, and Ortus nodded back, smiling, but he didn't stop to chat. He had business with Jaden.

Jaden's tent was quiet, and he had to call twice before the man emerged, half-stooping out to see who was demanding his attention.

"Get some clothes on, we need to talk," he told the Illusionist.

Jaden grumbled, but retreated compliantly to fetch his things. He reappeared a few moments later in a crumpled shirt and breeches, tugging on his boots, alternately hopping on one foot and then the other before throwing a cloak over his shoulders. Sleep still clung heavily to his dull eyes, and Ortus could smell wine on him.

"What's the hurry at this hour?"

"Let's take a short walk." Ortus was already striding ahead, and Jaden made haste to catch up.

"I've got business to take care of in the north, and I'll be taking your son along."

"What? Why?" Jaden wrapped his cloak tighter around himself. "Take your own boy along, or can he not sit in the saddle? You only need *one* squire."

"And you need *none*."

Jaden was outraged. "He's my son, and I say whether he goes with you or not."

Ortus stopped to study the other man. He knew Jaden had put Lorcan out of the tent when Maebh had moved in a while ago. The boy had slept out in the open all summer and into the fall until the weather had turned, and he suspected Lorcan now spent the nights at the goat shelter.

Jaden had no idea what Lorcan was capable of and what he might be setting in motion by treating him the way he did. Darkness thrived where shadows fell, and there was just as much potential in Lorcan for darkness as there was in Jaden. But, Lorcan was still young. There was more to Lorcan than what his father was and what Jaden had contributed to his existence, and Ortus held the deepest regard for the boy.

The Sorcerer didn't believe Jaden still had a right to decide where his son went, and he hadn't come to ask Jaden's permission to take Lorcan along – he'd merely come to inform him of the intention.

"Well, since you never paid for tuition or apprentice's dues, we'll just call it quits when he gets back, shall we?" he suggested.

Jaden was about to protest, but then changed his mind. Grumbling to himself, the man turned on his heel and marched off.

When Ortus got back to the pen, Lorcan had already fed the goats fresh hay, and he was refitting the door latch on the shelter so it would close more firmly. The sun was higher in the sky now, and it warmed away the frost on the grass.

Looking at the shelter, the Master Sorcerer thought the goats would be well taken care of for the winter – but the boy wouldn't. He'd need a tent of his own, or a tent to share, at least. Tents were in short supply at the moment because they'd had so many newcomers. Families with children always came first, and Lorcan was at an age where he was neither quite a man yet, nor a child anymore. Ortus didn't think Thaddeus knew how to handle the situation, and he'd have to speak to him when he got back. Either that, or he'd start handling this himself.

"That's looking good," Ortus told him when he was done with the latch. Lorcan looked at his feet, and it irritated the Sorcerer. "You keep doing that, son, but you really should look people in the eye. You apply yourself to everything you do, and you're smart. You have many Talents, Lorcan. Keep that chin up."

Half a smile tugged at the corners of the lad's mouth, and he fixed his gaze to Ortus'.

"The night watchmen said they've seen wolves around the grounds over the last week."

This didn't surprise Ortus. When the weather turned cold, all manner of predators became braver. The shelter might keep the beasts and the worst of the cold and ice out at night, but the longer the winter, the more likely it would be the wolves would come by day and take what they needed right from under their very noses.

Ortus had never been able to design wards that could hold off natural predators. Animals didn't bear ill will toward anyone or anything. They just tried to survive, and their instincts told them how. The new protections wouldn't respond to a few wolves wanting dinner, or a hungry fox coming for the hens to feed its cubs if someone had forgotten to lock up the coop at night.

"Well, then I suppose we'll have to post more guards," the Sorcerer mused. "But that won't be your concern over the next weeks. You'll have something better to do."

Lorcan tilted his head questioningly.

Ortus smiled. "I finished the Snow Globe."

Lorcan's eyes widened, and Ortus thumped his shoulder.

"The base you made fits the glass perfectly," he continued. "I cast the new enchantments last night, so all we need to do now is bring the Inner Haven to a place where no one will ever find it. We're going on a little trip."

"We?"

"We. You're coming along. You and Dean. It's time you got to know each other better. He's going to need your help, you know."

Ortus could see Lorcan didn't understand that right now, but he would. Things would start coming together once they were underway.

"Can I see the Globe?"

"Not here." The Fair was coming to life, and this was not for everybody to see. Also, now that he stood next to Lorcan, he decided the boy would need a bath and a new set of decent clothes before they saddled up, or they wouldn't be let inside the town walls of Ironstone. "Let's see if we can get some breakfast, and we'll discuss everything."

Seeing the sparkle in Lorcan's eyes, he was sure he was doing the right thing by both boys – and by The Fair.

Chapter Twenty-Five

ᘓ Bonding ᙙ

"So, what is it that you do again, exactly?" Dean asked Lorcan, but Lorcan didn't answer right away.

The boys' horses trotted a little way ahead of Ortus. This was Dean's first long trip in the saddle, and Lorcan hadn't spent much time on horseback before either, so traveling through the wooded highlands was slow going and taxing.

Neither of the boys had felt much like conversation after they'd left The Fair, but Ortus was confident they'd gradually warm to each other's company. Discovering they had some common ground helped. Their sore behinds from the long days in the saddle was their current shared misery, and they'd also started bonding against him over their mutual dislike for the unsweetened oatmeal he made them for breakfast every morning.

Despite the grousing, his own aching bones, and the realization that this was going to be his last long trip, the Master Sorcerer was glad he hadn't asked Mary to open a Portal for them. She could have gotten all three of them there easily and saved them a lot of time – they'd have walked in on their side of the Lightgate and emerged in Ironstone the next instant –

but this journey was all about *time*. The weeks they'd spend together were going to be invaluable for the boys' learning and for his own peace of mind.

Tethering The Fair to the Inner Haven had cost him years of his life, but he was determined to make good on his promise to Gwyneth and prepare Dean for his responsibilities – Dean and Lorcan.

"Well?" Dean insisted.

Lorcan scratched his shoulder. It was a gesture Ortus had become familiar with. Lorcan always did that when he wasn't sure if he was saying too much or being rude.

"I can create illusions," he finally admitted, summing up a part of what he was capable of.

"Is that all?"

Ortus knew Dean's reaction hadn't been intended the way it sounded, but Lorcan didn't seem to take offense. The next moment, however, something resembling a boa constrictor appeared directly on the path ahead.

The creature was twice the size of any of the Snake Sisters' *little darlings,* and it was made of a bluish-green translucent light. It grew bigger and bigger by the moment until it had reached the dimensions of a house before bursting like a bubble with a nauseating squelching sound. When it did, the horses shied, throwing both Dean and Lorcan before they bolted. Only old Bessie, Ortus' aging mare, remained calm. She'd seen a lot of things in the course of her long life.

Dismounting, the Master Sorcerer breathed a sigh of relief to see Dean scrambling to his feet completely unhurt and laughing, while Lorcan lay on his back, grinning.

"That was completely incredible!" Dean yelled.

Lorcan drew himself up on his elbows, smug satisfaction written all over his face.

"And completely insane," Ortus roared.

He was furious. How could an intelligent lad like Lorcan be so foolish? "You could have gotten yourself killed! You could have gotten *Dean* killed!"

The smile instantly faded from Lorcan's face, and he rose, beating the dirt from the seat of his pants. They were torn at the knees, and he limped slightly. Astoundingly, Dean didn't seem to have so much as a scratch on his hands.

Ortus was beside himself nonetheless. "You should be ashamed," he went on. "What if someone had seen you? I thought you were smarter than that, but I guess I was wrong." He instantly regretted his words, but couldn't take them back.

Dean went silent, and Lorcan stared at him for a moment before replying.

"I suppose you were," he replied simply.

The hurt in the boy's eyes was almost perfectly concealed behind the stone-cold façade he normally reserved for his father, but the Master Sorcerer could see it burn. It shamed him as the lad turned and walked away from them, adding, "I'll help you get the horses back and be on my way."

Dean looked back and forth between the both of them. He decided to go after Lorcan when Ortus couldn't bring himself to.

Ortus was glad his son had the sense to do that, and he took a moment to get a drink of water from his leather flask. He told himself he was angry at Lorcan, but that wasn't true. Mostly, he was angry at himself. There was a time for everything, and this was Lorcan and Dean's time to be young. It wouldn't be long before they had a great responsibility to shoulder. He had to make sure they understood they could only do this together, and he couldn't afford to lose either of them, but life was all about taking risks and making mistakes. Being young was all about taking risks only to see how things would pan out. He loved these boys, but Dean was the weaker of them, as Lorcan had just effectively demonstrated. All Ortus could do was hope they'd find their common ground, and learn to rely on each other on a different level.

When he was finally ready to go after them, it took him over an hour to catch up. They'd retrieved the horses and were sitting by the roadside, munching on some late blackberries. Nothing seemed amiss between the two, but when Lorcan saw the Sorcerer, he got to his feet and began picking up his things.

"Look, I'm sorry," he told the lad before Dean could say anything. "I don't want you to leave. I still want you with us. I shouldn't have said what I did."

Lorcan stopped what he was doing, but Ortus could see he had a hard time looking at him.

"I was worried. I'm always worried about you boys, but you're doing fine, the both of you." He paused, noticing Dean's brow creasing.

Lorcan faced back to him. If he'd expected another lecture, he wasn't getting it.

"Just don't kill each other before we get to Ironstone, will you?" Ortus closed hesitantly, half in earnest.

Lorcan looked at the ground before him, but then corrected himself and met his gaze firmly before raising a mischievous eyebrow to let him know he'd understood.

Ortus realized the lad would never be a man of many words. He'd seen enough of life to know it was too short for that, but he had more honor and pride in his little finger than his father had in his entire body.

"Kill each other?" Dean grinned when he gathered that his father and Lorcan had regained their status quo. "*He* would wet himself laughing if I tried."

Lorcan thumped him, Dean returned the gesture, and Ortus felt the unreasonable urge to scratch his shoulder.

Later that evening just before he fell asleep, Ortus heard Dean asking Lorcan quietly, "I don't suppose you could teach me to cast an illusion like the one you did today, could you?"

The Master Sorcerer held his breath, hoping for the best.

"No," Lorcan replied matter-of-factly and keeping his voice low. "You're not an Illusionist." He let that sit with Dean for a moment before continuing, and Ortus wondered what was going through his son's mind.

"Aside from what we can all do – you know, slow down other people's perception – every one of us is different in what we can do and how we work our magic, and I don't mean just Cine magic. Humans have magic, too, they just don't know it, most of the time."

Dean hummed. "Yes, but Cine magic is more powerful."

"Says who?" Lorcan returned gruffly. "We can manipulate the different forms of energy. Some of us can move particles or bend an animal's will to their own. I can make you believe you're seeing something that isn't there. So what? How is all of that so different from what humans can do, in the end? It's not, when you think about it. It just seems more *grand*, maybe." Then, he smiled at the younger boy and patted his shoulder. "Don't underestimate yourself. You're a great Artist."

Ortus had no idea whether Lorcan was just trivializing their Abilities for the benefit of a self-doubting friend, or if this was really how Lorcan felt about his magic. By the tone of his voice, he assumed it could be a bit of both. Dean... a great Artist... well, perhaps he would be, one day.

"Being an Illusionist might have been a little more *useful*," Dean grumbled.

Of course it would have been, but things were what they were. Dean had other strengths to draw upon: an open mind, a fearless heart, and a firm resolve to learn. Ortus didn't doubt he'd come up in their little community just fine.

Lorcan snorted a laugh. "Yeah. But I guess we're all just stuck with what we got. Take Rua Tine, for instance. He can't light a cooking fire without burning down his tent. I'll bet he wishes he could draw a picture and then change it with his mind."

Both boys snickered, and Ortus smiled. He wished he'd done this sooner. Perhaps Ironstone wasn't far enough away.

Chapter Twenty-Six

∞ Traveling ∞

With the Middlelands behind them, untended roads and overgrown paths led Ortus and the boys into the southernmost part of the Northern Forest.

Temperatures had dropped below anything comfortable, and Ironstone was still a good two weeks' ride northwest, so the earliest they'd arrive back at The Fair would be around the winter solstice if they didn't dawdle.

Bundled up against the cold with the hoods of their cloaks up and scarves covering the lower half of their faces, the boys were less watchful than they should have been as they rode ahead of him through the foggy woodlands.

They didn't even notice the ruins of the Tierney castle on the hillside until they'd nearly passed them. The irony of this didn't escape Ortus. Fate had a way of quietly pointing out the obvious. The world had changed so much since his father had fled this place, it was almost like they had no business being here. Perhaps the age of the Cine had irrevocably come to an end, and all that was left was to remember.

Ortus believed his father had done everything right, given the choices he'd been facing when he'd fled from his forefathers' stronghold. He'd protected those closest to him when he'd no longer been able to protect the people who'd worked and fought for them. So many people, both humans and Cine, had died. Ortus had witnessed the carnage in the inner courtyard after the king's men had broken through their last defenses. He saw it in his dreams even still.

When his father had gone into hiding and changed his name, it hadn't been for cowardice. He'd done it to keep his family alive. He'd done it to keep *him* alive.

On a whim, Ortus decided to make a detour to the castle. He led the boys away from the old hollow way they'd been paralleling and into the thicket. The desire to find his father's missing books had driven him back here often enough as a young man to remember which of the barely visible trails would lead them to the unkempt cobble road that snaked uphill toward the fortress.

If the trail had been difficult then, it was barely manageable now. Thorny black branches clouted their arms and legs. Dead wood lay decaying in the undergrowth, infecting beeches and pines with rot and fungi. The king of Trondenburgh had done nothing for this land after he'd claimed it. He'd merely razed and abandoned it.

"What is this place?" Lorcan asked, pulling his scarf down off his nose and chin as they passed through a hole in the outer defensive walls into what was left of the village of Tully.

The vestiges of the dwellings nestling around the upper walls of the bailey stood bare and gaping, like dark, demonic skeletons in the mist. They no longer had anything in common with the settlement as it had been before the siege. He'd watched the blaze tear through the village from a window in the keep just before his father had come looking for him to take him to the tunnel. His memory often played back how the flames had fed on the reed roofs and the timber-framed walls of the straw and clay houses.

Crows protested at the Master Sorcerer's presence as he passed the chapel with the boys in his wake. Black eyes watched them from the shells of the disemboweled stone buildings left standing around it.

The beech tree growing next to the little church ruin had tripled in size since he'd last come here. Its mighty boughs hadn't reached halfway to the gables then, but they'd invaded the space above the sanctuary completely over the last decades. Roots that had been below the earth then now strained against the building's cracked foundations, lifting the floor and walls in places.

"This was my father's home," Ortus said quietly, dismounting.

He slowly led his horse to the gatehouse, drinking in the silent gloom of the atmosphere. He almost regretted having brought the boys here, but perhaps they had to see this. Dean and Lorcan followed him through the sloping passageway into the courtyard, where they made halt.

Turning on the spot where he stood, Lorcan glanced around, his eyes wide. Ortus could see he was working it out.

"This is the castle from the Snow Globe," Lorcan mumbled, barely audible and more to himself than the Master Sorcerer or Dean.

Dean was baffled, and Ortus nodded. "It was destroyed during a siege when I was very young."

He recalled the bodies of soldiers and peasants strewn all over the cobble pavement where they stood, and gave himself a moment to banish the imagery from his mind. Then, his gaze caught on a pail on the rim of the walled well.

"Watch yourselves, please. We might not be alone here," he warned the lads and opened the leather thong that secured his dagger inside the sheath.

Dean warily sauntered to the keep's doorway, not taking him too seriously. "How did you get out?"

"By a secret tunnel," Ortus replied, swiftly scanning the courtyard and the black windows of the buildings around him before inspecting the pail.

The pail was nearly new, but fastened to the end of a frayed rope that had seen better days. Both the bucket and the rope were dry, so whoever had left them here hadn't been around, or hadn't been in need of water today.

"Can we see that tunnel?" Dean asked while Lorcan joined Ortus at the well, his eyes searching the compound.

There were no hoof prints in the muddy grass, no droppings on the cobble road or pavement in the yard, no well-worn paths around. Whoever was or had been here was probably alone.

"My father blocked it behind us," Ortus explained, "and I never found the entrance again later."

Lorcan looked at the pail before casting a quick glance down into the well as he considered the Sorcerer's findings. Then, he walked to the keep and pushed past Dean to enter it, signaling him to stay back. "And you and your parents went to Ironstone after that?" he inquired calmly to keep the conversation going.

Ortus hummed absently, his hand on the hilt of his dagger as he went over his options in case of an attack. "Well, my father, my uncle, and I did."

All at once, he thought he saw a shadow scurrying from the servants' quarters toward the gatehouse, but he wasn't certain. It could have been a girl or a young woman, or just a crow swooping low. Whatever it was, it was gone in an instant.

Dean took a peek inside the keep but didn't follow Lorcan.

"What became of your uncle?" Dean asked. "I never met him."

"He died of disease a time after we left Ironstone to go to the Middlelands."

Lorcan reemerged from the building, carrying a raggedy blanket. "Someone is using it as a sleeping place, on and off, at least," he informed them.

Ortus had thought as much, though he no longer believed there was anything really dangerous lurking in the shadows. The only thing they had to fear about this place was the stones coming loose from the crumbling buildings, or falling into one of the sinkholes that had opened up everywhere on the grounds.

Beyond that, angry echoes of the past seemed trapped here, and he felt they weren't welcome. He'd never noticed this before, but although he didn't think anything could purposely hurt them in these ruins, he wasn't inclined to make halt here for the night either.

The girl he'd caught sight of was likely a waif who was just trying to stay alive, and she'd have no interest in confronting them. She'd be scared to death of them and cowering behind a pile of stones somewhere in the bailey, or in the chapel until they left.

"Well, then put that back and let's end this little family history lesson," he told Lorcan. "Best be on our way." Arduously, he pulled himself up in his saddle.

Lorcan frowned. "I'd love to take a closer look around."

Ortus knew what Lorcan was thinking. He'd told him about his hunt for the missing books, and the lad had been fascinated by the prospect of what they might offer.

The Sorcerer often imagined they contained all the missing pieces, the explanations his own journal was lacking, and he wanted nothing more than to see the set complete again, but he believed his father had stowed them away elsewhere, or that someone had found them after the castle had fallen and either destroyed or taken them. A lifetime of searching here and in every library and book binder's workshop between the northern port of Saint Aeden and the southern city of Monksfort had dissuaded his hopes of ever recovering them.

"No. They're not here, Lorcan. There's nothing good here anymore at all – can't you feel that?"

Lorcan chewed on this for a moment, obviously trying to get a sense of what he meant. Dean didn't seem to understand, but that was inconsequential as long as Lorcan did.

Finally, Lorcan looked up at him. "Alright, then. Let's get to Ironstone."

"Tell us about Ironstone," Dean said, heaving himself back up in the saddle, and Ortus was glad for the change of subject, but he waited until they were clear of the bailey and its haunting desolation, as well as the waif who might still be hiding there somewhere.

"Well, Ironstone is a beautiful town," he told them once they were back in the forest. "The queen is descended from a long line of Unnaturals and understands our plight."

"You mean she's Cine?" Dean asked.

Lorcan still seemed distracted.

Ortus looked in his direction to get his attention. "No. *Fairypeople.*"

Lorcan snapped back to the here and now and tilted his head. "Fairypeople? Like Mary?"

Ortus nodded, smiling to himself. "That's right."

Mary had fled north from the Sudlands, just as Jaden and Lorcan had, only twenty years earlier after having lost her husband and young children to the third and final wave of persecutions against Fairypeople in the south. Her people hadn't been as farsighted and politically adept, or as willing to make concessions and forge alliances as the last of the northern families had. They'd fought their wars on battlefields and lost.

"Queen Aoife comes from a long line of Fairypeople. They've always been in Ironstone. They built it."

Dean smirked, shifting his weight in the saddle. "And the humans don't know that?"

Ortus smirked back. "They've forgotten. The northern Fairypeople were always very... human. Most of the Unnaturals living there don't know either, but she protects them. She's denied the Pope's Inquisitor the authority to bring charges against any free citizen of Ironstone, maintaining her right to try any offense committed within the city walls before her own court. The Dwarven are free citizens, and the Cine there are mostly half-human and know how to keep their secret. It's a big town with plenty of byways."

Lorcan thought about this. "The Pope's Inquisitor won't like that much."

Of course he didn't, but Thomas of Ornoa was a fool with a huge area of jurisdiction, and northern noblemen weren't always prepared to pay the costs his trials generated. People were poor here, and selling what little property they had never covered the expenses. Ornoa wasn't disinclined to take the bribes knights and aristocrats paid him *not* to attend their hearings. Of course, that also made Ornoa one of the Pope's least successful witch hunters.

"Oh… it's bound to be a thorn in the Holy Church's all-seeing eye alright."

But, this was Ironstone they were talking about. Ironstone would never fall.

Chapter Twenty-Seven

⍥ Ironstone ⍥

Virtually impenetrable by mechanical war machinery, the huge stronghold of Ironstone stood tall on the steep sloping hillside above the river Leigne. Its thick outer walls molded almost organically to the landscape, as did the high defensive walls of the thriving town nestling at its foot. Both the palace and the town had outlasted many centuries and their feuds, blights, and even the last plague.

The Master Sorcerer stated their business at the western gate, and they entered a labyrinth of well-tended cobble streets that led them past trim houses and two bustling market squares onward into the upper town. Neither Lorcan nor Dean had ever been in a town this size, and Ortus knew they'd have liked to make a few stops along the way, but he wanted to get to the palace.

A stately gatehouse built from limestone blocks marked the end of the commoners' right of way. The massive building had two levels above the portcullis and it was fully manned by archers on the battlements, though most of the guards seemed quite at ease. The Sorcerer showed one of the gatekeepers a coin he'd been given by the queen many years ago and the man let them pass. In the courtyard, two squires took their horses and baggage with the exception of the satchel Ortus insisted on carrying, and another servant led them inside the main building.

The Great Hall was alive with the buzz of guests. Ortus remembered how the house of Ironstone had always welcomed visitors from all over the continent and the Taigean Isles. This was a lot, even for Aoife, but it was good to see things generally hadn't changed here. He hoped they never would.

Two intricately carved oakwood thrones stood empty at the far end of the Hall upon an elevation of polished white marble. The king had passed away over a decade ago, and a merchant from the Winter Mountains had told Ortus of Queen Aoife's resolve never to sit on her own seat again for the loss of his guidance at her side.

This afternoon, she looked anything but lost as she stood amid a sea of chattering people and servants carrying platters of fruit and wine, laughing and talking. He found that he still loved looking at her as much as he ever had, and he watched her for a moment from the Hall's entrance before crossing the floor with Dean and Lorcan in his wake.

Waiting his turn to speak to her, he remembered how they'd played *catch* and *hide and seek* all over the palace and in the garden together as children. He recalled her long chestnut-colored mane falling open about her shoulders when she'd run along the never-ending corridors and arcades, and the way she'd smiled, a mischievous gleam in her eyes. Her hair was white now, and she no longer wore it open, but that playful twinkle was still there in those sky-blue eyes, and he thought she was every bit as stunning as he recalled her. If anything, the years had made her more beautiful. Perception was a strange thing: the good mental images you had of someone who meant a lot to you never faded, never wilted, but tended to grow in color and intensity.

He knew time had taken its toll on him at over sixty. He was an old man at this point in his life, but *old* wasn't the word that would come to mind when he looked at her, and he wondered how she would view him as he bowed when the crowd in their immediate space dispersed. Dean and Lorcan followed his example.

He was sure he'd arrived at the worst possible time for an audience, and he should be lowering his eyes respectfully instead of fixing them to the warm radiance of her gaze, but he couldn't help himself. It had just been too long, and a small wave of regret for the years he'd let pass swept over him.

"Your Majesty," he mumbled, and she made haste to motion him to straighten, letting him know how uncomfortable she was with the gesture, though it was appropriate form. They'd never bothered with protocol when they'd been young, but that was a lifetime ago, it seemed.

"Ortus, how good to see you," she said, smiling.

Dean had a tendency to miss his cues, and he had no idea what was expected of him. He didn't notice Lorcan straightening and stayed where he was until a kind-hearted steward nudged him, suppressing a grin.

Ortus stepped aside, giving the queen a view of the two boys he'd brought to the palace. "Queen Aoife, this is my son, Dean."

Dean gave another little bow.

"And this is Lorcan Aurum."

Lorcan's eyes seemed lost in the queen's for a moment. Ortus noticed how his features softened, but also how she seemed to ponder him.

"Let's find a quieter place," she finally suggested, and Ortus nodded, offering his arm.

She hooked her arm under his, quickly whispering to her lady-in-waiting that she'd be needing her cloak, and he patted her hand as they sauntered toward one of the two arching doorways to the left and right of the thrones. Somewhere behind him, Ortus heard the steward explain to Dean that there would be a meal waiting for both him and his brother in their quarters, and he left the boys in the man's care without correcting him.

From the corner of his eye, he saw Dean haughtily raising his chin.

"He's not my brother," the lad informed the steward more loudly than necessary.

The steward either wasn't listening or didn't care, and Dean obviously found that frustrating while Lorcan seemed amused. Most things had to be frustrating to Dean after having been in the saddle for so long, Ortus supposed. All the boy would need was something to eat and a rest, so he let it go as Dean shuffled off after the steward and Lorcan.

Simply enjoying Aoife's company in silence, he walked with her toward the south entrance of the palace, where he knew a tall, narrow door would lead them out to the gardens. By the time they'd reached it, Aoife's lady-in-waiting had caught up with them and helped her into a fur-lined cloak that appeared to have threads of silver woven into it.

Memories of building snowmen awoke in Ortus as they descended the stairs to the first of three wide plateaus, where the gardeners had set about wrapping rose shrubs in coarse burlap sacks.

Ortus noticed an armed guard following them. The tall, muscular man bore the bishop's blue and green crest on the tunic he wore over his mail shirt. He was keeping a discreet distance as they weaved in and out between the rockeries and the bare spring plots, but he was never entirely out of earshot. This was something Ortus would not have suspected in Ironstone, at least not inside the palace walls, and his heart sank.

"Times are changing all over the land," Aoife told him, picking up on his observations without elaborating as she took his arm once again, snuggling close. The merest whisper of melancholy clung to the words as she spoke them, and she was quick to change the subject. "Tell me, how have you been?"

Ortus chortled a laugh. "Very happy and deeply sad, but mostly hopeful, and stubbornly looking for light. What about you, my dear? How has life been treating you here in the north?"

Aoife thought about it briefly. "Very happy, deeply sad and completely determined to keep every light shining if I can. Dean is a handsome boy, certainly a light."

"He takes after his mother… as I'm sure Lorcan does, as well."

"He's a *very* special young man."

"I'd guessed as much."

"You must tell me all about your journey here. I haven't been to the Middlelands and the Northern Forest in a long time. Matters of state and religion have been demanding my *complete* attention here."

Going by what he was seeing, he assumed they had, but he didn't quite know where to begin telling her what she really wanted to know. Not with the bishop's man trailing along behind them, and he thought about it. She waited patiently, like she always did, and he didn't feel rushed as she quietly held his pace.

"I suppose you could say its people haven't found their way out of the darkness yet," he deliberated.

Casting a quick glance back at their shadow, she

locked her fingers with the Sorcerer's, and he felt her inside his mind, a small whisper of a voice asking for his help, so he gave her what he could. She was a Fairywoman, not a Cine, and her magic was different to his.

The bishop's emissary stumbled over a protruding stone on the cobbled path and fell, hitting his head so hard they heard the thump. One of the gardeners who'd been sweeping leaves noticed that he'd managed to knock himself out cold, and came running, calling a comrade for help.

Ortus and the queen continued on their way without paying the little scene any heed.

Aoife fought to keep a straight face. She failed almost as gloriously as Ortus did the moment they'd put a little distance between them and the injured man and the servants attending him, and she erupted in bursts of laughter.

"Sometimes, you just have to chase the shadows away, even if you know they'll not be kept for long." Ortus smirked, and she leant in to him, stroking his arm affectionately.

"Agreed," she said, and sat down on a bench overlooking the town and the forest beyond its eastern gate in the valley. The exquisitely carved sandstone seat might have been cool to the touch even in summer, but it warmed the moment she decided that it would, and Ortus was glad for its balminess as he took the weight off his own feet.

She looked around before leaning back slightly, not quite relaxing as she scanned their surroundings. "The Inquisition has reached us through the people," she informed him with a facial expression that didn't match the graveness of what she was saying, and he forced a smile, understanding.

"I'm sorry," he said. "I didn't know." He wasn't certain anymore that he could or should ask of her what he'd come here to request. "How?"

"It was bound to happen. Look at all of that…" She gesticulated down at the busy streets and marketplaces. "Isn't it beautiful?"

He had to admit that it was. Ironstone was doing well.

"I love this town. I thought I was doing the right thing for its people, but I made a mistake. I opened the gates for Ornoa myself by giving the guilds too much power and inviting the merchants in."

"The merchants?"

There had always been merchants in and around Ironstone, primarily the Dwarven and the faring kind who supplied goods to the markets and craftsmen. The Dwarven had settled here, as they'd done in most towns along the river Leigne. They'd traditionally specialized in trading in gold and silver craft, precious stones and glass in all its forms. The travelers from the Trading Roads came and went, bringing many kinds of desirable goods from the eastern Mizrahi and Bharat, and from the south; fine cloths, spices, salt, oil, wax and wine. Having a Merchants' Guild here in town was new.

Aoife sighed. "The Kontors in Saint Aeden were never a problem for me, but the new Merchants' Guild here demanded the same rights as the Craftsmen's Guilds. I was foolish enough to listen to my council and grant them most of what they asked for. A lot of our wealth depends on trade. But, that brought a lot of changes. Their influence is welcomed by most here."

He could imagine. He wondered how many of her councilmen were adding to their own wealth these days. "And now?"

"Well, it's a fact that there's a new era coming, and it's one I'm getting too old to handle."

Ortus was about to protest, but she stopped him.

"It's time for the younger generation to take charge. My granddaughter is getting married tomorrow."

"Fairyman?"

"No, but steadfast human. She's going to need someone with guts and glory in his family tree by her side, and I think I've chosen well." She looked convinced. "She's got her work cut out for her, but she's going to do what needs to be done."

"Does he know?"

Aoife shook her head. "Would it make a difference?"

"It might."

"This is not a love marriage, Ortus. This marriage is going to save Ironstone from the wolves." She paused, studying him. "You're still the dreamer you always were."

He hummed. Aoife hadn't married for love, but he had. He knew about the power of love, even if the love he'd married hadn't been his first and true love. His *true love* had sat in this very spot over forty years ago, telling him he was a dreamer, just as she was doing again now.

Despite this, he hoped the princess would still be permitted at least a glimpse at what love was capable of. She was going to marry a man she hadn't chosen for herself, but sometimes love grew in unexpected places, if it was nurtured. Sometimes unanswered prayers turned out to be the answer you were looking for.

"Maybe," he replied. "But what is life without a dream?"

She smiled, nodding more to herself than to him. "I'm happy to see you, I really am. I missed our little talks. But won't you tell me why you're really here?"

He drew a deep breath and suddenly wasn't sure of what to tell her.

She wasn't willing to wait for the answer this time, and her brow creased. "You haven't made the journey in years, and you're not calling on me because you've missed me so."

Holding her hand, he decided on good faith that he

wasn't going to lie to her. He owed her respect, and he didn't want to lie to someone he respected.

"I've managed to make one of my dreams – one of my father's dreams – come true," he said.

"That's good," she returned immediately, and he told her about the community he'd built.

It didn't surprise him to find that she seemed to take great pleasure in his descriptions of The Fair and the people who dreamt his dream too. She had a lot of questions about the Snow Globe and how Mary worked their new Portals. He did his best to answer them, but they hadn't gotten half way through everything he'd been hoping to explain to her when the bishop's man was back, hovering close by. Someone had fixed him up with a heavy bandage on his bleeding temple, and he was clearly in pain, but determined to do his duty.

Just moments after he'd resumed his post, a young woman joined them. She placed herself defiantly between the man and them, and Ortus could see the resemblance to Aoife in her features. She may have been about seventeen, and her hair was several shades lighter than the queen's had been at that age, but her eyes were the same, as were the curves of her lips and nose.

Rising to greet her, he gave a small bow, and Aoife's granddaughter beamed at him.

"Cassandra, this is my oldest friend, Ortus Greenleaf."

"I'm pleased to meet you," Cassandra said, and he smiled, picking up the satchel he'd set down by his foot before he'd seated himself.

"And I'm very pleased to meet you," he returned. "I have brought Your Highness a wedding gift I hope will please you."

He took the Snow Globe from the bag and handed it to her, watching her eyes light up in delight at what she was sure was the most wonderful present she'd ever been given by a stranger.

Chapter Twenty-Eight

‹ Greed ›

Cooper thought of himself as a businessman rather than a farmer. You couldn't run a farm without a certain knack for making good deals – or making deals good. He'd always done quite well.

No one could say he hadn't known to provide for his family, but his wife had left him years ago, and she hadn't been very supportive before that. His daughters had turned out disrespectful brats. He'd bent over backward to ensure they had a beautiful home to live in and food on the table. He'd taught those girls to read. He'd given them *everything*, and what had he gotten in return? *Nothing*.

Catherine, he'd decided, was probably no different, judging by how things were between them, but he'd be damned if he didn't make sure he got *something* for his troubles back from her. She was a greedy little wench, but she was a clever greedy little wench. The book she'd found – whether he believed she'd happened to come across it or not was beside the point – might be worth a pretty penny to someone who could put meaning with it, and he knew just the man who had contacts.

Smirking to himself as he dismounted and tethered his new horse to a post, he looked around, thinking Caius Fletcher wasn't doing too badly for himself. It had been a while since he'd last seen him.

He noticed the fat pig in the pen beside the chicken coop, and the sheds were in good repair, as was the house itself. War was a generous employer, he supposed, and a weapons-maker always made a living.

Taking the book from the bag he'd strapped to his saddle, he wondered exactly how much it would fetch. A Cine spell book was bound to be worth a little something, even if there were just a lot of maps in it. He wasn't inclined to accept anything in trade. He wanted money, and he was sure he'd get it because Fletcher was paid in the currency of whatever nobleman he was working for. Any king's silver would do, as long as it was plenty.

No matter whose picture was on the coins, they'd buy a new cow to replace the one he'd lost recently, a pair of good leather boots, or some pretty new crockery for pretty Catherine to break so he could punish her for it.

The cow would make sense if he decided to stay and try to weather one more season with the plantation. He missed having milk in his porridge. The boots were just vanity because he didn't really need them. But, the crockery – that was sheer genius, considering how much of his tableware lovely little Catherine tended to break.

Fletcher stood in the doorway of his house before Cooper could even knock. He didn't look too thrilled to see him, but then, no one ever did. He put on his most pleasant smile.

"I think I have something that might be of interest to you," he told the last Cine Duke's illegitimate son, holding up the book.

Fletcher glanced at the book and led him inside.

Let the bargaining begin, Cooper thought, and decided on the boots.

When he left the bower's house again not half an hour later, the silver coins he'd received weighed pleasantly in his pouch. He rode a little way into the forest, wondering what else he could sell to the man, and then stopped to glance back at the farm.

Fletcher already had a buyer in mind, it seemed. He stood on his porch, holding what looked like a dove, attaching a message to the leather ring on its leg. He whispered to the bird before he released it, and it became a jay. A second later, it was a magpie, and Cooper knew that another mile or so on, it could turn into a raven or a hawk. He hadn't been mistaken about Fletcher. He definitely had some form of contact with Unnaturals, or he wouldn't own a dovelen.

Perhaps there was something more to be gotten from this yet.

Chapter Twenty-Nine

❧ Family ❧

The dovelen found Ortus by the river where they made halt to rest the horses on their tenth day of riding back from Ironstone. It had the form of an owl when it perched in a beech tree almost right next to him as he filled his leather bottle in the stream. He was contemplating how far the next inn would be from here when it shrieked, catching his attention. He'd already guessed its true nature by the time it took on its dove-shape and revealed itself.

"Hold out your arm," he told Dean, demonstrating how.

Although Dean hadn't watched the bird change form and looked slightly irritated, he did as he was told, and the dovelen landed on his wrist.

Smiling, Dean understood, and he held the bird gently while Ortus plucked the parchment from its ring.

Caius Fletcher's distinctive scrawl wasn't getting any easier to read with the years, the Master Sorcerer discovered, but he was also aware that half his trouble was rooted in his bad eyesight as he squinted at the words his cousin had inked.

Fletcher didn't often seek contact with him. He wasn't good with people that way. He wasn't good with dovelens either, for that matter, other than from making a meal of them as though they were common pigeons. As far as Ortus could remember, Fletcher preferred other paths of communication when there was a need for it, so if he had something to tell him now that was so urgent he'd send a dovelen, then it had to be important.

"Anything wrong?" Lorcan asked.

Ortus corrected his mien to a smile and shook his head. "Nothing to worry about. A relative of mine has asked me to meet him, and I think I'll oblige."

Rummaging around in his saddle bag, he found a quill and a small flask of powdered ink. Licking the quill, he wrote his reply on the back of the parchment and rolled it up again to a scroll. Lorcan helped him tether it to the dovelen, and they watched the creature change into a swallow as it soared high above them in the sky.

"Lorcan, do you think you can find your way back to The Fair on your own?" he asked, full well knowing Lorcan wouldn't have any problem with that.

Now it was Lorcan's turn to look confused, but he just shrugged, casting a glance at Dean. "Of course."

Ortus shook a few coppers from his pouch into his hand, counted them and handed them to Lorcan. "Don't save them. Spend the nights indoors wherever you can. Tell Thaddeus Dean and I will be a day or two behind."

"I could ride with him," Dean said.

"No, you were asking after my family – this is your chance to meet my uncle's son. I want Lorcan to ride ahead so no one will send out a search party. We're late in coming home as it is."

Home. Had he really said that? The Fair was home to Lorcan, surely, but neither he nor Dean had considered it so up until now. Then again, they hadn't been back to his house in months, he realized. It occurred to him he might be ready to sell it in spring. Without Gwyneth there, and Dean at The Fair most of the time, it didn't seem worth holding on to anymore.

"Let's eat something and be on our way," he said, pulling a loaf of bread from one of the burlap sacks tied to Dean's horse. It was their last.

Each of the boys took their share.

"Restock at the next stop," he told Lorcan, "and watch your pouch."

Lorcan grinned. "I know."

"Don't leave the saddle with the horse in any stable, no matter how good the place looks."

"I know."

"Don't drink." He didn't have enough coppers for that in any case.

"I know."

"Watch your back."

"I know."

Ortus supposed he *did* know. This, and a whole lot of other things besides.

Dean burst out laughing, and the Master Sorcerer blushed, but couldn't help himself and joined in.

"I know you can take care of yourself," he said to Lorcan when they'd regained themselves, but then he let his gaze wander between Lorcan and his son. "*Both* of you can. Lorcan, don't think badly of me. In a family, you always care, and you always worry. You're a part of my family, so I'll care and I'll worry about you, *both of you,* as much as I like."

He caught an instant of bewilderment in Lorcan's eyes, and it bothered him to observe the inner conflict born from the uncertainties his own father had instilled in him, but he was sure Lorcan would find his way through it. His soul was strong. It was stronger than Dean's for all the batterings it had taken.

"You boys are going to run The Fair one day," he told them. "Together. Like Thaddeus and I are doing now. You're both equally important to me, not *only* for this reason, but *also* because of it. It's important that we take care of each other in this family, whatever happens, because we're not only responsible for each other's well-being – we're responsible for a whole lot of other people also. Their survival depends on our strength. We get our strength from our family's unity. Promise me you'll remember that."

Both boys seemed to find their feet especially interesting this morning, and Ortus huffed. He remembered what it was like to be young, though he couldn't recall his father ever having given him a speech like this. Missing Gwyneth had opened his eyes for a lot of things over the last two or three years. He'd let down his family often enough to have become familiar with regret, and the older he got, the deeper his guilt for every bad decision he'd made or good decision he'd failed to make ran.

"I mean it," he persisted. "Promise me."

"Yes, father," Dean finally replied, raising his chin.

Lorcan followed his example. "I'll remember. *We'll* remember."

Chapter Thirty

⍟ Plots ⍟

Thin snowflakes danced through the icy air as Maebh peeked out of Jaden's tent.

"Your son's back," she said without looking at him.

He heard her and yawned, rolling over on his straw mattress. "Great. That means *His Lordship* is back, too."

She wasn't so sure about that. Lorcan was leading only one horse to the enclosure, and neither the Master Sorcerer nor his son were anywhere to be seen. "I don't want to wait anymore."

Jaden got to his feet and stood behind her, wrapping his arms around her. "What's the matter?"

She was tired of being cold, and she was tired of the work around the camp. She twisted out of his embrace. "You told me last year this was only going to be temporary. You promised me we were leaving before the winter." She jabbed a hand accusingly in direction of the fairground. "It's winter."

"Aye, it is, dear," he muttered, drawing her back into his arms, "but we don't want to go rushing things."

"Rushing things?" She couldn't believe the nerve of him.

Observing Lorcan as he returned the horse he'd borrowed from the Trick Rider's daughter, she guessed the boy wouldn't be going back to mucking the goats. He'd grown; he was almost taller than Jaden, and she didn't believe he'd be taking nonsense from anyone anymore, least of all from his father.

Sometimes she wondered how Catherine was faring with Caleb, but she tried not to think about her daughter too intently. There was no point. It was doubtful she'd ever see her again.

"We do want to get that spell book, don't we?" Jaden said, referring to the leather volume he'd made the lad tell them about when he'd given him his last whacking for his insolence – probably *the* last whacking he'd ever dole out to Lorcan.

For some reason, the Master Sorcerer obviously imagined the boy was something special, something *better* than the rest of them. Soon after his first reading lesson, he'd off-handedly mentioned a spell book to Jaden, and Jaden had gotten all excited about it because spell books were rare. The Church had been burning any written documents by or about the Cine for decades.

When Lorcan hadn't been willing to share any further on what Jaden had always thought to be the Master Sorcerer's journal, Jaden had gotten really mad.

She knew it irked him that Lorcan might be more knowledgeable than he, though he'd never admit it. Maybe Lorcan really *was* clever. The Sorcerer seemed to think so, but this notion didn't sit well with Jaden, and when he'd finally found a reason to pick a fight with Lorcan, he'd vented a year's worth of anger on him.

Neither she nor Jaden could read, so they'd never have any use for that book themselves, but after what Lorcan had told him through the pain of several cracked ribs, he'd guessed it would have old Cine spells in it. That meant this book was valuable, though he hadn't let on to Lorcan. Old magic was *pure* magic, and Jaden knew someone in Shingelsforth who was willing to pay well for that.

"Come on, now," he murmured into her hair. "We're almost there, love."

"That's what you said six weeks ago."

"How was I supposed to know the old man would be away this long?" He let go of her and bent to open his clothes trunk. "Just look at these," he told her, handing her a book from deep within the chest. It vaguely resembled the Sorcerer's. "Rua did such a fine job on them, our buyer won't suspect a thing when he sees Greenleaf's book on top of the pile. Our little hedge wizard will be convinced he's getting five Cine books of spells, and the silver we'll get for the lot will be enough to get us settled anywhere we like."

Again, she didn't consider it very probable. He'd traded quite a few of their belongings for good inks and spent their entire savings on leather and vellum, but it seemed questionable to her that a man who'd be willing to pay a large sum in silver wouldn't be able to tell a real spell book from one Rua had put together in a few months. Granted, Rua was good, but she wasn't sure he was *that* good.

She hesitated to answer, and Jaden frowned. "Ah, for cryin' out loud, woman, what do you want from me?" His accent was thick as it always was just before he erupted, and she bit her lip as he turned away from her, tossing the book back into the chest. "Do I look like an alchemist? I'm doing this with or without you, you know."

An awkward silence hung over them for a moment.

"Alright," she sighed at last, folding her arms across her chest. She wasn't going to let him go alone and be left behind *here*, but he just needed to understand her frustration. "Fine. I'll see if I can find out if Greenleaf is here, but if he isn't, we're leaving tomorrow."

He shrugged. "Fine! We're better off with a head start anyway. We'll arrange a meeting halfway to Shingelsforth, and we'll be half way to Saint Aeden by the time he notices he's been robbed. Is that a deal?"

Studying him and the way he was looking at her, playfully pleading with her, she huffed a laugh.

"Well?" he persisted, and she smiled, wagging a finger at him.

"Alright. But don't you go back on your word."

Chapter Thirty-One

✂ Caius ☙

The run-down old building that currently served as the village alehouse in the tiny settlement between Shingelsforth and the Tierney castle was crowded. Just why Caius had chosen this of all places to meet, Ortus did not understand when he entered the main room with Dean in his wake.

The Master Sorcerer's nose scrunched up involuntarily. The heat and the sour smell of sweat, smoke, burned lard, and stale beer hit him hard after the long ride through the cold, clear winter air. Tugging off his heavy cloak, he pushed and shoved his way through the small room until he'd spied the man he was looking for.

"Go see if you can organize quarters for the night," he told Dean, hoping he wasn't going to regret that, but it was dark, and they had to sleep somewhere.

Caius had possessed the wisdom to get himself settled in as far away from where the heavy late-night drinking was going on as the confined space would permit. The dark-haired bower was languidly lounging back in what Ortus supposed would have to pass for a chair here, mercifully close to the window.

Knowing his uncle's son, he might have been here for hours already, watching the scene before him unfold in quiet amusement; clever long-limbed fingers curling around the handle of a mug that was balancing on his thigh, clever slate-gray eyes carefully observing his surroundings. He'd casually draped a leg over the chair beside his own, and none of the people standing had thought to challenge him for it. Obviously, he'd been saving him that seat, and he cleared it when Ortus reached him.

"I see you've found it alright," the younger man remarked, his gaze probing though his tone was friendly as he moved over, pushing the stool toward Ortus with his foot.

"That wasn't so hard. Just had to follow the stench and look for the worst possible pile of rubble with a pole above the door."

Caius leaned forward, his wicked grin revealing perfect, white teeth. "I'd have thought *Your Lordship's* sensitive nose would have grown accustomed to the aroma of the common folk by now, seeing as how you've been gathering the rabble around you all these years."

"I wasn't talking about the *aroma of the common folk*," Ortus returned dryly, unwilling to take the bait he was being thrown not fifteen seconds into the first conversation they'd had in ten years. "I was talking about your filthy reeking arse."

Barking a laugh, Caius thumped him on the back, almost spilling his ale.

"Well, at least you've finally developed a sense of humor."

He signaled the burly, red-faced woman of the house, who was plowing through the carousers, lugging about a jug filled to the brim with strong bitter ale. She nodded at him curtly and beckoned her daughter. The delicate, weary girl of about ten brought a cracked mug and set it down on the window sill next to Ortus. Slopping a generous amount of the dark amber brew on Ortus, the brewer poured him his drink. He wondered if it was as warm and flat as it looked. It didn't matter; he was thirsty, and if there had been any of the stew left in the encrusted crock her husband had just taken down from the fire, he'd have had a helping of that, too.

"A copper for three," the sweaty woman told him, looking him up and down as she placed a pudgy hand on her hip.

"Now, Maggie," the bower admonished her, and she cast him an irritated glare.

"You been hoggin' that chair there all night, and your friend here looks like he can afford it."

Caius was about to argue, but Ortus cut him off, raising a hand in an appeasing gesture.

"Maggie, is it?"

She nodded, returning her attention to him fully.

"I'll have all three and another mug for my son, and you'll have your copper."

He gestured at Dean, who was bargaining with her husband for the room. Caius glanced at the boy and nodded to him when Dean noticed.

The alewife considered this for a moment. "Let her know when you'll want your refill, then," she finally said and shuffled off, leaving them under the watchful eye of the child.

The girl seemed to know from experience not to let a stranger out of her sight lest he decided to skip out on them.

Ortus half drained his mug in one swig, grimacing at the consistency and the fuzzy, lingering aftermath of the beer on his tongue before facing back to Caius.

"Why did you want to speak to me?"

Caius raised his chin, his eyes narrowing. "You always cut right to the chase. That hasn't changed."

The bower took another sip of his drink before bending down to retrieve the leather satchel he'd deposited beneath his chair when he'd arrived, dithering a moment to tie the strap that had come undone from one of his boots.

He opened the bag's buckle fasteners and extracted a rectangular object from it that could have been a book. It was about ten inches long and about a third as wide, and he'd swathed in a waxed cloth, so Ortus thought that it must be of value. Setting the package on

273

his lap, Caius took his time about redoing the buckles of the satchel while Ortus waited patiently.

"You know," Caius began, laying his arms leisurely across the bundle, "I often thought that it was a shame we didn't stay in touch. I've missed out on getting to know that son of yours."

His cousin resembled his father in many ways, the Master Sorcerer thought, though he might not even realize because he hadn't met him.

Ortus remembered Tierney well. He vividly recalled his uncle's deep, melodic voice and laugh, the roguish, self-assured smile that had lit up his angular features, the straight black hair that had turned gray the year after the castle had fallen, and the strong, though slender hands that were so much Caius' own. He'd died of a diseased lung just before his second wife had given birth to Caius. Ortus, who'd been about the age his own son was now, had mourned him.

It was difficult to keep in mind that the outer appearance was all father and son might ever have in common.

Ortus smiled permissively, raising an eyebrow. "Maybe you're right," he admitted. "But then again, I'd have had to kill you at some point."

Unexpectedly to Caius, the Sorcerer half-rose and reached around him to recover his coin pouch from the bower's belt. He'd hardly have perceived him taking it from the lining of his cloak if he hadn't known to be wary and felt the brief movement of air about his legs while Caius had been tying his bootstrap – or pretending to.

The scoundrel had gotten unbelievably good at what he did over time, but this was one of the reasons they'd parted ways.

"You still can't keep your hands to yourself, can you?"

Caius sighed, playfully tilting his head, reminiscent of the little boy who'd had his behind whipped almost on a daily basis for not being capable of keeping his fingers out of the pastries and pies at the local bake house.

"Just wanted to make sure you can afford to pay the alewife." He smiled. "You do have a lot of mouths to feed."

Ortus snorted a laugh, mirroring the look on the other man's face as he tucked the coin pouch away. "Did you really have me come all the way out here to steal from me? Or were you going to show me something worth my while?"

Slapping his forehead like he'd just realized that this was why they were here, Caius unraveled the book from its protective wrapping while Dean pulled up another stool he'd swiped from somewhere. Ortus put a mug in front of the boy and watched him grimace at his first swallow.

From the wax cloth, Fletcher pulled forth a book. It was bound in dark crimson leather with a golden ivy border and a center piece depicting the same familiar repetitive pattern of infinity signs the Sorcerer had spent every day of his life staring at. Trying not to give away what he felt as he squinted at the second of the three books his father and grandfather had written on magic, he impassively directed his gaze back to Caius' inquiring eyes.

"That's a book," he stated flatly, as though it was nothing to be excited about. At the same time, he firmly lowered his heel on the tip of Dean's toe before the lad could say anything. "Dean, would you please go check on the horses? That boy by the stable didn't seem so bright to me – see he isn't feeding them moldy hay."

Dean did as he was told, catching on, but grumbling all the same at the prospect of having to go out into the cold again.

Caius' eyebrows knitted. "Well, that's not just *any* book," he said, insistently tapping a finger on the cover. "Take a closer look at it."

Ortus turned the tome over in his hands, his heart thumping in his chest. "Oh, I know what this is," he responded quietly, testing one of the clasps that held its covers shut. It wouldn't budge, but that didn't worry him; he'd find out how to open it. He'd eventually removed the clasps from his own because he'd found them to be quite annoying.

"I was right, then," Caius mumbled, leaning back. "This is one of your father's."

Ortus returned to him. "Probably." He drained his mug, and the brewer swept in to refill it for him instantly, eying the book with mild interest. She appeared to know Caius, and she hadn't thought to ask who he was, so he guessed that this was where Caius habitually conducted at least a part of his business.

"My father possessed quite a few books in his time. Where did you get it?"

"That's not important," Caius told him, holding up his own mug to the overwrought woman without looking at her. "But I would be willing to make you a good deal for it."

Of course he would be. Ortus hummed. "And what would be a good deal – to you?"

The bower rubbed his stubbly chin. "I don't want money," he said, and then the haughty superiority that generally resided within the glint of his eyes gained a different quality altogether. The nuances of his tone shifted to become softer, more compassionate. "I know you haven't got any. But, you do have something I could really use right now. Let's discuss this at my house in the morning, if you're willing."

Ortus didn't have to think about this. He would have done anything to have that book and the other one that went with it. He was convinced it would help him complete the enchantments on The Fair's protections, make them a fixed part of this world so that the ground it stood on would never be breached like the walls of his ancestors' castle. It was almost too good to be true.

He nodded. "Alright. How do I find you?"

"Follow the stench," Caius returned with a smirk, rising. "I'll be waiting for you. My wife – Loredana – makes a great breakfast."

Caius passed Dean on his way out, and Ortus watched them exchanging a few words before they shook hands.

"Count your fingers," Ortus warned him when he claimed Caius' chair.

Dean laughed. "I think he's alright."

Ortus patted his shoulder. "He is. He just hates to hear anyone say it."

Chapter Thirty-Two

❧ Dealing in Arrangements ❧

Ortus didn't have to look very hard for Caius' farm. The nameless settlement was comprised of a cluster of no more than ten or twelve hovels that housed some starving peasants, and a few farms scattered loosely around it. Two were in such bad repair, he didn't even bother checking them and one was a fouling plantation he couldn't imagine Caius running. The fourth place they came to looked right, though he still couldn't imagine what Caius had been thinking when he'd made his home here.

Things became a little clearer when he got a close look at the young woman who opened the door for them. Her eyes were brown one second and the color of glowing coals the next, if only for an instant. Loredana was a Shapeshifter. He couldn't tell what kind, but he could see she was with child. Her dress had been widened at the seams, and he guessed she was about seven months along.

"Come in," she told them, a warm smile on her lips as she led them inside the tidy, spacious house.

Ortus had to wonder how Caius had managed to steal her heart, and whether he was really aware of what he'd gotten himself into.

"I hope you're hungry," she went on. "We've got warm bread, cheese, milk, and eggs."

All of that was set out on a proper table with earthenware plates and cups, and Dean dug in as though this was his first decent meal in days.

After they'd eaten, Caius helped Loredana clear the dishes away, and he asked Dean to help her muck the pig sty. Dean was puzzled, but complied, leaving the men to talk.

Ortus hadn't told his son why they were really here. He'd lain awake half the night because he wasn't sure he'd be in a position to pay Caius' asking price for the book, whatever that would be, and there was no sense in getting anyone's hopes up.

Caius fetched the volume he'd shown him at the alehouse from a chest by his bedstead, put it down on the table and pushed it toward him as though they'd already struck their bargain. Caius knew he wanted it.

"You were going to tell me how much this would cost me, should I consider taking it off your hands," he reminded the bower.

"I was, wasn't I?" Caius smiled, folding his arms across his chest as he fixed his gaze to Ortus'. "Well, seeing as how you're a man who'd understand the burdens of late fatherhood, I think you'll agree with me that a man should make provisions for his family, just in case."

"Indeed." Provisions for a Shapeshifter might turn out to be a tall order, but the Sorcerer was willing to hear Caius out. "Can she control her – is it a wolf? Can she control her wolf?"

Caius' smile froze. "Even if she couldn't, I'd still be asking."

Going over his options, Ortus remained silent for a moment before answering. "She'd be better off with her own kind."

"She might. But there's not many of *her kind* left. This child is unique, and you know Loredana wouldn't stand a chance alone. Shifters raise their offspring in packs, but where do they go for help when there's no more packs? If something happened to me, they'd both be lost."

Ortus could well appreciate that. It might never happen, he told himself. Fletcher was almost fifteen years younger than he, and although his profession took him to a battlefield every once in a while, it wasn't as if he constantly stood in the line of fire. Loredana didn't look as helpless as he made her out to be either. What were the odds?

"Alright," he said. "You have my word."

Caius smiled. "Then that's settled. But I'll need a charm for the child."

Ortus studied him, bewildered. He'd yet to see a charm that could work any kind of magic, let alone a magic that would help a Shapeshifter maintain his human form. A lot of people were superstitious that way and believed in all kinds of nonsense, but to his mind, a Cine man and a Shapeshifter woman should know better, no matter who'd raised them.

"A charm…? *Really?*"

There was that mischievous gleam in his cousin's eyes again, and to Ortus' relief, Caius laughed.

"No, not like you think. I don't want a piece of metal dipped in some hedge witch's concoction. I want a token to seal our deal. I'm not going to give you this book on your promise alone. Promises aren't worth much at our age."

Ortus looked down at his hands, humming. "I guess you're right there. But no matter what token I give you, it won't be much use to Loredana and the child after I'm gone, so we'd just have to rely on the next generation then, won't we?"

Caius nodded slowly, almost unwillingly. "Aye. We would." He thought about it for a moment before continuing. "Just consider this: I could use help over the spring months here with the farm and a few orders I've taken on for the king, particularly since I won't be home all the time. If that *next generation* was to pitch in a little while getting to know Loredana and what she is, I'm sure it would strengthen the family ties as well as the relations between the people considerably."

Ortus scoffed. There *were* no relations between the Cine and the Shapeshifters. They had nothing in common other than that they were being hunted. Shifters rarely or never sought the company of the Cine, and the Cine stayed clear of pure-blooded Shifters for the same reasons humans did.

"Look, if it's help with the farm you're looking for, I'm sure I know a few boys who'd be happy to earn a wage," he said.

Caius leant forward in his chair. "But none of them would be the Master Sorcerer's son, *cousin*. You know I'd *never* let anything happen to Dean if he were to spend the summer and learn a trade from me. *Never*. This is *me* asking *you* to seal an agreement between us with something more valuable than a chunk of metal."

Ortus knew that, but implementing a sense of duty toward Shifters in his son had never been on Ortus' agenda, and a whole summer was a long time.

He'd already spoken to Dean about joining Lorcan in Thaddeus' employ. The boy hadn't been particularly enthusiastic about learning carpentry, but Ortus thought this would be a good way for him to assume responsibility while being close to Thaddeus and Lorcan. Dean needed to be present at The Fair as more than just Ortus Greenleaf's son, and he needed to practice his magic with Lorcan if they were going to manage and protect its people when he was gone.

Caius' eyebrow twitched upward. "Ortus, stop doting on him, or he's going to end up like you, teaching some filthy rich human brats to say their prayers in a language no one speaks. If you really want him to step into your shoes, then let him learn to stand on his own two feet for a bit. Let me teach him my trade and let him see for himself what more there is in this world, just until the end of summer. If he's willing, that is."

Ortus had to smile at that, but *he* wasn't willing.

He didn't think he was *doting* on Dean. He just wasn't prepared to leave his son here in trade for a book, or even a cause. Of course he wanted his father's book – but not at this cost. Family was family, but Caius was asking too much.

"No." He pushed it back across the table at the bower.

Caius sighed, and unexpectedly returned it to him, gingerly directing it with one finger. "So you can't guarantee my wife and child's safety, and you won't let your son do it either. That's a shame," he said softly, but without any bitterness. "Take it anyway."

Ortus didn't believe he'd heard right.

"Go on," Caius insisted. "It's yours."

"Are you sure?" Ortus thought that age must have mellowed the man. There was no way he would have given something like this away twenty years ago.

Caius leant back. "I am. Go on."

Reluctantly, Ortus claimed the volume, and when Caius nodded at him, encouraging him, he put it in his satchel with the book his father had left him. He hardly dared to believe he now had two out of three.

Rising, he twisted his father's silver ring off his fourth finger and handed it to Caius. "Your token," he said. "For the child. But I can no more speak for *all* of my people and how they'll think about this tomorrow than you can speak for *all* of Loredana's kind, so this is for your child only, and not for your wife's people."

Caius placed a hand on his arm. "Thank you."

Just then, Dean came back inside with Loredana. They appeared to have had a pretty good time despite the dirty job out in the cold. Ortus didn't doubt she had a good heart. In her human form. He wondered whether she could hold on to it when the wolf took over.

"You look like you've been discussing someone's funeral," Dean remarked, the smile on his face fading when he saw Ortus' severe mien.

Caius grinned. "In a manner of speaking. But not to worry – we'll both live long enough to make sure you keep moving in the right direction… and learn a trade."

Ortus almost hated the old scoundrel.

Dean snorted a laugh. "I don't think I'm going to make such a great carpenter."

Caius looked straight at Ortus, but spoke to Dean. "You could make a great bower."

Ortus frowned. "Or something else." He wanted his son at The Fair, and Dean knew it.

The boy smirked at him before turning to Caius. "I saw your equipment in the shed. I think I'd be interested in that."

"You don't say! I was just telling your father I'd like to take on an apprentice."

Dean beamed. "You would?"

Ortus plopped back down in his chair, telling himself he was going to regret this.

By the time Ortus was ready to leave after they'd discussed everything at length, they'd managed to agree that Dean would stay with Fletcher for the next two weeks to see if they'd get along. Ortus would check on him after that time, and they'd make a final decision. Dean seemed happy enough with that, though Ortus wasn't.

Before he mounted his horse, he handed Caius the satchel with his books. The bower cast him a bemused glance.

Ortus shrugged. "Since you've already got the most valuable thing in my life in your care, you may as well keep these two until I pick my son up again."

"What makes you so sure I won't sell them?"

Ortus tilted his head. "We're both too old for games, Caius, and I don't want that book – or any other – on the basis of a bargain like this. You could have asked me without offering me anything in return. But, I get the message. It's time we start trusting each other. Besides, if anything ever happened to me, you'd know those books would belong with Dean, and that Dean belongs with The Fair."

He knew this beyond a doubt, and he was sure it wouldn't take Dean longer than two weeks to figure out where his place was.

Caius smiled and awkwardly embraced the older man. "Alright. I understand that. I'll see you in two weeks. But I think you might as well save yourself the trip. He'll likely stay over the summer."

Ortus snorted. "Then so be it. He's nearly grown anyway. No sense in doting on him."

Chapter Thirty-Three

◌ Crossroads ◌

When Lorcan got back to The Fair, Thaddeus presented him with a tent of his own. He wasn't sure it was an improvement on the goat shelter as far as warmth went, but he gladly accepted it; it was clean, it was his own, and it was about as far away as possible from Jaden and the company he kept.

He worked harder than ever for Thaddeus in the days that followed. He was on the job, sorting nails and smoothing boards before most of the other workers were there, and he stayed to clean up and sort scraps long after everyone else had left.

The carpenter seemed to think he had an eye for detail and a steady hand, but Lorcan wasn't happy with the quality of his own work half the time, even if everyone else seemed to be. He'd never been good at anything but mucking the goats, and he could read now, but that was about it. He was, however, determined to learn because he had the ambition to one day own one of the wagons he was helping to build. He had a tent now, and he'd have that wagon sometime in the future.

They were working on three different prototypes at the same time to see which of them would be more practical. Thaddeus had drawn up the plans for them, and now they needed to get a feeling for the living-space and use the vehicles would offer. Lorcan already had a preference, but he thought they'd all be great because no matter how the walls were shaped, or what kind of chassis or axles they put underneath the frames, anything would be an unquestionable improvement on what they had today.

Having such a caravan would almost be like living in a house, he imagined, only that this house would have the advantage of being mobile.

All their belongings had to be mobile because they'd discovered that things that were anchored to the ground wouldn't move when Mary triggered a Portal. The Big Top had to be disassembled and the tents picked up if they wanted to take them along, but wagons and carts went through with no bother at all, so it seemed logical to build wagons to live in rather than keep rebuilding and repairing their already raggedy and worn-out tents.

The Big Top couldn't be helped, but they'd soon have their hands free to find a routine for that, thanks to the caravans. Whatever other pavilions or booths they had, they'd find solutions for them, too, he was sure. Thaddeus had convinced everyone this was the way to go, and Lorcan didn't doubt it, especially with the number of refugees they had coming in all the time now since the new Inquisitor had taken up his work in the area. Lorcan was humbled to be a part of what

Thaddeus was doing. They'd have *homes* again – all of them – despite everything.

To Lorcan, the best part was that, in addition to saving them time and effort, the caravans would give them the comfort of a bed up off the ground and a door that would lock. That was going to be a new experience of privacy all round. He'd never had that luxury before. There wasn't a prudish soul among them, but a real door was a genuinely attractive thought, and their little project group got a lot of volunteers who were ready to help with this and that and even submit ideas. Not all of those were feasible, but they were generally inspiring nonetheless.

Lorcan had many ideas of his own. He sketched them out for Thaddeus in his journal, but they were often too elaborate to implement. The more down-to-earth things he dreamt of simply involved having a table and some chairs in the caravan he'd build for himself. Maybe there would even be a shelf for the books he might have when he could afford them.

The shell construction of the model he was currently working on would be roughly finished by nightfall, if all went well. He pretended it was his as he fitted the last tongued and grooved board to the side lattice.

In his mind's eye, he could already see what this caravan would look like when it was up on wheels and painted.

Andrea, the Bear Tamer who'd been a famous painter's apprentice in the Sudlands, had shown him the colors they'd be using for it. He'd made a sketch of white and yellow flower patterns to decorate the portions around the door and the window shutters, and Lorcan thought they'd look beautiful.

He was worlds away when he realized Thaddeus was speaking to him.

"Take a break and walk with me," the burly man told him, not appearing his usual happy self.

Descending the ladder he was standing on, Lorcan worried. "What is it?"

"I have to tell you something. Let's just walk."

Thaddeus kept his gaze trained on the ground ahead until they were out of earshot of the others.

"What's wrong?" Lorcan persisted, observing the older man shuffling about, huffing warm clouds into the cold afternoon air. "If I'm not fast enough, I can do better. I just like to have everything straight and I still need a while for that, but—"

"It's not that, lad." The carpenter cut him off. "Look, your father and Maebh were seen leaving the fairgrounds yesterday morning, and they haven't come back."

Lorcan didn't quite understand. That wasn't unusual. Jaden came and went as he pleased. He always had, and everyone knew it. They were probably enjoying some privacy in the bushes, or cheating some merchant or other out of a bottle of wine.

"So?"

"They had their belongings with them. They're not coming back, son."

Lorcan snorted a laugh. "We should be so lucky."

The other man's mien didn't lighten, and Lorcan began to wonder.

"No, you must be mistaken. I mean, where would Jaden go?"

Thaddeus sighed. "He left a map with one of the Snake Sisters. Freya was supposed to give it to Ortus when he gets back tonight, but she thought it strange, so she came to me with it."

He handed Lorcan the creased scrap of parchment. Unfolding it, Lorcan didn't know which way was up, at first. The lines and landmarks depicted on it were badly executed, and the amateurish labeling of places and roads didn't consistently go in the same direction. That aside, it was still too good to have been drawn up by Jaden. Jaden didn't have that kind of patience with a quill – not that he owned one – and why would he?

"My father can't read. How could he have written this?"

"Apparently, he had help from Rua Tine."

Rua played cards with Jaden, so that might have made sense, but the rest didn't.

"Why would my father want to have Rua draw a map for Ortus?"

"He said he was meeting someone to acquire a book of spells that would be of great interest to Ortus, and he wanted to strike a bargain for it – but not here. He said he and Maebh were going to start over somewhere else."

He remembered the night Jaden had beaten him for not obeying when Ortus had argued with him. Jaden had wanted to hear all about the Sorcerer's spell book, and Lorcan recalled telling him what he wanted to know and that it was one of three, in the end. He'd felt terrible for it right afterward, but he'd tried to put it out of his mind because it seemed so inconsequential then. He couldn't say exactly how, but there was some connection here, and Jaden was going to lay some kind of crooked deal on the Sorcerer. Where would Jaden have gotten the means to bargain for a book of spells? This was all wrong.

"Do you know where this crossing is?" he inquired, and Thaddeus nodded, running a finger along one of the roads.

"This is the Old Trading Route due west. It's a little over two days' march from here, halfway to the Northern Forest."

Lorcan tried to envision it, and he found it wasn't too hard. Placing a hand over the parchment, he spread his fingers, and a bluish-translucent miniature of the forest appeared to rise up out of it, taking on dimension. Thaddeus watched patiently as Lorcan made it turn so he could see it from different perspectives, and a part of an abandoned hollow way became visible through the trees. Eventually, the forest vanished, and more and more of the path revealed itself. Tollhouses and mills, bridges and road marks came into sight and disappeared again.

"You're getting so good at this, my boy," the Master Sorcerer said, startling both Lorcan and the carpenter. Lorcan dropped the map, and Ortus levitated it up from the ground and took hold of it, looking pleased.

"You're back," Thaddeus remarked, and Ortus smiled wearily.

"Just stopping over, by the look of things." He studied the map intently.

Lorcan looked around. "Where's Dean?"

"Staying with that relative of mine I was telling you about for a few weeks," he replied absently. He cast Thaddeus a glance. "I've already spoken to Freya, and I'll be leaving at first light."

"I'll come with you," Lorcan said.

"I don't think that's a good idea," Ortus replied. "Freya said he wanted to talk to me alone."

Lorcan was about to object, but Thaddeus cut him off.

"He's right. Besides, with all the new people coming in, I need every good man I can get here to help with the wagons."

Realizing he'd been misread, Lorcan shook his head. "Then take someone else," he suggested. "It doesn't have to be me, but don't go alone."

The men looked at each other, and Ortus barked a hearty laugh. "What, do you think I can't take care of myself, boy? Your father will be wanting to vent. Then, he's going to tell me how much better things are elsewhere. After that, he's going to ask a ridiculous ransom for whatever book he wants to sell me, and I'm going to tell him to go to hell. End of story."

Lorcan could feel the heat rising in his cheeks. Of course the Master Sorcerer could take care of himself. The trip to Ironstone had taken a toll on him. Ortus was stiff and he looked tired, but Lorcan was sure he could hold his own against anything Jaden would have to offer.

"It's not that," he mumbled. "It's just... I know my father, and I think he's up to something."

Ortus huffed amusedly, and then fixed his gaze to Lorcan's.

"I know," the Sorcerer assured him a little more softly. "Look, I can't tell you what to do. I can't forbid you to come. But I *can* tell you this: I think you shouldn't give him that much of your attention anymore. He's made his choice, and you're almost a man, so don't give him the satisfaction of letting him think you need to talk this over with him. Let me deal with whatever it is he wants as a parting gift from our community in case he left here with the impression he could sell us out on some level, and then we'll just let him be on his way. Let him go, Lorcan. I know it's tough, but this is how he wants it, and trust me, he's made this decision in your favor without even knowing it."

On the brink of wanting to say he was afraid Jaden was capable of more than just betrayal, Lorcan could see the sense in everything the Sorcerer was telling him. Ortus knew people, and he knew Jaden.

"We'll talk some more when I get back," Ortus closed. "In the meantime, you help get those wagons up and running, alright?"

Lorcan found himself nodding, looking at his feet.

It didn't feel right, but he was willing to believe he was overreacting. A part of him really was mad at Jaden for denying him closure. Jaden was a fraud and a liar, but he was his father, and the tiniest amount of respect for their relationship should have drawn at least a short farewell from his lips, but it hadn't. He knew Ortus was right in that he shouldn't waste his time on the man, but he couldn't help himself, and perhaps the mixture of resentment and distrust that was stewing his innards was clouding his judgement.

Ortus made a point of catching his gaze and tilted his head. "I'll see you in a few days, then?" he insisted, and Lorcan straightened his back.

"Alright. I'll see you then."

With an uneasy feeling in his gut, he watched the Master Sorcerer walk away from them and disappear somewhere in the maze of tents.

Thaddeus thumped his back. "Come on, let's get moving so we'll get a roof on that caravan tonight. I want to see that."

Reluctantly, Lorcan followed the carpenter back to the worksite, but the knot in his stomach churned and grew with every passing minute. The longer he thought about it, the more convinced he became his anxiety had nothing to do with the unspoken goodbyes. It was raw concern for the man who'd been more of a father to him in the past few weeks than Jaden had managed in all the years before.

They finished putting the roof on the wagon while Mary decorated a birch sapling with colorful ribbons and bands for the rounded gable, and some of the other women brought salads and bread so they could celebrate and drink to their achievement together tonight, but Lorcan had no head for it.

He made up his mind that he had to talk to Ortus again, but when he got to the Sorcerer's tent, the man was already gone.

Chapter Thirty-Four

☙ Metamorphosis ❧

"He's not coming," Maebh mumbled, pacing with her arms folded across her chest as evening descended like a silent cloak on the empty winter fields around them. Heavy clouds were moving fast and low overhead, and the icy air smelled of snow.

She was sure the old man was mocking them. They'd waited at The Fair until they'd heard from one of the horse trainers when Ortus planned to be back. Rua had written the right day on the map, but where was the Sorcerer? Maybe he didn't have the map yet, or he'd decided he simply wasn't interested.

"Relax. He'll be here," Jaden patiently responded from where he was hunkered down on the frozen ground, leaning against the signpost with his head back and his eyes closed. "You should know him better by now. He's too curious not to show up. And if he doesn't come today, he'll be here tomorrow. Let's give him a bit of time."

Maebh thought her lover sounded way too comfortable, as if he didn't have a worry in the world and was about to have a nap. She couldn't imagine how he could be so laid back and collected, but that was just so like him. Nothing ever seemed to make him nervous.

They'd come here to steal from the hand that had fed them, whatever else Ortus was to either of them, and she was getting giddy and anxious. Doubts started cluttering her mind, confusing her. Waiting for so long by the old road marker in the bleak midwinter certainly played a part in that Maebh wasn't so sure anymore if she wanted to do this. The Master Sorcerer was no fool. What if he saw through Jaden's illusion, or what if he wasn't distracted from her sufficiently by it? She was chilled to the bone.

Toward the end of her patience, she was inclined to think it might be a good idea to just pick up and go back the way they'd come, but Jaden seemed positive their strategy was going to work out. He'd planned this the way he planned everything: with every confidence that nothing could possibly go wrong, and who was she to disagree? Jaden Aurum was the sweetest dream she'd ever had, and she didn't want him to think she didn't trust his judgement. He was everything she'd missed in Caleb.

"Come here," he gruffly ordered her, sitting all the way down.

He stretched out his legs and reached up a hand to her, patting his thigh with the other. Inviting though the offer was, she didn't much care for his tone.

"Please," he added, rolling his eyes at her.

Reluctantly, she folded herself onto his lap and

nestled into his chest. To her surprise, she discovered that he was warm as though he'd just come out of bed. He was always warmer than she, somehow, but she wouldn't have thought he'd be this cozy there on the frozen ground. Despite herself, she relaxed against his body.

The Fair wasn't where she wanted to spend the rest of her life; it wasn't where either one of them wanted to grow old. They weren't going to sleep in tents until they grew gray and useless, and they didn't want one of the new wagons Thaddeus' lot were building. They weren't going to die poor. Jaden often told her stories of places she'd never seen. He knew the most interesting people everywhere, it seemed. This was destiny calling. It had to be, and she wasn't going to mess this up.

Finally, Ortus came into sight and there was no going back. She got to her feet, wiping her sweaty palms on her skirts.

"Are you ready?" she inquired softly without turning around.

"I am," he replied. "Are you?"

She took a deep breath and held it for a moment. "I think so."

Ortus looked tired, she realized when he was close enough for her to see his face. He dismounted stiffly, not acknowledging her. The soles of his boots crunched on the rime as he strode past her to stand in front of Jaden, pushing his fists into his sides while

Maebh took his horse's reins, gently stroking its muzzle.

"What are you *doing* here, Aurum?" the Sorcerer inquired of the Illusionist, leering down at him. "What are *any of us* doing here?"

He cast an irritated glance at Maebh, who stopped edging around the dark brown, patting her neck. She was genuinely fond of horses and hated that she'd probably have to put the old girl down so Greenleaf couldn't follow them when they had the spell book. It was a shame.

Jaden rose and straightened. Then, from beneath his cloak, he brought forth a book bound in dark green leather. Maebh knew it was one of Rua's forgeries, but it vaguely resembled the Sorcerer's own volume. He was cloaking it to fool a weary magician whose eyesight was failing and who might be inclined to see what he wanted to see, *longed* to see after years of searching for it, if they could believe Lorcan.

"I thought you might like to expand the collection," Jaden offered, his tone alight with the dancing underscores of his accent, and he smiled pleasantly.

Ortus' eyes widened, and Maebh heard his breath hitch even from where she stood behind the horse as the elderly man reached for the tome. Jaden snatched it back before the Master Sorcerer's hand could touch the binding and destroy the deception. She was relieved to find Jaden had captured all of his attention.

The Sorcerer's eyebrows arched. "Where did you get this?"

"Does it matter?" Jaden grinned smugly. "I know you've been looking for it."

"I want to see it," Ortus demanded. He didn't appear to notice Maebh rummaging through his saddle bag behind his back. Either that, or it was so irrelevant to him he couldn't be bothered rebuking her for it.

"Tell me what you'd do with it first." Jaden was playing for time, and Ortus was buying in. Maebh knew he didn't care why the Sorcerer would want to have it. This wasn't about the magic. This was just about the silver.

"You probably don't have the slightest inkling of what you've got there." Greenleaf snorted. "It's next to no good on its own, if that's really what I think it is – but I'd have to see it to find out, wouldn't I?" He paused, but Jaden remained firm, clutching the fake volume by his side without indicating the least bit of ambition to give it to the other man.

"Well, then what would you be willing to pay for it?" Jaden smirked.

Maebh knew he couldn't see her from where he was. He'd be fuming if he discovered she hadn't found Greenleaf's spell book, but it wasn't there like he said it would be. The Sorcerer couldn't possibly have it on him, and if it wasn't in his saddlebag, he must have either left it at The Fair or hidden it elsewhere before he'd come.

Ortus released a warm breath into the icy air, and his stance changed. "What, are we talking silver, here? You know I can't pay you that much."

Jaden laughed as Maebh came back around the aged mare, steeling herself for Jaden's reaction.

"See?" he said to Greenleaf, not paying her any heed. "And that's what's wrong with you. That's what's wrong with your Fair. You've been living on a prayer for years now, and you don't have more than a few hellers to your name. You've put every guilder you've ever made into The Fair for – what? A decade now? And it still won't pay for itself. You have powers well beyond those of most people I know, and you're stubbornly refusing to use them to help yourself the way you could if you had any guts. The Fair is a washed-out dream. It's a lost cause, and so are you, old man."

Standing next to him, it occurred to Maebh that maybe they were, too.

"At least I know where I belong, and I don't have to put others up to steal from people," Ortus plowed on, his voice a little higher in pitch and louder in volume as he faced Maebh. "Unlike some. What were you looking for, dear? What is he after?"

Cringing both inwardly and out, she didn't know what to say. If she'd found what she'd been looking for, the horse would be dead, and she and Jaden would be long gone by now.

"Where's your spell book?" Jaden wanted to know then, suddenly standing by the mare and rummaging through the saddle bag himself.

Ortus' face turned to stone, his eyes hard and cold as he spun around. "Has he been putting ideas in your head?" he spat at Maebh, and she shuffled about uncomfortably, her gaze darting back and forth between the Sorcerer and Jaden, but Jaden stoically ignored her.

"Where is that spell book?" Jaden repeated, a growl beneath the words as he vanished and reappeared in front of the Sorcerer, grabbing him by the collar. "Look, we don't want any trouble – we just want that book."

"You don't want any trouble?" Greenleaf snapped. "Let go of me! You wouldn't know what to do with it…" he trailed off, finding himself immobilized.

"Go ahead," Jaden hissed at Maebh, trying to keep the restraining spell he'd been practicing in place as Ortus struggled and strained against both it and the hands that were holding him.

Maebh's heart hammered in her chest. They'd talked about this, but she didn't think she'd actually have to go through with it. Why couldn't he just have had that book in his bag?

"Where are you keeping it?" Jaden roared.

Maebh found it hard to concentrate. She could see Greenleaf's astonishment plainly reflected in his eyes just before it turned to horror. She *felt* his innards churn. Large and small veins began bursting as he went to his knees, desperately attempting to shield himself against her invasion of his body and mind, but it was too late. She didn't mean to go this deep or inflict this kind of agony, but she had no grasp on what she was doing. A human wasn't a rat or one of the dogs she'd been practicing on with Jaden, and before she knew it, she'd lost control.

"Don't..." Greenleaf pleaded, gritting his teeth.

From a distance, she heard Jaden's voice telling her to stop, but she couldn't reverse the damage, nor could she repair it.

Why had he not fought her? He was supposed to be a Master Sorcerer – why had he not pitted himself against her?

Just then, she heard the nastiest noise she'd ever perceived. It came from somewhere inside of the Sorcerer's head: a sharp *pop*, ever so tiny, yet profoundly final, and she knew Ortus Greenleaf wasn't going to get up again.

Snowflakes danced in waning daylight.

Looming over Greenleaf, Jaden started shaking him. "Where's the book?" he yelled in his face, but got no answer.

Maebh was grotesquely aware of the diminishing timeframe within which he might obtain the information he was seeking.

She observed Greenleaf as he arduously tried to keep breathing. She'd messed this up, and she wondered if Jaden was going to forgive her.

Unexpectedly then, the Sorcerer's eyes cleared, and he seemed to focus. His features contorted, but he fixed his stare to hers. Around his pupils, she saw a silver aura that hadn't been there before, and she found herself immersed in its radiance. She'd never seen anything more beautiful than the silver, and she couldn't look away even though Jaden was yelling at her, trying to pull her back from Greenleaf, but she just couldn't leave him.

Soon, a glittering flurry of magic made from the silver swirled outward from the Sorcerer toward her, mixing with the falling snowflakes. She breathed it in deeply without knowing she was, and the changes that the whirling particles evoked within her manifested on her skin almost instantly.

Greenleaf continued watching her, laming her thoughts by repeating strange words into her mind, perhaps from the book they'd meant to steal from him, words that twisted her body and reshaped it to form something else entirely.

She still felt the Master Sorcerer's eyes on her long after death had claimed him, but her vantage point had changed.

Everything had changed.

At first she thought she'd fallen over, but she soon discovered that she couldn't get up anymore because she was lacking legs and feet to stand upon. Looking around for Jaden, she saw him retreating from her in his confusion. Fear and disgust molded his expression as he stared at her, and she wanted to scream, but all that she could muster was a rasping, hissing sound.

He started running, and she followed him, the muscles of her body undulating with incredible speed. She wanted to explain that she hadn't intended for any of this to happen. She hadn't intended to disappoint him.

He stumbled and fell, and she curled around his leg to be close to him, sinking her fangs into his soft flesh so she could taste his blood, tearing through the muscle and envenoming him to make him stay with her.

Stay he did, and when the poison reached his chest, it slowed his beating heart until she could barely hear it anymore. The woman inside the king cobra tried to attach her mind to his, tried to tell him things that were irrelevant now, things she no longer understood and finally failed to remember, but when she sensed death closing in on him, she couldn't disentangle herself from his scattered thoughts.

The last human emotion that formed was regret, and the last remnant of her human soul was torn to pieces trying to escape Jaden Aurum's doom.

Chapter Thirty-Five

❧ The Mark ❧

Waking up from the first rays of sun shining in his face, Lorcan was exhausted, sore, and freezing. Another hour of rest would have been good. For a moment, he was tempted to turn over and ignore the obtrusive light in his eyes, but he had to get moving if he wanted to catch up with the Sorcerer.

The damp moss and pine twigs on the forest floor hadn't made for a very good bed, he discovered, as he stretched his aching limbs beneath the thick woolen blanket one of the Snake Sisters had given to him for his new tent at The Fair. He'd cocooned himself within its warm lining, but roots and sharp stones had dug into his back, and the cold had crept into every bone of his body. He knew he shouldn't have made halt to lie down in the open on a night like this – it could have cost him his life – but he'd been too tired to think straight. He'd lit a small fire and kept it going until sleep had claimed him, and that was the best he could have done for himself.

Casting off the blanket, he looked around as he rose. He was alone, and the woods were still. Loosening the knots in his muscles, he tried to get his circulation going, wiggling his toes in his cold, hard leather boots, and rubbing and blowing warming breaths at his numb fingers.

The road he'd been following was just a stone's throw from where he'd slept. The crossing he'd seen on the map wouldn't be far now. He was aware he must certainly have missed the rendezvous; Jaden and Maebh would be long gone by now, as would the Master Sorcerer, but it was a place to start looking. Ortus hadn't come back the way he should have unless he'd passed him while he'd been asleep, but Lorcan doubted it.

If he found any tracks that would tell him they'd been at that crossing the previous evening, he might see which of them were heading in which direction, at least, and he'd catch up with Ortus sooner or later. The old man might be disappointed in him for disobeying, but he'd understand, in the end. He'd have to.

Lorcan no longer felt the need to tell his father what a jerk he was. He might have been tempted to if he hadn't had time to think about this, but he wasn't going to embarrass himself to someone who didn't care whether he lived or died. He had nothing to say to Jaden, nothing that would have meaning to either one of them. Contrary to what Ortus might think, he was past that.

And, he wasn't a child that needed to be spared anything; he wasn't the Sorcerer's son who needed to be kept out of harm's way for the sake of his father's peace of mind. Sometimes, he thought Ortus was confusing him with Dean. Dean would never know how both lucky and unlucky he was at the same time.

No, Lorcan's gut told him this was going to end badly, and the woman his father was trying to impress had a lot to do with that.

If Maebh had been just another of Jaden's expendable lovers it wouldn't have mattered, and he would have wished them both farewell and good riddance, but there was something seriously wrong about her and this meeting and *everything*.

He made haste to roll his blanket up and tie it to his backpack. Shouldering it, he couldn't really fathom what to expect of the day, but he was underway in any case, and he'd find out what was going on here and think of something to remedy it, if necessary. He wasn't afraid of choosing a side that wasn't Jaden's.

Keeping to the road, he soon cleared the woods. The open fields to either side of the path were frosted white. The heavy haze seeped through the layers of his clothing, breathing an icy promise of the winter yet to come.

He thought he saw a deer grazing by the side of the road in the distance, but when he got closer, he realized it was a horse. The dark mare with its long, shaggy mane seemed familiar, and when he recognized the saddle he'd put on her himself so often for the Sorcerer, his stomach lurched. He began running.

There was no way the Master Sorcerer would have left old Bessie to roam the countryside over the night.

Horses were expensive, and Cine people were accustomed to tending to what they had. Apart from that, Ortus was very fond of Bessie.

Lorcan called to her, struggling with his baggage. His heart hammered in his chest. She met him half way. He didn't have anything to give her, so he just rubbed her muzzle before examining her. There didn't seem to be anything amiss. There were no wounds that he could see, and the saddle and stirrups were intact. Even the saddle bag was still there.

"Where's your master, Bessie? Where is he?"

The mare snorted as though in reply, shaking her mane. She would know, he thought, but couldn't offer an answer – or could she?

"Show me," he encouraged her, pulling himself up into the saddle and patting her neck. "Come on, show me."

Slowly, the old horse trotted up the road toward the crossing while Lorcan scanned the way ahead and the fields around him for activity or any sign of Ortus or Jaden.

They hadn't gone very far before he spotted a motionless form lying on the frozen ground ahead. Sliding off Bessie's back, he dropped his things and felt sick when he realized who it was. There was no need to hurry anymore.

Edging toward the Sorcerer's dead body, he kneaded his hands fiercely, not knowing what to do with himself. Eventually, he knelt down and scratched his shoulder as he studied Ortus' face, trying to concentrate on what might have happened here, but he felt the absence of his mentor like a void in time.

Trying to block out the pain, he first looked at the ground around the Sorcerer's body. There was no sign of skirmish. Then, he let his hands and his gaze roam over the Sorcerer's body. There wasn't a single bruise or scratch or any other kind of mark on him anywhere, as far as Lorcan could tell, but people didn't just lie down and die in the middle of the road unless they were ill or there was dark magic involved.

He didn't think Ortus had been ill. That left magic. The unusually wrought position of the body and the bloodshot eyes testified to unnatural circumstances of death, though Lorcan couldn't imagine which.

He couldn't say if he was shaking from the cold or something else that was making him tremble, but there was a sense of loss like he'd never felt before. Tears leaked down his cheeks as he sat back on his calves in silence. No matter how he wiped at them with his sleeve, willing himself to stop crying, the hurt kept spilling over until it had all but emptied him out.

When he finally got to his feet, he tried to think of what to do next, but his mind was as numb as his fingers were, and it was hard to focus. Raking a hand through his hair, he scanned the area around the crossing more closely.

Where were his father and that wretched woman? Had Ortus encountered them here at all? Did they have something to do with his death? The path from fraud and trickery to murder was steep, but it was thinkable. A searing rage threatened to consume him as he started stomping about, searching the rock-hard ground for tracks. Of course, there were none that could have told him anything.

After a while, something a little way into the field caught his eye. Lying by a bush, there was another body, and when he'd reached it, he recognized his father.

Jaden was lying on his side, but he wasn't dead. Not yet.

Bending over him, Lorcan took note of the agony distorting Jaden's ghostly features, and it startled him. His father was breathing in ragged, shallow gulps and didn't seem to register his presence. Lorcan knew he was beyond help even before he'd laboriously turned him on his back to get a better look at him.

"What happened to you?" he mumbled, searching for wounds.

He found several bite marks on his hands and arms, but he couldn't place them because he'd never seen any quite like them before.

For a moment, Jaden's vision unexpectedly seemed to clear, and he came to. Staring at Lorcan with bloodshot eyes, the man grabbed the neck of his shirt firmly, pulling him down to him.

"The snake," Jaden whispered, foul breath wafting into Lorcan's face. "Look out for the snake."

The thought that the bite marks might belong to a snake hadn't occurred to him right away. He'd never actually seen a snake bite. Freya and Brunhild had never been chewed on by one of their "darlings" – not that he knew of.

"I will," he said. "I'll watch out." He patted the hand that hadn't been hurt, and Jaden seemed to acknowledge that. "Papa, what happened to Ortus? He wasn't bitten by a snake."

"You're wrong," Jaden stammered, panting and salivating heavily before his eyes turned upward, whites showing just before he was shaken by a fit.

Lorcan held him by the shoulders, helpless. Then, Jaden's life-force slipped away.

Sighing, Lorcan waited for a few moments before shutting his eyes. He knelt with him for a while before getting to his feet, wiping his runny nose on his sleeve.

All at once, something else came to mind. "Where's Maebh?" he mumbled, wondering if she, too, would be lying close by.

Perhaps she'd fled either before or after what had happened here, but maybe she was still somewhere close by and hurt or scared. She might be in need of help, and whatever he'd thought of her, he wanted certainty she wouldn't be injured and bleeding to death a few feet from where he was.

Rising, he turned about slowly, searching for his father's lover in the open lane and the underbrush. He called her name as he retraced his steps up the path to where he'd left the Sorcerer's body.

A light dusting of new snow gave way beneath his feet as he walked, and he'd almost given her up when he caught sight of a tiny scrap of dark red fabric beneath the winter-dead twigs of a gorse. It was part of a piece of clothing, he realized, almost completely hidden by the undisturbed rime-coated cloak that covered it. His heart sank at the thought of finding yet another body – especially if it was that of someone he'd known.

Cautiously, he approached the cloak and what might be there underneath it, but it appeared to have been simply discarded in the brush. Not knowing whether to be relieved or not, he was more puzzled by the discovery than anything else.

Why would the woman take her dress off in the lane, if indeed she had taken it off herself freely? It could have been ripped off of her by robbers or highwaymen who'd passed through before or after Ortus had died. They might have raped and killed her, and disposed of her corpse in the woods, or taken her with them. There was no way of knowing. He'd already started to turn away, frantically scanning the area again, when a slight movement within the folds of the cloak caught his eye.

Fear prickled along his spine, but his curiosity got the better of him, and he picked up a stick that looked sturdy enough to bludgeon the unfortunate rodent that might be hiding there.

Using the end of it to push some of the coarse woven cloth aside and stir the dress that he was sure had been Maebh's favorite, he discovered that it was far too heavy, like it was either frozen fast to the grass or had something else, something bigger inside of it. Poking about more intently, his efforts revealed a snake coiled tightly inside the bodice, vainly hiding from the cold.

He could tell it was probably fully mature, but it was an unusual species he couldn't name, and he stepped back from it instantly, his brow knitting as he scrutinized it from a distance. Its long body was covered in shiny, black scales, interspersed every few inches with thin, blood-red stripes that perfectly matched the color of the dress beneath it.

The creature was almost frozen stiff and didn't move when he fully uncovered it, but Lorcan was sure it was still alive. Something about it felt very wrong. It wasn't native to these parts, and he asked himself how it could have gotten here unless someone had brought it. Maebh? Jaden? Some other person who'd been here? Jaden had warned him of a snake, but he hadn't counted on this.

Undoubtedly to him, this was the snake that had bitten Jaden, but Ortus hadn't died of a snake bite, and he hadn't found Maebh's body yet. He knew there was a connection, but he couldn't put his finger on it.

Every instinct told him to do away with the reptile, and he drew his dagger, cautiously inching toward the snake again so he could get close enough to sever its head from its body.

It was vicious. It had killed once, and it would kill again because that was its nature. It would kill him, too, if it got the chance. He could have sworn it was watching him, and he was ready to bolt at its slightest movement, but it stayed completely still.

Freya and Brunhild had never failed to point out to him that snakes were no different to any other predator in creation. They only killed for food, and they weren't interested in trouble unless you brought it to them, but he couldn't help himself – he'd always hated snakes with a passion, and he especially hated this one.

Telling himself it needed to be taken care of as quickly as he could manage it, he placed one of his boots' heels firmly on its head, expecting it to start thrashing and writhing in protecting itself, but it didn't. It remained perfectly still, and that baffled him.

For reasons he didn't understand, he couldn't bring himself to bear down on it with his full weight and start cutting into its flesh as he'd intended. He hesitated, asking himself what he was doing, what he was waiting for, but killing the snake when he didn't know what it was that was troubling him about it seemed rash, all at once.

He bent to pick it up the way Freya had taught him, but still, the snake remained motionless.

While gripping it so it could neither strike at nor get away from him, the skin contact sent a warm tingling sensation rippling through his body. An image of Maebh's face began to form in his mind, fading in and out of sight like a ghostly shadow, a screaming mess of confusion and agony. Then, he noticed for the first time that the cobra's eyes weren't at all serpentine. They were blue.

Turning the reptile stiffly about in his bewilderment, he saw that the hood behind its delicate head bore a strange symbol he recognized from somewhere, but it took him a moment to remember where he'd seen it. The red scales formed a shape similar to a Y, and it looked like a mark he'd once seen in Ortus' copy of the Bible, the special one the Sorcerer had gifted him. He recalled that it was on a picture of a man named Cain.

The story of Cain and Abel was one of the first stories he'd read and talked about with Ortus, and Ortus had told him that the artist who'd drawn the image had probably used a very old symbol to represent God's warning to all of mankind. It meant to show that its bearer was a murderer.

Slowly, he released the breath he'd been holding. He didn't know what to make of all this, but he was willing to think about it. As things were, he couldn't kill the beast before he'd gotten to the bottom of this somehow, but he had to make sure it wouldn't harm anyone else if he took it back to The Fair with him.

Keeping a good hold of the creature, he slid the satchel he'd been carrying off of his back, and awkwardly opened the fastening with one hand so he could empty it on the ground and place the snake inside. Having done that, he quickly secured the cord and put it aside so he could shake the frost from the cloak and dress. Gathering the cloak, he bundled the dress and his belongings carelessly inside and fastened it to Bessie's saddle along with the satchel.

Then, he got busy finding a place in the nearby grove where he thought the earth might be soft enough to dig at least a shallow grave for one of the dead, and dragged Jaden's body there. Bessie couldn't carry two back to The Fair, and he didn't feel that it would be right to leave him where he was.

He had no tools, and it took him the better part of an hour to realize he couldn't jab so much as a narrow trench in the cold ground with only stones and his bare hands. When he finally gave up, he did so with a roar of anger and defeat, startling the crows that had been watching him amusedly from the trees. He threw the rocks he'd been trying to loosen the ground with at them, but they laughed at him hoarsely, and he wished them all to hell.

He didn't have a prayer for his father's soul, so in the end, he just silently covered Jaden as best he could with branches and dead leaves. Jaden had made his life what it was, and he'd left Lorcan with nothing but emptiness and shame. Words couldn't make the situation any better. Jaden hadn't been a father to him, but Lorcan had done his duty as a son and buried him in the earth instead of leaving him to the crows. He thought it was what his mother would have called *the right thing to do*.

The other *right thing to do* now was to bring home the Sorcerer's body to The Fair. Ortus was the man he'd spent the last years wishing had been his father.

He had no idea how he was going to explain this to anyone, least of all Dean.

Chapter Thirty-Six

ೞ Shame ಲಿ

There were no footprints in this part of the snowy forest besides Lorcan's. Only a deer had crisscrossed the trail he was using and left its tracks in intervals on the thick blanket of white. The world was so quiet, it seemed almost as though it had stopped.

He was exhausted and wet through by the time he reached the glade where The Fair had set up camp. The tingle of the protective enchantment that encompassed the grounds lapped at his skin as he slowly neared the invisible wall of the Outer Haven. Both relief and dread tugged at his heart. He was relieved to find the new defenses firmly in place beyond Ortus' death, just as the Sorcerer had promised, but he dreaded passing through them onto the grounds, so he stayed hidden between ghostly bare birches and black oaks for a while.

"I'll bet you never thought you'd carry him home like this," he mumbled, stroking the mare's muzzle as he leant his forehead against her neck.

On one hand, he thought how wonderful it would be if Ortus could have lived to see his new wards hold. Any ordinary protective enchantment bound to this world ended when its creator left it, but the magic

Ortus had created here wasn't anchored to the soil its originator would be buried in. It would remain tethered to the spirit of The Fair for as long as its people carried it. Ortus had crafted a masterpiece, and Lorcan thought it honored his memory in the most wonderful way.

Still, another part of him wished the Sorcerer had failed and the grounds had relocated in his absence. The thought shamed him, but if The Fair had moved, he wouldn't have to go in there right now with a heart so heavy that he could hardly carry it in his chest.

Someone would have to send for Dean, if they hadn't already done that, and he couldn't imagine facing him. Life would never be the same again for either of them.

He asked himself what Ortus would have wanted for his son. The Sorcerer had always been so afraid for the boy though he'd never outright said it. Lorcan honestly didn't know what Dean would do now, given the choice of staying with The Fair or the relative he was visiting.

Finally, he mustered the courage to step out of the grove and into plain sight of the Cine community.

"Come on, let's get this over with," he told Bessie, and they moved through the intermediate space that separated one reality from the other.

The smith was the first to take note of Lorcan, and he dropped everything when he saw what Bessie was carrying across her back. Soon, a whole crowd of people had gathered around him as he led the mare to

Thaddeus' work place.

A jumble of voices assaulted him, but Lorcan couldn't hear clearly what they were saying. He didn't much care to. He wanted to talk to the carpenter before he spoke with anyone else, and stoically kept going.

Someone insulted him, letting everyone know that Lorcan's father was most likely to blame for the Master Sorcerer's death. Another man yelled at him, calling him names and ordering him to tell them what had happened. One of the Equilibrists shouted that Lorcan was as rotten a scoundrel as his father was, and that he should be banished at once.

There was no point in starting a discussion in the middle of all this commotion, so he ignored them all, keeping his eyes trained on the ground ahead. Thaddeus would know what to do, he was sure, and he was better at talking to people. They tended to listen to him.

Then, he bumped straight into Rua Tine, who'd purposely put himself in his way. A raging ball of fury formed in his stomach.

"You!" he said, but that was as far as he got before Rua derailed and hit him in the face so hard, he went to the ground and blacked out.

When he came to, he found himself lying on a mattress of straw. Mary was tending to his bruised and swollen cheek. It felt as though there was a goose egg in between his skin and the bones behind it. He was cold despite the fire going in the small brazier in the tent's center, and he didn't think he wanted to sit up.

"Come on, you should try to drink some warm broth," Mary told him, and he pushed up on his elbows to take the cup she was offering.

"Where's Thaddeus?"

"Talking to Rua. Calming things over, as much as he can. Lorcan, no one really believes you had anything to do with it – and Rua is a fool who ran face first into this with his eyes closed. He's plain scared. They're all scared. You have to tell us what happened. They all just want to know. *I* want to know."

He looked at the cup in his hand and set it down.

"Honestly? I have no idea. Ortus was already dead when I found him."

Mary seemed to accept that. She turned to lay another log in the fire mold.

Why would he have come back if he had set out to help his father, and what would he have had to gain by Ortus' death, or by coming back if he'd had anything to do with it?

He knew what she thought of Jaden, what *everyone* thought of Jaden. And, they were most likely right. But where was his place in all of this? Where would he still fit in when they'd buried the Sorcerer? He'd always be the son of the man who'd been involved in the death of their benefactor, their protector, their leader… their friend.

He could never expect to be forgiven for that, even if he hadn't done anything wrong. People would never look beyond that. People were what they were, whether Cine or human, and he was what he was.

Gathering himself, he rose and picked his cloak up from where Mary had laid it out to dry. It was still as wet as his boots were – the boots Ortus had organized for him before they'd left The Fair.

Peering through the tent's entrance, he could see it was getting dark, and there didn't seem to be anyone about. They were probably all at the Big Top. That was where they held council, and they'd have a lot to talk about tonight. He wasn't sure he'd want to be around after they'd closed.

"Where are you going?" Mary asked.

"Away," he told her. "I don't think I should stick around. No one is going to want to hear what I have to say, and I don't have all that much to tell them."

"Rubbish." She sounded convinced, but he wasn't. "It's not safe," she continued. "What would you do, love, and where would you go?"

"I don't know."

He really didn't.

It didn't matter where he went or what he did, though. Anywhere would be better than here right now. He registered the hurt on her face. Mary had always been good to him, and she meant well.

"Maybe I'll be back when all this has blown over," he offered, but he didn't think it ever would.

"Wait," she called after him, and he stopped. She handed him a piece of parchment with a seal on it. The

Tierney family crest was embedded in the blood-red wax; a beech leaf with two stars above it in each corner of the crest. "Thaddeus thought you might need this. Open it when you've cleared this part of the forest."

She hugged him and pressed a kiss to his cheek, and he knew he was going to miss her so much.

Chapter Thirty-Seven

❦ Partings ❧

Dean thought he should feel something, but he didn't. Not the icy winter wind biting the ends of his nose and ears, and not the tentative shafts of sunlight spilling through the bare branches of the oak beneath which they were laying his father to rest. He felt neither cold nor hot nor anything in between.

He'd been peeling willow switches for arrow shafts at Caius' fireside when he'd heard the gentle tapping of the dovelen's beak on the window shutter. Recognizing the hawk for what it really was by the tingling sensation its magical origins sketched into the lining of his stomach, he'd known something was wrong the moment he'd let it into the house.

That was the last thing he remembered *feeling*.

Caius had lifted the bird off the table and carefully turned it on its back as it traded brown feathers for the pure white plumage of a dove. Dean had untied the note from its leg, but he'd handed it to Caius and taken the dovelen from the fletcher's hands in exchange for the message he didn't want to read.

He recalled the silence that had filled the room.

The same silence still filled his heart and his mind now as he stood staring down at his father's coffin beside its hole in the frozen ground, Thaddeus on one side of him and Caius on the other.

Thaddeus had carved the Tierney family crest into its lid. Oddly, Dean kept thinking Lorcan would have done a better job, but Lorcan wasn't here.

No one else would ever see that crest, so it didn't really matter, but he was sure the leaf was too broad, and it was crooked, and the acorns looked puny.

It was almost ridiculous: his father was dead, his best friend was gone because he blamed himself, and all Dean could think of was the rendering of a stupid crest on a stupid box. He was sure that wasn't right, but what, exactly, was right anymore?

Lifting his hand in a waving motion, he willed the leaf in the middle of the emblem to reshape. Its lobes drew inward toward the median line, defining the knobs more distinctly, and the acorns shifted and churned, growing in size until he was satisfied everything was as it should be.

Caius startled, but didn't say anything. Thaddeus didn't appear to notice.

Lorcan would have.

Dean knew none of this was Lorcan's fault, but he wished his friend would have stayed and talked to him.

He was convinced that if anyone was to blame, then it was he himself. He shouldn't have insisted on staying with Caius. He should have gone back to The Fair with Ortus and done what his father had asked of him. He should have… He should have.

He'd seen his father's body, helped lift him into the wooden casket before they'd put the lid on, and he understood why Lorcan had left. Nothing remained of the Master Sorcerer in the empty shell Lorcan had brought back from wherever he'd found him. Nothing.

Dean wanted to remember the indulgent grin the old man always had for him, the animated expressions of his face no matter how tired he was or how often he'd answered his endless questions late at night. He wanted to remember the weathered hands writing or crafting or patting his shoulder affectionately. He wanted to remember his father as he'd last seen him, reluctant to leave him behind but proud that he was old enough to make choices for his own life.

He wanted to remember all these things, but right now, try as he might, he couldn't even recall the sound of Ortus' voice. His mother's was still clear in his mind as the day she'd passed away. Some of the conversations they'd had before she'd left them had lodged firmly in his brain in every detail, but it was as if some power beyond his grasp had decided to silence Ortus' voice forever.

There was no priest, and this wasn't holy ground, but Thaddeus and he had chosen this spot near the Outer Haven over the graveyard where Gwyneth lay because this was the only way the community Ortus had built could safely say their goodbyes. Ortus belonged here more than he did in the graveyard.

Dean barely heard Thaddeus speak of the things his father had done for their people, the lives he'd saved and changed, and the sacrifices he'd made. Despite his will to try, he found it just as hard to concentrate on Caius' short speech, than on what any of the other people whose life his father had touched said afterward in turn. He only snapped back to himself when the bower gently pushed him forward so they could lower the casket into the hole, three ropes, three men on each side, six in all. It was remarkably heavy, and Dean wondered yet again how Lorcan had managed to get his father on old Bessie's back by himself to take him home.

After it was done, they dropped the ropes in after the coffin, and Caius bent to pick up a handful of soil. He filled Dean's palm with it, nudging him, and Dean tossed it into the grave, flinching at the dull thud the dirt made when it hit the box. Caius picked up another handful for himself and tossed it in as well. Thaddeus followed. Some of the children had cut witch hazel twigs and dropped them on the casket instead of the soil.

Watching as nearly two hundred people paid their respects, each in their own way, Dean didn't know how he was going to live up to what Ortus had asked of him – of him and Lorcan. He wasn't prepared. He didn't want the responsibility. He might never be ready for the task.

"You should stay," Thaddeus said when Caius and he were the only ones left at the grave aside from the diggers. The two stayed back respectfully.

Dean was at a loss and looked to Caius, who'd already fetched their horses from where he'd tethered their reins.

The bower studied him for a moment. Dean could see he was torn between a promise and a plea.

"My cousin's son has an obligation to his family right now," he finally said, choosing the needs of the living over those of the dead.

Thaddeus chewed on this for a moment. "I'm aware of that, but he has obligations here, as well." The burly man locked his gaze to Dean's. "I can understand that you need time to yourself, my boy, believe me. We've all lost so much. I know you'll be back, though, just as I know Lorcan will be back."

Dean wasn't convinced of that. There was nothing here for either of them, it seemed.

"Look," Thaddeus continued, "we'll be breaking camp in spring, but we'll be back right here every winter for the next three, so you'll know where to find us, and if you don't happen to be looking for us in winter, you'll find markers here that'll tell you where we went."

Dean smiled weakly and nodded. He wasn't too good at reading markers, but Lorcan would find them, he was sure – if he ever really did come back.

All Dean wanted now was to leave this place behind him and not have to think about it anymore, not have to take the silence anymore, not have to look at the hole in the ground with his father's casket in it anymore, so he turned and heaved himself up into his saddle, and followed Caius into the forest.

Chapter Thirty-Eight

☙ Pikes and Tadpoles ❧

Catherine sat quietly on the thick, straight branch that jutted out over the steep river bank. Her feet dangled lazily into the water, and she watched it ripple and curl around her ankles. Its coolness felt glorious on her bare skin in the warm summer sun.

Someone had warned her to watch out for the huge old pike that was said to take the toes off children if they hung them into the stream, but she didn't believe everything she was told anymore. She was no longer a little girl who'd believe in the scaretales the old wives would tell while they did their laundry a bit further up river where the stream was wide and shallow. They liked to distract themselves from the monotony of their day's work with gossip, and a lot of it revolved around things that simply *couldn't* be true.

But, even if there was a monster pike in these parts, she'd dare the scaly, pointy-toothed creature to try to disturb her ruminations. In fact, she thought she'd love to see it.

"Bring it on," she mumbled absently, smiling. *"I'll boil ya in your skin."*

She'd done that with one of the rabbits she'd

caught in a snare some weeks ago – if more by accident than Ability.

Had they seen her, the washerwomen would have had her in shackles, waiting for the new clergyman and that new book of his that told him how to recognize a Shifter by daylight and a Cine by night, but no one ever watched her, so they'd never find out. They were dense, and they talked so much, they didn't pay proper attention to what was going on around them. Much like the new clergyman.

If the clergyman paid attention, he'd have known who needed help and wouldn't have been sitting in his cozy little house, eating his meals by a warm fire while children had been starving to death all around him last winter.

If the washerwomen paid attention when they were down by the river, they would see Catherine taking food from their satchels to ensure *she* wouldn't starve to death *any* winter.

Most people in the village were as dense as rabbits, and the rabbits Catherine caught were as dense as the people were.

The small, frightened animal she'd accidentally fried had still been alive when she'd found it. She'd pulled her knife from its leather sheath to end the creature's suffering, but then she'd felt its terror and hesitated at the unexpected, raw sensation.

She'd felt its heartbeat, thumping, jumping, hammering in what she'd at first believed to be her own chest. Then, she'd realized she was somehow both inside of herself and inside the rabbit's skin – in two places at the same time, seeing two fates unfold; panic and death on one side of reality, and a thin, dark-haired girl viewing panic and death on the other side of it.

She wondered if it had been like this for her mother.

The rabbit had twitched and writhed and made sounds that shook Catherine to the core. Watching and feeling the animal die had seemed like an eternity even though it had only been mere seconds until it stopped moving once she'd let go of its *essence* – or its *essence* had let go of *her*. She wasn't entirely sure which, at first, and she'd dropped the knife and taken a few steps back from where she'd stood.

The hollow, oozing eyes and the smell of death had imprinted themselves in her memory, and she'd sunk to her knees and cried because she hadn't meant to be cruel.

Not like this.

She wasn't *like* Maebh.

She'd *never* be like Maebh.

She'd been confused, and she'd felt herself burning up as though a sudden, severe fever had taken hold of her, but she had been *aware* of her doings. She was *aware* whenever she triggered without meaning to, whether it was to suggest a thought to someone, move a very small object just a little way with her mind when she was terribly mad or sad, or blend in with the backdrop so she wouldn't be seen right away, which she was best at.

She'd realized this could happen any time again if she wasn't careful to control herself, with a rabbit… or any other living being. But, Rebecca had told her it was possible to control a Talent, and she believed that.

She'd come to the conclusion her own inner distress had caused the boiling heat within the little animal's body because she'd never experienced emotions that weren't her own before. The more she thought about it, the better she understood. Controlling her emotions was the key to controlling her Abilities. Her Talent was certainly worth having – or it would be, once she'd found out how to master it. Her life was full of moments that seemed to evade her, but this day had served to teach her she could control even death if she learned to control her fear of it.

No, she was certain she'd never be *like* Maebh in any way, and she wasn't going to end up like Rebecca, either.

One day, all of the village girls who'd looked down on her ever since she could remember would wake up to find she'd risen above them. The village drunk's daughter would show those arrogant, stuck-up, prissy maidens what she was really made of, and she'd put them in their place. She was convinced she could be someone; *really be someone*. She could be whoever, or *what*ever she chose to be. She could become a Lady, or a duchess, like Lady Tierney, who'd ruled the castle when it had been grand so many years ago, or even *a queen*, if she wanted; a queen with wealth and power who could rebuild the castle from the ruins. She'd reign over these lands, wearing the finest clothes, and she'd have the best of everything those village girls could only dream of.

Every last one of the silly little boys who'd laughed at her and pointed whenever she'd encountered them on the village road or in the woods would discover that the girl they'd made fun of had become a woman who was far above them. She'd turn their heads, and they'd stare and be sorry they'd ever laid eyes on her, but never their hands, and she'd strike them down like the dogs they were, if she chose to. No one – *no one* – would ever laugh at her again, or she'd have their tongues torn out.

She'd make them all see how wrong they'd been about her, and she'd move on to greatness while they lived out their pitiful, meaningless lives in fear of tomorrow, of illness, of hunger... and... perhaps of her.

So, bring on the big ugly pike, she thought again then; it would serve her well for practice.

She was curious if she could willfully repeat what she'd done to the rabbit, if she put in an effort right now. She hadn't found anything about a Gift like hers in the book she'd hidden from Cooper just yet, but she wasn't half done with it. Reading it by herself was a trial, and the texts were difficult. As far as she could tell, they were more about the magical properties of ores, minerals, and plants than controlling a Gift anyway, but she hoped for something more useful down the line.

Catherine believed improving her command of words would help her considerably with the book, so she'd been dragging Caleb to church every Sunday over the past year, and she'd been spending more time than ever with Cooper. Cooper was quite good about giving her the reading practice she needed, and in addition to that, he was teaching her how wealthy people ate, spoke, and behaved.

She also just kept trying to utilize what she had in a practical way while she was putting meaning with the texts she was working on. If she had a means to funnel and concentrate the tingling sensation in her body and in her mind that went along with the almost audible buzz she felt when she unintendedly moved small objects, or, as more recently, fried that bunny, she'd likely get the hang of it even if neither of the books ever turned out the information she was searching for.

The pike would be bigger and stronger than a rabbit, and it was a clever predator; it would have more fight in it. She was sure if she could channel her energy toward a creature like that, she might be able to tackle different challenges altogether very soon, but she had to be careful.

She thought most Cine who got caught weren't. That's what her aunt kept telling her father whenever they spoke of Maebh, or rather, whenever *Rebecca* spoke of Maebh while her father did his best to ignore her, getting steadily drunk as he was inclined to do whenever his sister-in-law got started on another round of *let's speculate.*

Shapeshifters, Cine or Witches were hung, or burned, or drowned, or beheaded *before* they were burned, if they confessed, but that was as much mercy as they'd get, Rebecca never tired of reminding them. She'd often wonder aloud whether her sister would be stupid enough not to confess if she got caught.

A good headsman would kill with one blow of his blade-heavy sword if a Witch was to be beheaded before she was burned. A clumsy one with a dull blade might miss, and he'd need several attempts to sever the backbone.

The bleeding, writhing being at his feet wouldn't feel the mercy in that, Catherine reckoned, and she didn't think she'd confess to anything if the bishop's men came after her. She'd never witnessed the execution of a Cine before, but she'd been to the disastrous beheading of a murderer once. The executioner, who'd just taken over the family business from his father, hadn't been paid because he'd blundered the job.

There had been a lot of fear in the air that day; not just the murderer's, and so much that she'd almost been able to taste its heavy sour aroma on the tip of her tongue. It had been exciting, somehow. Events like these could easily get out of hand, and everyone present had, at the very least, been nervous – even the king's soldiers, who'd kept their hands on the hilts of their weapons, and the clergyman, who'd kept his on his holy book.

People who were afraid could be more dangerous by far than any old pike biting children's toes off, and that applied to murderers, soldiers, and clergymen alike – death wasn't always swift, and life wasn't always worthwhile at any cost.

It wasn't worthwhile at all if you were weak.

Catherine was tired of being weak, and if practicing to cook a fish could put an end to that, then let's have that fish, she told herself and meant it.

Her thoughts soon shifted back and forth between one thing and another as the afternoon wore on without so much as a sighting of the alleged monster, however. Just before she was about to rise and walk back over the bough toward the grassy river bank, a lanky, red-haired boy roughly her own age, sixteen at most, caught her attention.

She knew him from the village, though they'd never spoken. She'd heard from Rebecca that he'd come to stay with relatives a while ago, learn his uncle's trade, and help out on their farm. Since she'd never had a reason to approach him, it had been all the same to her. She had other worries than to think about a boy who apparently spent most of his free time with his drawing coals. Rebecca had gone on and on about the expensive parchments he squandered on sketches of the mongrels that skulked about the squalid huts, and portraits of the men and women who lived there.

He must have been there for a while without her noticing, but he hadn't been aware of her presence any more than she had of his, and when the boy looked up to find her staring at him from not ten feet away, he startled. Eyebrows quirking as his head jerked back, he turned to leave, trying to hide the clear glass jar he was holding in his hand. Such an invaluable and striking object was rare to the world Catherine lived in, so it caught her eye, and she was curious, in part about the jar, and in part about its owner.

"Hey," she called out, not moving. "Wait!"

She didn't assume that he would, but he stopped in his tracks with his back to her.

"You're that weird kid that lives in the woods most of the time, aren't you?" he said, making more of an uncertain statement of it than a question.

A small, haughty smile tugged at her lips. "And you're that weird kid that draws things half the day – so?"

Hesitating, the boy slowly faced her, still concealing the jar behind his back, and looked her firmly in the eyes. "I'm not *weird*."

"Well, neither am I," Catherine stated assertively, folding her arms across her chest. "So I guess that makes two of us. I'm Catherine Salt."

"I know who you are." He shifted his weight from one foot to the other and back, and awkward moments passed in silence so Catherine assumed that he'd either not taken the hint or simply wasn't intent on telling her his name. Both notions irritated her, but she wasn't about to ask. It didn't matter anyway. The jar did.

Finally, he brought it out from behind his back and hugged it to his belly, looking first past her shoulder, and then at the ground, where his foot was tracing patterns in the dirt. She watched him hem and haw, her brow crinkling, and wondered why he was still here, and, more interestingly still, what on earth he'd be keeping in that jar.

"Tadpoles," he offered eventually, nodding to himself as though he'd heard echoes of her thoughts, and she climbed down from the tree to get a closer look at his prize.

"Indeed," she determined, squinting in bewilderment at the minute creatures scuttling around in the murky water as he held the vessel up to her face. What a prize *that* was.

She discovered there were ones in it close to losing their tails, while others had barely hatched. "They'll eat each other in there, you know," she told him, and he looked shocked.

"No, they won't," he snapped, his lip pulling upward in disgust.

"Yes, they will," she persisted defiantly. She knew these kinds of things because she'd observed them, and, in her experience, this particular law of nature didn't just apply to tadpoles. "If you put too many of one kind in a closed off space together, they'll start fighting over who's boss." She paused, scrutinizing him, before adding another bit of personal knowledge. "It's not always the big ones that win; it's the ones that are a little bit *faster* than the others."

There was another moment of silence as she gloated. It was the kind of silence she was vaguely familiar with whenever you told someone things they didn't want to hear or couldn't process. She knew it would be best to let it go, but the boy didn't seem to be heading off in a hurry anymore.

"What are you going to do with them?" she inquired, toning down pleasantly, and she could see the corners of his mouth pull upward into a vague smile.

"I want to do studies of them."

Unexpectedly to her, he set the jar down by his feet and reached behind him, making her withdraw in alarm and reach for her knife, but he didn't seem to realize that he'd made her jump. He pulled several folded sheets of parchment from beneath his shirt where he'd tucked them into the back of his pants, and she released the breath she'd been holding. Not that she wouldn't have been able to handle him, but she'd thought she might have underestimated the boy.

Moving a little closer to Catherine than she was comfortable with, he almost knocked the jar over as he smoothed out the creases in the paper to show her what he'd been working on. Taking one of the leaves from his hands, she examined the sketches he'd done of mature bull frogs and toads, and she had to admit they were quite impressively executed, although she couldn't fathom why anyone would actually be interested in drawing frogs. They were unspectacular to look at, disgusting while alive, simply everywhere around these parts, and, worst of all, lurking inside her shelters after a downpour. They were edible, at best, when turned on a stake over a fire long enough.

"Okay..." she mumbled indifferently, caught between humoring him for reasons she herself couldn't understand and telling him that this kind of thing was never going to win him friends. "And...?"

He snorted a little laugh as though he was a tiny bit annoyed with her in the way that an older brother might be annoyed with his ignorant younger sister, and her eyebrows knitted in a frown.

"*And*, when I'm done with this series, I'll have the whole metamorphosis detailed step by step, and I can analyze how they change."

Catherine sighed. "The meta-*what?*" she grumbled, genuinely puzzled by his motivations. He was serious about whatever it was he was doing, and since he didn't seem to be as dense as most of the village fools, she was inclined to believe that there would be some reasoning to it. "Why are you doing this?"

"Because–" he began, but paused as his glance darted to some distant place behind her again, as though there was something there worth seeing. She looked over her shoulder to where he'd directed his eyes only to find there was nothing there at the edge of the forest but trees and bushes and a jay soaring low, weaving in and out between the branches.

When she faced back to him, he was gone. He'd left the jar with the tadpoles, and although she was slightly irked by his sudden disappearance, she suspected that he was close by and scolded herself for having fallen for his cheap little thimbleriggers' trick.

Picking up the jar, she didn't let on that she was in the least bit surprised or bothered by his absence. She never let *anyone* see what was inside. Resolutely, she strode over to the water's edge, peeled off the thick waxed fabric that closed the jar off, and stretched out her hand with it like she was about to pour its contents back into the river where they'd come from.

"No!" he called out then from a bough high up in the same tree she'd been perched in for the most part of the afternoon, and a smirk stole across her face, though she didn't look up just yet.

"Why*ever* not?"

She heard leaves rustling, and twigs snapped. He was as inept as he looked; he probably never climbed trees, and she was sure that watching him descend was going to be very entertaining.

"Just... don't," he implored her. More twigs snapped as he slipped and plummeted a few feet downward before he got ahold of a branch that didn't crack under his weight.

She heard him muttering to himself under his breath, and a chuckle escaped her before she could smother it.

Still clutching the jar, she folded her arm back against her chest, resting the cool glass against her breast and waited; it would take him a while to get back down, if he managed to do so in one piece. When she finally did look around for him, it was just in time to see him falling the last few feet to the grassy bank, grimacing and wincing as his tailbone bruised.

He'd be sore tonight, but she wasn't worried; he'd be sleeping in a soft bed of his own, she presumed, since she knew that the aunt and uncle he lived with had only one other child to care for and were not poor. Not like her father, who'd traded the last of their chairs just the previous week for something he'd apparently needed more urgently, and had been cowering on the dirt floor of the near-empty hovel, drinking away his regrets when last she'd seen him.

"I went to a lot of trouble getting those," the boy told her in earnest, brushing himself off as he straightened, narrowing his eyes at her.

She flashed him a condescending smile and huffed as she handed him the precious object with all of its content, and he replaced the makeshift lid carefully.

"Well?" she insisted, and he looked bemused, probably wondering why she didn't question how he'd gotten up there so fast in the first place.

"Well what?" he returned disconcertedly, and she rolled her eyes.

"You were going to tell me why you're fixing to draw how they change before you pulled that little... stunt."

He grinned. "That wasn't a *stunt*," he confessed, and added more softly, "That was *magic*."

"Yeah, right." Catherine felt her heart hammering in her chest, but she didn't know whether to believe him or not.

She thought it unlikely. He was probably just trying to make himself seem more important than he really was. Oddballs were inclined to do that, though he'd rather struck her as being smarter than that. He had to know how dangerous a conversation of this sort could turn out to be. Maybe she'd given him too much credit, maybe he was leading her on. Or, maybe he was telling the truth.

Whatever this was, it was getting beyond what she was good with right now. She began walking away from him, but he kept up, hurrying to hold her stride.

"What are *you* so afraid of? You have magic, too," he flung out at her.

She was startled again, though she left her knife where it was this time and merely quickened her pace, refusing him an answer.

"You *do*," he repeated tenaciously, "I *know* you do because I can feel it."

Chapter Thirty-Nine

❦ Light ❧

Dean sat cross-legged on the river bank in the morning sun, studying the firefly he'd caught in a jar the previous night. He'd brought some parchment and a few charcoal pencils, but he doubted he'd get any decent detailing done with those today. He'd misplaced his quill and hadn't gotten round to making a new one yet.

Secretly, he marveled at how Catherine never seemed to grow tired of watching him draw when he was working on something new. They'd met here most every day over the summer when she wasn't cleaning that creepy old man's house.

Sometimes, she'd already be here, waiting for him as though she'd slept somewhere nearby, and sometimes she'd come later in the day, but he'd never see her or feel her presence before she was standing next to him or looking over his shoulder – never before she allowed him to. He could generally perceive magic and the proximity of a Cine close by, he'd learned that much in his time at The Fair, but Catherine was a mystery to him, if a pleasant one.

Dean found that he enjoyed her company because she was easy to talk to and didn't take offense at the slightest discordance. She was different to most other girls he knew, even and especially those at The Fair.

She was neither quite human in that she didn't seem to have the need to be noticed all the time, nor did she display many of the traits or tendencies so typical to the Cine he'd gotten to know over the last years. She was just as passionate about the things she did as most of his father's people were, and she was stoically determined to finish any task she'd started in a very Cine kind of way. What she *didn't* do was talk about herself or what she really wanted or needed. She wasn't the queen of drama most other girls at The Fair or in the village were, and she didn't expect anything of him.

Catherine's sense for quiescence was a breath of fresh air, but she was also good at prodding a conversation onward when she felt he wanted it, letting him think he was taking the lead. He'd caught on to that, but only because his father had been a master at that method of communication, and Dean had developed a sensibility for it. He didn't mind when she did that because he knew it was just her personality, and that didn't make him uncomfortable. She was probably the only person in the world who really understood him because she was as caught between the worlds as he was.

Talking to her, he'd never have guessed she was the gravedigger's daughter if Loredana hadn't told him. Catherine was interested in Cine history and science and a whole lot of other things besides, but she was also trying so hard to be human most of the time that he thought her magic colored her somehow darker whenever she made use of it than she might otherwise have been.

He guessed it was because of the midwife. He'd met Rebecca when she'd come to help deliver Loredana's baby.

He didn't think the woman had a real Gift. She was just extremely observant and wary of and for Catherine, although Loredana's exceptional nature remained unbeknown to her.

Catherine had told him Rebecca was always at her to remember how dangerous using magic could be, and how it might make her reckless if she got in the habit. Perhaps a Gift lost its power if you didn't use it, and maybe this was why Rebecca didn't have one.

Rebecca was more likely to be accused of sorcery than Catherine nonetheless. Rebecca dealt in life and death, and death was always in close proximity to where new life began. That, and she sold elixirs and salves that were bound to get her in trouble one day if they didn't do what she promised they would.

Despite her watchdog, Catherine still had a generous amount of mischief in her, and it outweighed the other things he didn't want to think about too intently. It contrasted her natural beauty and elegance, and he valued the friendship they shared for what it was – a summer of adventure that lessened his emptiness. He loved every new distraction she found for them when he wasn't drawing, or learning how to shape bows and make arrows for various arms and ranges from Caius.

Curling up in the warm dry grass beside him as he thought about the insect's wings, Catherine didn't look as though she felt much like adventures or anything else remotely strenuous today.

She'd been cleaning again the day before.

"That place you told me about," she mumbled, "are you going to go back there?"

"Don't know yet," he returned absently, not taking his eye off the parchment right away. "They're so plain in the daylight, aren't they?" He showed her the picture.

One moment, the firefly he'd depicted was just a drawing, lifeless and drowning in lines and smudges; the next, it began rising from the parchment, turning this way and that as it gained its third dimension. It stretched its limbs and wings, giving small crackling noises, and he directed the insect to train its eyes on Catherine.

"Well, they would be," she muttered. "If they drew attention to themselves by day, there would be none of them left for the night because the birds would get them all."

Reaching out, she nudged Dean's creation gently with her finger. It deflated instantly, fell back onto the parchment and became a drawing once more.

She hummed, pleased with herself.

He knew she hated insects. He also knew exactly what she was talking about and cast a quick glance around, but there was nobody there.

"Same as with the Fairyflies, huh?" He didn't know why he'd said that, but it pulled her from her lethargy.

Eyes wide open at him, she leant up on her elbow. "Have you ever seen any of those?"

Laughing, he shook his head. "No, but I'd love to. I'd love to study them and make some sketches."

She grinned, slapping his arm playfully. "That would be the only reason, of course. But, would you recognize them if you saw them?"

He'd never seen a picture of the beings in any of his father's books. "I'm not sure, but I know seeing isn't everything. I think I'd know what they are by how they feel."

Now it was Catherine's turn to laugh. "You're silly, you know that?"

Dean grinned at her. "Yeah, but I guess we all have our handicaps. I can't change solid things' shape or see things others can't the way my father did, or like my friend Lorcan can. Not *yet* anyway. But I can slow down someone's perception of me for a moment, I can feel traces in the air of an enchantment that's been cast. And I can *feel* when someone has a Gift. It's not much, but I'm working on it…" he trailed off, fixing his gaze to hers, waiting for her to laugh at him, but she didn't.

"Sounds strange, I know."

"Not at all. I think I can *feel* magic, too, but not the way you describe it." She paused, seeming to think on this. "Your father could actually *change solid things' shape and see things others can't?* Like turn a stone into a flower? And did he have visions that layered real time?"

"Yes and no."

He put down his coal pencil and rubbed his blackened fingers on a rag he'd brought. He didn't want to talk about Ortus, or how he'd only found out at fourteen that his father could turn a stone into a cup, or a bee into a firefly.

He'd never actually seen Ortus do this, but he'd kept hearing it from other people. Ortus had claimed spells like these, spells that served not just to *cloak* but *alter* physical matter, disturbed nature's balance. He'd never really appreciated why Ortus had refused to show him, though.

How could one bee less have tipped the scales of the entire world? There were so many bees, the sum total of them wouldn't change if you turned just one into something less stingy and prettier, he thought, but he'd been giving his father the benefit of the doubt all summer long, trying to find out how small changes affected things, and trying to find out how to encourage change in physical matter.

Catherine probably wouldn't comprehend that. She never worried about *little things*.

"Can you see the silver?" he asked her instead of elaborating on what she'd really wanted to hear.

By her baffled look, he knew he'd lost her.

"Silver?"

He grinned. "That's how we recognize each other. Well, it's how we do it if we *can*. Not every Cine can." He couldn't, and he'd been wondering about her.

She didn't respond.

"The Cine have different eyes to humans," he explained. "They have a silver rim around the irises, but humans can't see it. I can't, either."

"Then how did you know about me?"

"Because you use your magic often, and I felt that," he lied. With her, he'd just guessed, based on what he'd observed before she'd let him into her confidence and allowed for that kind of closeness. She was like a bee some power of nature had deemed necessary to be disguised as a firefly, but he felt the traces of her magic swirling all around her when she was as near to him as she was now.

"I don't," she grumbled.

Maybe she wasn't aware of it. To him, the energy that surrounded her, the life-force he felt when she was open for him was much like the charge in the air around Lorcan, and he didn't need the silver Ortus had described to him to know they were both more talented than he'd ever be, unless he could find out what made the world's scales tip and what didn't, and how that would give him a better grasp of what he wanted to do with himself.

He smiled. "You do. You're good at it. You just don't know *how* good."

She smiled back, and surprised him by pressing a hurried kiss to his cheek as she rose.

"Gotta go," she told him. "Meet me here tomorrow. Don't be late. I have to show you something."

Her kiss burned on his cheek long after she was gone, and he couldn't concentrate on the insect anymore, so he opened the jar and let the creature go, looking forward to the next day and whatever new light it was his Fairyfly had planned for them.

Chapter Forty

ᛓ King of the Castle ᛞ

Observing what she perceived as the depth of silent wonder on Dean's face as they neared the ruin was the most fun she'd had in ages. Over the past weeks, Catherine had learned a thing or two about Dean. One of them was that he wasn't easy to impress. She'd never have guessed he'd be so taken with this place, but he obviously was.

He looked completely enthralled as they passed through what was left of the gatehouse, almost as though he could see what she did every time she came here. She could have sworn she saw a hint of recollection reflecting in his gaze when they crossed into the inner courtyard, but she was sure he didn't have that kind of Ability. He couldn't possibly have memories of a place he'd never been to, yet the look he had about him made her wonder for a moment.

"Isn't this great?" she asked.

He appeared a bit preoccupied, blinking away a speck of dust that had gotten in his eye. "Yes," he returned, minding his feet. The toes of his shoes kept catching on the uneven mess of cobbles and gravel. "And you come here all the time?"

She nodded, and he perked up, smiling at her before adopting that peculiar make of silliness she so loved about him. He jumped up on the treads of the crumbling stairway leading to the servants' quarters and did his own version of a little jig, spreading his arms and waving them like he was giving the performance of his life.

"Well, you could have shown me sooner, dear Lady," he hollered. "I do so love it! Look at me: I'm the king of the castle! Applause please, applause!"

A stone came loose beneath his weight, pulling several others with it as he danced, and he nearly fell. Catherine rolled her eyes. He was so beyond clumsy, even if he himself thought otherwise. No wonder he hadn't been here before. His uncle would have been reluctant to let him wander so far from home for fear he'd kill himself. If anyone missed him this afternoon, they'd probably accuse her of attempted murder for bringing him. Showing him around, she'd have to make sure he didn't break something, or she'd have to lug him all the way back home.

Exploring what was left of the old keep, she described the rich tapestries and paintings that had once adorned its walls to him; the thick auburn carpets and the huge lard stone mantelpiece around the hearth that retained the heat of the fire long after the flames had died down. She told him how they'd warmed the children as they'd slept here on the coldest of winter nights, and he listened closely. She explained about the chunky oak table in the middle of the room, where maps had been drawn and councils held, and then she led him to the entrance of the concealed stairway that went underground to the secret room beneath the Great Hall and the hidden tunnels.

Her stomach fluttered at the thought of sharing a knowledge she'd been so stoically keeping to herself. It was strange, and it didn't feel quite right, but she wanted him to know she, too, had something of value. She wanted him to know she trusted him enough to show him the things that had meaning to her, and she *wanted* to believe he wouldn't betray that trust, *needed* to believe he'd be loyal and true to her. He'd come into her life just in a nick of time.

He was her friend.

He *was*, wasn't he?

"How come you know so much about this castle?" he inquired casually as they moved toward the smooth steps leading downward, and she stopped.

Timidly, she took his hand. It was a strange sensation, and a gesture she wasn't at ease with, but it wasn't born from the sort of affection Cooper claimed a right to inflict upon her. There was nothing *dirty* about it, though she might have felt something for Dean that wasn't entirely *pure* either.

She told herself it was just a skin contact necessary for what she was about to convey to him – if she could manage to keep her nerve. She could feel his bewilderment at her touch without looking at him and fully understood what he must be thinking. He was about to withdraw, but she insistently held on to him, dragging in a deep breath when she finally lifted her eyes to his.

She searched his eyes intently, trying one more time to find the silver he'd mentioned every Cine had in them. She couldn't see it, but she wondered if it would have any effect on what she was about to try on him.

"Do you remember what I asked you yesterday?" she asked. "The layering of one reality over the other?" She was aware of how small her voice might sound as he held her stare.

Her heart was thumping so wildly, she thought he must surely hear, or feel her hammering pulse through the flesh and skin of her hand. But, she'd made it this far, and she'd have to follow through now, she told herself, taking his other hand as well.

He remained perfectly still, his gaze unwavering though his eyebrows quirked and his jaw was firmly set while he waited to find out what she'd do next. Registering his sweaty palms, she found he had something of a rabbit caught in a snare. Doubt reared its ugly head. Perhaps this hadn't been such a good idea, but it was too late to turn back.

"Can you bear with me, just for a little while?" she heard herself say, and he nodded impulsively.

"Okay... don't be afraid."

"I'm not." He was lying.

He was afraid. *She* most certainly was, but mainly because she didn't know if this was going to work. If it didn't, she'd look like an idiot.

She'd never tried to show anyone images from her mind before. She'd only whispered words into Cooper's or Rebecca's head, and she'd fantasized about planting pictures there to go with those words, pictures of ghosts that would haunt Rebecca's dreams and ghouls that would hurt Cooper the way he'd been hurting her, every time he closed his eyes.

She'd thought about it all morning as they'd walked, torn between the prospect of attempting to share this with Dean or sparing herself the embarrassment if it didn't work. Courage had won, in the end. Dean wouldn't laugh at her even if he failed to see what she wanted him to.

He wasn't mean or dangerous. Not to her. She was stronger than he and had nothing to fear from him in any case, so it was *safe* to let him into her world, or in on her failure to do so; he was already in her castle, so what harm would there be in sharing the rest of it?

If he saw the castle as it had been through her eyes, he'd understand what her particular Gift was all about. He'd understand what *she* was about. No one else did, but she thought if anyone would really *want* to know her for no other reason than because he might actually *care*, then it would be Dean.

Catherine began concentrating first on the steady rush of blood coursing through her veins, and then on his, edging toward pulling his life-force to her own. She didn't want to hurt him, she just wanted to align him to her and *feel* him so she could anchor his perceptions to her own long enough for him to see what she did and believe. Her heartbeat was the measure, and the echo of his own became the complementing tone to it.

Gently tugging at his cognizance by lowering her own guard sufficiently to draw him in, she found that she could suddenly see herself through his eyes. She felt all of his anxiety, all of his uncertainty and even his empty, rumbling stomach, and she nearly jumped. It was too much; releasing him bit by bit, her awareness returned to her own consciousness, but she wasn't alone inside of herself. His presence was there within her mind just as much as hers was inside of his.

This was it. This was what she'd intended.

Making sure not to let go of Dean's left hand so as to keep their connection, she looked around at the derelict building's walls, floor, and ceilings.

She willed the shadow-like, missing particles of matter time had long since carried away to return, and they gradually reemerged from the deep folds of the space they'd once occupied, the space they'd been *meant* to occupy all along. Stones and plaster appeared to move back into place, pillars and columns resurrected from the rubble, doors rematerialized from the ashes and returned to their frames. What was broken became whole again.

The biting smell of smoke and burning tar from the torches in the room below rose up, filling the air about them, and observing Dean's eyes as they widened, she knew he was hearing, seeing and feeling it, too.

Neither of them spoke as she led him down the stairs that were now perfectly intact, where a warm golden glow illuminated the floor mosaic. Crossing it to where the stone protruded that would open up the portion of the wall revealing the chest, she could hear his breath rattle and wheeze, and she felt his heart racing, as though he'd been lifting heavy weights. Looking at him, she discovered that a sheen of sweat had formed on his face, and his shirt was drenched.

"Are you alright?" she asked, halting, but he just nodded resolutely, unwilling to stop.

She'd had no idea what her magic would do to him, and she was afraid of harming him, but he seemed determined to go on. Clutching his hand more firmly, she held them both back for a moment and tried to pace his hammering heart. It only took a few seconds, and she told herself she'd have to be more careful and perhaps delve into his consciousness a little more intensely, if she could, without losing his awareness. She instinctively knew that if she went too far, he might not remember what he'd seen – he might get lost altogether.

"I'm fine," he said impatiently then, sounding almost irritated, and she nodded curtly.

A few more steps closed the distance, and she bent down, lightly blowing on the surface to open the vault. He helped her drag out the wooden trunk, and she let go of his hand as she lifted the lid. Tilting it back all the way, she was sorely mindful that breaking the contact might break off the connection – but it didn't. The room remained unaltered.

Rummaging through the contents of the chest as he fished out two beautiful ivory figures and admired them, she brought forth the one object – the *only* object – she knew he'd really be interested in.

He set the figures aside and took the book from her hands as if he were touching something of untold value, and she felt a twinge of regret for having left the other one with Cooper. She wanted it back because she wanted to show Dean *both* books. It didn't seem fair; one was incomplete without the other, and this was like giving him one shoe, or the hilt of a knife without a blade.

"Where did you get this?" he asked, barely breathing as he stared at the golden ivy and infinity patterns on the cover.

All at once, she found herself expelled from his thoughts and excluded from his mind. The quality of the moment struck her as odd, but she had other worries since it was dark in the room now. Scrambling toward the small niche by the stairs, she groped around for the candles she kept there, the firestones and the bit of kindling she'd need to light them.

"I think it was left here for me," she told him.

"Left here for you? By whom?" He sounded as though he didn't believe her. *She* wouldn't have believed her, she supposed. It did sound a bit far-fetched.

"The last Lord of this castle was my grandfather." It was funny to hear herself putting forward something that sounded so preposterous, but it was true.

A spark cracked, and a flame came to life as she struck the firestone and the kindling ignited. Dean just stared at her, and she wasn't sure if he was doubting her words or doubting her sanity. She felt awkward. Perhaps she shouldn't have told him. There was no benefit in it. *None.*

He might think she was bragging, though this was nothing worth bragging about. Having a nobleman's bastard hadn't done a thing for her grandmother's reputation. It hadn't made her wealthy or given her any kind of advantages. If anything, it had made life harder on her grandmother. She realized it might make life harder on her, too, if Dean's mien was anything to go by.

Throwing her head back, she laughed at the irony of it all, taking the edge off the situation, and he looked relieved, somehow.

Then, he went back to trying to open it, and she quietly watched him struggling with it for a while. Finally, he was forced to admit defeat.

Another grin tempted the corners of her mouth, but she stifled it in its beginnings, crouching down beside him and gently reclaiming the volume. She had no idea how she was going to handle it this time, but something always came to mind.

"Here, let me show you."

On an impulse, she brought it to her lips and kissed both clasps in turn, completely convinced of what she was doing, somehow. So many times her instincts had been dead-on, when it came to her Talent, and she was slowly learning to put trust in them.

The clasps instantly came undone, and she began leafing through the book, almost tenderly. She loved everything about it; the texture of the leather binding beneath her fingers and spicy smell of it, the grain of the parchment and the color of the ink that had been used to pen the words upon its pages.

Dean grew tired of waiting. "Can I have it?"

Snapping back to why she'd brought him here, she quickly surrendered the book to him, and he started turning the pages, skimming the texts reverently.

"Have you read any of it?" he asked absently.

She hadn't told him she could read; he just automatically assumed she could. That was Dean. He came from another world.

"I have, but it's difficult to understand."

"It is..." He hesitated to ask, but it seemed extremely important. "It's about the magical properties of things in this dimension and in others… Would you let me borrow it for a while?"

"No." Plain and simple.

There was absolutely no way. Even if she hadn't managed to read all of it and couldn't understand most of what she'd read, it belonged to her. It belonged *with* her, and it belonged here in the castle. It had been safe here all this time; survived the war, the fire and the years upon years that had passed. She needed it to stay where it was, and she never wanted to have to ask anyone to return it to her if she wanted to look at it.

Leaving the other one with Cooper had been a mistake, she knew that now. Cooper had dismissed most of what was in it as redundant, and the rest as fairytales and fantasies of times past, but she knew better. Dean knew better.

There had to be a reason why the magician had gone to the trouble of hiding these books down here. The knowledge stored in them had been recorded for a reason. She didn't have a clue what good it would do her, but she was sure it had to do with her.

If she was to trust Dean with this one and he managed to lose it, she'd hate him for it. No, it was better off here. He'd just have to deal with it.

"Let's look at it together here," she suggested, "Maybe we can make sense of it together."

He seemed to accept that, and moved the volume so she could see the passages he was studying.

Leaving the secret room some time later, she took note of how unusually withdrawn Dean appeared, but she supposed he'd get over it. He wasn't one to bear grudges.

He was her friend.

Chapter Forty-One

෬ Heritage ෭

Dean didn't know what to make of it.

He'd wanted to tell Catherine he'd been at the castle before and that he knew who'd written the book she'd so proudly presented to him. He might even have claimed it for his own, but it hadn't seemed like the right thing to do in this situation. It wasn't the one his father had carried around with him, but it looked very much like it, and he was sure that the same hand had penned the words within, so, technically, it was his.

Catherine had been so happy at the castle until they'd gone down into what she'd called *the hidden chamber*. He'd never seen her so excited about anything before, and he loved that look on her face. Telling her she wasn't showing him something new would have taken away from the moment, and he hadn't wanted to get into telling her how he was connected to the place.

Perhaps she hadn't been joking when she'd declared that the last Lord of the castle had been her ancestor, but it seemed more likely to him that she just wanted to believe it. Catherine wanted to believe a lot of things, and he wouldn't be the one to take any kind of hope away from her. He simply couldn't.

They were friends, after all.

Walking back to Caius' house in the gloom after they'd separated in the forest, he realized she was his *only* friend at the moment, though she certainly kept her secrets as well as he kept his.

Catherine was different from most people he knew, and her wit and companionship had managed to fill the aching emptiness inside of him, over the summer. For that, he was grateful. He couldn't tell if there would ever be more between them than that, and he wasn't sure he wanted there to be, but this was *a lot* for the *nothing* he'd found himself with after he'd decided not to return to The Fair right away. Finishing his apprenticeship with Caius was important and it had helped distract him from the loss, but the hurt was still there, as was the indecisiveness as to what would come next. He didn't have to think about these things when he was with her.

For some reason, he wanted to turn around and go after Catherine to return the kiss she'd given him and hold her to see if that would chase away the shadows that haunted him, but how would that look, and what would she derive from that?

Even if that messed up Troll she called *father* didn't miss her if she didn't come home at night, Caius would start searching for him. The only rule Caius expected him to keep was that he be home by nightfall. This hadn't been so hard to stick to at first because he hadn't felt much like leaving the farm until he'd met Catherine.

It was almost dark now, and he couldn't help but wonder whether she was really going home like she said she would, or if she'd be heading back to the castle instead. He knew she didn't mind the dark as long as she was out in the open, and she'd probably make the trip in half the time without him tagging along. She was used to covering long distances on foot, and he supposed she spent a great deal of her time roaming the countryside – and dreaming that old fortress back to life.

Entering the Fletchers' cottage, he was welcomed by the smell of thick rabbit stew with vegetables from the pot over the fire.

"You're late today," Loredana muttered, only briefly lifting her eyes from her sewing. The baby was asleep in her cradle by his aunt's rocker. "Saved you some food. Bowl's on the table."

He was famished. Catherine was bound to be, too. She'd shared some apples with him, and they'd picked berries in the woods, but he was always hungry nowadays, and he had no idea what she survived on.

Ladling a generous amount of stew from the pot over the hearth into his bowl, he felt almost guilty. No matter where Catherine was going to spend the night, she wouldn't have anything as good as this.

Loredana waited until he'd seated himself on a

stool by the fire and eaten a few spoonsful. "You been out with that girl, haven't you?"

The undertone in her voice lent her words a troubled sourness that spilled over into his food.

"*That* girl?"

"Don't get smart with me. You know exactly who I'm talking about. That Salt girl."

He chose not to answer and continued wolfing down his stew, whether or not he tasted what he was eating anymore. It was hard to digest: here was Loredana, a Shapeshifter, calling Catherine *that girl*. He didn't think she knew about Catherine's disposition. At least he'd never spoken to her about it. She simply had no liking for Catherine or her family and didn't make a secret of the fact. It wasn't hard to *not like* Catherine's family, but Catherine wasn't Rebecca or Caleb. Catherine was Catherine.

"Is there any bread?"

His aunt put down the shirt she was working on and fetched a small loaf swathed in a cloth from the shelf farthest from the fireplace. Handing him half, she watched as he broke little pieces off and soaked them in the rich broth at the bottom of his bowl before popping them into his mouth.

"She's bad news, Dean. You don't really know her, and you'd do well to keep away."

He got that his aunt was worried about him, but he had no intention of discussing Catherine with her right now. It wasn't like he was going to make any life-changing choices centered around Catherine, but Catherine didn't deserve to be talked over like this.

He'd learned from his father's cousin that diversion was a good means of dealing with unpleasantness or uncomfortable topics of conversation when it came to Loredana, so he abruptly changed the subject.

"Where's Caius?"

Sighing, Loredana pulled the pot from the heat by using a hook to haul back the sturdy chain fixed to its curving handle. "Away."

She caught hold of the handle with a rag and took it down, setting it on the floor.

Dean guessed no one else would be eating here tonight. "I can see that. Where to?"

She was reluctant to answer and seemed annoyed. He could see her choosing her words. "Look, we might be leaving here soon."

He swallowed the bread he'd been chewing in one hard lump. What did she mean by *we*, and what would that entail for him?

The arrangement they'd made before Ortus' death wasn't anything permanent, and the summer was almost over, but he hadn't thought about what would come when his apprenticeship ended.

He didn't want to go back to the house where he'd spent his childhood, but he didn't want to return to The Fair either – at least not yet. The doors that led to his future had been locked with him on the wrong side of them after his father had died. Even today, he still felt like he was on the wrong side of it most of the time.

Except for when he was with Catherine.

"You're thinking of going somewhere else?" he asked casually, trying to sound as though as though it didn't bother him.

"We're *thinking*, yes." She fixed his gaze to his. "But we'd like you to come with us. We're family. It's what your father would have wanted."

He doubted it.

Ortus had wanted him at The Fair.

If his father had wanted him to live as a human, he wouldn't have taken him to The Fair. He wouldn't have shown him that wonderful other world and started teaching him to use his magic. Well, what magic he had. Ortus wouldn't have kept telling him how important he and Lorcan were for the survival of the Haven that protected The Fair, and how they needed to stand together. But, his father had put way too much faith in him and Lorcan. They didn't need a half-blood there who couldn't measure up, no more than they needed Lorcan, it seemed. Lorcan certainly didn't need The Fair.

Having lost his appetite, Dean pushed his bowl away, and Loredana patted his arm before crossing the room to the heavy chest by her bedstead. It was where she kept the things she valued most; a new-looking dress that didn't fit her anymore – but might again one day, since hope prevailed when all else was lost, she claimed – some dried flowers from her wedding day, and a few other odds and ends.

Arduously moving the trunk aside, she knelt on the reed rug and pulled back one corner of it to reveal boards Dean hadn't been aware of beneath it.

He rose to get a better look when curiosity got the better of him. The boards were loose, and they covered only a small section of the floor, just enough to conceal a hidey-hole of sorts. Watching Loredana pull them up one by one as he hunkered down beside her, he realized this was the second time he'd seen this kind of thing today.

When she'd set all three boards aside and the little cavity in the ground lay open, she brought forth two books that looked much like the one Catherine had shown him earlier that day. His breath caught.

She smiled as she handed them to him. "These were your father's. He asked us to keep them safe for you."

One really was his father's. So this was where it had gone… He'd nearly gone crazy looking for it. At first, he'd thought it might be at The Fair, but when he hadn't found it there, he'd assumed Lorcan might have taken it and grudgingly let it go, for now. He'd been sure they'd meet again, and he'd resolved to punch him for it when they did. Now he had to acknowledge he'd been wrong, and again, he felt a pang of guilt for having believed Lorcan would steal from him.

The other book was almost identical to the first, but

for the color of the leather; Ortus' was green, and the one he hadn't seen before tonight was light brown. They were the same size, and the golden ivy patterns and infinity designs in the center of the front covers were the exact same as those on Catherine's, which he now assumed was likely the third of a set. It was a strange thought, but one that seemed logical the more he pondered it.

"Thank you," he told Loredana absently and retreated to his little room under the rafters, taking a candle along to study his prize.

The clasps, he found, opened for him in the same manner they had for Catherine. He couldn't wait to show her, on one hand. They'd have a lot to discuss. But, did he want to go down that road with Catherine and all of her shadows?

Chapter Forty-Two

०ॐ Rumors ॐ०

Dark shadows heralded the waning of the misty afternoon into drizzly evening. The windows of Caleb's hovel were alight, and Catherine wondered if he'd come home early today. She was almost glad to find it was only Rebecca, stirring a pot suspended over the hearth.

"Close the door," her aunt muttered without looking up. "See if you can find some clean bowls and spoons for us somewhere. I couldn't."

Catherine frowned, but she wasn't going to let Rebecca's tone spoil her day. Caleb had sold every stick of furniture they had, but she'd cleaned the bowls and left them out back in a basket by the bucket she'd washed them in. Baskets and buckets were in good supply now that Cooper had no need for them anymore.

It wasn't long before the door opened again and Caleb appeared, dragging a sludge of mud and dead leaves in with him.

"Give us a hand, girl," he ordered her.

Dropping his tools on the floor, he staggered toward Rebecca, drawn by the smell of her cooking.

Catherine picked up his shovel and pick ax and set them in the corner.

Caleb's clothes were disheveled and covered with mud, and he smelled of mold, death, and ale, as he always did. He struggled for a moment to get out of his threadbare wool coat and then dropped it, too, on the floor. Catherine hung it on a nail.

"Where have you been?" Rebecca asked, handing him a bowl of stew. The tone of her voice was so sour, Catherine hoped it wouldn't spoil the soup.

He motioned to Catherine to fetch his bottle from under his mattress, and she did, thinking that coming home may not have been such a good idea after all.

"I planted old Farley down in the church yard today." Uncorking the brew, he took a swig. "His son wanted him laid in deep, with all those wolves scavenging around the cemetery at night."

Rebecca handed Catherine a bowl and then filled her own. "I hadn't heard about that yet."

"Ah." He shrugged, sitting down on the floor, his bottle next to him. "He just wanted the old man deeper in, that's all. Closer to where he's going, I'd say. I told him I charge extra to go further down."

He grinned smugly at Catherine, revealing yet another missing incisor, before he tucked into his meal. She didn't think he'd have a tooth left in his mouth by winter.

"Young Master Farley refused to pay up, but his wife got into it with him. She went on and on about there being strange things afoot here lately, and that loosened him up," he continued as Catherine sat down opposite him, avoiding the boards that covered the hidey-hole. Rebecca looked disdainfully at the filthy floor and decided to pull the straw mattress across to them to sit on its edge.

"Did you get what you asked for?" Catherine wanted to know between spoonsful of warm goodness.

The wild herbs Rebecca gathered in the woods and put into her soups made them taste differently every time. Catherine recognized most of them, but she doubted she'd be able to copy her aunt's brilliant recipes exactly.

Caleb, whose taste buds were past telling barley from spelt, never mind thyme from nettles, pulled a small leather coin bag out of his rope belt and tossed it over to her, winking. "Got nearly half the fee again, and old Farley's safe from the wolves at the Devil's heel."

Rebecca set down her bowl, reached over and snatched the pouch from Catherine. She emptied it into her careworn palm. "Looks like it's a bit short, if you ask me."

"No harm in getting a pint on the way home."

With a scowl, Rebecca slipped the coins back into the pouch, but held on to it. "What's this about wolves, again?" she asked pointedly.

Caleb chewed noisily while he answered. "Ah, it's just talk. A pack took one of the goats wandering free around the miller's pen last week just before dusk when he was gettin' ready to put them inside the shed. It's his own fault – he was too late in the day. He said he saw 'em himself when they came out of the woods. Four or five big'uns tore straight into the goat and carried the pieces off back into the woods with them. Somehow, the bones turned up at the cemetery."

He took another drink from his bottle and held his bowl out to Catherine for more soup. She ignored him. Rebecca got up to fetch him some more.

"Some of the old biddies that like to come and pray in the first Mass saw them and started squawkin' about werewolves in the graveyard." Bleary-eyed, he shook his spoon at his sister-in-law in amusement. "I told them what it was and to go ask Miller, but the tale had already made the rounds and people would rather believe the tale than the truth, and that's for sure."

"Why won't the clergyman put a stop to this kind of thing?" Rebecca wondered.

Caleb snorted a laugh. "Why would he? Our dear Father Briggs is young. More people in the church, more money in the coffers." He pulled a long draught from the bottle, emptying it, before wiping his dirty sleeve across his mouth. "Besides, there's talk of more than just wolves going around, and I think he's just dyin' to look into that with the help of that book of his." His eyes were glassy from the fire of the alcohol. They settled on Catherine in a way she didn't like one bit.

She saw the accusation in his scrutiny, there as it

always was when the drink wrapped around his brain and laid his thoughts bare. He knew what she was, and she was his daughter, but he hated her for it all the same. She held his gaze. Finally, he turned his attention back to his stew, shivering.

She could feel his latent fear and the anger growling beneath the surface of his addiction. She knew that neither her mother nor she was to blame for his life not having worked out the way he'd perhaps hoped it would. He was the only one to blame, not a wife who'd left him, and least of all their little family secret.

"There's always talk," Rebecca bit out, "any time a pig goes missing or someone gets the ague, people blame an *evil eye* or some such nonsense."

"It's different this time," he said quietly. "Gilbert and Lance were at the alehouse a few nights ago, claiming they saw Shifters changin' in the woods just before the bones turned up in the cemetery."

"They're ruffians and drunks." Rebecca scoffed. "No one listens to them."

"And that's where you're wrong. People *are* listening," Caleb returned. "They're saying the Shifters and the Cine have been hiding, getting stronger, that they've been biding their time 'til they can strike."

Rebecca collected the empty dishes. "Old wives, looking for a reason for a bad harvest. A few bones in the graveyard and the drabble of drunks isn't proof of anything."

"Yeah, well that Shearer girl claims she's seen a witch dancing a pattern near the old castle." Sucking on the inside of his lip, Caleb ventured another glance at Catherine. "Said there was a girl up there dancing around a circle of runes, singing things in a tongue she didn't understand. Now who would do that, I wonder? What decent person goes up to those old ruins?"

Catherine tried to contain her amusement, but her mouth was faster than her brain. "Laura Shearer, apparently."

She couldn't remember ever seeing Laura Shearer up at the castle, and she most certainly didn't dance around in circles up there... aside from once or twice in the Great Hall, years ago, when she'd witnessed a ball held in honor of the Duke's birthday.

Caleb didn't seem to see the humor in her remark. A muscle twitched in his cheek. "What have you been up to, girl? Are you set on conjuring disaster on us?"

"Of course not, you idiot," Rebecca spat. Snatching the spoon he was still holding from his hand, she grabbed him by the shoulder and forced him to look at her as she spoke in hushed tones. "You, of all people, know better than to start looking that direction. Catherine's Talent is no one's business and that's how it's going to stay. You drink too much, Caleb, and your tongue gets too loose. The girl likes her solitude, that's all. Don't you think we'd know if she was up to mischief?"

Catherine decided this meal was over and rose. Half-listening to the argument that ensued between her father and her aunt, she got busy fetching some water and washing up the dishes, thinking he should have married Rebecca instead of Maebh. He might still have all his teeth if he had.

It struck her as odd that he'd mentioned the Shearer girl up at the castle. If Laura was spreading rumors and people were looking for causes for their misfortunes, she'd have to be careful when she returned there with Dean in a few days.

Neither prayers nor penance, nor the hanging of a Shapeshifter or the beheading of a Cine would cure the rot in the corn or take the fungus off of Cooper's trees, but people believed what they wanted to believe when times were tough. She was no fool – this winter was going to be really difficult, going by what she was seeing all around.

Even Cooper was having a hard time. The old man had told her he hadn't seen this kind of crop failure since his youth when an old hedge witch had cursed a farmer's field after the man had refused to marry her daughter and claim the whelp she'd birthed. He had taken to watching her with measured scrutiny, and she'd been waiting for him to ask if she'd ever wished any harm on his acres.

She'd have loved to tell him how she'd passed her mind through his plum grove with malevolent intentions after the very first time he'd taken her, hating him with every fiber of her being. She smiled at the notion of the shrinking life-force within the heart of the trees as her silent scream punched through them, their limbs recoiling in shock.

The pestilence had started there, and it had spread to all of the rest of his orchards and then to the crops. A coincidence, surely, but not one she'd share with Cooper for all he claimed to know of how magic worked.

He'd never asked her openly if she had a Talent, and she was certain he wouldn't believe his attentions toward her warranted anything except her gratitude for the lessons she was getting from him.

Lessons she wouldn't need after today. She had Dean.

"The old bastard won't be living with the losses," Caleb's words broke into her musings. "He'll be pulling out and heading back east where he came from. He told me he's still got relatives he can live off of there."

Cold shock settled in Catherine's chest at the half-heard conversation and she turned to Caleb with sudden interest. "Who's leaving?"

"Cooper. Didn't he tell you?"

"When?"

Caleb took a moment to stretch before answering. Hard labor, hard drink, and a heavy belly made him lethargic. "Most likely in the morning. The roads are still good, and he wants to be on his way now that he's made up his mind. He's paying me to keep an eye on his place until spring; not much, but more than nothing, and not a lot to do for it either."

Turning the news over in her mind, she realized that if he was leaving, he'd take everything of value with him. He hadn't told her, and she wouldn't have known if Caleb hadn't mentioned it, so that meant he intended to take her book with him, too.

Without a backward glance, she flung the door open and ran out into the night, Rebecca's shrill cries unheeded as she plunged through the underbrush and onto the slippery path to Cooper's farm.

Chapter Forty-Three

∾ Judgement Day ∽

Her legs burned and her lungs felt near to bursting by the time she made it to the grove of shriveled fruit trees marking the boundary of Cooper's property. No stars or moonlight penetrated the thick clouds overhead, but she knew the way with her eyes closed.

She'd last seen the old farmer two days before. Thinking back on it now, she should have known something was up with him. He'd presented her with the gift of a red scarf from the trunk in his daughters' room when she'd walked in the door. She'd fancied that scarf from the first time she'd seen it because of the shine and sparkle of the beadwork on it.

He'd watched her incessantly as she'd worked, his eyes following her every movement and he'd forced his bloated body on her twice before she'd even made him dinner.

Yellow light spilled out of the windows as she neared the house, and she could hear voices inside. Cooper was hollering something indiscernible at the top of his voice, and a girl shrieked repeatedly, though not from pain. Catherine was only mildly surprised and wondered whom he was shagging.

Standing up on the weathered porch, she peered inside. She couldn't see Cooper or anyone else in the main room, but several large trunks had been set on the rug in the middle with a few chests of tools balancing on them, quilts, some pots and kettles haphazardly thrown on the pile. He was obviously leaving early.

There was room for more in the wagon he kept in the barn, but she doubted he'd take any of his furniture. If what her father had said was true about him going to stay with his wealthier relations, he wouldn't need it.

Walking around the side of the house, she tried his daughters' bedroom window. The shutters weren't closed, and there they were: Laura Shearer and Cooper, wallowing in the sheets Catherine had washed the previous week. The girl was riding him like there was no tomorrow, bare breasts bobbing, enjoying herself with every thrust of her hips as Cooper swore and cursed beneath her in a way she'd often heard him do when he wasn't as close to getting what he wanted as he would have liked to be.

From that, Catherine gathered, she had at least a small time window.

She let herself into the house by the back door and lifted the quilts and chests off of the heavy boxes. None of the boxes had locks on them, and she searched them one after the other. She hadn't gotten to the third one when the screaming and groaning in the next room stopped.

The silence was infuriating, and Catherine felt her teeth clenching in anger and disappointment. What now?

Plodding footsteps sounded on the plank floor, and she was briefly torn between heading for the door and facing Cooper. She opted for the latter and sat down on the chest she'd just searched, folding her hands into her lap and trying to look bored, as though she'd been waiting for him.

Cooper hadn't bothered to put on his pants for his excursion to the bucket, or wherever he'd been headed. He was shocked to find her there, but didn't flinch. He just closed the bedroom door behind him.

She looked him up and down in disgust. Gray hair pasted to his round skull, chest, and legs, red-faced from exertion, slick and spent as he was with his belly hanging down over his wrinkly member, he was a pitiful sight to behold.

The good news was that he wouldn't be her problem anymore after tonight.

"Catherine!" he stumbled, looking around for clothes or a blanket, perhaps. "What a surprise!"

"Yeah, but you love surprises, don't you?"

She watched him pull a pair of workpants from under his bed and put them on.

"Oh, you know I do." He looked a little more comfortable with something on. "But tell me, to what do I owe the pleasure of your company at this late hour?"

"I know you're busy." She smirked, nodding at the other room. "No rest for the wicked." She heard more footsteps. No doubt Laura Shearer was looking for clothes, too. She'd have to resort to the chest at the foot of the bed, since her own lay scattered by the fireplace.

"I hear you're leaving in the morning," Catherine continued.

He nodded, fidgeting. "Yes, I'd have told you, but I've just decided."

She hummed. "But you still have something that belongs to me."

His brow creased. "I do? I don't recall…"

"My book, Cooper. You have my book, and I want it back."

"Your book?"

Cooper didn't just love surprises. He also loved games, but Catherine was in no mood for games tonight.

"You know which book," she said quietly.

He slapped his forehead and gave a little laugh. "Oh, that old thing." Then, his mien darkened, and a dangerous glint entered his eyes as he leant toward her. The smell of his sour sweat and bad breath assaulted her senses. "I don't have it anymore."

She couldn't believe it. She wanted to hurt him, and he recoiled from her a little way, as though he felt it.

She rose. "Where is it?"

He moved around her to the fireplace and picked up Laura's dress and undergarments. Bundling them carelessly, he opened the bedroom door a crack and threw them at the waiting girl. Catherine caught a glimpse of her by the dresser.

"I've sold it," he said without offering any further explanation when he returned to Catherine. Pushing his hands into his sides, he smiled as though he had every right to.

Catherine didn't care if he shagged every sheep in the Shearer's flock and went to Sutrailia, but she couldn't grasp why on earth he would have sold her book until she realized what his smile meant. He'd bargained away one of her only and most precious possessions. He was mean and he was ugly both inside and out, but selling her book was the lowest thing he could have done to her and he knew it. She could plainly see he got a kick from watching her now, and she loathed him beyond anything she'd ever felt before.

His eyes danced with glee, and his voice was smooth as silk as he drew closer to her, reaching out and stroking her arm with one finger. "I've sold a lot of pretty things, in case you haven't noticed, darling. But that book... it fetched a pretty penny."

Actually, she hadn't noticed anything else missing in his house last time she'd been here. She'd had other things on her mind besides counting Cooper's inventory. His finger on her arm bothered her to the point of wanting to throw up.

"Got myself some new boots for the trip," he added, taking her hand in his, and the stench of him made bitter bile rise up into her throat.

She told herself to keep breathing. She was on the brink of exploding, but forced herself to stay calm. "Who did you sell it to?"

"What is it to you?" He laid her hand on his hip, pushing it slowly toward his groin. "You'd never be able to buy it back."

"But you would," she growled, close to tears as she snatched her hand away, and he laughed.

"Tell me again why I should? You've been using up my time, eating my food and stealing from me. I think you've broken so much of my crockery, it's only fair that I get some form of reimbursement. Look, you're not dumb. I've got another girl waiting for me back there." He waved a hand in the general direction of the bedroom. "She might be about ready to leave now, but we could have a lot of fun together tonight if I asked her to stay another while."

Catherine wanted to hurt him, *really* hurt him.

It wasn't so hard getting into his mind. He was only human, and he had no defenses against her. She'd left hints and thoughts there before, but this time, she wanted to leave something more than that. She wanted to cause damage and see him writhe for all of what he was and what he'd done to her, and for the humiliation of what he was doing now.

Seeing herself through his eyes and seeing him through her own, she felt the blood course through his veins, warm and fast, and she willed it to get even warmer as she heard his heart pumping in her ears.

Pain, she thought, and pain was what he got when she began assaulting the muscle tissue with heat and anger, burning tiny holes of rage in it.

Clutching at his chest, he went to his knees, and she feigned concern, helping him lie down on the floor. She observed his contorted face with some satisfaction.

"Are you not feeling well, Cooper?" she asked kindly, crouching over him as he struggled to fill his lungs, his eyes wide and his mouth working without making more than a moaning sound. A new sheen of cold sweat covered his doughy face, and he grabbed at her with the strength of a dying man.

She knew he couldn't answer, and she perceived the infinite, crushing tightness in his chest, but she wasn't afraid. This wasn't *her* heart, wasn't *her* agony. It was *his*, but *she* controlled it, and it felt good to be on the giving end.

"Must be the bad conscience that's giving you heartburn, *dearest,*" she mocked him, casting a quick glance at the bedroom door as she pulled his hands off of her and moved away a little, just out of his reach. The door was still shut.

Continuing to concentrate on the muscle in

Cooper's chest, she found she could see the holes in its walls increase in size, and blood began seeping through, oozing into the cavity of his chest. She'd watched the miller cutting up a freshly butchered pig's heart for his dog once, and Cooper's resembled it to a fault. Fascinatedly, she dug through the fissures and tears and into the chambers until the blood began clotting.

How often had she thought her blood was clotting inside of her when he'd raped her? How often had he hurt her so badly during the first months, she'd hardly been able to walk? She'd bled even when it wasn't her time, and he'd taken her again and again despite that. She'd been in constant pain, and now it was *his* turn to suffer. He was *never* going to hurt her or anyone else again.

The old man was barely conscious anymore, and she wanted him to die, the way he'd made her die inside a hundred times.

He made a gurgling sound when she rolled him on his back, and she saw that he'd wet himself. How that fit. He'd be facing his maker with pissed pants.

"Are you afraid?" she whispered. "Afraid of the dark?"

Leisurely, she took out her knife and ran the blade along his belly, playing with the thought of cutting off the part of him that had tormented her most as a final act of justice before she rammed the steel into him, but then she thought of something much better. He'd taught her to write, and write she would, so God would certainly not mistake him for anything else but what he was.

She spelled the word D-E-M-O-N out on his middle, carving it deep into his skin. He moaned and bled, and he bled and moaned.

When she was finished, she put her lips to his ear for a final goodbye, the tip of her knife resting against his jugular. "I. Hate. You."

Then, two things happened at once.

The bedroom door banged all the way open on its hinges, and Laura Shearer flew past her toward the front door, screaming like a banshee. Her big breasts were no longer bare, but bobbing hectically as she ran straight into Caleb, who'd been just about to enter with Rebecca in his wake.

Gripping the pallid, hysterical girl firmly by the shoulders, Caleb peered past her and saw Catherine on the floor. She held the blood-smeared knife in her hands as Cooper took his last breath and vomited into his own mouth.

Caleb was so shocked, he let go of Laura.

Laura couldn't stop screaming as she attempted to flee, but she tripped on the first porch tread – the one with the loose board Cooper had always been meaning to fix – and landed face first in the mud.

Rebecca grabbed the hatchet Cooper had put by the door so he'd remember to take it along in the morning. She lunged at Laura from behind before the girl had even turned, and rammed the blade into her skull with everything she had.

The screaming abated instantly.

Catherine got to her feet, dropping the knife. The look on Caleb's face as he tried to wet his lips told her he couldn't find words. Blanching as he doubled over, he emptied his stomach on the floor.

Rebecca pulled the hatchet out of Laura Shearer's head with a squelching sound and carried it up to the house. For a moment, Catherine thought she was going to use it on her, too, but she just put it back where she'd found it.

"Up with you, Caleb. There's work to be done. You have two more to put down deep, if there's any more room in hell."

Caleb gathered saliva in his mouth and spat a few more times before he could straighten, but when he did, Rebecca thumped him on the shoulder, and he mumbled a curse.

"Off you go," she told him again. "Get your gear and find a nice patch of earth that'll have them."

Casting one more incredulous and hateful glance at Catherine, Caleb hobbled away to the old farmer's shed.

Absently, Rebecca wiped her nose on the back of her hand as she stared at Cooper's body, smearing a speck of Laura's blood on her cheek.

"Well," she finally said to Catherine, "I guess we have some work to do here ourselves now, don't we?"

Catherine felt so tired all at once, she could have lain down where she was and gone to sleep. She didn't have a clue what Rebecca was talking about.

"Don't just stand there, girl," Rebecca persisted, taking a few steps toward her. "Go fetch me the sheets off of the beds. We'll need two. One for him and one for her. We're going to have to clean up this mess."

When Catherine still didn't react, Rebecca shook her. "Listen to me! We have to get this done tonight, or they'll string the both of us up tomorrow. Don't you understand? We have to take care of this *right now* and leave this place!"

Catherine understood just fine. She'd killed Cooper. He'd deserved it. Rebecca had killed Laura. Maybe Laura hadn't deserved it. But, both she and Rebecca would hang for what they'd done if she didn't start moving. So, she did.

Chapter Forty-Four

✂ Stealing the Light ✄

Rebecca navigated Cooper's wagon along the Old Trading Road due south for the first twenty miles in silence, then she let Catherine take the reins.

Catherine was just as tired as Rebecca, but she didn't complain. The thoughts that tumbled around inside her head wouldn't let her rest anyway.

Every time she closed her eyes, she saw Cooper and the smug grin on his face when he told her he'd sold her book. He'd been like a parasite on her, eating its way into her flesh over all these past years. She'd thought that cutting him and the diseased skin out of herself would bring on a sense of satisfaction, but he'd won their little game in the end nonetheless. She'd sent him to hell for what he'd done to her, yet he mocked her even still.

He was the reason she had to leave here now.

Not that there was much keeping her in this godforsaken place – nothing aside from Dean.

The idea of leaving Dean made her want to jump off of the wagon, but Cooper and Laura Shearer had robbed her of the choice, and there was no satisfaction to be had from that. It was as though she needn't have bothered with Cooper at all. She could just as well have walked away, if her searing rage had let her.

Perhaps revenge was only sweet if the people who truly deserved to suffer lived long enough to feel the kind of pain they themselves had inflicted upon others.

Catherine hadn't expected Rebecca to react to Laura Shearer as quickly and resolutely as she had, and she was grateful to her aunt, but she was no fool. She realized Rebecca hadn't done this just for her; she'd done it to save herself and Caleb, too. If Laura had gone screaming to her parents and spread around what she'd seen, the clergyman would have had them all on trial for the crime Catherine had committed. Even Caleb was smart enough to understand that.

They'd worked together quickly to clean Cooper's house and loaded some of his things as well as his hens onto the wagon. Anyone who happened to come by this morning would think he'd left just as he'd planned.

Then, they'd picked up their own belongings and Rebecca's distillery in the cover of darkness, while Caleb had buried the bodies in the soft earth on top of old Farley's rotting corpse in the graveyard.

Catherine wondered whether the relatives Cooper had been meaning to visit would await him, and if they'd miss him when he didn't show up. She doubted it. She didn't think anyone would really miss Cooper, as opposed to Laura Shearer.

"Just keep going until we get to the next big crossing," Rebecca told her, wrapping a blanket around herself against the cold night air before she leant against her and closed her eyes. "Don't stop for anyone."

For a moment, Catherine was tempted not only to stop the wagon, but to turn it around and go back to the castle for the book, at least, but she knew she couldn't chance it. Rebecca would never let her. She hadn't even let her go back to Cooper's house to look for the locket she'd lost when she'd discovered it was gone.

If anyone saw them with the old farmer's wagon now, they'd be done for.

***

Dean searched for Catherine when she didn't come to the river the next day. He combed the woods and checked all of her favorite haunts, but he couldn't find her anywhere.

The filthy toothless drunk who called himself her father lay in a stupor on the floor of his hovel, not making much sense, and no one had seen Rebecca.

The creep whose house Catherine cleaned was also gone, Dean discovered a day later, but Caius told him Cooper had been planning to leave for weeks. He'd been selling what was left of his livestock and his belongings. Dean couldn't recall that she'd mentioned it, but she rarely talked about him, aside from making jokes about how sloppy he was. Perhaps she hadn't known.

For some reason, he felt the need to look around the old farmhouse. Finding the back door unlocked, and he let himself in. Cooper had taken most of his things, but what struck Dean as odd was that he'd left the place so remarkably clean and tidy.

Or Catherine had, he thought when he found her locket beside the bed in the main room.

***

Unloading the wagon in front of the deserted house where Charlie had been born, Catherine discovered that one of Cooper's hens hadn't survived the two day trip in the basket. The other six had pecked it to death.

"That's what becomes of the weak," she mumbled as she took the dead bird out and inspected it to see if it would still make a meal. She hadn't realized Rebecca was standing right behind her.

"Just don't make the mistake of thinking strength is the opposite of weakness," her aunt said, shifting the weight of one of Cooper's chests of crockery from one hip to the other.

Catherine turned, narrowing her eyes at Rebecca. "Well, then, what else would strength be?"

"It's weakness in disguise, Catherine, nothing more. Some are just better than others at hiding it. I've told you before: none of us were born to power, even if you think your *Curse* can make you strong. Trust me, you're all alone in that basket."

Returning her attention to the chicken in her hands, Catherine found that it was already half-eaten by maggots, wiggling and squirming on the bloody patches where the other hens had pulled its feathers from its skin.

She let out a yelp and dropped the carcass, disgusted and frantically wiping her hands on her dress.

Rebecca smiled.

Catherine hated her.

***

The old Tierney castle was the last place Dean had yet to search. His heart sank when he physically felt Catherine's absence as he walked the last yards uphill to the gatehouse, the locket burning a hole in his hand. He wanted Catherine to be there and safe, but he had little hope that he'd find her.

He wanted to tell her he'd been worried – but didn't know if she'd want to hear.

He wanted to show her his books and see her face when she saw the resemblance – but he didn't know if he'd dare.

He didn't want things between them to change – but he did.

Ever since he'd felt her in his mind and seen what she saw, the images and impressions she'd left behind had been haunting him.

She'd been haunting him.

She had powers he could only dream of, but at the same time, he knew he wouldn't want them for fear of the nightmares they must give her. Past and present merged in the place where she'd taken him, and all of it inside of her head. It was too much for one person, yet she made it seem as though it wasn't near enough. She didn't create illusions, she lived and breathed them. He didn't think she was aware of how thin and brittle the line she was walking really was.

On the long march here, he'd imagined telling her it was his grandfather who'd written her book, but he couldn't begin to guess how she'd react. Of course, she'd wonder why he'd kept this to himself the other day, and he'd have to admit it was because he'd been so overwhelmed. She knew he tended to be, and she'd forgive him for that, he was sure.

Provided he found her.

A mild breeze whispered through the waxy leaves of the red beech next to the chapel as he crossed the courtyard, and for a moment, he thought he saw her scuttling around the corner. Blending in with the backdrop was a part of her Talent she'd almost perfected, though it was beyond him how anyone could overlook her.

He couldn't tell whether or not she had the silver in her eyes because he was so much human that he couldn't see it, but he liked to imagine her overall aura being as layered as she was. It could be made up of so many colors more beautiful than some old metal from beneath the earth. Nature had the most wonderful pallet to choose from.

He thought most of Catherine's colors could be brighter than the fresh greens of spring or the fiery carmine of the beech he found himself looking at as he was chasing her shadow.

They *could* be, if she wasn't so driven by the ghosts that haunted her, the ghosts she called to haunt her.

Having been inside her mind, he knew this castle and the book were a part of that. They were a part of who she wanted to be.

From the corner of his eye, he caught more movement in the boughs near one of the crumbling walls farther up. Smiling to himself when the squirrel he'd seen leapt from one branch to the next, he went inside the chapel and his gaze wandered to the window where she told him she liked to sit and think, breathing in the scent of the seasons as they came and went. He thought it was the perfect place for her.

Only, she wasn't here.

She'd abandoned it, whether alone or with creepy Cooper, and perhaps she was right to have done that, in the end.

***

Catherine didn't accept what Rebecca had told her.

Rebecca was wrong.

Catherine knew she wasn't *cursed*. She was *blessed*. And, she may not have been born to power, but she was sure she was entitled to it because she was strong. Her blessing and her strength would ensure her power, one day, she was certain. She just needed to gather her strength and think.

Scouting around the back of the house, she discovered a small shack. It was in bad repair because it had stood empty even longer than the house itself, but it would do to keep the chickens confined for now, so she brought them there in the basket and released them after she'd tossed the dead one into the bushes a little way into the woods for the foxes.

There was a well in the yard, but the water looked murky and foul, not even fit for the hens, so she went to the river to fetch a few bucketsful while Rebecca got started on sweeping and unpacking.

It was a long walk to the stream and back. The water sloshed all over the hem of her skirts, soaking through her shoes, but all she could think of was the book she still had at the castle, and Dean.

They'd agreed Caleb would tell anyone who asked about them that Rebecca and Catherine had decided to leave and head for the next town where they hoped to make a better living. That was believable enough, but would Dean accept she'd up and left without even saying goodbye?

***

Remembering how he'd seen the keep through Catherine's eyes, its Great Hall was disappointing when Dean entered it. He supposed that no power on this earth would ever restore it to its former state.

None, except for maybe the power of Catherine's imagination.

Descending the stairway to the hidden room, he knew he'd no sooner find her down there than he had above ground. It felt wrong to be here when she wasn't, somehow, but he told himself he wasn't *doing* anything wrong. He just wanted to have another look at the mosaic floor, and he wanted to see inside the vault again, while he was at it.

He recalled where she kept the candles and was surprised to find a whole stash of them, along with firestones and kindling. Some of the candles had been burned down to stumps, but some were still quite new. A tinge of guilt niggled at him as he set about lighting one after the other to methodically illuminate the whole of the floor, but he vowed to replace them as soon as he could because Catherine surely couldn't afford to.

Portions of six artfully designed hexagons became visible in the buttery glow around the centerpiece. Borders of young ivy set in gold leaf lined their outer rims, tendrils intertwining as though they'd grown there and were determined to go on doing so until they'd succeeded in completely walling in the images depicted there. He hardly dared to breathe as he took in what he'd only glanced at a few days ago, but the centerpiece captured his gaze entirely.

Looking at it, he was suddenly convinced he knew the nobleman it showed and his dark-haired Lady with the striking gray eyes, both dressed in rich, flowing cloths of blue and silver. The ruler and his wife held hands, as if in mid-stride at a dance, surrounded by a hundred pinpoints of light like stars. He thought the couple might be on a journey through time because they appeared so peaceful and content, as though time had no meaning amid the luminescent orbs.

Studying the circumjacent sections as he continued placing candles on the floor, he saw that they were parts of a whole that fit the somewhat sentimental theory that had begun to form in his head.

Right above the middle section, there was a continuation of the night sky with the Milky Way as he knew it, only more vibrant. The light was far more prominent against the dark here.

The portion to the left of it showed a sorcerer conjuring the sky and stellar constellations that moved toward the uppermost part from the palms of his hands. Dean thought he had to be one of the most powerful wizards in this or any other world if he could command the stars – command the light itself.

He'd definitely been around Catherine too much, he decided with a smile as he lit the next candle directly opposite the previous one, revealing another part of the art.

There was a wolf, its gleaming eyes directed at a haunting full moon that looked like it was also a part of the night sky above the nobles. A man stood fearless at the beast's side, his sword in his hand and ready to fight.

On the hexagon to the lower right of the centerpiece from where Dean was standing, he saw a tree. It was a beech in winter, maybe, its branches bare and inclined in one direction, as though a steady wind had been training them to sway and stretch out to a place just beyond their reach, just beyond their heart's right for all the years of the tree's life.

The portion below the centerpiece depicted a scale, weighing several books against a crossbow and a sword on a background of faded rust. It made him think of the main reason he'd actually decided to light the candles in the first place, and he crossed the room to where the singular stone protruded from the wall. He took care to go around the mosaic, unwilling to tread on the images now that he'd really looked at them.

Kneeling, he placed both hands on the smooth surface of the wall and tried to copy what Catherine had done. Blowing lightly around the edges of the stone, he watched in fascination as it came free, and very soon, he had access to the vault and the chest within.

***

Catherine set down one of the two buckets she was carrying, and opened the door of the henhouse to take the other one inside. A panicked chicken flew straight at her, trying to escape, and she dropped the bucket.

"No!" she shrieked, and all at once, the water halted in its course through mid-air, suspended in defiance of gravity as the light of late afternoon caught on the floating droplets scattered about her like dust. Her stomach clenched and tingled as she tried to grasp which of her mind's muscles she'd just utilized to make this happen. She drew a sharp breath, and then it was over; the water spilled, and the last of the hens fled past her legs and out into the yard.

Nothing like this had ever happened before. She'd never commanded inanimate matter. Peering around, she was glad to find Rebecca was still busy in the house and hadn't seen her.

Curse, indeed. This was the best thing that could happen to anyone.

She tried to imagine Dean's face and what he would have said if he could have been here. A smile tugged at the corners of her mouth. An invisible barrier had fallen, and something told her this was only the beginning.

***

Catherine would be fine with this, Dean told himself

again as he lifted the lid of the chest, but even if it wasn't, Catherine wasn't here.

The book was right on top of everything else, and he took it out to compare it with the other two in his satchel. Holding them together cover-to-cover was like completing a puzzle when he looked at their spines. Together they made up the same tree he'd just been contemplating near the bottom of the mosaic. The middle one depicted the trunk and the crown of the ancient oak, and the books to the left and right showed its branches and roots joining to a full circle around the tree.

He put his own two books down and brought Catherine's to his lips. It opened for him just like it had for her. Time slipped by and minutes turned to hours as he studied the maps in it. The texts that went with them and the explanations in the new book Loredana had given him made sense when he connected them to his recollections of the lessons his father had taught him. There was so much here to learn and discover, the prospect made him forget where he was and why he'd come here. One by one, Catherine's candles burned down until he was down to the last stump, and that left him with a number of difficult choices.

***

After she'd rounded up the hens, Catherine went back inside the house. It reeked of damp and mold, and

Rebecca had lit the years-unused fireplace, so the biting smell of smoke added to the stink, but this was better than another night outside on the wagon.

"Get your stuff sorted," her aunt barked, unfolding a blanket on the bed she intended to use.

Catherine set her bucket down by the door. It was only half full, since she'd left the hens their share of what she hadn't spilt.

"Well's foul," she said, and crouched down by the fire to warm her hands. Inspecting them by the yellow flickering light, she had a brief flash of Cooper's blood still on them, but it was gone again as quickly as it had appeared.

Rebecca talked on and on behind her about clearing the sludge from the well, but she barely heard the woman over the draft pulling at the flames in the hearth. Sparks flew as the heat cracked open pockets of resin in the pine wood, and she concentrated on the glowing particles, trying to bend their will to her own as she'd done with the water. Some of them floated for a moment before continuing on their way upward to the chimney.

Anything was possible.

Anything.

***

Dean put Catherine's locket into the chest and closed the lid before tucking all three books into his satchel.

He told himself it was alright because he didn't think Catherine would come back, and it would be foolish to leave her book, the third of *his* set, here for just anyone to find. It had been his grandfather's life's work, and his father had spent another lifetime looking for it. It was a knowledge that belonged with his people.

Caius and Loredana would be leaving in the morning. He didn't yet know what he would do then, but he'd made up his mind he wasn't going with them. Perhaps he'd wait around another few days in case Catherine changed her mind and came back, but he doubted she would. It was strange how the people he cared for always seemed to fall off the earth without saying goodbye.

Walking through the gatehouse on his way out of his ancestral home, he did not look back.

***

Burrowing into her blanket, Catherine listened to Rebecca's steady breathing as she slept. Sparks from the fireplace drifted all over the little cabin, glowing like stars before they burned up and turned to gray ashes.

They reminded her of the first November snow falling silently around her between the bare branches in the forest when she'd been small. She closed her eyes. Pushing the image of Cooper's wide grin away, she tried hard to imagine Dean there in the flurry, walking next to her through the dancing flakes, but all she saw was a girl who looked a lot like her. A girl who also answered to the name of Catherine. The only difference between them was the blood on her hands when she raised them to her face, stealing what little there was left of the light.

***

If you enjoyed Stealing the Light, read *Into the Dark – Dies Irae Book Two*, and follow Lorcan as he makes a new life for himself in Ironstone, but soon discovers that – even there – the hunt for the Tainted is on, while Catherine is forced to join a troupe of traveling harlots to survive…

The third Dies Irae Series novel, *Gates of Eventide – Dies Irae Book Three*, takes Catherine, now queen of Trondenburgh, back to the old Tierney ruin, where she unearths vengeful ghosts from the past that threaten to destroy her future, while Lorcan travels deep into the Sudlands and all the way to Loegria to make up for a terrible mistake – and puts himself into mortal danger.

Fairyflies is a short Dies Irae story, where we meet Cooper's father, a mercenary, who is taught that not all superstitions are mere figments of the imagination…

Fire is the second short Dies Irae story, where we learn what brought Lorcan to The Fair after his family is forced to flee from the massacres in the Sudlands.

Fairypeople is the third short Dies Irae story, where we encounter Mary, a wise woman and one of The Fair's oldest residents, and find out how a young fairyboy with a noble background comes to join the traveling carnival.

Other titles by the author

Trading Darkness – A Dark Fairytale

Tales from the Midnight Forest –
A Shifter Collection

Amberflame – A Short Dragon Shifter Story
Amélie – A Short Wartime Shifter Love Story
Aura – A Phoenix Shifter Mystery
Artemis' Wings – A Raven Shifter Novella

Please consider leaving an honest review for
Stealing the Light.
It'll take only a moment,
and it will cost you absolutely nothing. Thank you!

You can visit the author's homepage at
https://www.lisahofmann.net/